The
LANGUAGE
OF
HOOFBEATS

Center Point
Large Print

Also by Catherine Ryan Hyde and available from
Center Point Large Print:

Take Me With You

**This Large Print Book carries the
Seal of Approval of N.A.V.H.**

The
LANGUAGE
OF
HOOFBEATS

Catherine Ryan Hyde

CENTER POINT LARGE PRINT
THORNDIKE, MAINE

This Center Point Large Print edition
is published in the year 2015 by arrangement with
Amazon Publishing, www.apub.com.

The text of this Large Print edition is unabridged.
In other aspects, this book may vary
from the original edition.
Printed in the United States of America
on permanent paper.
Set in 16-point Times New Roman type.

ISBN: 978-1-62899-427-8

Library of Congress Cataloging-in-Publication Data

Hyde, Catherine Ryan.
 The language of hoofbeats / Catherine Ryan Hyde. — Center Point Large
Print edition.
 pages cm
 Summary: "When Jackie and Paula's teenage foster daughter Star
disappears with Comet, their disapproving neighbor's spirited horse, the
neighbors are thrown together—far too close together. But as the search
for the pair wears on, both families must learn to put aside their animosity
and confront the choices they've made and the scars they carry"
 —Provided by publisher.
 ISBN 978-1-62899-427-8 (library binding : alk. paper)
 1. Lesbian couples—Fiction. 2. Large type books. I. Title.
 PS3558.Y358L36 2015
 813'.54—dc23

                                                                2014046987

1. Jackie

We were more than halfway to this new town whose name I'd forgotten again, and something was brewing in the back of the van. Not with the kids. With the pets. Given the two choices, we were probably getting off easy.

First I tried ignoring it, but there was a clear escalation of minor hostilities involved. The cats were all tucked away in individual carriers, but the dogs were loose, and carriers would not stop Peppy, the youngest dog, from harassing cats. Nothing would. Except maybe a county's worth of distance.

I looked over at Paula in the driver's seat. Her small features and fine, straight nose in profile. She was staring at the road ahead and didn't seem to notice. Maybe she was lost in thought. It wouldn't have been the first time.

I looked over my shoulder at the kids.

"Quinn," I said. "See if you can stop Peppy from picking on the cats."

Before he could leap into action—and with Quinn, that would not be much of a time lag—Paula said, "He shouldn't take off his seat belt while we're moving."

I have to admit this: it filled me with a sense of comfort to know that Paula was mentally here in the van with us after all. That we were still within her scope of conscious awareness.

"Peppy," Quinn barked, and it was funny to me, the way that tiny-for-his-age eight-year-old tried to make his voice sound authoritative. But, of course, I didn't hurt his feelings by saying so. "Come! Now!"

Peppy leaped onto Quinn's lap, and the van fell blissfully silent. Quinn wrapped his arms tightly around the little troublemaking beagle mix and slipped a finger under his collar for good measure.

"Good job, Quinn," I said.

"Thanks, J-Mom," he said back.

The girl, Star, withered me with one of those classic teenage death-ray stares of disgust. Armando never stopped looking out the window. He looked intense, maybe even more so than usual. Possibly over the line into distressed. But with Mando it was hard to tell.

I sat forward in my seat again, feeling a sense of relief at leaving the problems in the van behind me . . . well, literally behind me. If only for a moment.

"How much longer?" I asked Paula. "We must be getting close."

"I'm not sure. Look at the map."

I plowed through the glove compartment and found the map. Unfolded it. But I'd forgotten the name of the little town again. As I think I might have mentioned. So I used my finger to search in a broad radius east of the Bay Area, hoping to stumble on it and be reminded. It didn't work.

"What's the name of this damn place again?"

Paula's brow furrowed, but she said nothing.

"Sorry. I mean, this place. This very nice place."

"I swear you have a mental block."

"Possibly. But I'll get over it. Can you please just remind me?"

"Easley. As in, 'We could Easley be happy there.' "

"As in, 'We could just as Easley live someplace else.' "

I didn't look up from my map when I said it. Coward that I am. I didn't bother to look over to see if Paula was miffed. It pretty well went without saying that she was. Or maybe "hurt" would be a more honest way to say it.

"Sorry," I said. For about the tenth time in as many days. "At least I can't forget it again. Now that I've so memorably used it in a sentence."

I found the dreaded town of Easley on the map. Before I could stop myself, I blurted out, "Holy crap, that's a long way." Not that I didn't know where it was. Not that I hadn't driven there. Once. But it hit me all over again, in a different way. Far more real.

"From where?" Paula asked.

"I'm not following."

"A long way from where?"

"From where we live. Lived."

7

"Right. I know. But the point I'm trying to make is that we don't live there now. So maybe you can reset your odometer. The one inside your head. So you're not measuring distances from a place that's not even relevant anymore."

I fell silent.

I'd like to claim I was doing the suggested internal work. I wasn't. I was bathing in a moment of grief. It had never occurred to me, before that moment, that Napa County was no longer relevant.

We stood in the cavernous living room of our new rental home. The floors were hardwood; the walls, wood-paneled; the massive fireplace, stone. Words echoed. The kids and pets were elsewhere, checking out the new digs. The place was empty except for Paula, who I sensed was about to leave as well. She had a veterinary practice to tend to. Not that it wouldn't wait a few minutes. But I knew her. She wanted to be there. She wanted the discovery of something new.

"I'm going into town to check out the new clinic," Paula said. "Hopefully, the moving van will get here while I'm gone. I'm sorry to leave you alone with all that. Don't unpack anything. Don't do anything I should help with. I'll be back as soon as I can, and we'll tackle it together."

"Where's Star?" I asked. "I haven't seen her for a while."

"She's not in her new room?"

"She wasn't last time I looked. I could go check again."

"No, it's okay. I'll see if I can find her before I go."

Paula trotted up the carpeted stairs, her boots making a muffled brushing sound with each step.

Quinn trotted into the living room, followed by three of the four dogs—Cecil and Jocko, the black Lab–type dogs, and Wendy, the poodle mix.

"I like it," Quinn said.

My heart filled up, the way it always did when Quinn was . . . well, anything. When he was what he always was. When he was Quinn.

I wanted to invite him to come sit with me, so I could pull him close and put one arm around him. But there was nothing to sit on. I reached one arm out anyway, and he came close and tucked underneath it. Quinn never tired of being close.

"You don't mind having to share a room with Mando?"

"No. But I think *he* does. Maybe we could clean out that big barn for him."

"Did he say he minded?"

"No. But I still think so. You know he'd never say anything like that."

"The barn. Hmm. Maybe. We'll see. Let's go with this for now."

Paula trotted down the steps again, shaking her head. Then she disappeared out the front door. A wave of heat washed in and made me feel weak and tired.

"Have you seen Star?" I asked Quinn, looking down into his small face. His hair was red, not bright red but a dark coppery color, and wild. His skin was almost absurdly freckled. It was hard to look at him without smiling. "We're not sure where she is."

"Think she ran away again?"

"No. I wasn't thinking that at all."

"I can't find the cats, either," Quinn said. "Not one of them. It's weird. Like aliens came or something."

"The cats are in the master bedroom. So they can't slip out the door in the confusion."

"They don't get to go outside here?"

"Not right away. You have to keep them inside for a while in a new place. Until they understand that it's home."

"Oh," he said. "I didn't know that."

Quinn hadn't experienced pets before coming to us. And we'd stayed put until now.

The front door opened again, along with another blast of heat. Paula leaned in, her fine blond hair windblown, but in a way that looked nice. Paula always looked nice, no matter how hard she didn't try.

"I don't see her," she said. "But don't freak out. It's a big property. Lots of places she could be. And I don't have much time. So the fact that I couldn't locate her in about thirty seconds does *not* mean she ran away again."

"I wasn't worried she ran away again."

"Then why did you want me to go find her?"

"Oh. Because . . . I was worried she ran away again."

Paula shot me a crooked, slightly rueful smile. She reflexively pushed her wire-rimmed glasses higher on the bridge of her nose. Paula always reminded me of those teen movies about the nerdy girl who turns into a beauty at the end of the film—by taking her glasses off and not much more. But Paula was beautiful with them on. Then again, so were the girls in the films.

Then she disappeared, pulling the door closed behind her.

I looked back down into Quinn's eager, hopeful face.

"Want me to go find Star, J-Mom?"

"If you can. That would be great."

He ran to the door, followed by the small galumphing canine herd. All except Peppy. I ventured a guess that, if I were to look, I'd find Peppy sitting outside the closed door of the master bedroom.

Quinn held up his hand like a stop sign, and the dogs skidded to a halt.

"You stay here," he told them, sternly, imitating a tiny version of an adult disciplinarian. "Until you know this is home."

He ran outside, slamming the front door.

I looked around the living room as though more appealing options might suddenly appear. The heat, the emptiness, the sheer monumental nature of the task of building a household all over again, the fear of the hypervisibility so unavoidable in small-town living—it all ganged up on me at once. I wanted to flop onto a couch, or a bed. But that was impossible. So I flopped onto the hardwood in a corner of the massive room, my head in my hands.

The dogs settled on all sides of me, which felt comforting.

A few minutes later the front door creaked open again, so I looked up. Dark dots swam in front of my eyes from the pressure of the heels of my hands.

Quinn looked relieved, so I felt a slight relief as well.

"You okay, J-Mom?"

"I'm fine, honey. Just hot and tired."

"Star didn't run away. I found her."

"Is she coming home?"

"I'm not sure. Maybe not very soon."

"Where is she?"

"She's across the road talking to a horse."

2. Clementine

I stood at the living room window, holding back the curtain with one hand, alarmed to see someone on our property. Anyone. I'd given no one permission to come onto the place. It was only a young girl, but that's not the point. The point is more about simple property rights. If this girl had been raised correctly, she would have known better than to do such a thing without express permission.

And especially she had no right to go anywhere near Comet's corral.

"Vernon, who is that?" I asked.

Vernon was sitting at the dining room table, as usual, his temple on one palm, reading the paper and ignoring me. Or not fully hearing. I could never tell. And I was never sure which was worse: if he could completely tune me out, or if he was perfectly aware of every word I said but choosing not to reply.

"Vernon!"

Still nothing.

I rapped on the glass, hoping to frighten the girl away. No response.

It seemed to be my lot in life these days, wondering whether I was invisible to those around me, or just a nuisance they chose to ignore.

"Vernon, there's a stranger on our property, and I want to know who it is. And I'm not going to stop talking to you about it until you look up from your newspaper and take some responsibility for the fact that I exist."

A deep sigh from him. Then he looked up. Our eyes met. Just for a moment I wished I hadn't pressed the issue. Then he looked away.

"You're the one standing by the window," he said, "so you would know more about who it is than I would."

"I told you. It's a stranger."

"If it's a stranger to you, it's likely to be a stranger to me."

It was my turn to sigh. But mine was less resigned. More agitated. I was quite frustrated, and in no mood to make a secret of it.

"You are absolutely maddening," I said, but under my breath. It was not a remark I intended for him to hear.

I opened the front door, the heat of the day blasting me in the face. I stepped out of the glorious air-conditioning and into the summer sun.

"You there!" I said.

The girl glanced at me over her shoulder, still leaning on the top wooden rail of the horse corral.

I couldn't tell how old she was. I'm no good at that anymore. The older I get, the more they all look like children to me. She could have been as young as thirteen or as old as sixteen. Her limp brown hair was long, and cut into bangs in front, but bangs that were too unkempt, and hung over her eyes. Her skin was bad, breaking out in blemishes.

The way Tina's had been at that age.

I quickly set that image outside myself and slammed the figurative door on it as hard as I could.

Then that impudent girl just looked away from me and back at the horse again. She reached a hand out, and Comet approached it, which made me furious for reasons I couldn't quite sort out.

I stormed over to the corral.

"Now see here. This is private property, and that horse belongs to this family, not to you. I'll thank you never to set foot on anybody else's property without getting their permission first."

Still she had her hand out to Comet, who nuzzled around in her palm.

It just about made me see red.

"Are you listening to me? Can you hear me? That horse is very high-strung and not safe to be around, and I will not be responsible for your medical bills if something goes wrong, because I did not invite you here."

I heard a voice, a little boy, yelling.

"Star!"

That's what he called out. I had no idea who the boy was, or why he would call out that word. It certainly didn't sound like anybody's name.

I watched him jog up to where we stood.

"Star, J-Mom is looking for you. I think she wants you home."

At that point I tried on the idea that Star might be a silly name for the girl, but I still wasn't sure.

The girl ignored him.

"Is this your sister?" I asked the little boy. It may seem as though it should have been obvious, but they looked nothing alike. Maybe one of those modern families where each child is melded in from a different marriage.

"Sort of," he said, which was meaningless.

"Who on earth are you?" I asked him.

He pointed across the road to the empty rental, the big rambling wooden farmhouse. "We're moving in. Right there. I'm Quinn Archer-Cummings. This is Star."

"Now why on earth would I not know they rented that place again? Wouldn't the real estate people think I'd want to know? How can any-body even keep a secret like that in a town the size of Easley?" Though, at the back of my brain, it did register that we were scheduled to get a new large-animal veterinarian in the area, and that vets have to live somewhere, like every-body else.

Of course, my words were not serious questions directed at the little boy, but he didn't seem to know that.

"I dunno," he said with a shrug. "I just got here.

16

Star. Are you coming, or not? What am I supposed to tell J-Mom?"

"Tell her I'm busy," the girl said.

The little boy stood a moment, watching his own feet, as though fascinated by the way his athletic shoes sat on the dirt. Then he shook his head and began to walk away.

"Little boy," I said, because I'd forgotten his name already. I could only remember that it was something odd.

He stopped and turned back to me. Finally, someone who seemed to notice that I existed.

"Why do you call your mother 'J-Mom'?"

It was none of my business, I supposed, but I was curious. And he might be too young to know it was none of my business, so I'd likely get an answer.

"The 'J' is for 'Jackie,'" he said.

"But why don't you just call her 'Mom'?"

"Oh. So I don't get her mixed up with my other mom. P-Mom. The 'P' is for 'Paula.'"

"How very interesting," I said.

He waited for a moment, as if I might say why I found it so interesting. Then he crossed the road and disappeared back inside the rental house.

I looked at the girl again. Of course, she did not look back.

"I'll thank you to go home now," I said.

"Why are there all these burrs in his coat? Don't you ever brush him?" She had a wispy, high voice.

Insignificant. As though she doubted her own right to speak. "And his mane and tail are all tangled. It looks like he hasn't been brushed in a year."

"I told you before. He's very high-spirited, and it's not safe to— Wait a minute. Why am I even answering that? That horse's coat is none of your concern. Now, I've asked you to leave these premises. Are you going to do that or not?"

She never once took her eyes off Comet. She ran a hand down his gray neck, under the darker mane, as though feeling the smooth muscles to get a better sense of him. Each time she came to a burr, she picked it off and dropped it at her feet outside the corral.

I decided it was time for Vernon to sort this out. Not me. After all, he is a big, tall, heavy man, if not a particularly young one anymore, and if there is trouble, I should not be left alone to face it.

I stomped back into the house.

The air-conditioning hit me in a way that made me stop and sigh. It flowed over me like water, as though I had just dived into a swimming pool on a sweltering day. I'd been so distracted by the impertinence of our intruders—well, the one of them; the boy seemed polite enough—that I'd lost track of how much the hot sun had sapped me.

When I had collected myself, I walked to the dining room table and pulled the newspaper out of Vern's hands.

"What?" he said.

"She won't leave. I think you'd better deal with it."

"She?"

"Yes. She."

"Doesn't sound very dangerous."

"It's not about danger. It's about whether she has a right to be here." Then, as an afterthought: "And it's about legal liability. What if she's injured getting too close to Comet? As the property owners, we'd be held responsible." Then I wished I'd started there, because it sounded better, and was really much more to the point. "Even her little brother couldn't make her leave. So that's two of them who've come on our property uninvited, though at least the boy seemed reasonably polite. But the girl. The girl is anything but."

Vernon sighed and rose from the table, levering up with the help of his hands. The way he'd never used to when we were younger.

I watched from the living room window.

He walked outside, and over to the small corral. Comet snorted, and threw his head a few times, the way he always had when approached. The way he had not done with the girl, which I guess I should simply have found perplexing. But it brought up far more emotion in me than just that.

For perhaps thirty seconds they exchanged words, and then the girl walked back across the road where she belonged.

I thought, *Now what was I doing wrong?*

Vernon came back inside, and walked right past me like nothing had happened. Like nothing needed to be said.

"Wait. Aren't you going to tell me what happened?"

He shrugged. "Not much to tell. She went home."

"But she didn't go home when *I* asked her. I want to know why she didn't go home when I asked her, but she did for you."

Vernon shrugged again, and moved off toward the dining room.

"Wait!" I said, and he did, though I could tell he was not happy about it. "I really want to know."

A pause. One I thought he might never fill.

Then he said, "Maybe because I asked her nicely."

He settled at the dining room table and took up his paper again.

I sat across from him. "I just learned something interesting," I said.

No response.

"It's a rather amusing thing."

Still nothing.

"Don't you want to know what it is?"

"Sure," he said, but it didn't sound very convincing.

"Those children across the road have two mommies."

No reply.

"You have no thoughts on that?"

"Not really."

"You don't think it's funny?"

"I don't really care about it one way or the other. I don't care what the neighbors do. It's their business, and none of my own. You're the one who wants to know everything about everybody. So long as they keep to themselves, I don't care."

"They're not doing a very good job of keeping to themselves so far."

"If you ask them nicely, they do."

Then I decided I was getting nowhere with him, as usual, and chose to end the conversation and go have a talk with these new neighbors instead.

3. *Jackie*

Star and the moving van showed up at exactly the same time. So the movers were standing right behind Star, tapping their feet—well, one was tapping his foot, anyway—as I brushed the hair out of her eyes and asked if she was okay.

She pulled her face away from me sharply. In front of an audience.

"I'm fine," she said, "but I don't think they take very good care of that horse." Her voice sounded stronger than usual. More than I was used to. Hell, any words from her were more than I was used to. "I think you should have Paula go look

21

at the horse," she added. "Make sure he's okay."

"Well, she can't do that without the owner's permission, honey."

Tap. Tap. Tap.

See, this is the problem with a big family, with multiple kids. They always need something, but everything is always happening at once. You know they need you, but there's never much time to follow through. And yet I was the one who'd wanted the big family. The bustling household. Because I'd been an only child, raised by parents who barely spoke, either to each other or to me. So I loved the commotion. Paula would have been happy enough with just Quinn, but she went along with Mando and Star to be supportive of me. And I went along with the four dogs and five cats to be supportive of her. I like animals, but I'm not sure I needed nine. It was Paula who had to take every one that needed taking.

In any case, at moments like this I understood why my parents had stopped having kids after me.

"Right," Star said. "Fine. I knew you'd be no help at all."

She pushed past me into the house, bumping my shoulder.

I looked up at the movers.

"Sorry. Family stuff."

The foot tapper handed me a clipboard with a paper to sign. Without comment.

• • •

Before a single stick of furniture made its way into the new house, the lady from across the street showed up on the welcome mat. She knocked, even though the door was standing wide open.

"Yes," I said. "Can I help you?"

She was middle-aged or older. I guess I should say she was of indeterminate age. She could have been fifty or seventy; it was hard to tell. Her hair was styled as though stuck in the 1950s, with not a single hair out of place. Which seemed odd in this rural environment, though I'm not sure why. She was almost bizarrely short, and a bit heavy, her body shapeless and soft-looking with age and, I guessed, lack of use.

"I'm Clementine D'Antonio. My husband and I own the property across the road."

I made my way to the door and stood face-to-face with her, as much as that's possible with someone two heads shorter. Both Paula and I are about five foot ten, so I'm used to looking down at some people. Just not quite so far. I wanted to invite her in, and I would have. But I was held back by knowing there was nothing inside to sit on.

"Jackie Archer-Cummings," I said.

I held out my hand, but she didn't shake it. Which was awkward. And a clue to her nature, if I'd been on my game and able to absorb it.

"You're not the new veterinarian," she said. It didn't sound like a question.

"No. Not personally. That's Paula. My wife."

In my head, there was a slight pause before the word "wife." Because I had to push it out. It was always a little hard with new people, though a lot less so in Napa. Still, there was no way we were going to hide. And, actually, nowhere to hide even if we'd been so inclined.

In the real world, I'm guessing the pause was imperceptible.

She didn't answer. I couldn't read anything by her face, and it was starting to make me uneasy.

"I'd ask you in, but there's literally no furniture."

Two moving men came up the walk behind her, each carrying one end of our couch, shrouded in protective plastic and wrapped with tape. We had to move aside to let them through, and I was relieved by the distraction. Then I realized there was now something to sit on, if I wanted to invite the neighbor in. But I didn't. By then I quite definitely knew I didn't.

"Well, it was nice of you to come over to welcome us," I said. I looked into her face. It's hard to define what I saw there, but my heart fell as a result of it. Still she didn't speak. "Oh. Got it. That's not why you're here at all."

I sighed deeply. It was hotter with the door wide open. The house had stayed fairly cool when closed up. It was making me feel a little unsteady on my feet.

"I guess you'd better come in," I said.

I think it was pretty clear by my tone that I was less than thrilled with the prospect. But it was one of those life moments when you've only got exactly what you've got to work with and no more.

She walked in. Short, tight steps, as if her muscles didn't stretch far. She looked around, taking stock of the place, which seemed an odd thing to do with a house that's empty. I wondered if she'd been inside the place before.

We sat on the still-wrapped couch, the plastic crackling uncomfortably under us. My bare legs immediately began to sweat and stick to the plastic below the hems of my shorts. Clementine sat on the very edge, barely touching the couch, like a bird balanced on a perch. For an awkward moment, no one spoke.

"I understand that teenage girls are drawn to horses," she said, in a voice that made it sound as though she understood no such thing. As though she understood nothing. "But that horse is very highly strung, and a person could easily be injured getting too close to him. So I really think it's best if you keep your daughter over on this side of the road where she belongs. I hope you understand. I don't mean to sound overly harsh, but there are liabilities involved. I don't want anyone being injured on our property."

"Of course," I said. "Of course I understand." Meanwhile, my head swam, wondering how I was supposed to make Star do—or not do—anything. "I'll certainly try."

Clementine's head rocked back. "That's an odd answer. You do have control over your own daughter, don't you?"

I took a deep breath. A moment to sort out what to say, how much to tell.

"The problem is . . . we don't really know Star all that well. Yet. She's only been with us for about three weeks."

"Been with you?"

"Yes," I said, thinking this woman should stop asking questions and go away now. "Been with us."

"So she's not your daughter?"

"We're fostering her. We take in foster kids. Two of our kids we're fostering, and the little one, Quinn, we fostered him for two years, but now we've legally adopted him."

Immediately I wished I'd told her less. Not because there was anything wrong with what I'd told her, but because she deserved less, and I found myself circling the wagons, protecting myself and my family by wanting her to know as little about us as possible.

"Oh," she said, drawing the word out long. As though she'd had a dozen questions in her head and this answered all of them. "Of course. I should have known that. Of course you wouldn't have your own children."

"Excuse me?" I was mad now, and wishing Paula were with me. She was better at situations like this. More graceful and gracious. I just got ticked and fired back.

"I only meant—"

"I know exactly what you meant. And we could have had our own children. Paula and I are both perfectly capable of giving birth to children, and we could have gone that route. We foster and adopt because we believe there are too many children no one will take. Through no fault of their own. And we feel bad for them. And it's just something we wanted to do."

"I'm sorry if you took offense," she said.

But it didn't sound all that heartfelt. And the very phrasing suggested she was not sorry at all. It was not nearly as good as saying, "I'm sorry. I see now that what I said was offensive." Her statement almost seemed to put the blame on me for being too sensitive.

I looked up to see Mando standing in the entryway to the living room, near the stairs. He'd frozen there, obviously aware of the tension.

"Excuse me, ma'am," he said when it was clear I'd seen him.

"Me?" Clementine asked, thinking he was addressing her.

"No, he's talking to me," I said. "Maybe just give me another couple of minutes with our new neighbor, Mando."

"Yes, ma'am. I was just wondering if I could go look in the barn."

"Of course you can. You can go look wherever you want."

"Thanks," he said, and disappeared.

I looked back at the neighbor lady, hoping she had no more questions, yet at the same time knowing I would not be so fortunate.

" 'Ma'am'?" she asked.

"Armando has a mother, and he feels loyal to her, and so he doesn't think of us as his parents."

"But she must have abused or neglected him, or he wouldn't be here."

I breathed a moment before answering. I was right on the edge of throwing this difficult person out of my new house.

"No. She didn't. Not at all. She . . ." But then it occurred to me that it was none of Clementine's business what she did. Nothing on this side of the road was any concern of hers at all. ". . . just can't take care of him right now. Now if you'll excuse me, this is a very busy time, what with the moving men and all." I stood. She didn't. "So I'm going to have to excuse myself."

"We haven't really solved the basic problem," she said. "Of your . . . foster daughter. Getting too close to the horse."

"Why don't you let that be our problem?"

"Fine," she said, and stood stiffly. "But I want to go on record as saying that if any of your family

28

gets hurt while on our property without permission, you'd best be prepared to pay your own medical expenses."

"Fair enough," I said, just wanting to end things with her.

She stood a moment. I mentally willed her to leave. Just as I was right on the edge of asking her out loud, she stamped across the hardwood and out the front door, forcing two moving men—holding two lamps each—to jump aside.

I looked up to see Quinn watching from the stairs.

"You okay, J-Mom?"

"I think so," I said.

He came close, and we sat on the couch together.

"I put the dogs in my bedroom," he said. "So they can't accidentally get out."

"Thank you, honey. That was very smart. See, you're thinking better than I am. I never even thought to wonder where they were."

"And I put a water bowl in there for them so they don't get too hot. I mean, thirsty. Because it's hot."

"Good work. Very good thinking."

"You shouldn't let that lady make you feel bad," he said. "I think she's just not a very nice person."

I smiled, and it felt like the first time in a long time. I stroked his wild hair back off his forehead. "I think you're right about that, honey. I think you're a pretty good judge of people."

I found Mando in the barn, sitting on an old and faded bale of straw.

"It's awfully hot in here," I said.

"I wouldn't mind that, though."

I had only been speaking about the present moment. Clearly, his mind was deeper into the future. More in a planning mode.

I sat next to him, and he shifted over to give me room.

"You'd rather be out here by yourself, wouldn't you?"

He turned to look full into my face, his own face hopeful and maybe a little scared. His jet-black hair was short enough that it stood up straight if he didn't slick it down carefully after getting it wet. And he'd been sweating, so it stood up. He was wearing jeans and flip-flops, and a plain white T-shirt. The bulk of each upper arm was wider than Quinn's waist. He was a big, solid boy, and it was hard to see him as barely thirteen.

"Yes, ma'am."

"Jackie. Please."

"Jackie. I know you always say that. But that doesn't feel right. It doesn't feel respectful."

"It really is, though, if that's what I want. Please see if you can get used to it."

"I could try. No offense to anyone else in the family. You know. About wanting to be out here."

"None taken. I know privacy is important to you."

"Yes, ma'am. I mean, Jackie."

"You seemed a little upset on the ride out."

"It's just strange, you know? Leaving a place you've lived in all your life."

I snorted a sarcastic laugh. "Tell me about it. But we'll get used to it here."

I stood up, stretched my back. Looked around.

It was old and shabby, the barn. Slivers of light filtered in between the boards. Birds' nests and cobwebs decorated the high corners.

"It's going to take an awful lot of work to make this livable."

"I'll do all the work."

"Tell you what. When Paula comes home, we'll talk about it."

A big sigh from him. A happy sigh. Or as close to happy as Mando seemed to get. "Thanks," he said.

I smiled, leaned down. Put one hand behind his head, pulled his face in close, and kissed him on the forehead. When I let him go again, he looked shy and embarrassed, but not particularly unhappy.

4. Clementine

When I got back to the safety of my own house, Vern was sitting in his stuffed easy chair in front of the television, watching one of those shows about bass fishing. He did now and then, and it always struck me as strange. I can see the point of fishing well enough, though I wouldn't care to go myself. But watching fishing on TV? It hardly seems like a proper spectator sport. I always felt you should watch other people do things you never could or would do yourself. Bullfighting. Skydiving. Tackle football. That sort of thing. If you can do it easily enough, you should just do it. That's what I think.

Vern used to go fishing. Back in the day. In the "before" of our days together. Before all the heartache, as he put it. By now he'd wound down to mostly the newspaper, the TV, and the occasional long, hot bath.

I sat down in the chair next to him.

"I have to tell you the strangest thing," I said.

"Okay," he said. Without ever taking his eyes off the screen.

"One of the women who just moved in across the street is the new vet. You know. The one to take over Dr. Raymond's practice now that he's retired."

"What's strange about that?"

"That's not really the strange thing. Well, it's a little strange, thinking of a small woman tending to all those bulls and horses."

"Have you met her?"

"Not yet."

"Then how do you know she's small?"

Listening to the bass fishermen on TV while we

were trying to talk was starting to get on my nerves. I wanted to grab the remote and turn it off, but Vernon can get cranky over a thing like that.

"Because she's a woman, and women are small compared to men. Look. You're getting me all off track. I want to tell you the strange part. The woman I was just talking to—not the vet, but the other one—she calls the vet woman her wife." Silence. Except for the bass fishermen. "You're not saying anything," I said.

"I'm waiting for the strange thing. Was that it?"

"Of course that was it. Are you teasing me just to give me a hard time? She calls this other woman her wife. Like they were married."

"They probably are. That's legal in this state now, you know."

I felt myself getting angry. Angry at Vern for not thinking this odd thing was odd, and at the state of California for changing everything, and the Supreme Court of the United States for letting them. And at the bass fisherman for talking over us and making it hard for me to think. All of life was suddenly getting under my skin.

"I just don't like it," I said. "I don't like it one bit. This was always a nice town. And now suddenly here these people are right across the road, and I don't like how they talk about being married, like there's not the slightest thing wrong with it. Like I wouldn't bat an eye at that. And I don't like that rude girl who comes over here and

33

leans on the corral and reaches her hands out to Comet without even asking if she can come on the premises. And that boy—"

"You said the boy was polite," Vern interjected.

"Not that boy. Turns out there are two boys. A little one and a big one. And the big one is really big. Big enough that even you might be scared of him. And I don't think he's American. His name is . . . Oh darn, I don't remember now what his name is, but it has an 'o' on the end and I think he's Mexican or Spanish or something. And I just don't like having all of this going on right outside my house, where it gets to be part of my life, too, and there's nothing I can do about it."

Vernon clicked off the TV. It was sudden, and it surprised me. The silence was stunning after all that noise, and it should have been a relief, but it wasn't, because there was something strange in the air between us. When I looked up at Vern, he was staring at me. He didn't say a word, and he didn't look mad, but it was a strange stare. In thirty-three years of marriage, I didn't ever recall seeing quite that look on his face. He looked almost as though he was curious about something, something that could be found in me, and if he looked harder he might locate his answer.

He scratched near his hairline, and a few wisps from his thin, sandy island of remaining hair trailed onto his forehead, and he didn't seem to notice. I wanted to brush them back into place. I restrained myself.

A few seconds passed, until I felt I couldn't take it anymore.

"Why are you staring at me with that strange look on your face?" I asked him.

Here's what he said for an answer: "What *do* you like, Clem?"

"That's a very strange question," I said, hoping to put the matter to rest.

"I don't see why. You always used to like things, just like anybody else. You know. Before things got so bad like this."

He didn't say anything about Tina, or mention her name, but I swear I could hear it as clearly as if he had. When he stopped talking, I could hear the echo of her name, the one he didn't say, hanging in the silence, like the way the peal of a church bell stays in the air long after the hand that rang it is gone. Except this was a bell no one had rung.

I didn't know what to say. Words were stuck in my throat.

So he went on.

"Now we watch the news every day, and you tell me all the things you don't like about the world. And you meet new people, and you tell me all the things you don't like about them. But what *do* you like? I don't even know anymore. I know you think I'm being sarcastic, or saying all this to criticize, but I'm not. I really want to know."

That seemed to knock loose my ability to speak.

"This is a perfectly ridiculous line of questioning, and I refuse to dignify it with any kind of answer at all."

"You sure it's not because you don't know, either?"

I jumped to my feet, brushing off the front of my dress as though it were spattered with this conversation and I could dismiss it just that easily.

"I won't listen to another minute of this," I said.

And I went into the kitchen to start that pork roast for our dinner.

After a few silent minutes, I heard him click the TV back on. The bass fisherman had caught something. I guess the show wouldn't be interesting for long if they never did.

I woke up in the wee hours of the morning, already knowing something was wrong. Yet there was nothing to know it by. It reminded me of the times when Tina was little, and I'd wake up with a thought in my head—well, partway between a thought and a voice—saying I should go and check on her. And sure enough, by the time I got into her room, she'd have a fever or so much congestion it was almost hard for her to breathe.

A mother knows.

But I wasn't even a mother anymore. Or was I? When you've only ever had one child, and she's gone, are you still a mother? Maybe. But I don't even know.

I opened my eyes.

Vern was sitting up on the edge of the bed, fully dressed. He had that thin jacket on, the one he usually wore to church. He wasn't moving at all, just sitting there, his back to me, the slump in his spine and shoulders telling a tale I didn't care to hear.

I lifted my head to get a better view, but my nightgown was all caught and bunched beneath me, and it held me at my throat—a more literal version of how trapped I suddenly felt. I didn't want to lift up to rearrange it, because I didn't want him to know I was up. Something bad was afoot, and I was convinced that all it needed to arrive was for me to prove myself awake.

As my eyes began to adjust to the light, I saw Vern's big old leather suitcase sitting on the blanket chest at the foot of our bed—the one he used to take to that mountain lodge when he would go up there for a week of hunting. Another thing he used to do before, but no longer did. Another part of life lost, now that it was after.

I swear I made no movement or sound, but he turned his head. Just a little. Then he turned it away again.

"You're awake," he said. I couldn't tell if he was relieved or disappointed.

"What are you doing up?" Then I immediately

wished I hadn't asked, because I knew he would tell me.

"Going away."

"Hunting?" I asked, hopefully.

"No."

"Where are you going, then?"

"I don't know."

That sat on the bed with us for a moment while I readjusted my nightgown, so it would be the one thing in my life not trying to strangle me.

I thought he would say more on his own. I was wrong.

"How can you be going away if you don't even know where you're going?"

"I guess I'll get a room somewhere."

That was when the shaking started. In the bones of my thighs, and in my hands, and in a place at the base of my throat, but deep. That had never happened before.

"Why?" I asked. I had to. I didn't really want to, but it had to be done. He didn't answer. And I waited a long time, shaking. "Yesterday you asked me a question, Vern, and when I didn't give you an answer, you accused me of not knowing the answer."

"I know the answer," he said.

"Then why won't you say?"

"I've just been sitting here trying to think of a way to put it that's not needlessly cruel. And I'm still not sure there is one."

Those words echoed in my gut—a kind of reverberation, as though they were physically moving through me. My mouth felt dry, and my brain was becoming disconnected, as though I were just about to fall asleep and couldn't fully absorb my surroundings. Not instead of the shaking, but in addition.

"I think now that you've come out with a thing like that," I said, "you have to finish." My voice sounded calm. But it didn't sound mine. At least, not to me.

"I feel like I don't know who you are anymore. Like you're someone different. You know. Since . . . all the heartache."

Again, he never said "Tina." I'd been meaning to tell him to go ahead and say it, since I always heard it anyway, but it seemed too late by then.

"That changed us both," I said.

"But the person you are now . . . This is the hard part. I don't want to be cruel. The person you changed into . . . I don't like her. I don't want to live with her anymore."

Inside myself, I let go of my grip on okay. Usually I cling very tightly to okay, but sometimes it slips too far away, and then it's easier just to give up.

"Is this about what I said last night? How I don't like those new people? Would you honestly hold it against me for not liking having those people so near?"

39

"No." He still hadn't turned to face me. "It's not that. Well. It's not just that. It's not that you don't like *them*. It's that you don't like *anybody*. Or anything. And it's that I'm just not happy. We only get one life, and I don't know why I sit here day after day, watching mine tick away, when I know I'm not happy. We're not happy together, Clem. Can you honestly say otherwise?"

"We're just the way we always were," I said.

"Right," he said. "That's exactly what I mean."

I didn't answer. Didn't or couldn't. It was all too hard to sort out by then.

Then, after a shaky pause, he asked, "Don't you even *want* to be a person who likes something?"

"Oh, Vern. Please. Just because I didn't answer the question doesn't mean I don't like anything, or even want to. You just didn't give me time to think."

He glanced partway over his shoulder at me. As if he might glimpse a bit of hope. "Okay. Take all the time you need. Think. What do you like?"

We froze that way for the longest time. I really have no idea how long, but it dragged out. Despite the fact that I knew the answer early on.

Nothing. Not a damn thing.

After a time, he rose, and took up his suitcase, which apparently was already packed, and told me he'd be in touch when he found a place to settle.

And that was it.

Thirty-three years of marriage. Just like that.

• • •

I never got back to sleep. I didn't even try.

I made myself a cup of tea and sat at the kitchen table and felt myself tremble. The moon was out full, bathing the horse corral, and I watched Comet fret and pace in that pen I knew was too small. Watched him trot from one side to the other, having to break gait far too soon.

I wondered if he did that every night, and I just didn't see.

I wondered which of us was more upset, and who I felt more sorry for, him or me.

5. Jackie

"I'd appreciate it if you'd come along," Paula said to me. "To help me handle the horse."

"If she even lets you get near the horse," I said.

We were at the breakfast table, all five of us, eating waffles with fresh local strawberries. Star was silent, her face tipped down toward her plate, her hair drooping over her face. Yet I guessed—or sensed—that she was hanging on our every word.

"I think we should go over there all ready to give that horse an examination," Paula said. "I don't think we should be tentative. Some people don't give their animals all the care they need—they forget, or they can't afford it—but not many owners are cruel enough to say no to care if it's

41

offered. Especially with no expense to worry about."

"You haven't met *this* person," I interjected.

"I still think we should assume she'll say yes. If she doesn't, we just walk home again. Nothing lost. But the way we approach the situation might make all the difference."

"Hmm," I said. "I don't mind holding a lead rope. But wouldn't it be better to cross-tie him in the barn?"

"Potentially. If she'll let us take him out of that corral. But that's a bigger if."

"I can help you handle him," Star said. "He's calm around me. He likes me."

Paula shook her head. "I don't think that's a good idea, kiddo. I'm not saying you couldn't do it. Or even that you couldn't do it best. But there's already some friction over you going onto their property. I think you should stay here."

"I'm going across the road with you."

I waited to see how Paula would respond. She'd always been a good disciplinarian, Paula. Because she never lost her cool. With one exception: if someone neglected or abandoned an animal. How do you think we ended up with so many? But outside of animal cruelty, she had this amazing equanimity that I'd been observing for nine years and still didn't fully understand. She just said what needed to be said, without clouding the situation with her own agenda. Without mixing in her own anger. Yet she was less likely than I was to take any crap from the kids. Well, from Star. The other kids rarely gave any crap anyway.

"If you want to come close enough to watch me give the exam," Paula said, "that's fine. But I insist you stay outside the line of their property."

Star huffed a bit, but said nothing in actual words.

"Let me knock," Paula said.

I was more than happy to hang back a few steps, Paula's big medical bag in the dirt at my feet.

She rapped sharply at the door a few times, and then we stood and waited. I glanced around at Star, who was standing at the edge of the road on the D'Antonios' side, and suddenly wished she hadn't come along. That she'd stayed inside. I knew it would make Clementine armor up just to see her there. But it seemed too late to repair the situation.

Paula looked back at me, asking without words if I thought it was time to give up the idea that anyone would answer the door. I shrugged.

Just as I did, the door swung open.

There stood the tiny Clementine, in her nightie, her hair a shocking mess. She squinted into the light as if opening her eyes for the first time that day.

"I'm sorry we woke you," Paula said.

"You didn't wake me," Clementine replied.

Then we all just stood there, with nothing being

said. I remember thinking, *Don't say I didn't warn you, Paula.*

Paula broke the stalemate. "Paula Archer-Cummings," she said, thrusting her hand out for Clementine to shake. "I'm the new veterinarian."

"Yes," Clementine said, staring at Paula's hand as if she'd never seen a hand before. "I know that."

Not surprisingly—at least, not to me—she never shook the hand she'd been offered, and in time Paula dropped it to her side again.

"I thought it might be the neighborly thing to do to offer to take a look at your horse. No charge. Just a courtesy between neighbors."

Clementine's eyes narrowed into slits. "You thought no such thing," she said. "That girl"—she thrust her head in the direction of Star, standing awkwardly in the dirt road—"told you I'm not treating him right. Didn't she?"

I felt my molars grind together. But Paula only smiled. "Just a courtesy between neighbors," she said again. "Unless you feel he's had a checkup recently enough."

"Well," the old woman said, and then paused. As though buying time. Searching for excuses. "I suppose it *has* been a while."

"When was he last seen? Do you remember off the top of your head?"

"Well, he's my daughter's horse. She made sure he got plenty of attention. Too much, I thought. Always having the vet or the farrier in and out of

44

here, like he was just about to fall off the face of the earth if she didn't."

"Ah," Paula said. "Got it. And now your daughter's gone off to college . . ."

Clementine's eyes narrowed again, and a long and awkward silence fell. "No," she said at last.

Everyone waited, thinking she would elaborate. She never did.

"Well, I'll go ahead and get started," Paula said. "Can we take him out of that little corral and cross-tie him in the barn? It would make things easier."

"No. Don't take him out. He's too hard to handle. What if he broke away?"

"Okay, then. In the corral it is. I just need his halter and lead rope."

"It's hanging in the barn."

"Maybe you wouldn't mind fetching that for us, and then I promise it's the last we'll ask of you all morning."

"But I *would* mind," Clementine said, her face an impenetrable mask. I had no idea what she was thinking, or feeling, but there was something underneath all that stoniness. But she was clearly not going to let us see it. "I would mind very much. I don't go into the barn."

"Okay," Paula said. "Fair enough." Though, frankly, I'd be hard-pressed to think of anything that sounded less fair. She turned to me and said, "Jackie, will you please go see if you can find it?"

45

"She won't have any trouble finding it," Clementine said. It sounded like a complaint. Then again, so did everything she said. "It's hanging on a hook on the wall just inside the barn door."

Then she slammed her door and left us standing there.

Paula looked around at me, and we shrugged at each other. Then, in spite of the fact that she'd asked me to do it, we walked together to the barn. I think she'd assumed she'd have to stand with the neighbor lady and make conversation the whole time. Clementine's slamming herself back into her house seemed to have changed the landscape.

"Told you she was a horrible woman," I said.

"I don't really think of her as horrible."

"Seriously? Then what is she, if she's not horrible?"

"I guess she seems kind of . . . scared. And sad."

"You're a freaking saint, you know that, Paula? Do I tell you that?"

"Upwards of three times a week," she said.

But it wasn't really saintliness. That was only the nicest way to say it. It was just Paula. It was the way she was wired. Level, unlike me. It was generally good, but, like anything, it cut both ways. The upside was that she didn't get as excited as I did. The downside was that she didn't get as excited as I did.

We found the halter and lead rope hanging just inside the barn door. Paula lifted them down, and

46

you were right. We're having trouble handling the horse. But you knew that, didn't you? Because you were watching out the window the whole time. And I'm sure it gave you great pleasure to watch us fail. Paula's a good vet, but you're not giving her what she needs, insisting the horse can't even be moved to a place where she could properly restrain him. He's not impossible, but he's nervous, and she needs access to his hooves. And it's not worth a bruised bone or a broken foot. So I'm going to suggest we let Star come and stand by his head. She's sure she can settle him down. Don't think I don't already know how much the very idea of that ticks you off. But you either care about that horse or you don't. Paula thinks there are some problems with his hooves. They're overgrown. They're not self-trimming. Plus she thinks he might have a touch of thrush. Which probably isn't that serious now, if he even has it, but it can be very serious if you let it go. So what's it going to be?"

Clementine peered past me, shading her eyes against the slanted early sun. "My husband, Vernon, [ha]s a long-handled rake, and he rakes out the [ma]nure two or three times a day, just so we won't [hav]e those issues."

"[W]ell, regardless, you have the issues. Horses' [hoov]es need a lot of care. So what's it going to

"[Yo]u know I don't want that girl on my [prope]rty."

blew on the top strap of the halter, and on the top of the coil of rope that had been draped over the hook. I watched a thick cloud of dust swirl around in a beam of early light slanting through the door.

"How long do you think it's been since anybody took that down?"

"If I had to bet," she said, "I'd take a chance on more than a year."

Paula slipped into the corral by ducking between the rails. The horse threw his head, bouncing it up and down with his muscular neck, as though nodding. I saw his nostrils dilate. I trusted Paula to handle just about anything, but I got a tingle in my gut just the same.

She approached the horse, rope in one hand, halter in the other. He pivoted on his back hooves and turned to trot away. She stopped him in his tracks by standing right in front of him, arms out to both sides, speaking to him in soft syllables that were more horse and less English. After ten or eleven stops, he stood tentatively and let her slip the rope around his neck. Haltering him was easy enough, but as she led him over to where I stood outside the rail, he stopped and reared up. Paula planted her feet, the rope tight in her gloved hands, and spoke to him again.

It took a few more tries before she could lead him over to me. I was beginning to hope he'd never arrive.

"Get a pair of gloves out of my bag," she said. "I don't want you to get rope-burned."

"This is making me nervous. I'm not as good with the big animals as you are."

Actually, I wasn't as good with any animals as she was. Who could be? Even little Peppy was too much for me half the time. I loved the hell out of them, but getting them to knuckle down and behave was a whole other subject.

"Don't be. He'll pick up on your nerves."

"Does that advice come with step-by-step directions?"

She twisted her mouth at me, shaking off the joke. "Do your best with him. Please. This is important to Star."

I sighed, and dug out a pair of leather gloves. "Wouldn't it be better to tie him to the rail?"

"Not necessarily. Depends on the horse. Some get panicky when they hit the end of that rope. I'd rather have somebody at his head."

"Like me!" Star called from the road.

I'd had no idea she could hear us. *Good ears,* I thought.

Paula waved her suggestion away, then turned her attention back to me.

"Hold tight to the rope, but if you feel yourself being lifted off your feet, let go. I'll follow him and pick up the rope. I have a feeling this guy'll do better if his back's not against the wall."

But he lifted me off my feet, pulling me into the fence. Immediately. And almost every time. He was okay when Paula wanted to look into his eyes and ears. But the rectal thermometer was a nonstarter. And only once did she manage to check one of his hooves. And only briefly. Just long enough to know that his hooves very much needed checking.

"She doesn't like me," I said, when Paula had ducked out of the corral again. "I think *you* should ask."

"It didn't seem that she liked me any better. Just be polite. Don't let your feelings about her get the best of you."

As I scuffed through the loose light-brown dirt to Clementine's door, I saw her watching through the window. Half-hidden behind the curtains. The minute I saw her, she jumped away. As if she never meant to let on that she cared enough to watch.

Before I could even knock, her door swung open. She was dressed now in a flowery dress, her hair carefully combed into place.

"What now?" she asked. As though I'd been getting on her nerves all morning. But it was the first we'd come face-to-face that day.

I stepped in closer, and lowered my voice. I knew I couldn't handle this the way Paula had, so didn't want to be overheard.

"Okay, lady," I said. "You'll be

48

49

"Yes, we've been all through that. 'Without your permission.' That's what you said. You don't want her coming on your property without your permission. And, as you can see, we have her standing very respectfully in the road, because you haven't given your permission yet. But I'm asking if you will now. For the sake of the horse."

"His name is Comet," she said.

"And?"

"That's all. You keep calling him 'the horse.' Like he doesn't have a name. He has a name. It's Comet."

"Fine. For the sake of Comet, will you let Star stand at his head?"

Clementine clucked her tongue and did not answer.

I decided to break out the big guns.

"Unless *you'd* like to do it."

I'd made an observation. It seemed to make her angry not so much that Star stepped onto her property—although maybe that, too—but that the horse seemed to like the girl, and to calm down around her. I was guessing that meant Comet was better with Star than he was with his owner. Then again, Clementine wasn't really his owner. He belonged to a mysteriously absent daughter. In any case, it seemed this woman couldn't handle the horse, either. And I was betting everything on that theory.

Her face clouded briefly. "Do what you have to do, I suppose."

Then she slammed herself back inside again.

I motioned to Star with a big sweep of my hand, and she trotted up to the corral. Comet put his gray muzzle up close to her face, and she blew lightly into his nostrils, and he made a soft, rumbling, almost-whinnying noise deep in his throat, which I can only describe as highly communicative and surprisingly contented. He blew back, with an audible huffing sound.

"Keep talking to him," Paula said. "Keep his attention."

She ducked back between the rails of the corral and ran her hand down the back of one of his hocks. He danced away again. But Star kept whispering into his ear, and the third time Paula went for the hoof, he let her have it.

I looked up to see Clementine watching us through the window again, cobalt-blue mug of coffee in one hand, face dissatisfied and dark.

6. Clementine

The veterinarian lady came back to the door and knocked, but this time I wasn't surprised, because I'd been watching out the window. I'd seen her coming.

When I got up to answer the door, I felt that

shakiness again. Mostly in my thighs. I don't think it had gone away in the meantime. Not really. I think I'd just been getting used to it, focusing off it as best I could. My mind felt like a balloon floating a mile over my head, anyway, which made everything seem distant and unreal. But every time my shaky legs had to hold me up, it was a hard sensation to deny.

I opened the door.

Behind the vet lady on my doorstep, I saw the girl and the "wife" packing up leather gloves and a stethoscope, and some other things I couldn't quite identify. I saw the girl pick up the halter and head for the barn, and I thought, *No. No, don't let her do that. Don't let her go in that barn like she owns this place. One of you grown-ups do it.* But I didn't say so. I wasn't being polite, exactly. It just would have taken more energy than I knew how to muster.

"How is he?" I asked.

"Seems to be in good overall health. But I definitely recommend you make an appointment with a farrier. And if he says he has to take Comet into the barn and cross-tie him, I suggest you let him do it. Even if I have to tranquilize the horse beforehand. His hooves need attention. They need to be trimmed, and the frogs need to be cut back and cleaned. And they may need to be picked out really well once or twice a day, depending on what he finds when he cuts them back."

"Does he have thrush, or doesn't he?"

"Not a bad case. A couple of spots looked suspect. But I don't have farrier tools on me today. I have some at the clinic, but I don't have them in my 'farm call' bag. I should, but I don't today. So I can't really get in there to see as much as I'd need to see to offer a real diagnosis."

"So his hooves may be just fine."

"No. They're not. A horse can go lame just from having his hooves so overgrown. It changes the way he stands. I've seen horses go lame for weeks after getting a proper trimming, because suddenly they're using all their muscles in a different way. Even though it's the right way. So, listen. I'm on my way in to the clinic, and I'm meeting this afternoon with John Parno, the farrier who was Dr. Raymond's choice. I'll pick up a business card and have Jackie bring it over. Or Star."

"No!" I said, even more vehemently than I'd intended. "Don't send that girl. You or your . . . the other person. One of you grown-ups. Please."

I don't know why I even bothered with that charade. I knew Johnnie. I had Johnnie's number if I'd wanted it. It was all just a big well I didn't care to dive into.

"Okay," she said. And with that I thought she was going to leave. And I wanted her to. Instead, she said, "How often does he get out of there?"

I said nothing for an uncomfortable length of

time. My face felt a little hot, which embarrassed me, and I could only hope it didn't show.

"That would be my husband's department," I said, finally.

"Oh. Okay. May I speak with him?"

"No, you may not." Then, because she looked at me oddly, I added, "He's not here."

"Oh," she said. "I see."

"Besides. I didn't ask you to come over here and tell me how much exercise to give him. In fact, I didn't ask you to come over here at all. This was supposed to be a health checkup. You're a vet, not a fitness coach. This was supposed to be about his health."

"That's a pretty important factor in his health. It's also why his hooves are overgrown. They're not self-trimming."

I looked past her to see that the horrible teenage girl was back from the barn, staring daggers at me.

"Thank you for looking him over," I said.

I closed the door quickly.

I thought I could close everything I didn't like about the conversation outside. Heaven knows, I'd been doing a good enough job for the past almost-two years, keeping situations shut out. I knew Comet needed to get out of there. I knew he needed more exercise. But day after day I managed to go from morning till night and keep such thoughts at bay. I assumed I could do the same now.

I was wrong.

It's different when someone else sees it, and says it to you out loud. Just like it was different to hear Vernon say he wasn't happy. If I had wondered before last night about whether he was happy, I likely would have decided no, I didn't think he was. But it's different out loud.

But it made it harder to breathe, thinking of Vernon, so I pushed that out the door as well. But nothing pushed—at least, not quite the way it had always used to.

I watched out the window to make sure they were all really gone. After they went back home, I breathed a little more. But not enough. Not nearly enough.

My hands shook as I punched the numbers into the phone. Not that deep trembling, but a violent shaking that almost made it hard to hit the right numbers. I knew that when I spoke, my voice would shake, too, and I hated the thought and the feeling. But by then the phone was ringing, and Emmy had caller ID, so it was too late to back out.

For a brief moment, I tried to think if I had ever been so deep-down terrified. But of course I had, and I remembered when right away, and that only made it harder when she picked up the phone.

"Clementine?" she asked, in place of hello.

"Yes," I said, because I thought short words, and

very few of them, would best keep my shaking a secret.

But then there was a silence. A long silence. And she didn't seem to want to fill it. I began to wonder why I thought she would, or how she even could. After all, she was not the one who knew why I was calling.

"I wondered if you talked to Vernon," I said. I know she heard it, what rocky shape I was in, but what could I do about that?

I heard her sigh.

Emmy had never been my biggest fan, but we got along okay. I think she liked me better than Vern's other sister did, but it's hard to know these things if you don't ask. We had nothing against each other, and we never fussed or bad-mouthed at each other. We just weren't all that close.

"You have to give him time," Emmy said.

"So you did talk to him."

"What if I did?"

"I need to talk to him, Emmy. I need to know where he is."

In the silence that followed, which I swear was only a second or two, I was staring at this spot on the stove, and it hit me. *I don't know where he is. He's gone, and I don't even know where.* It was the most panicky feeling, like the crust of the earth opened, or I'd broken right through it, and there was nothing solid under my feet. Nothing to hold me up anymore. I didn't know what to grab onto. I felt like I was falling, but I was sitting in a chair by the phone, so I had no idea how to steady myself to stop the fall.

"He'll let you know where he landed when he lands," Emmy said. "And when he's ready to let you know."

"But it's an emergency."

"What kind of an emergency?" she asked, sounding more than a little suspicious.

"I'm all alone here with Comet, and he needs to get out and exercise, but I can't handle him."

"Oh, Clementine," she said, and my heart fell, due to the way she said it. "That horse has needed to get out and exercise every day since Tina . . . passed. And all of a sudden, today it's an emergency?"

I wanted to tell her about the nosy neighbors, and how it's harder out loud, but I didn't think she'd understand and besides, it was too much energy. So I just said, "I don't even know how Vern used to rake out that corral."

"You don't know how to move manure from one place to another with a rake?"

Then I felt more humiliated than I'd felt for a long time, and all I could say was, "But . . ."

"I'm sorry," she said. "But those are his wishes."

And she very gently hung up the phone.

I tried not to look in the direction of the stove again, because last time I did so, the earth nearly swallowed me up. I just kept looking at the phone, and I dialed up Emmy's husband, Arthur, at work. He was a contractor, and worked for his own self, and could take calls on his cell phone on the job. So I didn't feel like I was disturbing him.

"It's Clementine," I said, three times, because there was a lot of noise on his end. "I'm just wondering if you heard from Vern."

"No," he said. "Why?"

So I could tell he had no idea what had happened.

"Just looking to round him up," I said, trying to sound casual. But I doubt I succeeded. Plus, in over thirty years I'd never once called Arthur for the purpose of rounding up Vern.

"Ask Emmy," he said. "If anybody knows, she would."

And that was that.

Well, not quite it wasn't. I also called Vern's other sister, Amelia, but no one answered the phone.

So I went and lay down on the bed.

That way if the earth opened up on me again, at least I'd be horizontal, and maybe more able to cope with the falling. If there was something else to do in a situation like that, I swear I didn't know it. If I'd ever needed to know such a thing, most likely I would have asked Vern.

7. Jackie

"He's quite the problem," I said, as we were walking back across the road together.

Star had long since shut herself up inside the house.

"I don't think there's anything wrong with him," Paula said.

"I meant his temperament."

"So did I. He's fiery. On the high end of normal, I'd say. I think he's behaving the way most fairly young horses would if they never got out and got any exercise."

"What makes you think he never does?"

"Well. The dust on the halter."

"Maybe they bridle him and take him out."

"In which case I think his hooves would be self-trimming. They have the look of a horse who doesn't ever get the opportunity to wear them down. But there's another thing. Even more definite. Did you notice the gate?"

"The corral gate?"

"Right."

"No. What about it?"

"It's nailed shut."

"You're kidding. How do you nail a gate shut?"

"It's got three pieces of two-by-four across it. And they're nailed in place."

"Whoa. Think Star noticed that?"

"I have no idea. But I wouldn't exactly point it out to her. She's worried enough about the horse as it is."

"And he's still somebody else's horse," I added.

"Exactly," she said.

At the end of her day, Paula brought home barbecued chicken and biscuits from one of the few takeout places in town. It was surprisingly good, I noted, sneaking a piece in the kitchen before calling the kids to eat. She was nice about bringing home dinner at least half the time, because when I was alone all day with three kids and my art—especially during summer vacation, with everyone home—getting dinner on the table could be a lot.

Mando set the table with paper plates in wicker holders, and stacks of paper napkins, and Quinn washed his hands carefully, including under his nails with a brush, and arranged the food on serving platters. It was my favorite time of day. Even Star, sitting limply at the table, her chin in one palm, hair hanging into her eyes, couldn't ruin it for me.

"What did you kids do all day?" Paula asked, settling at the table.

"I'm not a kid," Star said.

"I'm teaching the dogs tricks," Quinn said.

"What kind of tricks?" I asked.

"Can't tell you. It's a surprise. When they're all ready, we'll do a big show for you."

"All the dogs?" Paula asked.

"No. Not Peppy. All Peppy does is sit in front of your bedroom door and wait for the cats to come out. Also I walked all around the property, all the way to every fence. Did you know there's a big creek that runs through here? I was thinking maybe there are fish in there. But I don't have a fishing pole. Do you think there are fish in there?"

"Might be," Paula said. "We can get you a fishing pole, and you can find out for yourself."

"I don't know how to fish."

"You've got all summer to learn. What about you, Mando?"

Mando's head jerked up, as though he'd just been jostled out of sleep. "What? Me? Oh. Um. I started cleaning out that barn."

Paula's brow creased the way it did when she was figuring things out. "Why would you clean out the barn?"

Mando shot me a wounded look, and I instantly felt like a sack of crap. If not multiple sacks of crap.

"Oh, Mando, I'm sorry. It was all this flap about the horse. I forgot to talk to her about it. I'm really sorry."

He shot Star a brief look, and just for a split second I thought I could see what he was thinking. That we spent time on Star that should have been evenly divided among everybody. And it was true; we did. I'm not sure if it was avoidable, but it was true enough.

Paula chewed faster. Swallowed. Set down her fork. "Talk to me about what?"

"Mando wants to make that old barn his room."

"Really? Why?"

I turned to Mando in case he wanted to speak for himself. But he looked like an actor, frozen, staring into the lights onstage, desperately searching for his line.

"He needs more alone time than we do," I said, and watched a little breath ease out of him.

"Does it have electricity?"

"It has a line going to it from the power pole," Mando said. "But the light doesn't work. I tried replacing the bulb. Maybe it's just a bad fuse or a flipped breaker or something."

"Do you know how to check that?"

"Yeah," Mando said. "The breakers seemed okay. But something's wrong."

"We could get an electrician out here to take a look," Paula said.

I looked from her face to Mando's, and it hit me all over again why I loved her. Why I loved them both.

"Thank you, ma'am—Paula."

"It doesn't have a bathroom, though," she added.

"No, ma'am. But I don't mind that. I'll go before bed. I don't get up in the night anyway."

Paula bit down on a drumstick and chewed for a few moments. I could tell she was in one of her thoughtful modes. "Only thing is, I don't want anybody thinking we stuck you out in some drafty old barn when the idea was supposed to be to give you a room in our house. But if we can get it in some kind of shape that your social worker would approve of, and if you're careful to tell her that it was your idea, and that you really prefer it that way . . ."

"It could be really nice out there," he said.

And then a silence fell.

"Star," Paula said. Loudly enough that it should have startled the girl. But she didn't so much as twitch. "What did *you* do all day?"

Star only shrugged. She never stopped eating. She never even paused.

"You don't know?" Paula asked. "You were there, weren't you?"

I wondered if it was a subtle way of asking if she had gone back to see the horse. But I didn't interfere.

"I did nothing," she said with her mouth still full. "I sat in my room and did nothing."

"How do you do nothing all day long?"

"It's easy."

"Quinn and Mando found plenty to do."

On that note, Quinn, who liked tension less than anyone, piped up again. "That wasn't even everything, what I told you. I made a kite. But it didn't

64

fly. Also it broke. And then I watched my hour of TV."

"Jackie used to make beautiful hand-painted kites," Paula told him. "Maybe she could teach you."

"Did they fly?" he asked, turning his attention to me. "Or were they just art?"

"They were both," I said. "They were flying art. I used to sell them through one of the wineries in Napa. But that was before we met you."

"Will you teach me?"

"Of course I will."

"Promise?"

"Promise."

I felt like I was saying too little to Star. I wasn't a natural when it came to family communication. I didn't do it by feel. And I was always accusing myself of doing it wrong.

"Did you watch your hour of TV, Star?" I asked. She was still avoiding everybody's eyes.

"No," she said, like that had been the dumbest question in the world. "There's nothing I want to watch. I'm not going to sit there and watch cartoons for an hour with Quinn."

"You can pick a different hour, you know."

"There's nothing on I want to watch. Any hour."

Everyone ate in silence for what seemed like a painful length of time.

Then Star said, "I don't think that horse ever gets out to run. He needs to run. He told me so."

65

Quinn snorted laughter. Star raised a hand to smack him, but before her hand could follow through, she instinctively met my eyes, and froze.

"Don't you dare," I said. "Ever."

She dropped her hand. "But he was laughing at me."

"You said the horse told you something," Quinn said. "Horses can't talk."

"He didn't say it in words, stupid."

"How did he say it, then?" Quinn asked, surprisingly unguarded for a boy who had just avoided being smacked by his sister.

Star turned her eyes up to Paula. In them I saw something I'd been looking for in Star as long as we'd known her. And which had always come up missing. It's hard to find just the right word for it, but something about engagement. Something that was the opposite of remaining utterly detached.

"Paula, when a horse is sick, or hurt, or needs something, can't you tell?"

"Usually," Paula said. "Sometimes I can see it with my own eyes. Other times I'd say, yes, the horse has a way of communicating pain without words. I can't always put my finger on how."

"Exactly," Star said. "That horse needs to get out of there."

"Star," I said. "He's not ours."

"I think you should call the Humane Society," Star said, visibly more agitated. "Have him taken away."

Paula shook her head. "They won't take that horse away from those people."

"You don't know that. Unless you call."

"I do know, Star. I've been a veterinarian for twelve years. I know the legal minimum for animal care. It's a low threshold. It's what the animal needs to survive. Food and water. Minimal shelter, for some animals, like dogs. But it can even be an overhanging porch, just to keep them out of the rain. It's not the same as what they need to be comfortable and happy."

"Well, that sucks!"

Star was on her feet suddenly, dropping her napkin and bumping the table. I steadied my glass of iced tea. Quinn and Mando both flinched.

"Star," Paula said evenly. "Sit down. Finish your dinner."

"I won't sit down!" she shrieked.

"Star," I said. "Paula took a lot of her own time this morning to go look at that horse. You shouldn't be talking to us like we don't care."

"It's not *enough!*" she shouted, wound up in that thunderstorm of teenage rage that carries its own unbreakable momentum. "You don't care *enough!*"

She stomped away from the table, leaving her mostly uneaten food on the plate. We all winced when the door to her room slammed.

I looked over at Paula. "Should we go in there?"

"I don't think so," she said. "I think we should

67

let her cool down. Nothing we say right now is going to make any difference anyway."

I looked at both of the boys, one after the other, and they both smiled weakly and looked away. Just for a moment, it crossed my mind how happy the family had been before we took Star. For what would prove to be the first time of many, I wondered if adding her to the family had been fair to them at all.

After dinner, Paula slipped a business card into my hand. "Do me a favor and run this over to the house across the road."

"Ick," I said. "Hate to talk to her on a full stomach."

"You don't have to talk to her. Just stick it in the door, or under the flag on the mailbox or something."

So I put on my shoes and walked across the road.

It was dusk by then, and the light had a dusty quality. I looked around at the landscape, only to be immediately reminded that there was nothing out here to see. Just flat brownness. The heat of the day had broken, leaving the air neither hot nor cool.

I saw no lights on in the house across the street. No truck parked in the dirt, as there had been the day we moved in. No movement, or signs of life.

Except the horse.

He never took his eyes off me. He tossed his

head and snorted, and stared at me every step of my way to the door.

On the way back to the road, I veered closer to his corral, for reasons I couldn't quite sort out. He was a beautiful horse, with a long mane, darker gray than his mottled coat, and a dark forelock that hung over one eye. It was hard to look away from him.

I stood at the rail for a moment or two, and he looked at me, and I looked at him. He didn't behave nervously, but he didn't seem relaxed, either. Just fixated on me. Like there was something he needed to say.

"Oh my God," I said. Under my breath. "Star was right. You need to get out of there."

Paula was getting ready for bed when I got back upstairs. She went to bed early, because she got up before dawn. She was standing in front of the mirror over the dresser, brushing her hair, and our eyes met in the reflection.

"That guy whose card you just delivered," she said, "John Parno. The farrier. He and his wife want to take us to dinner."

"Us?"

"Yes, us."

"Wouldn't it be better if I stayed home with the kids?"

"He has to get used to it, Jackie. He has to. Not just for our good, but for his own. The only way he's going to accept our both going away is if we do it often enough so he starts to notice we always come home."

"We don't have a babysitter."

"We do. John recommended one. Their family has been using her for years."

"Won't they need her when we go out to dinner, then?"

"I doubt it. They have no children. She's the sitter his parents used for him when he was a kid."

I breathed a few times, feeling the way my gut filled up with anxiety on Quinn's behalf. But Paula was right. We couldn't only go out one at a time for the next decade, until he was eighteen and off on his own.

"Okay," I said, though I noticed it didn't sound too confident. I sat down hard on the bed. "Maybe she'd sell us that horse."

"Where did that come from?"

"I guess I feel bad for him, too."

"She said he belongs to her daughter, though."

"So I guess the question is whether her daughter is coming back. Which I don't really want to ask her. Because she doesn't seem to want to talk about it. And because talking to her is about as entertaining as going to the dentist for a root canal. Except without all the fun anesthetic."

Paula smiled crookedly at me in the mirror. "It's a small town. It shouldn't be too hard to find out."

8. Clementine

I woke in the night because Comet was restless. He was whinnying, and I could hear his hoofbeats drumming. Not like he was running. He couldn't get up much of a head of steam to run in that little corral anyway. More like he was stamping his feet, or rearing up and coming down hard.

It bothered me, and I figured it bothered the neighbors.

So I said, "Vern!"

Nothing. But then, Vern slept like the dead. Always had, as long as I'd known him.

I rolled over and slapped my hand down to hit him on the arm, but my hand just kept going. By the time it thumped the mattress on the other side of me, I'd twisted my rotator cuff in my shoulder and had to yelp out in pain.

I sat up in the half dark, rubbing where it hurt.

The moon was full, dead full that night, and it poured in through the windows, where the curtains blew in, looking all filmy like a ghost. I kept the windows open at night in the summer, in the heat, so I wouldn't have to run air-conditioning, which I don't like the feel of when I sleep. Besides, that's too expensive.

For a minute I just stared at the open bathroom door. I think I was half-asleep and half-awake, because it took longer than it should have to realize Vernon wasn't in there.

Then I remembered.

It filled me with this sense of dread that I'm not even convinced I can describe. It hit me, right in that moment, that maybe this was real and maybe it would always be that way.

When Vern first left, it didn't feel real. I figured he'd be back by nightfall, hat in his hand, telling me things had to change for us to give it another go. And I would have promised to do better, and I swear I really would have tried.

But sitting up in bed, watching the moonlight thread through those blowing curtains, it hit me that I might never get the chance to try.

It wasn't that same feeling I described before, like falling. Not at all. It was more like just a blankness. Like a nothingness. A thing that didn't even make sense. I knew so little about how that would feel, how that would be, that it was like a thing that couldn't possibly exist at all.

I put on my robe and my big fuzzy slippers, and went out front to see if I could tell what was amiss with Comet.

There was nothing wrong that I could see. No people or animals around, no strange smells on the wind.

He noticed right away that I was there, and he stopped his fussing, and he stood stock-still and just looked at me. So still it made the hairs on the back of my neck stand up a little bit.

Then he lifted one front hoof and started to paw at the ground.

He used to do that with Tina, when she had him tied to the hitching post by the barn. She'd be saddling him up to go for a ride, and he'd stand there and paw and paw and paw. She said it meant "Hurry up and let's go already" in horse language.

But there was nowhere for us to go.

I did something I hadn't done in a very long time. As long as I can remember. I walked over to his corral and put my hands on the top rail, and he held stock-still again, and then pawed the earth another time or two. Just for a minute I had this mental image of me as a matador and Comet as a bull, ready to charge, but he did no such thing—just fixed his gaze on me and waited to see what I had in mind.

"When exactly did you and I get to be enemies?" I asked him.

He seemed a little curious to hear my voice. Like he was surprised that I would talk to him. He didn't have any answers for me—not that I expected any. But it was clear just by the way he stood his ground that the word "enemies" was not entirely off base.

But, then again, maybe I was wrong about that, because a minute later he came ambling over to the rail, like to come visit with me, and I swear that scared me even more than the charging-bull routine.

I hurried back inside and got myself into bed.

But I never got back to sleep.

In the morning I walked outside again, to see if I could figure out where Vern kept that extra-long-handled rake. You could catch most of what Comet dropped in there without even going in, unless he dropped it dead center.

The minute I stepped out into the cool, Tommy Smith came by in his pickup, running his paper route, and lobbed a paper right onto the stoop near my feet, where I swear it landed not a foot from the previous morning's paper, and slid until it hit its twin and stopped. He had been doing this for years, and had good aim. He waved at me before driving off.

I looked down at the papers and thought, *What are you bringing those for? I don't read the paper.* I thought about whether I should call the newspaper office and tell them to stop delivery. But the answer to that question was the answer to whether Vernon was coming back, so I just stepped over them and kept going.

I looked for that rake in the toolshed, and everywhere something could lean against something else outside, but I never found it, which could only mean it was in the barn.

I guessed maybe I'd have to get my car out of

the garage, if the old thing even started, and go get a new rake at the farm store. I didn't drive it much, so maybe the battery had held a charge and maybe it hadn't, but without Vernon to do the shopping and errands, it would soon be time to find out.

I stood a few feet away from the corral and looked at Comet, and got the strangest feeling. Like it was him, but it wasn't him, all at the same time. Like I remembered him from somewhere, but that's just plain foolish, because there's nothing to remember. He's always right there. I was tired from my lack of sleep, and just for a split second I couldn't sort it out.

Then it hit me. He looked like the horse he'd used to be when Tina was here. That's where I remembered him from. From his other self, before.

"You're looking unusually handsome this morning," I told him.

I separated off a flake of that good alfalfa hay and tipped it over the fence into his feeder. While I did, I noted that his water trough looked a little scummy with algae, and I had no idea what to do about that when it happened. That was one of the things Vern knew for both of us.

One of many.

I looked at Comet again, sticking his soft-looking nose in the feeder. Everything finally clicked together, and then I had to question what was wrong with me that it had taken me so long to sort it all out.

His coat was perfectly smooth. No burrs. No foxtails. No clumps of old shed that hadn't quite fallen out on their own. In fact, you could even see the little ridges in his coat left by a curry comb. And his mane and tail had no tangles. Every hair was perfectly separate, and fell perfectly into place alongside every other hair.

I looked at the house across the street, but nothing and no one was up and stirring.

"Why, you little . . ." I said. But then I trailed off, because I don't like to curse. Although, if I ever made an exception, it would be for that rude girl.

I wanted to go over there and pound on the door and take her to task, but it was too hard to know what to say. How do you say to someone, "How dare you make my horse handsome like he used to be?"

Besides, I was still shaky and tired. And it was easier to cut a wide path around the newspapers and go inside and start a pot of coffee and just let it all go by.

9. *Jackie*

I stepped out of Quinn's room briefly to knock on Star's door and make sure she was around.

"What?" she called through the door.

I confess I was relieved. Deeply relieved. I could hear Paula letting the babysitter in, and it was no time for Star to disappear. So of course this was the moment she was voted most likely to.

"Just wanted you to know we're going."

"So?"

"Just letting you know is all."

"That you're going."

"Right."

"So go."

I sighed and walked back to Quinn's room. He was lying on his back on the bed, looking at the star stickers on his bedroom ceiling, tears running down both temples. All four dogs were wedged onto the bed with him, and he had one hand each on the backs of Cecil and Jocko, the two big guys.

"How're you holding up, sweetie?"

"Couldn't you take two cars?" he asked, his voice strained and a little whiny.

I sat down on the bed, right up against his hip. Pushing dogs out of the way. I brushed that wild copper hair off his forehead. "Honey, we don't even have our second car out here with us yet. We all came together in the van, remember?"

"Oh. That's right. But I forgot how we're ever supposed to get it back."

"Marcie and Fran are coming out to visit this weekend, and they're going to drive it out to us."

"And then how do they get home to Napa?"

"They're coming out separately. In two cars. And going home together."

"Oh," he said.

I pulled a tissue out of a box beside his bed. Wiped his tears away. Held it to his freckly nose. "Blow," I said.

And, of course, he did.

"Couldn't one of you go in *their* car? Not Marcie and Fran's. I mean the people you're going to dinner with. Couldn't one of you go in their car?"

"I knew what you meant. But they're meeting us at the restaurant, because they live a long way away."

"Oh." I watched his chest hitch with little sobs like hiccups.

"Want me to run through it again?"

"J-Mom," he said, chastising me, "I could say it by heart."

"Well then, go ahead. It might do you good."

He sighed deeply, but it was a hitchy sigh. "My something-conscious mind is a funny place, because it always thinks just because it happened before it'll happen again. But really it's not more likely to. In fact, the odds of it happening to one kid with two different pairs of parents all in one lifetime are practically . . . I forget the word. But, like, probably it won't."

"Very good."

"I don't like the word 'practically' in there, though. You can't absolutely promise me."

"No," I said. "You're right. I can't absolutely promise. Life isn't like that. But I can absolutely promise you we'll drive very, very safely."

I looked up to see the babysitter standing in the bedroom doorway, a round woman in her sixties with thin, colorless hair. Wagging dog tails tapped the bedspread.

"Clara Bowe," she said. "Please, no jokes. I've heard them all before. What's wrong with the little guy? Gets sad when you go out?"

"Come on in, Clara," I said. "We're happy to meet you." Then, to Quinn, "You want to tell her, or should I?"

"You go," he said.

"Have a seat," I said to the babysitter, and patted Mando's bed, which Mando wasn't using. In fact, I suspected he hadn't used it for days. She settled her bulk onto the bed carefully, as if her bones hurt. "This is Quinn. Quinn had a very big tragedy in his life. When he was in kindergarten, his parents left him with a nanny for three weeks to go on a South American vacation. But there was a bus crash up in the mountains. And they were both killed. So now Quinn is with us, which he likes. But he does *not* like it when we go out together. He's pretty okay when we go out one at a time, or take two cars. But knowing we're both driving somewhere in the same car gives him anxiety. A lot of it."

Clara clucked her tongue. "Poor little guy." She reached across the space between beds and ran her fingers along his chin. He flinched, just a little, because he hadn't seen it coming. "We'll get along just fine. And your . . ." An awkward pause as she—I was guessing—questioned whether to call us his parents. ". . . they'll be back."

"I was hoping you'd stay with him and talk to him until he goes to sleep. He likes word games and guessing games, and they help take his mind off his anxiety."

"Of course. Of course I will. That's no problem. And the other kids?"

"I think Armando is out in the barn. You might see him or you might not. But don't worry about him. He's thirteen and very self-sufficient. And Star I can just about guarantee you won't see, and for your sake, I hope I'm right. She definitely doesn't need babysitting. She's fifteen."

"Oh my goodness," Clara said. "She's old enough to sit for the other two."

Quinn rolled his eyes wildly and made a noise like he was being strangled. "Nooooo! Don't ever leave me alone with just Star!"

I smiled, probably a bit sadly, and brushed his hair back off his forehead. "Star's not the baby-sitting type," I told Clara. "She's . . . unpredictable."

I pulled to my feet, and Quinn's panic escalated three or four notches. I know because I felt each notch in my own gut.

"You're going?"

"Pretty much, kiddo. Try not to worry. And if you have to worry anyway, tell Clara, and she'll help you."

I kissed him on the cheek and let myself out. It's best not to linger in that moment. Otherwise, his anxiety and my anxiety over his anxiety can mix together and become a very big monster. Overwhelming.

I looked around the house briefly for Mando, even though I knew damn well I'd find him in the barn.

Then I found him in the barn.

He was sitting on a sleeping bag in the corner, under a small lamp, reading. Leaning over his book with his signature intensity. He didn't immediately see or hear me. I looked around the place. No hay or straw anywhere. Perfectly clean concrete floor. He'd even begun putting up Tyvek sheeting on the inside of the walls for insulation. It looked about one-third done.

"Hi," he said. "You guys leaving?"

"We are."

"How's Quinn?"

"Weepy. But not in a state of utter panic."

"Want me to go check on him while you're gone?"

"I think he'd like that. It would be nice. I think the babysitter will be good with him, but—"

A movement high in the corner of the barn caught my eye. When I looked up, I saw some kind of frightening specter. A whitish mass, with intense, dangerous-looking eyes glowing at me in the dim. I jumped, then made some kind of strangled noise.

"Don't freak out," Mando said. "It's okay. He's okay. Don't be afraid of him. It's just the barn owl."

"We have a barn owl?" I was embarrassed at the breathiness in my voice, and the way I held one hand to my chest. That owl really had given me a good scare. I looked more closely and realized why he hadn't initially looked like a bird to me. It was the way the feathers on his face obscured his beak. It was partly the light, of course. The electricity was fixed in the barn now, but Mando wasn't using the big overhead light. Plus, barn owls are just spooky.

"We do," he said, sounding like that was not such a bad turn of events.

"I guess we'll have to look into how to relocate barn owls. Maybe Paula will know."

"No! Please don't move him. I like him. And he . . . well . . . I don't want to say he likes me. I don't know if owls like anybody. And I don't want to start sounding like Star. But he's . . . okay around me. We sort of have an understanding."

I looked up at the bird again. He stared back at me. Which I still found unnerving. "Well, I sure wouldn't want him looking at *me* like that while *I* sleep. But if you like him . . ."

"Actually, he's mostly out hunting while I sleep."

"So you *have* been sleeping out here."

He looked down at the olive-drab sleeping bag. He didn't speak. He seemed almost ashamed.

"It's okay. We're okay. I was just curious. See you soon."

"Ma'am? I mean, Jackie? When are your friends coming with the other car?"

"Funny, I was just talking to Quinn about that. This weekend."

"Oh. Okay. Good."

"Worried about the hearing?"

"A little bit. I know you say not to worry . . ."

"Right. Don't. I'll take you there if I have to take the only car we've got. If I have to rent a car. Hell, if we had to hire a cab to drive us all the way back there, I'm not letting you miss that hearing. I promised."

He nodded a few times. "I don't know why I worry about things I know I shouldn't worry about."

"Everybody does."

"Really?" His eyes came up to meet mine. Maybe eager to feel that connection between the inside of his head and everybody else. Then the corner of his mouth twisted into something almost akin to a smile. "Bet Paula doesn't."

I had to smile, too, at that. "Okay, maybe not everybody. But I bet more than half the people in the world right now are worrying about something that really is going to be okay."

The minute I got back in the house, Paula said, "There you are. Where were you? We're going to be late."

"Just checking in with Mando," I said. I did not say, *Oh, look, you're just like everybody else. Worrying about something that's bound to turn out fine.* But I thought it. "I just forgot to tell Clara one thing."

"Okay, but make it quick, please. I don't want to be late."

"Forgot to tell me what?" Clara asked, sticking her head into the living room.

"Our cell numbers are on the side of the fridge. Do me a favor and keep half an eye on the house across the street. Star is *not* supposed to go over there and see that horse, but I think she's been sneaking. If you see her there, please ask her to come home. But don't get into a fight with her if she doesn't. Just call us."

Clara gave a little salute. And then Paula grabbed my elbow and towed me out the door.

John and his wife, Mary Jo, were younger than I expected. Younger than we were. I don't know why I expected otherwise, especially with the babysitter thing to tip me off. Something about the rural environment, and a tough job like shoeing horses, just seemed to go with older and more experienced men to me. Silly.

For about the first ten minutes, almost until we ordered, Paula and John talked shop.

Then he suddenly looked at me and said, "This must bore you to death. I apologize." He had a nice face, handsome in a clean-cut sort of way, and a scar on his jaw that I wondered about. I wondered if he'd been kicked by a horse. And if something like it could happen to Star. Maybe even that night, while we weren't around to take care of things.

"I'm used to it," I said.

Mary Jo said, "I'm used to it, too, but it sure bores the hell out of *me*." She had fine features and butt-length brown hair, and wore makeup that I figured must take hours. "You must want to know something about the town. Or the people. You must be curious about something more like local gossip."

She beamed a smile right at me, and I tried to smile back, but her remark gave me a touch of heartburn. Because anyone who will gossip *to* us will gossip *about* us. I tried to take a deep breath and talk normally. I opened my mouth with no idea of what would come out.

Here's what came out: "What do you know about the horse across the road from us?"

Her smile deflated immediately. She exchanged a look with her husband. "The horse? Or the people?"

"Both, I guess."

John shook his head. "Really tragic thing. Very bad. Worst thing's happened in these parts as long as I've been alive."

I looked over at Paula, who was reading her

85

menu. Then back at John and Mary Jo across the table. They were just waiting, as if I were about to express my thoughts on the tragedy. But I had no idea what they were referring to.

The moment dragged on.

"She doesn't know, honey," John said.

"How can she not know?"

"Honey, they've only lived here barely a week."

"Oh, that's right."

Another long, awkward moment. Paula set down her menu. Not so much like she needed to engage in the conversation. More like she'd decided what to have. Frankly, I doubt she'd been listening. Her attention is unusually single-pointed. If she was reading the menu, chances are everything else in the room passed her by.

John and Mary Jo looked at each other, and I could see them mentally flipping a coin to see who had to talk. Then Mary Jo looked down at the table and John sighed, and I knew he'd lost the toss.

"Vern and Clem had a girl. They only ever had the one kid. They wanted kids real bad. Would have had a whole herd, I think. But they tried and tried for years, and nothing. And then Clem got pregnant with Tina. Right around the time people were telling them they might have to adopt, it happened. I know they tried for another, but Clem was close to forty by then and it was just a lot of miscarriages, and it broke everybody's heart. So it was just Tina. I knew Tina, too," he said. "Pretty well. We were only two years apart all through school. We both knew her."

"Kind of an odd duck," Mary Jo said. "But nice. I'm not saying she wasn't nice. I'm not speaking ill of the dead."

"Oh, she died," I said. Somehow that was an option I'd not yet considered. So that answered that question. She was not coming back for the horse. I don't mean to sound unsympathetic. I felt for my unpleasant neighbor. I did. More than I was really prepared to feel in that moment, in fact.

"Yeah, just a couple years back," John said. "Maybe not even quite that."

"How did she die?"

Another uncomfortable glance between them.

"I think she had some emotional issues," Mary Jo said, leaning in and lowering her voice. "She was . . . troubled. Everybody knew it. It was just one of those things you accept."

John said, "When she turned twenty-one, they bought her the horse for a birthday present. She never really got a job or left home or anything. I don't know if she ever would have. I think they thought the horse would calm her down. You know. Give her something to do. Something to . . ."

"Live for," Mary Jo said, jumping in to finish the sentence.

I had a bad idea I knew where this was going. It was building up in my gut, like the uncomfortable precursor to nausea.

"And it seemed to work for a few years," John added. "But . . ." And then he seemed to stall.

"She killed herself?" I asked.

They didn't want to say it, and I needed to get it said.

" 'Fraid so. Hung herself in the barn. And Clem was the one to walk in there and find her. Hasn't been the same since, I'll tell you. She was never exactly Little Miss Sunshine, but she took a very bad turn that day."

I realized suddenly that my hand was over my mouth. I had to move it to say what I said next. "Oh God. That's why she doesn't go in the barn."

"Doesn't she?" Mary Jo asked. "After all this time?"

"She told us she doesn't."

A silence fell, and lasted. And the waitress came to take our order. And I hadn't so much as glanced at my menu, except in those first awkward moments after sitting down, and I had no memory of what I'd seen. So I signaled to Paula to order first. She ordered roast turkey breast with scalloped potatoes, and that sounded good enough that I ordered the same. The Parnos both ordered steak.

When the waitress left, Paula said, "See, Jackie? It's like I always tell you." Then she addressed the other couple. "I always tell Jackie, and we always try to teach the kids, if you meet someone you don't like, or who doesn't treat you right, try to reserve judgment, because you don't know what that person's going through, and it's probably not so much about you at all."

"That's a very good attitude," Mary Jo said, nodding too much.

"So, John," I asked, getting the conversation back on track. My track, anyway. I couldn't dismiss the loss of Clementine's daughter, and I certainly didn't mean to minimize it. But right in that moment I was mostly worried for my own. "Have you done that horse's hooves before?"

"Oh yeah. Bunch of times. Tina had me in four times a year like clockwork. And that was back when Comet got tons of exercise, got ridden constantly, and got his hooves picked out at least twice a day. So they didn't need all that much, but she had me out just the same."

"Trouble handling him?" Paula asked.

"Not a bit. Never. Nothing wrong with Comet. He's just pent up. He needs to get out and blow off some steam."

"We put your card on their door," I said.

"Oh, she knows my number if she wants to call. She just doesn't call."

"Maybe her husband will."

Another look passed between them.

"Oh, you don't know that, either," Mary Jo said. "Vern left. Right around the time you moved in."

"Left? For good?"

"Hard to say," John added. "I heard he's holed

89

up at one of those extended-stay motels with the kitchenettes in Franklin County. Never know how these things'll go."

I glanced over at Paula, wondering if she'd say it again. About how we should always reserve judgment. She didn't. I supposed it went without saying by then.

"I guess this is what I'm really curious about," I said, mostly to John. But definitely to the other side of the table. "She acts like she doesn't care about that horse. I mean, she treats the horse the way you treat an animal you don't care about."

"I know," Mary Jo said. "It's a shame."

"Beautiful horse," John said. "Cost them a bundle. Shame to see him go downhill like that."

"So . . . what do you think?"

They both just stared at me.

"About what?" Mary Jo asked.

"Do you think she cares about the horse?"

Silence while they chewed that over. I guess it was a hard question.

"The reason I'm asking is because our foster daughter just loves that horse. She's made some kind of connection. And it just seemed like she'd be good for him and he'd be good for her. But I have no idea if Clementine would ever part with the horse."

"I doubt it," Mary Jo said.

It made my heart fall. Because that would have solved everything. At least, in my head it would have. I'd been living in this transitional happy place where that one final tying up of loose ends could make Star whole. Whether it was the real world or not was unclear. Probably not, because things are rarely that easy.

"So you do think she cares about him."

"Tricky," John said. "Not sure. That's a very good question. Well . . . this is my expert on human nature right here." He pointed at Mary Jo. "What do you say, honey?"

"I think she cared about Tina more than anything else in the world. And now I think . . . I think she sort of . . . is having trouble keeping the two things apart."

Which made so much sense it made my chest ache on behalf of our horrible neighbor. Did Clementine's having her reasons for being horrible help her case? Probably. But it was too much to sort out emotionally. At least in that moment.

"Tell you what," John said. "I'll give it a couple of days, and if she hasn't called me about his hooves yet, I'll just show up at her door."

10. Clementine

It was only a few days later when Johnnie Parno came knocking on my door at about ten thirty in the morning. And I certainly hadn't called him, or asked him to come. Probably I *should* have called him, but I hadn't. It's not the kind of thing a person is likely to forget having done.

To make matters worse, when I opened the door, he was standing there with five or six newspapers in his arms, which he handed off to me. I dutifully took them, like I'd wanted them all along, but meanwhile I was thinking to myself, *See what bad shape I'm in, that I never even thought what it would say to the locals, letting them pile up like that?* I felt humiliated, but also more than a little bit helpless, because I could no longer see such obvious things all on my own.

I looked past him and saw that girl was with him. It's not that I didn't remember her name, that girl. I did. But it was a silly name, a word that should never be a name on anyone, and I just found I resisted saying it, that's all.

She was bent over his big canvas shoulder bag of equipment, taking out metal files and long-handled clippers and blades and arranging them on the ground. And I had no idea why she would be doing that, rather than Johnnie doing it himself. Or, actually, even why *he* would be doing it. Somewhere, yes, but why here and now was a mystery.

Meanwhile, I hadn't managed to push out a word, which was getting awkward.

"Johnnie," I said.

"Morning, Clem."

He was wearing his leather farrier's apron and a

battered gray cowboy hat, and he tipped the hat to me. He looked so grown up. He'd been a boy of only two when Tina was born, and it was easier, somehow, to think of him as just a boy. But there I was looking in the face of this handsome, fully grown man, and all I could think was that if Tina had kept growing older she'd be this much of an adult herself now, minus two years. But that might not have been true, really, because adulthood had never been Tina's strong suit, not even when she was twenty-four. What she would have been beyond those years is lost to me forever.

"Don't recall our having an appointment, Johnnie."

He shook his head in a way that dismissed my argument, but good-naturedly. "Now, now, Clem. Let's not go all through this. It's high time, and you know it."

"Because that nosy vet told you so."

"Like I wouldn't have known it anyway, just because I know all on my own that I haven't been out here for two years. But yes, she told me what she saw when she gave Comet his exam. That's not nosy, Clem, that's just standard procedure between professionals, you know that. No charge today. Courtesy call."

For reasons I can't quite explain, it caused a flare of anger in me.

"Now why do people keep doing that?"

"To be nice?"

"But you're all treating me like I don't have the money to pay my bills. I pay my bills, young man. I've been taking care of my own expenses since before you were born. You can just send me a bill like you do everybody else."

"Yes, ma'am," he said. "Anything you say. We'll just get started."

My eyes shifted past him again to the girl, who was just standing there, arms limply at her sides, waiting for him.

"What's *she* doing here?"

"Well, it's like this, Clementine. I've got two choices. Have Dr. Archer-Cummings come over here and give Comet something to calm him down, or put that young girl at his head. And you know we don't like to tranquilize unless it's absolutely necessary. Now I hear you don't want her on the property because you have liability concerns, but let me put your worries to rest on that score. I've deputized her as my assistant. Which means my business insurance covers us both today. So we'll just go ahead and get started. Halter and lead rope?"

"I know where it is," the girl said. "I'm the one who put it away last time."

Before she walked off to the barn to get it, our eyes met. I felt silly, because I was still holding that armload full of dusty papers. I expected her to gloat at me, because she'd won this round. But instead her eyes just shifted back away.

I made a special point of not looking out the window while they worked.

"So, does he have thrush or doesn't he?"

Johnnie was back at my door, and when I looked past him, his things were all packed up and the girl was gone. I felt a sense of relief all out of proportion to the moment.

"Couple of spots, yeah." He held up a metal can of something, like the size of a pint of house paint, but without my reading glasses I couldn't read what it said. "He'll need his hooves picked out two or three times a day for the next few weeks, and this stuff brushed in. Get it as deep down into the grooves on each side of those frogs as you can get it, which'll be easier to do now, because I cut them way back. You can use a regular paintbrush, provided it's a stiff one, and good and clean. But I'm thinking you might not want to do the job yourself, and I'm not quite sure how you're going to work that out."

My head spun for a moment, because I expected him to say I should ask Vern to do it for me, and when he didn't, I knew that meant he knew everything. Probably everybody did. And I do mean the world spun inside my head, literally, like in that moment when you think you might pass out. I was that embarrassed.

"I'll work it out," I said, though I hadn't the slightest idea how.

"There's that girl across the road."

"When did you get in cahoots with her, anyway?"

Johnnie held both his gloved hands in the air, the way someone will do to show you he's unarmed. "I'm not in cahoots with anybody, Clem. I'm not *for* anybody or *against* anybody, except I'm on Comet's side. I just want him to get the care he needs."

"And you're saying I don't?"

"I said no such thing."

"I'll hire a boy. Some local teenager."

"Except Comet likes that teenager who was just here better than anybody. But it's your decision."

"Yes," I said coolly. "It is."

He seemed to take the hint. He handed me the metal can.

As I took it, I said, "Put this on the bill, too." Then I thought better and handed him back the can. "Do me a favor and leave this right outside his gate, since that's where it'll be needed anyway. Why keep it in the house? Comet never comes in."

He smiled a crooked smile, tipped his hat, and left me alone.

I had to lie down for a while, just to recover from the stress of it all.

The whole of that day and the next went by, and I didn't call any local boys to ask them to do the job. Every time I started to, I thought about what if they got hurt on my property doing some casual work for me, especially if they were minors. And if they were older than that, well, then they were all off at college, or working some serious job of their own. It just seemed so complicated, and without Vern here to help sort it out. I kept trying to think of somebody, but then the whole idea would tangle back on itself, until my brain was overloaded. I felt like I was blowing fuses in my head.

I felt bad about it, too.

And I felt mad. At Vernon. What a time to go away and leave me alone to cope with a thing like this. I didn't wish any harm to Comet, heaven knows, but this was a big undertaking.

By the following night I was so tangled up in guilt and dread and anger that I couldn't get to sleep. And don't think that didn't make everything harder, all the sleep I was missing. I've always been one of those people who doesn't function well unless I get my eight hours on a regular basis.

It was a little past midnight when I heard the sound out front. Just a minor sound, like something tapping on metal. If it had been cooler and the window had been closed, or if our bedroom had been around at the back of the house—and if I hadn't been wide-awake—I doubt I would have heard it at all.

I crossed to the window and looked out. What I saw did not surprise me in the least.

That girl from across the way was right inside the corral with Comet, and she was holding one of his hooves, and he was allowing it. She had a flashlight tucked under her chin, shining on the hoof. And she was brushing something in there with some kind of brush. It wasn't hard to figure out what. Or why.

I took a deep breath, and when I let it out, all those pent-up feelings came out with it. All the irritation, and the guilt, and the worry. All the sense of my brain being overloaded like one of those electrical outlets with too many power strips plugged in at once.

You'd think it would have made me furious—I sure would have thought so—but it didn't. How could it? She was doing what Comet needed done. She was doing what I wasn't.

I watched for a time, then slipped back into bed without ever letting on that I'd seen.

11. Jackie

It was a little after midnight when I woke up. I have no idea what woke me. If there was any sound, I didn't consciously register it. But a couple of times in nights past I'd wakened up and gone to the window—just as I did two or three dozen times each day—to make sure Star hadn't snuck over to be with the horse.

Surprisingly, in all this time I hadn't caught her.

I moved a cat off my chest and slid out of bed carefully, so as not to wake Paula. I went to the window. When I saw Star there, I wasn't surprised.

She was in the corral with Comet, doing something with his hooves, which seemed pretty reckless and dangerous to me. Then again, the horse looked content enough to let her work. Even so, it was dangerous, if only because of the reaction it would bring if Clementine caught her.

I watched for a minute, surprised at how hard it was to know what to do. How to handle it. I wanted to go out there and yell at her, ground her, forbid her. But we'd done all that already, and it wasn't helping a bit.

I needed Paula.

I hated to wake her. But I did anyway.

I sat on her side of the bed and stroked her hair so she'd wake up gently. I didn't want to shock her awake.

"Hmm?" she mumbled. "What is it, honey?"

"I need your help."

She blinked a few times. I could see her pulling herself from the depths. Then she sat up and looked me full in the face. "What's wrong?"

"Star is over there right now. Actually in the corral with the horse. I wanted to handle it, so you could sleep. But I'm just so out of ideas. I just

99

really don't know what to do anymore. I mean, we talk to her and talk to her and talk to her . . ."

"Maybe it's time to listen," she said.

Even half-asleep, Paula does life better than I do.

We were still in our robes and slippers when we crossed the road. Star never saw us coming, because she was bent over, with her back to us. I'm not sure how long we could have stood there undetected if Comet hadn't given us away. He tossed his head once and gave a little rumbly whinny, blowing our cover.

Star turned, and dropped what she'd been holding, and Comet spooked and danced over to the far rail. Even in nothing but moonlight, Star's panic was easy to see in her body language. She opened her mouth to speak, but I held my finger to my lips and pointed to Clementine's window.

Somehow she seemed to get it, in that moment, that we weren't about to come down on her like a ton of bricks. She tiptoed through the loose dirt to the fence. When she spoke, it was in a suitable whisper.

"I would've stayed away if she'd gotten somebody to do his hooves, but she never did. It's not fair."

"Come on out here," Paula whispered, and Star ducked between the fence rails.

We all three stood, with Star in the middle, leaning on the top rail and staring at the horse. We were so close that our sides were touching, which is good, because we could speak very quietly that way.

Why we stayed there at all, I'm not sure. It would have made a lot more sense to take her back home, turn on a light, and discuss it. But we'd come to try to get her to tell us about her bond with the horse. How it felt. Why it seemed more important than anything, even with all the trouble it could bring down on her. On all of us. Somehow the horse just seemed too much a part of the conversation.

Well, I'm guessing. Whatever the reason, we stayed.

"Tell us why this feels so important," Paula said.

I could feel the last of the tension breathe out of Star, who was wedged right up against my hip.

"Because he needs me," she said. "And I need him. We were meant to be together. I know we were. You can even tell from our names. Comet and Star. Like we're meant to be together forever in the sky. He can talk to me. He's trying to tell everybody what he needs, but I'm the only one listening."

"That's not true," I said. "Paula listened and gave him a checkup. John listened and did his hooves."

On that note, Comet walked over from the far side of the corral to join us. I swear I could see a perfect reflection of the moon in the dark, liquidy pool of his eye.

Star threw her arms around his neck. "But he didn't tell me he wants a checkup. He didn't say his hooves hurt. He says he needs to *run*." Nobody said anything for a time. It was Star who broke the logjam. "Maybe we could buy him from her. But I don't guess you'd want to spend all that money on something nobody wants but me."

"No, we would," I said. "It's not that we wouldn't. It's that I don't think she would sell."

"But you haven't asked."

"I put out some feelers with John the farrier and his wife. We discussed it over dinner."

"That figures," she said.

"Meaning what?"

"Bunch of grown-ups all sitting around discussing what's best for the horse. But nobody asks the horse."

"Come on, honey," Paula said, swinging an arm around Star's shoulder. "Let's go home."

"I can't," she said. "I have one more hoof to do."

I looked at Paula and she looked at me. More light would have helped us communicate. I shrugged. Probably we should have told her to come right home. I don't know. It's a hard question. I'm not quite sure how to tell a girl who loves a horse to leave an infection in that horse's

102

hoof when anybody with an ounce of humanity would put medicine on it. Especially if there was an open can nearby.

Paula nodded, which was nice, because I didn't have to.

We waited for her to finish.

While we were waiting, Paula whispered in my ear. "Think that was a metaphor?"

"Which part?"

"Bunch of grown-ups sit around talking about what's best for the horse. But nobody asks the horse."

"Oh, that," I whispered. "Right."

Like the way a poor foster kid must feel just about every day of her life. I didn't answer the question of whether I thought it was a metaphor, because it seemed like an unanswerable question. It probably was, whether Star had consciously meant it to be or not.

We walked back across the road together, leaning in on Star, each with an arm around her shoulder. As though she needed help holding herself together. Which was not entirely outside the realm of possibility.

"Will you at least *ask* her?" Star said to neither one of us in particular.

"Yes," I said, knowing this was one I could handle alone. "I can't make you any promises about what will happen. In fact, I'm not optimistic at all. But I *will* ask her if she'd consider selling us the horse."

"Thank you," Star said.

To the best of my recollection, it was the first time she'd ever used those two words in my presence.

I didn't get right back to sleep. I didn't even bother trying.

I sat at the dining room table with my laptop, and spent more than an hour composing a letter to Clementine. My instincts told me it would be better than talking face-to-face. Because she could read it in private, react to it in private. Think about it, maybe even get used to the idea, before responding. Maybe we'd get something better than her first, most bitter knee-jerk reply.

I was as conciliatory as I knew how to be. I was careful to ensure she didn't feel pressured. And no guilt trips. Or, at least, as few and as short as possible. I reminded her that the horse would be right across the road. That she could still see him every time she looked out her window. That he would live with a veterinarian, and get the best of care. And be ridden all day long by a girl who adored him.

I did my best to appeal to her humanity.

If indeed she has any.

Then I was immediately sorry for that inner comment. I shouldn't even think things like that, but Clementine made it extra-hard not to. I really did understand why she clung to the horse. I just hoped she could move beyond it now.

I hit "Print."

I tried to go back to bed, but the letter kept tugging at me. It was downstairs on the dining room table, and it wouldn't leave me alone.

In time I got up again, and tied on my robe and slid into my slippers. I tiptoed downstairs, folded the letter into thirds, and sealed it into an envelope. Then I walked it across the road.

The horse never took his eyes off me the whole time. I wedged the letter in between the door and the jamb. He made no movement. He made no sound. I wanted to tell him I was trying. But I didn't want to do anything to wake Clem.

It still took a long time to get back to sleep.

By the time Marcie and Fran were scheduled to arrive the following afternoon, my lack of sleep was catching up with me big.

I fed the kids in the kitchen, knowing they wouldn't want to eat as late as the grown-ups that night. I made chicken hot dogs, which were Quinn's favorite, with potato salad and pasta salad from the deli counter at that little market three miles down the road into town. I even let them have sodas, which I knew I might regret come bedtime. It's always harder for a kid to sleep with a belly full of sugar.

Quinn was worried that he would already be asleep by the time Marcie and Fran arrived. He asked three times when they were coming. Three times I told him they hadn't called yet with a progress report from the road.

"But even if you miss them tonight," I said, "they'll be here till Sunday."

"Oh," he said. "That's good."

I looked over at Star. She had just one hot dog on her plate, with no condiments and no bun. She was stabbing a fork into it repeatedly.

"You okay, Star?"

"You didn't ask her yet. Did you?"

"I did ask her. I sat up most of the night writing her a very nice letter. And I stuck it in her door. And this morning I looked, and she'd taken it in."

Star only stabbed harder. "Well, that's no good. You should have asked her in person. This way she can just never answer."

"I'm not sure if you've noticed this, Star, but she's not the easiest person in the world to get along with."

Star snorted more theatrically than necessary.

"The reason I wrote a letter is because I wanted her to be able to think about it. In private. I thought if she felt cornered, that would only make things worse. I did what I thought was most likely to get us a yes."

"What if it's not a yes *or* a no? What if she just never answers?"

106

"If I haven't heard back by the time our guests leave on Sunday, I'll go ask."

Fran was my favorite. Marcie was okay. I liked them both. But Fran and I had always clicked. So I was happy when Marcie and Paula assigned themselves to barbecue duty, and Fran and I got to sit on lounge chairs in the front yard, surrounded by sleeping dogs and drinking imported beer they'd brought as a gift. Our favorite brand, and we couldn't even buy it in Easley.

The sun was almost down, and it slanted into my eyes, and I shaded them with one hand. I looked out at the landscape through Fran's eyes. It looked even worse. Flat. Brown. Dusty. Dry. Thoroughly unremarkable.

As if reading my mind, Fran said, "This place, It's so . . . what's the word?"

"I'm trying to clean up my language for the kids," I said.

She brayed laughter, and I realized I'd missed her. Even though it hadn't been long at all.

Fran had a shock of very red—very unnaturally red—hair, and the more she sweated, the bigger her hair. It was coarse and wavy, going to frizzy in damp conditions. It was big that night. And she wore intense colors, always. In this case, a vivid-yellow sleeveless shirt and pants. Highway-safety bright.

"It's so . . . rural," she said.

"Oh, yes. It's all of rural."

"Do you hate it?"

"I don't like it. I sure wouldn't have chosen it. But you know how it is."

"No. How is it?"

"I knew when I got together with Paula that we'd go where her work takes us. I knew there were too many vets in Napa County. It was too hard to get a good practice going with all that competition."

"Yeah," Fran said. "Paula's worth it."

"She is. Isn't she?"

I shaded my eyes again and watched Paula brushing extra marinade on the mahimahi as it grilled. It hit me all over again, how worth it she was.

"You two have always been so perfect for each other. I envy it."

"You and Marcie aren't having trouble, are you?"

"No. Not at all. It's just so . . . *real* on our side of the fence."

"It's real on everybody's side of the fence. You just don't see the real through the fence."

"Tell you a secret," she said. "But you can't tell."

"Who would I tell?" I swept my arms wide to take in my dusky, mostly uninhabited environment.

"There are still phones, you know."

"I don't gossip."

"That's true. You don't. What's up with that?"

"Are you going to tell me, or not?"

"We're trying to get pregnant."

"Whoa. That *is* big news. Which one of you?"

"Me. We talked about adopting. You know. So we could be saints, like you guys. But we really want it to be ours."

I winced a little. People didn't always think before they spoke. I tried to tell myself that she really didn't mean Quinn wasn't ours. If I'd brought it up, she'd have apologized for an hour and convinced me she'd meant no such thing. Maybe it was more that they simply couldn't picture how "theirs" an adopted child would be. Because they'd never tried it.

Part of me wanted to lash out and remind her that the baby they were trying to have would be biologically hers but not Marcie's. Part Fran and part donor. But that was just trading one offense for another.

I wanted to be more like Paula. See the best in people. Give them the benefit of the doubt. But it stung.

Of course, while I was thinking all that, I missed a lot of what she was saying.

She stopped talking suddenly, midsentence, and it brought me back. I looked up to see what she'd seen. Clementine was tossing a flake of hay into Comet's feeder. And staring daggers at our side of the road.

"Whoa," Fran said. "Neighbors none too

friendly, huh? I can just see what she's thinking: 'Gaaaa! There used to be only two of them, and now there are four! They're multiplying! They'll take over the neighborhood!' Now you know how it feels to be in the minority, lady."

My heart fell as I watched Clementine cross the road in our direction, feet stamping hard in the dirt. And her daggerlike glare, now that she was closer, was clearly focused on me.

"Should we run?" Fran whispered in my ear, still in joke mode.

"Nowhere to run to," I said.

The dogs sat up and wagged, but as she got closer Wendy hid under my lounge chair, and Cecil and Jocko flinched and moved closer to the house.

When she was a few steps away, Clem reached a hand into the pocket of her flowered skirt, pulled out a folded sheet of yellow paper, and threw it in my general direction. The breeze caught it and blew it back behind her head, and she stepped on it as she walked away, grinding it into the dirt.

I looked up to see Paula and Marcie standing over our chairs.

"What was that all about?" Paula asked.

"I don't know," I said. "But it wasn't good."

Paula walked over to the yellow paper. Picked it up and shook dirt off it. Looked at it without unfolding it. Then she brought it to me, held it out, and just waited for me to take it.

"What are you giving it to me for? I don't want it."

"Because it's for you. It has your name on it. Right there."

I took the note. Opened it, my hands shaking just a little.

It was handwritten in a loopy scrawl, with lots of exclamation points and double underlining.

Dear Jackie Archer-Cummings,

Absolutely not!!! I cannot believe you would even ask such a thing!! This is why I didn't want you or your veterinarian 'wife' or that difficult child of yours anywhere near my horse, my property, or my life. Because you take liberties!! Now you're acting like Comet is yours, or at least should be! I'll have you know he belonged to my daughter, who died of cancer at the young age of 24, and he's the only thing I have to remember her by!! And he is NONE OF YOUR BUSINESS!!!! Please don't force me to say this to any of you people ever again!!! And don't ever again suggest that you can get him away from me! I don't care how much you offer to pay, because money has nothing to do with this!! I've never seen such rudeness in ALL MY LIFE!!!

—Mrs. Vernon D'Antonio

Within a hailstorm of other emotions, that signature—combined with the claim that her daughter had died of cancer—made me painfully sad.

I was so caught up in her outrage that I forgot three people were watching me, waiting to hear the news.

Paula said, "Well?"

"In short, she's not going to sell us the horse."

"Ooh. That's bad."

"You want to tell Star, or should I?"

"Let me," Paula said. "I do better with tantrums than you do."

The food was on the dining room table long before Paula got back. We finally broke down and started eating, because there's nothing worse than cold fish. But I didn't want to start without Paula, and I'd mostly lost my appetite anyway.

I had one ear trained for noises from upstairs, but I never heard a thing.

"Sorry we didn't have room to put you up," I said.

"Three kids," Marcie said. "I'm surprised you have room for everybody's elbows."

"I don't even want to ask how the motel is."

"Basic," Fran said. "I'm being as polite as I can."

My head snapped up when Paula walked into the room.

"How'd she take it?" I asked.

"Too well."

"Is that a joke? No such thing as too well."

"I hope you're right," she said.

And that was all we really cared to discuss in front of the company.

We never really got to discuss it later, either, because I fell asleep on the couch while they were talking, and Paula had to lead me up to bed.

It was after two in the morning, I would later learn, and I was having a dream that was nothing but hoofbeats. No visuals at all. Just a gray screen of nothingness, and the sound of hoofbeats.

Then I opened my eyes. I thought I might still hear them, but so faintly it was hard to know for sure. Plus I was half-asleep, and not positive whether the dream had let me go.

I blinked at the ceiling for a moment or two.

It crossed my mind that maybe it was only Comet, and not a dream at all. We heard his hoofbeats often enough in the night. But this was different. This was a continuous set of galloping hoofbeats fading off into the distance. This was a horse who could run without ever hitting a fence.

I was seized with a bad feeling, and I swung out of bed and ran to the window—nearly tripping over Jocko—just to prove myself wrong.

In the moonlight I saw Comet's corral empty, the gate yawning open, swinging back and forth in the breeze. The three pieces of two-by-four that had once held it shut lay scattered in the dirt.

I ran to Star's room and banged on the door, then tried the knob. It was unlocked, so I threw the door wide.

No Star.

Her closet door was hanging open, the dangling lightbulb on, and half her scant collection of clothes was gone. Her school backpack was gone.

I turned suddenly to find Paula in the hall behind me.

"What's all the noise, Jackie? What's going on?"

"We've got problems," I said. "We've got big, big problems."

12. Clementine

I thought if I marched across the road and threw that letter into my rude neighbor's face, I'd feel better. My anger was so hot and so huge that I needed a break from it. It takes a lot of energy to be that angry, and I didn't have what it took. I was beginning to feel like a big raw nerve from all these problems, compounded by lack of sleep. I needed relief.

But the wind caught the letter and blew it away. Which is not to say the direction the letter took was the problem. The problem was that I thought delivering it would help to resolve things, but I was wrong.

No sooner had I slammed my way back into the house than the phone rang, and I knew it was her. I just knew it. Calling to argue some more, probably. So just at that moment when I really, physically needed the relief from all this upset, it felt like my life turned up its own volume.

I stormed over to the phone and snatched it up.

"What?" I shouted. Literally shouted. "What do you want from me now?"

Silence on the other end of the line. In that silence, I knew I had been wrong about who was calling. It's as though the silence had a voice—though it sounds nonsensical to say so—and the voice was not hers. Not anybody's who lived across the way. Still no words, but I heard a faint clearing of a throat, and that was all I needed.

"Vernon," I said. Soft, like a whisper.

It had been a long time since anything soft had floated through my world.

"Clementine," he said in reply.

Then we were still, and I had that grand relief I'd been after. It was cool, like running water. It seemed so foolish of me to think he'd be gone forever, just like that. That I'd never hear. Never know. Of course it was Vernon. Of course.

"Where are you?" I asked.

He hemmed and hawed a little, then said, "That doesn't really matter."

115

It did to me, though. A lot.

I rushed to cover over the way I'd answered the phone. "I must have sounded awfully rude. I was just—"

But then it hit me how important it was not to say. I'd been just about to rant to him every detail of how furious I was with the neighbors across the road. Talk about being a slow learner! That was exactly what had sent him running for the door in the first place.

"Look," he said. "I know I can't just walk out of there, just like that."

I lowered myself into the chair by the phone, and that sweet relief got wider and deeper, and I just felt around in how wonderful it was, and how much I'd needed it. "Of course not," I said.

"There are a hundred details we have to take care of. Property to split. Arrangements over belongings, and . . . well, you know. Things like that."

My mouth felt suddenly dry. The relief dried up like the last of cooking water when it evaporates from a hot pan, right in front of your eyes. But nothing came in to take its place. I felt nothing.

"You don't even want to . . . ?" But somehow I couldn't go on.

"What, Clem?" he asked, sounding gentle. For a change.

"I can't believe you don't even want to . . . try."

"What do you think I was doing all those years,

116

if I wasn't trying? Look. I'm sorry. I didn't call to be hurtful. I want to give you a phone number. You know. In case of anything really urgent."

My whole life is really urgent, I thought. But he was still talking.

"Clem, these past few days . . . It's almost hard to say it in words. It's like I've been carrying three or four anvils with me everywhere I go, and I finally got to put them down. It feels like . . . Remember when I used to smoke two packs of filterless Camels a day? And then I quit. Just like that. It was damn hard. In my head. In my body, it was like I got well. But it's a weird feeling to get well when you never even knew you'd been sick. I thought it was just normal, how I felt. And then it got better, and I thought, *Damn. So this is how I was supposed to feel all along.*"

Which makes me a sickness, I thought. But I couldn't speak, and didn't want to even if I could have.

"I can't give that back, Clem. I'm sorry."

I realized I wasn't breathing—or, at least, not enough. I pulled a full breath, and it felt awkward. Not at all like something I'd been doing every minute of my life.

"So take down this number, okay? But, please. Just for emergencies only."

"It's probably on the caller ID," I said. "Unless you blocked it."

"Oh. Right. No. I didn't block it."

"How will we split property and belongings if we only ever talk in emergencies?"

There were more questions, but I was afraid to ask them. We had nothing, really, except this house and the land, and our Social Security checks. So what did it mean to split this place? Would we have to sell to split?

I looked down at my hand, holding the phone. It had drooped down away from my ear, and I hadn't even known it. It broke through and frightened me when I saw how much it was shaking, that hand, and how I was looking at it like it wasn't even me.

I think Vernon might have been saying something, but I'm not sure.

I brought the phone back to my ear.

"I don't know what to do about Comet," I said. "He's got algae in his water trough, and a touch of thrush. And his hooves are supposed to be extra-clean until it clears up, but I don't even know where that long-handled rake is. I don't even know how you used to do that."

"You don't know how to move manure with a rake?"

"That's almost exactly what Emmy said."

"When did you talk to Emmy?"

"Never mind."

"It's in the barn. The rake."

"Oh. I was afraid of that. I guess I'll have to go out and buy a new one."

"You can't buy a rake that long, Clem. I made

118

that myself, by welding two extra handles onto it. Don't you remember? I did that for you, in case you ever needed to use it. I was never so afraid of Comet that I wouldn't even go through the rails into his pen."

"Well, I don't know what to do, then."

"It's simple, Clem. You go in the barn and get it. Don't you think it's time you went in the barn?"

"No," I said, and my voice got much harder all of a sudden. "No, I think it's time to call Ernest Tate Construction to send out a few of his men to tear the damn thing to the ground like I wanted to but you would never let me."

"Well, before they start tearing, tell them to bring out the long rake." Then he cleared his throat softly and started off in a different tone. "I didn't want it to be like this, Clem. This is not what I started off to do. I'll see you."

And he hung up the phone.

But that was a lie, that last sentence. He wouldn't see me. And that was exactly what he had called to say.

I slept like the dead. And I have no idea how, or why. I guess my body finally snapped and took the sleep it needed. I slept the way Vernon used to always sleep. When I woke up, it was nearly light, and I was groggy and couldn't clear my head. It felt like my head was stuffed with cotton. There was no room left over for a single thought.

I sat up on the edge of the bed for a long while, slowly clearing my brain. I looked at the upstairs phone, sitting on the nightstand, and I thought, *I can't keep doing this. I can't stumble through every day like the walking dead, telling myself I don't know how to do what needs to be done. He's gone, and I just have to figure something out. Like it or not.*

I scrolled through the directory of numbers to see if Johnnie Parno was still in there from when Tina used to call him. When I saw that he was, I got tired again, and thought maybe I'd wait until right after I made myself coffee and some breakfast. But I knew I would lose my nerve again. I could feel it. So I went ahead and called.

He picked up on the second ring, and he was in his truck. I could hear the road noise, and the sound of his engine.

"Hey, Clem," he said. "Horse troubles?"

"I was hoping you could tell me the best way to clean algae out of a water trough."

"Sure. Lot of people drain the thing and scrub it out by hand, but if you ask me, that's doing things the hard way. Here's what I like to do. I like to go to the pet store over in Stafford and get three or four of those really big goldfish. Put those guys in a tank that big, they grow huge. Like monsters. Like the carp that people put in their koi ponds. They're a relative of carp, those goldfish. Anyway, you just drop 'em in there. And you never have to

120

change the water, because the horse does it for you, by drinking it down and triggering the valve to refill. So there's always fresh oxygen for the fish. And you never have to feed the fish, because they eat the algae. And so long as no hawks or eagles come by to go fishing, you're golden."

"And they don't scare the horse?"

"Never met a horse who cared. Besides, they tend to dive for cover if a shadow comes over the tank. I have to go by there today or tomorrow for a big bag of kibble for the dogs. Want me to pick you up a few fish?"

"That would be very nice. Thank you."

I took a breath, and it felt cleaner than the breaths I'd taken before. Suddenly I felt as though things were looking up. I had solved a problem. I had taken a small weight off myself. I had found an answer, and proved there were other people in the world to ask besides Vern.

Despite its being one weight of many, I felt, for the first time in a long time, like there might be a light at the end of my tunnel.

"Also," I said, "I still need a boy to clean that corral and look after his hooves. You know anybody?"

"Hmm," he said. "Let me think on that and get back to you."

And we said our good-byes and hung up.

I walked downstairs and made myself half a pot of coffee, for the first time ever. Every single morning since Vern had left, I'd made a full pot, and then the minute I'd heard it dripping I'd realized my mistake. That morning I made just enough for me.

While it was perking, I stepped out onto the front stoop to fetch the paper. My back twisted a little, bending down to get it, so I was careful to straighten up slowly. I was thinking I'd call the newspaper office after breakfast and cancel the subscription.

"Well, good morning—" I said out loud, in the direction of the corral.

I had intended to say, "Well, good morning, Comet." But before I could even say the name Comet, I saw there was no Comet in the corral to say good morning to. The gate was swinging open, and Comet was gone.

13. Jackie

We called Marcie and Fran on their cell phone, and we circled back and met up where our road intersected the two-lane highway into town.

It was full-on light. Maybe even close to seven o'clock, though I wasn't wearing my watch. We all stepped out of our two respective vehicles and stood in that mostly uninhabited landscape, and I swear I heard at least three of us sigh. Almost exactly at the same time.

One of them was me.

I leaned back against the grille of our van. "So much for 'They couldn't have gotten far.'"

"If she's smart," Paula said, "which I think she is, she'll stay off the roads. Plus, we know how much she cares about the horse. And he'll need water. A lot, if they're in traveling mode. So probably she's making her way along one of the creeks."

"Yeah, that makes sense," Fran said. "It's wooded over the creeks." She pointed to the proof of her observation. "Which answers your original question about how you hide something as big as a horse."

"Wait," I said. "There's more than one creek?"

"Oh yeah," Paula said. "There's a whole network of them running through this valley."

I said nothing, and neither did anyone else. For a time. I can't speak to their silences, but mine was full of the most painfully deep disappointment. I realized in that moment that Star was gone. She'd succeeded. Gotten away. Which is not to say she'd never be found, of course. But it was no longer likely that *we* would find her. Now. Before things got ugly.

Until that exact moment, I hadn't known.

I'd been pretty optimistic when we'd first launched our search party. I mean, I'd heard the hoofbeats fading away. How hard could it be to catch up to them in cars? I think I'd honestly believed we'd have that horse nailed back into his corral before the sun came up. Before Clementine even had time to scream.

I looked at the early sun lighting up the ribbon of trees lining the creek. Correction: *one of* the creeks. Watched it stretch seemingly forever into the distance, to fork into new creeks, also well covered.

I had not a scrap of that optimism left.

"Here's what I think we should do," Paula said. "I think Fran and Marcie should keep driving. Just on the off chance they can see anything from the road. Jackie, I think you should go back home. Deal with whatever comes up there, and stay by the phone. I'm going to drive to the nearest big town that rents ATVs. No idea where that would be, but I'll figure it out. Then I can search off-road."

"Keep driving *where?*" Fran asked.

"I don't know," Paula said. "Anywhere. They could be anywhere."

"I think . . ." I said. Then I stalled. Because it was hard to say what I needed to say. It wasn't a happy set of words. "I think maybe we shouldn't be searching for her at this point at all. I think it's gone past that."

Silence.

Fran said, "I know you don't mean we should do nothing."

"No, I don't mean that. I mean maybe the pros

need to be searching at this point. I think it might be time for the police."

"Easley doesn't have police," Paula said.

"What kind of town doesn't have police?"

"The unincorporated kind."

"There's no law enforcement in Easley."

"No, of course there is. There's the sheriff."

"Oh. The sheriff. Well, maybe that's who it's time for."

Paula slipped off her denim jacket, because it was already warm out. She wore a sleeveless shirt underneath, her upper arms strong-looking and tan. "If that's what you think, then make the call when you get home. We're going to keep looking."

Half a mile down the road from our house, I saw it. Parked in front of Clementine's, its light bar spinning red and white. I wasn't close enough to read what it said on the car, but if the sheriff was the only law enforcement in Easley, then it must have been the sheriff.

I was surprised at the fear reaction in my gut. As if I'd been caught robbing a bank. I tried to remind myself I had not personally stolen anything.

I pulled up in front of our garage and stepped out. Just as I did, the flashing lights cut out, and the car—which indeed said Sheriff on the door—pulled away. I thought I saw Clementine sitting in the passenger seat. Up front. I thought I saw her looking at me as they drove away. But from the distance and the angle it was hard to be sure.

It all happened fast.

I stood there in the middle of the dirt road, feeling half my fear drain away, leaving a jumble of emotions I couldn't even imagine untangling.

Then a movement caught my eye. I saw a uniformed figure crouching on the balls of his feet in the dirt by Comet's empty corral. Someone was still there.

I walked across the road.

"Good morning," I said, still too far away to see much about who I was saying it to.

"You Dr. Archer-Cummings?" he asked, without getting up or turning around.

"No, sir. I'm Jackie Archer-Cummings. Paula Archer-Cummings is the doctor. I'm not the doctor."

"Ah," he said. "The doctor's wife."

I thought it was unexpected for someone here in Easley to get that right the first time. I didn't say so.

Instead, I said, "I came home to call the sheriff. But you saved me the trouble."

He levered to his feet and offered his hand to shake. "Yes, ma'am. Dennis Portman. Sheriff's deputy."

His hand was big and rough, but warm.

"Was that my neighbor I just saw go by?"

"It was."

"Am I allowed to ask where she was taken?"

"Hospital," he said simply, and began to examine the ground again.

"Is she sick? Or injured?"

"Depends on how you look at it," he said, which answered nothing.

"I guess it's none of my business. I was just concerned."

He paused. Sighed. He was tall and broad-shouldered. Solid. Blond. Short-haired. Young. Suddenly everybody was younger than I was. I wondered how that had managed to sneak up on me.

"Our original goal was to get one of the doctors out here to sedate her. But that's a dicey thing when a person lives alone. What if she takes a fall? Or needs something? Can't really dope her up and leave her all by herself. We hate like hell to go the hospital route, because it'll cost her a bundle. All she has is her Medicare, and she'll get stuck with a big piece of the bill. That's why my partner drove her in. Save her the cost of the ambulance at least."

I knew in my numb, frozen gut that the expense would be ours. In time. After the criminal trial would come the civil one. Of course, that was the least of my worries. It was a worry, but it was just one more.

I looked at the dirt, where he was looking. He was squatting again, examining the two-by-fours scattered by the gate. Without touching them.

"Any chance that horse busted himself out?"

"No, ma'am," he said.

It had been such a thin thread of hope—barely the width of a human hair—my wild grasp at a scenario in which somehow the two disappearances were unconnected. What could the chances have been? One in a thousand? But it felt so hopeless and sickening to have it ripped away so quickly, and so completely. I wished he'd let me keep it just a moment or two longer.

"He could have hit that gate. Right?" I asked, even though it was over.

"Yeah," Officer Portman said. "Theoretically. Let's say he did. Let's say he knocked out those two-by-fours by hitting the gate. Clem says they were nailed in place. Which, really, when you think about it, makes us half want to put the thief in jail and half want to give 'em a medal. Hell of a thing to do to a horse for a couple years on end. And I can see how he might get anxious to break free. But if he did, one of two things would happen, the way I see it. The two-by-fours would break. Or the nails would pull out. Probably pull out on the nongate side. But here you have three two-by-fours lying in the dirt. Completely free on both ends. And here's the really important question. Where are the nails?"

He swept one arm, pointing to an arc of ground. No nails. I did see a claw hammer lying in the dirt.

"No, what we have here is a case of a person

128

prying out the nails with the claw of a hammer. But not dropping the nails. Or dropping them and then picking them up later. Picking up the nails but leaving the hammer lying right there in the dirt. I'm still working on that one. Why someone would go and do it like that."

"Because she cares about the horse," I said. My lips felt numb, and my voice sounded half-unfamiliar to me. "She didn't want the horse to step on the nails."

We stood in silence for a time. He was looking straight into my face, but I didn't dare look back. The moment seemed to stretch on for a long time. Too long. The sun had risen from its slant at the eastern edge of the sky, and it shone into my eyes, half blinding me. I wanted to convince the sun not to keep rising, the morning not to progress. What could it possibly bring but more trouble?

I decided to break the torturous silence myself. Just to get it broken.

"Maybe Clementine could come home and *we* could look after her. We live right across the road."

He continued to squint into my face for a time. His face looked friendlier, softer, than I expected law enforcement personnel to look.

"You should know she thinks your foster daughter stole the horse. Then again, it sounds like you think so, too."

"I think so, too."

"Okay, then," he said, with a sigh that sounded weary. "Let's go on across the road and I'll start my report."

"I am *so* exhausted," I said as we stepped inside. "I feel like I'm dying. I know your time is valuable, but what would you think about my taking a minute to start a pot of coffee?"

I could hear the dogs barking from Quinn's room, but they must have been closed in.

The deputy said, "I don't see how the earth would spin off its axis if I were to wait that long."

I disappeared into the kitchen while he settled at the dining room table.

My hands shook as I tried to separate one filter off the stack. It felt good to do something with no sheriff's deputy watching.

Then it hit me that I was being rude.

"Coffee for you, Officer Portman?"

"Dennis'll do."

"Dennis. Coffee?"

"I wouldn't say no to a cup."

A minute later I had the pot set up and ready to drip, but I regretted it, and wished I'd moved more slowly. Now I'd have to go out and talk to Dennis.

I smiled tightly as I joined him at the dining room table. He had a clipboard out, with a form on it. A blank report. He was tapping the edge of the board with a pen. It made me nervous. Well. *More* nervous. Of course, I didn't say so.

I sat down and tried to smile.

All four dogs came barreling into the dining room with Smoky, the long-haired gray cat, running ahead of them. Smoky jumped up onto the table, arched his back, and hissed at Peppy, who had been chasing him. The other three dogs greeted the deputy.

I looked around to see Mando leaning into the room.

"You're back," he said. He didn't look at me once. He was frozen in plainly visible fear. His eyes never left the deputy. "Where's Paula?"

"Still out looking."

"Oh. Too bad. I was hoping you found . . . I was thinking, maybe I could go back to . . . you know. My room. Now that you're here with Quinn. I mean, I did what you asked. Stayed with him. But you're home now . . ."

"Absolutely," I said. "Thanks for looking after him while we were gone."

"Sure thing," he said, and disappeared.

I looked back to Dennis. "Our foster son. Armando."

"So you have three?"

"Yes. Two foster kids, Mando and Star. And then Quinn, our eight-year-old, is ours now. Adopted." An uncomfortable silence. "You need that for the report? This really doesn't have anything to do with either of them."

"Just making conversation. Actually."

Another awkward silence.

I pulled Peppy up onto my lap so Smoky could get away, which he did.

I realized I was stilted, frozen. Terrified. I knew it showed, but I had no idea how to fix it. I couldn't make my mouth work.

He tossed his pen down with a rattly noise that startled me. "Mind if I tell you a little story before we get started?"

"Um . . . no. Of course not."

"Okay, good." He settled back in his chair. "I got a brother, quite a bit older than me. He was a teenager when I was born. So of course I idolize him, and always did. But, truth is, he's just a really good guy, and it's not my imagination. Everybody thinks so. He still lives around here. Has three kids. He and his wife, Marie, now you just couldn't find a better set of parents. Like two people you'd read about in a book on parenting, but the story might seem too good to be true."

He paused, and I could hear the coffeemaker huffing and dripping. I wished it would hurry up and brew, so I could get away from the table again. I had no idea why he was telling me this.

"Then last Christmas, his older boy, Jake, goes and steals a car with two friends and takes it for a joyride. And I have to go out to the house and arrest him. You catch my drift here?"

I wanted to. So I paused a moment before answering. But I didn't catch his drift. At all.

"Um . . . no. Sorry. I don't think I do."

"Kids do stupid things. Even kids with good parents do stupid things. They're kids. No matter how you raise them, they're going to take a cruise through Stupid Land. I'm telling you this because you seem really uncomfortable, like everybody's going to judge you. Like you just moved here, and you're new, and something bad happened, so everybody's thinking you're bad. But most of the reports I fill out are on the locals. Every now and again I'll catch somebody speeding while just passing through here, but mostly if I make an arrest, it's one of us. You know? So I just want you to relax and tell me what you know. Without you thinking anybody's looking down on you. Blaming you."

"I wasn't thinking that," I said. But I was so relieved that I felt myself needing to fight back tears. So that's how I knew I was lying. And it didn't seem right to lie to a guy who was being so honest with me. "Okay, that's not true. I was totally thinking that."

"Right. So take a deep breath. And maybe go get us both a cup of coffee. Just black for me, please. And then we'll get this report done with the least amount of wear and tear possible on everybody."

"Now. For starters, how long has this foster girl—Star, is it?—been with you?"

"Oh. Um. Not long. I'd have to look at a calendar. But . . . not much more than a month."

Dennis rocked back in his chair again. "Oh, well. Then I can't see where you get off blaming yourself at all."

I laughed. Just a little. Shrugged just a little.

"It's a talent of mine," I said.

Paula came through the door about ninety percent through the sheriff's report.

"In the dining room," I called out. Then, when she stuck her head in, I said, "That was fast."

"Oh. Yeah. Well. No rentals within a couple hours of here, and then I started to think you were right. Time to report it. I see you got that taken care of." She strode over to the table and held her hand out to Dennis, and he stood and shook it. "Paula Archer-Cummings," she said.

"Nice to meet you, Doctor. My partner and I've been meaning to stop by the clinic and welcome you to town. Sorry we didn't get to it yet."

"I didn't even have to call it in," I told Paula. "He was here when I got home. Clementine is in the hospital over this."

Paula's eyes flew wide. *Like she really needed more bad news,* I thought. *Like any of us did.*

"What happened?"

I looked to Dennis. Because I really had no idea.

"I don't know if it's entirely accurate to say 'over this,'" Dennis said. "Over a lot of things, this being the most recent. Everybody's been waiting for Clem to snap like a dry twig. If you ask me, this should've happened the day she found Tina dead. I'm guessing you know about that, a small town being what it is. I'm sure she's been falling apart at some level all this time."

Paula sank down at the table beside me, looking drained and uncharacteristically helpless. Still, it felt good not to be in this alone.

"On the outside, though," he continued, "nothing. I mean, anybody could see the effect it had on her. But she held it together. Then Vern up and left. And she held it together. But this morning. Waking up and finding Tina's horse gone. He was pretty much the last family member. That was the straw that broke poor old Clem's back. But it was a breakdown long overdue."

"But *the hospital,*" Paula said. Still clearly in that shocked awe. "Was she hysterical?"

It hit me that I should have been asking a lot more questions about my neighbor's welfare. Like maybe I'd allowed my own disasters to take precedence in my tired mind. I felt selfish and callous. But really it was more that I'd been intimidated, as if I had no right to inquire.

"No. Not at all. She was very calm. Too calm. I remember thinking, and I even said to Bobby—my partner, Bobby—she's taking this too well."

My mind flashed back to the night before. Paula coming downstairs after talking to Star. Saying she'd taken it too well. I hadn't known what she meant by that. Now maybe I did. But it didn't feel like last night I was remembering. So much had happened since then. It felt like I was remembering something from last week. Or last month.

"She told us some very detailed stuff, very lucid, like how she'd been missing sleep. She slept last night, but for some days before that she hadn't been sleeping well at all, which might be part of it. Anyhow. After a while she started repeating herself. And then she was just saying the same things over and over. Like her brain or her mouth got caught in some kind of a loop and she couldn't break out of it. That's when we got concerned. We wanted a doctor to come out and give her a sedative. But with her living alone and all . . . Too risky. So Bobby drove her over to Tri Counties."

I turned to face Paula. "I was thinking maybe she could come home and *we* could look after her." A dreadful idea, but it had seemed like a necessary one back when I'd thought of it. I no longer remembered why, but it was too late. I'd said it out loud.

Paula nodded. A lot. Too much, really. "That seems like the least we could do."

"Well," Dennis said, sounding none too sure. "I can look into that, anyway. I don't know but what they might want to hold her for evaluation. Plus, I can't say Clem would be any too happy about coming home to that arrangement. Then again, when was Clem ever happy about *any* arrangement? Let me see what I've got left for this report. If anything. Hmm." He ran the pen down the form, tapping it here and there. "I didn't really ask you too much about Star's background."

"We don't know much about it," Paula said. "Nobody does. She lived all her life with a mother who was mentally ill but undiagnosed. And nobody reported a child living in an unsuitable home. Until the day someone finally did. Now the mother is institutionalized. Probably permanently. Certainly longer than Star'll be a dependent minor. But there's really no way to go back and know what her life was like in that house."

"She won't tell anybody that?"

"She won't tell anybody much of anything," I said.

He pursed his lips, and I could tell he didn't like what he was about to say. "You know you have to report this to her social worker. And so do I."

I glanced at Paula, an obvious question in my eyes. But the question nearly went without saying by then. Paula called Janet when Janet needed calling. Paula kept Janet up to date. Reported events, got permissions, and asked questions. I found Janet intimidating. Though, really, she wasn't. She was just an authority figure in my life. Paula didn't have the same issue.

She nodded her assent to me. She would handle it. Again.

"Yes," she said. "We do know that."

14. Clementine

I don't take well to a hospital bed, because I don't like the feeling of being helpless. But in this case, I was mostly unaware I was even lying in one, until Denny showed up to fetch me home.

I don't even know how long I was there, though I'm embarrassed to admit it.

All I know is that Bobby Talbot took me in that morning through the emergency entrance, like I'd been shot, or been in a car accident, or something more dramatic than just being upset. And he waited with me, like I was a little girl and he was my worried father. I kept telling him, that whole time . . . well, I don't remember what exactly. I'm ashamed to say so, but it's true. I don't remember what I kept saying, but it felt important. I knew I was saying it repeatedly, but it seemed necessary. It seemed right. Like to do otherwise could create a problem.

But I make it sound like a choice. Really it was just a thing that seemed to do itself, even though my mouth was involved. My own voice seemed to work all on its own that morning.

They took me into a big room and I sat on a gurney, and a doctor I didn't know came in and pulled the curtain around in most of a circle so it was just me and Bobby and the doctor. He was very young, the doctor, and looked like he was from India or some such place where people have dark skin. That made me uneasy. Not that I care about the color of skin, but why not a doctor from around here? From this county, or the state of California? Or maybe at least a doctor from the United States of America. You'd think that would not be asking too much.

I was aggravated by it, and under any other circumstances I would have said something. But I was still saying that other thing, though I can't remember what it was exactly. I'm fairly sure it was something about Comet—something designed to help Bobby and Denny get on the right trail and get him home to me, even though his being gone seemed like a dream—but I can't remember the specifics.

I might have been saying it to the foreign doctor by then, but that part feels a little hazy as well.

Then he rolled up my sleeve and gave me a shot in my arm.

At first it didn't make any difference. But pretty soon I stopped talking. It felt good to stop. Even though I know I said it was very important, what I was saying. But after a minute it didn't seem so important anymore, and that was a relief.

After that, I really can't account. I just don't remember much after that at all.

• • •

When I woke up, I was in a hospital bed, and Denny was there, sitting at my bedside. He was wearing jeans and a short-sleeved shirt, and cowboy boots. So he must have been off duty and on his own time.

Whatever they had given me had worn off some by then, because I remember being irritated. Because I don't take well to a hospital bed, as I think I've mentioned.

Except when I had Tina, I'd never had to submit to one, because I was never sick a day in my life. Well, my adult life. I had my tonsils out as a young girl, and I stayed overnight for it, but I'm not counting that, because young children always feel helpless. I'm sure I was used to the feeling when I was six.

Denny said, "Welcome back to the living."

I tried to speak, but I felt a little wobbly, like I'd been drinking, which I rarely if ever did. Maybe twice in my life, but I remember the feeling. I hadn't liked it then, and it was no better now.

I took a deep breath and tried to pull myself together. I had to really focus on the words.

"When do I get to go home?"

"Right now," he said. "We're just waiting on a nurse with a wheelchair."

"I don't need a wheelchair."

"You don't get a choice in the matter. Everybody

140

checks out of the hospital in a wheelchair. It's policy."

"It's demeaning."

"It's the way it is, Clem. Accept it."

I sighed and closed my eyes, but as soon as I did, I could feel myself wanting to drift back into the depths again. So I opened them, and I fought. I fought to stay awake, and clear. I felt like I was in enemy territory, and I needed to stay sharp. I needed to protect myself from all kinds of things I knew I didn't want.

Denny said, "You're welcome, by the way. For the fact that you get to go home. They wanted to hold you for a three-day psych evaluation, but I talked them out of it."

"That's just plain insulting. I'm not crazy."

"They didn't think you were certifiable. They thought you might be cracking under stress. But there's no real reason to think you're a danger to yourself, so I got you sprung. Don't want to send you into medical bankruptcy. But the doctor, he insists you go on taking this sedative for at least a week. He gave me a prescription. We'll stop and get it filled on our way home."

That reminded me of something, but it took an embarrassingly long time to remember what. Something Denny or Bobby had told me before Bobby drove me away that morning. Even though they told me maybe five times or more, I still couldn't remember what it was. My brain was not right. I told it to perform, and it wouldn't listen.

Then, suddenly, just as I gave up on remembering, it was there. Fully formed in my brain.

"You said I was not to take sedatives at home, because it's dangerous to be alone and sedated."

"I did indeed," he said. "Which is why I got you some guardian angels to look after your well-being."

I felt my brow furrow. "Who?"

"That doesn't matter now, Clem. Let's just get you home."

"Who?"

"We'll talk about it later, okay?"

"Who?"

"Jeez, Clem. You sound like an owl. The only people who live close enough to do it for you. Who do you think?"

"No. Absolutely not. Just leave me here."

"Too late. Already checked you out."

"Well, check me back in. I won't go home. I don't want those people in my house."

"Jeez, Clem," he said again, and rocked back in his chair. The plastic moaned when he hit it with his weight.

He's a big boy, Denny. I watched him grow up, and we knew in the second grade he was going to be big. He played a little football in high school and college, some kind of back. A something-back. Not a quarterback, but one of those who get out there and hit. There was some talk of his going

142

pro, but I don't know if he wasn't good enough or didn't want it. Maybe both. He drifted into law enforcement, which is probably better, because you can do it longer. Retire at a reasonable age. Not be all washed up in your thirties. And I think the morals are better.

He said, "Now, your parents both died before I was born. So I apologize for not knowing this. But was one of them a mule?"

I snorted. "Certainly not, and I don't find that funny."

"Ah. Got it. They both were."

"If I want to stay here, it's my right."

"Wrong. If a hospital says it's time to go, you have to go."

"If I refuse to let those people into my house, then it won't be wise to release me. Will it?"

"Clem. You haven't been in a hospital recently, have you? You got any idea how much it costs per day? That's a rhetorical question, by the way. Because you don't. Trust me. You don't. You can't even guess. Whatever you guess, go high, and then multiply by three or four and you might get close."

"I have Medicare. They pay the costs."

"They pay around eighty percent. That's why a lot of seniors have gap insurance. Medicare supplements. But it doesn't seem like you do. Unless you've got some insurance cards you didn't show us that morning. And when you find out what you're on the hook for twenty percent of, you'll be climbing into that wheelchair. And that's if they even choose to cover it. They might just say it wasn't serious enough, and you should've been kept at home."

"I don't care if it's hundreds of dollars a day."

"Hundreds of dollars a day, Clem? Is that a joke? Try thousands."

"Couldn't be thousands."

"Shall I get your bill?"

"No," I said. "No."

I knew then that he wasn't bluffing. I could tell he really was anxious to show me that bill. He couldn't wait for the chance to prove what he was saying. So it really did cost thousands of dollars a day to be here, and all I had to pay it out of was my monthly Social Security check.

I wondered how much I already owed. That's when I noticed my brain had cleared a bit. Something about already owing more than I could afford. That woke me up, all right.

"Take me to *your* house, Denny."

He laughed. Really laughed out loud, like I'd told him a good joke.

"And put you where? Me and the wife and two kids in two bedrooms and seven hundred fifty square feet? You want to spend a few days strapped to the roof of my car? Outdoors, that is, because there's no room for the car in the garage, which is full to the rafters with all the stuff we got no room for in the house. No, you have a perfectly good house, Clem. And you're going to it. I know you're none too fond of the neighbors, but you'll be sedated. So why should you care? That's the whole point of the pills. Take the things you can't tolerate and make them slide right off you, and you don't even care."

Just then a big, horsey nurse showed up with a wheelchair. And I knew I'd lost the game.

"I'll clear out," he said. "So you can get back into your street clothes. Nobody likes those damn gowns that fall open in the back."

"Least of all me," I said. "You better pick up plenty of those pills. I might be taking a double dosage."

He just shook his head. Like he was dismissing my words. Which didn't exactly feel good. But it was better than being treated like I hadn't spoken at all.

15. Jackie

Paula took the first shift at Clementine's house. It's a good thing she did, too. By the end of that day, I had almost literally hit a wall. Not completely literally, in that it was not an actual wall. But I hit the end of my ability to keep moving through all this. That part was very real.

It smacked me hard when that sheriff's deputy, Dennis, pulled up across the road. He had

Clementine in the car with him, but it wasn't a sheriff's car. Just a regular car, some kind of silver sedan. And he was out of uniform. Clementine's head was dropped back, her mouth open. I felt inordinately relieved that she was in no position to look at me.

It was after eight, and getting on to dark. Not full-on dark, but getting there fast. Quinn had been tucked into bed, and Mando was on his own in the barn. Fran and Marcie were back at their barely acceptable motel, giving us our crisis time alone. Paula and I had been sitting on lounge chairs out front, surrounded by dogs, drinking that good beer our friends had brought us and waiting to see what would happen next. When it happened—when he brought Clementine back—that's when I dropped off the edge of the earth. I could feel it. I hit the end of my tether, and that was that.

Paula jumped right up and walked across the road, and I just slumped there in my chair and watched it all play out. Watched Paula talk to Dennis for a minute or two, and then watched them help Clementine out of the car and into the house. I knew I should get involved, but *should* had nothing to do with it. I was broken.

A good ten or fifteen minutes went by, and the light continued to fade. All I could think about was Star, alone, out in the middle of nowhere, with no bed to sleep in. No way to get indoors for the night. Star out there alone on a lovely hot summer's day had been a less panicky feeling.

When the door finally opened across the street, it was Dennis who stepped out. Not Paula. He walked across the road and stood over my chair. The dogs thumped their tails against the ground and looked hopefully into the air toward his face.

"How're you holding up?" he asked.

"A perceptive question. Not well at all."

He sat down on the lounge chair that had so recently been Paula's.

"Wish I could tell you we have some kind of good lead or something, but we have exactly nothing. Oh, and your wife told me to tell you she's going to sleep on the couch over there tonight. She doesn't want to leave Clem alone, even for a few minutes. Not until she gets more of a bead on how safe it is. Like whether Clem tries to get up on her own. That kind of thing. You can go over there if you want, but she's not coming back tonight."

"I can't go over there. I wish I could, but I can't. I seem to be stuck."

We both watched the evening fade for a minute or two. It was dark enough that if I hadn't already known what he looked like, I wouldn't have learned much in that light. I could hear crickets, and I didn't remember having heard them in Easley before. I couldn't imagine they'd just sprung into action that very day. I figured I must be more present now, in this perfectly excruciating moment when my fondest wish was to be absent.

"When this first happened," I said, "all I could think about was Clementine. What she would say. How much trouble she would cause. Would she sue us? Would she press charges? Would she be irreparably damaged by something we maybe could have prevented? And now the sun is down, and all I can think of is that . . . child . . . I know she doesn't think she's a child, but she's fifteen. That child from a sheltered, abused, neglected background. Out there all by herself. Well. She has the horse. But I don't think that's as helpful as she probably thinks it is. She didn't take any notice-able amount of food, at least not from us. What's she going to eat? What's she going to cover herself with before she goes to sleep tonight? How's she supposed to survive out there?"

Another long pause, full of crickets. I looked over at Dennis in the dark, wondering why he wasn't saying anything.

"Oh," he said. "Those weren't rhetorical questions. Well. I don't know. I do know a healthy kid can survive a long time without eating. But not very long without water. Especially with these hot days. So that's one reason why we figure she's moving along that network of creeks. Because they both need to drink. Both her and the horse. But that creek water'll serve the horse better than it'll serve the girl. If she has no way to filter it, I expect it'll make her mighty sick. Cryptosporidium.

Giardia. We've got it all. Looks clear, but looks can be deceiving."

I pulled in a breath that was going to be a sigh. But somehow I wasn't up to the effort. "I'm being rude again. You seem sufficiently off duty. Can I get you a beer?"

"I wouldn't say no to one bottle. Then I'll scoot on home."

I made my way into the house, in spite of the lead weights in my limbs, and pulled the first beer of the second six-pack out of the fridge. Popped the cap and brought it out to him in the dark front yard.

It felt great to collapse again.

"This is the good stuff," he said, peering at the label in the dark. "Where do you even get this around here?"

"You don't. We have a couple friends visiting from Napa, and they brought it. Or *had*. *Had* friends visiting. I think they'll head out in the morning. They're trying to stay out of our way, and we can't really have much of a visit with all this going on. So . . . this stuff in the water you were talking about. Can it be fatal?"

That's when I realized I'd hauled myself into the house to get him a beer for no more important reason than to postpone asking that question.

"I guess anything's possible, but I doubt it. Might make a person *wish* they were dead. Might even work in our favor. If she feels bad enough, maybe she'll call this off and come home. Depends on how stubborn and determined she is."

I squeezed my eyes closed in the darkness. I had no idea if he could see it or not.

"Got it," he said. "Highly determined."

"I keep forgetting you never met her. If you had . . ." Then I had to think for a minute. Find a proper way to finish the thought. "She's a hard kid to love. That's the nicest way I know how to say it. She wants everybody to keep away. She makes it hard to feel for her, you know? She's got a tough shell. I know there must be a scared little girl in there somewhere, but I swear I've never seen it. Then again, this doesn't exactly bolster my theory. This was a bold move, what she just did. But I still can't help thinking she must be scared out there. So nobody's seen her at all?"

"Nobody. And don't think they don't all know to be looking, too. If she comes up anywhere . . . steals from a trash can to eat, or shows her face on a road . . . we'll get a report."

"But you're also actually *looking*, right?"

"Absolutely. We had a helicopter up looking today."

"Seriously? Easley has a helicopter?"

"No, Easley's lucky to have a traffic light. The state highway patrol has a helicopter, and they put it up today in support of our search. But they saw nothing, which is another reason why we think she's moving under the line of trees along one of the creeks. Comet is a big horse. Not all that easy to hide him in plain sight."

"I don't even know if she has a saddle," I said. It was the first I'd thought of it. It moved a jolt of fear through me, but my brain hadn't put the fear into words yet.

"Not unless she has her own somehow, or stole one that wasn't reported yet. Because Comet's is in the barn."

"Maybe she's not even still with the horse, then. How do we know he didn't throw her twenty minutes out? She could be lying somewhere with broken bones, all by herself."

"Well, if the horse turns up somewhere without her, that'll definitely change our style of search. She have any experience around horses?"

"I have no idea. See? There's so much I don't know about her. I thought I'd have time to learn before people started asking all these questions I can't answer."

A silence fell. I watched the first stars begin to glow on the horizon. I didn't wish on one, because I was too low on optimism, and in no mood to allow myself to be vulnerable. In my peripheral vision I watched him roll the neck of his beer bottle between his fingers.

"You know," he said, "I admire what you two are doing."

"Taking in foster kids, you mean?"

"Yeah. Can't be easy."

"Some days it's easier than others. Today, not so much. So I take it you're not one of those small-town folks who think kids need a mother and a father."

"Kids need love," he said. "End of story." Then, after a pause, a little more bottle rolling, and a long drink, "I can't speak for everybody in town. But I don't think you're going to hit a lot of hate. I think some people might say stupid things, because they're not used to it and they don't understand. But probably nothing like real deep prejudice."

I laughed out loud. I couldn't help it.

"What?"

I pointed with my chin to the house across the road.

"Oh, what?" he asked. "Clementine? Hell, Clem's not prejudiced."

I laughed even harder. You'd think it would have felt good. But this was not that kind of laughter. "Are you kidding me?"

"Not at all. Bet you good money. Guarantee it. Clem doesn't have a prejudiced bone in her body. She hates everybody. One thing you can say for Clem, she's an equal-opportunity hater. No matter who and what you are, she'll judge you for it."

I smiled, and realized I did feel a tiny bit better. Because it wasn't just me. Everybody saw it. Everybody knew what my neighbor was. It made me feel like the whole world was on my side.

"Which means she'll press charges," I said, losing that slight mood gain and then some. "She'll put that poor kid behind bars in some juvenile detention facility, and we'll never get her back, and that'll be it for her. Last chance gone."

"First things first," he said. "First we've got to find her. I guess I'd best be getting home to the wife and kids. Get a good sleep and start again in the morning."

"One more thing before you go. On a scale of one to ten, how unhappy is my neighbor to have us keeping an eye on her?"

"Hmm," he said. "Let me do a little math in my head on that. I'd have to say . . . ten. But you're not the only thing that ever registered a ten on Clem's unhappy scale. If it helps any to know."

If it hadn't been a few hours until my turn at Clementine duty, it might have. But, things being what they were, it didn't.

I fell asleep on the lounge chair outside, because I wanted to postpone that moment of getting up and going to bed without Paula.

I woke up a few hours later because I was cold.

I took myself and the dogs inside and upstairs. I checked on Quinn, retucked him. Then I flopped on top of our bed, fully dressed, and fell back asleep. Just before I drifted off again, I wondered if Star was cold, too. If so, it was a problem not so easily solved. Not the way it just had been for me.

• • •

When I opened my eyes, it was light, and Paula was in the bathroom getting ready for work.

"You'll want to go over there," she said when she saw I was awake, "but I really don't think you need to be there every minute. I'd say go check in at least once an hour. See if she has to go to the bathroom. She seems to know enough not to get up on her own. Which is good. She's a fall risk, so I'd rather you walk her there to be safe. And give her one of those pills every four hours. They're on the kitchen table. With a full glass of water, if you can get her to drink it, so she doesn't get dehydrated. She had her last one at six a.m."

My heart sagged and my stomach twisted at the idea of having to do any of that for a woman I couldn't even bear in detached conversation.

"Did she say anything to you?"

"No. She's too out of it."

"Good. Here's hoping that lasts. Did you sleep?"

"Yeah," she said. "I slept some."

"Could you come here a minute?"

I wanted to say something, but it was something scary. If I said it too loudly, maybe Quinn would hear it. Or the Universe might overhear me and get ideas. Or I might hear it myself.

She came and sat on the edge of the bed.

"Remember the other night when we were talking to Star over there by the horse corral? And you wondered if that line about 'asking the horse'

154

was a metaphor? There's something else she said that night that I can't get out of my head. She said, 'Comet and Star . . . together forever in the sky.'"

I waited. She said nothing. Like she was assuming I'd go on. Make my point.

"What about it?" she asked when I didn't.

"That doesn't seem kind of . . . ?"

"Not following."

"Together forever in the sky. Don't you think it has this kind of . . . afterlife quality to it?"

"I don't think that's how she meant it."

"How do you think she meant it?"

She thought that over for a time. "I think she was being overly poetic," she said. "But . . . honestly? I have absolutely no idea."

We sat quietly for a moment. Maybe thinking. Maybe frozen.

Right around the time I realized I was going to cry, that it was inevitable, Paula got up to finish getting ready to go.

See, this was the moment we tended to drop out of sync. When Paula's upset, she doesn't necessarily turn to me. To anybody. She just handles it. I don't know how, but she does. I'd been trying to teach her how different it is for me. For nine years. But it's an easy thing for her to forget, because it's so far outside her own experience.

Halfway into the bathroom she stopped. Looked back at me. I can only imagine what she saw in my face, but it made my point.

She came back and sat on the edge of the bed and held me. And of course I cried. A moment earlier, I'd been about to cry because she hadn't reached out to me. Now I was crying because she had. Whether that makes me insane or human is hard to say. Maybe some combination of the two.

"You remembered," I said.

"Because you know enough to be patient teaching an old dog."

After a minute or two I said, "You'll be late." Even though I didn't want her to go.

"Yeah," she said. "That's right. I'll be late."

16. Clementine

I woke with a start, as though I'd been having a dream that some stranger was in the house with me. But then I couldn't remember if I'd been dreaming or not. It was just a feeling.

My eyes opened wide, and it was true. Someone had broken into my home. He was standing right there in the bedroom doorway, staring at me. He was young, like a teenager, but big enough to be dangerous. And brown-skinned. Not American-looking at all.

In my head I screamed long and loud—really bellowed it out—even though I know no one lives close enough to hear. Maybe those awful people across the road, but probably not even them. But it didn't come out the way I heard it in my head. It fed back to me as a little squeak. The way a mouse would scream if you frightened it. The pills I was taking had everything off-kilter.

He just stood there, looking at me. He tilted his head at the squeak. Like it was a language he might figure out how to translate.

"Take whatever you want," I said, my voice shaking miserably. "Just don't hurt me."

He tilted his head the other way. "What?"

"Whatever you came to steal, just steal it and go."

"I didn't come to steal anything." He seemed surprised, maybe even insulted, that I would think so.

"What are you doing in my house, then?"

"Jackie asked me to come over and check on you. It's just me. Armando. You met me already, remember? I live right across the road."

My eyes flickered closed, and I breathed a few times, trying to let off the fear. But, as I did, I felt the sedative try to draw me under again. At times like this, when I needed to be sharp, I hated those pills. But I did not intend to stop taking them anytime soon. If I did, I might have to absorb what was really going on.

I pried my eyes open again, and the boy was still there, leaning in my doorway now, his huge shoulder against the jamb, staring at me.

I felt anger well up.

"Well, that was a very thoughtless thing for her to do. Sending some big young man to almost give me a heart attack. You go tell your . . . You go tell her to come over here herself if she's supposed to be looking in on me. The rudeness. Why, I never."

The boy didn't move.

After a few seconds he said, "Why would it give you a heart attack? You've met me. You know I'm your neighbor."

He seemed to have an unspoken complaint, but I ignored it.

"Why didn't she come herself?"

"She's teaching Quinn how to make a kite."

"Oh, what an airtight alibi! Playing with one of her kids, and she can't take a minute out."

"She promised him. She doesn't like to break promises."

"She also promised to look in on me."

The big boy sighed and pulled himself up straight. "I think she hates coming over here." And he said something else, under his breath. I didn't hear it word for word, but it seemed to have something to do with his now knowing why.

"What did you say?"

"Nothing. I'll give her the message."

I have no idea how long I lay drifting, but when I opened my eyes, she was standing over my bed, holding a glass of water.

"So," she said, "just when I thought you couldn't

get any more offensive. I send my foster son over to check on your welfare, and you assume he's broken into your house to rob you blind. And you don't even remember that you've met him before. I'm guessing all Latinos look alike to you?"

The hard edge of anger in her voice made me mad. I didn't have the energy to express it, though, so I just told the truth.

"Those sedatives throw everything off."

That seemed to knock her out of whatever agenda she'd come over here to advance. At my expense.

"That's probably true," she said. "Maybe I should have thought of that. I'm sorry. Here. I have your pill. Unless you don't want to take them anymore. The doctor wants you to, but I guess it's up to you."

"I'll take it." I knew there was something heart-breakingly ugly waiting for me just outside the veil of medication.

She helped me prop partway up in bed, and put the pill on my palm, and handed me the glass of water. I took the pill with just one little sip of liquid, and tried to hand the glass back. She wouldn't take it.

"Paula says you should drink a full glass with every pill. So you don't get dehydrated."

"Then I just have to go to the bathroom more, which is awkward. It was very embarrassing when she had to walk me there."

"That's just inconvenient," she said. "Dehydration is dangerous."

I sighed, and drank half the water.

"Good," she said. "Something to eat? You must be starved."

"No. I'm not hungry."

"I think you haven't eaten since before . . . this . . . happened."

"I ate."

"When?"

"Your . . . friend made me some soup."

"You mean my *wife?*"

I avoided answering.

"Look. Lady. You may not be a fan of it. But we're legally married, like it or not. You can disapprove all you want, but that won't make it any less true."

"I might also have eaten in the hospital," I said. "I don't quite remember."

She sighed. Pulled the drinking glass out of my hand. Too roughly, I thought.

"I could warm some broth."

"What kind of broth?"

"Broth. You know. Chicken broth, for example."

"I don't have any."

"We do. It's not homemade, but it'll get some kind of nutrition in you. Maybe not much, but some."

"Maybe later," I said, and she sighed again. "That was a pretty flimsy excuse for not coming over here yourself." Truthfully, I no longer remembered what the excuse was. I just remembered the feeling—that it was flimsy.

"Look. Lady. I've got three kids who need my—" Then she stopped in midsentence and looked down at her shoes. "Well. Two. Normally I have three kids needing me."

I felt the whole middle of my body, from my shoulders to unmentionable places, fill with sickening dread. Because she'd reminded me of what had started all this.

"Oh, my," I said. It came out a breathless whisper. "He's gone, isn't he? Comet. Is he still gone?" My heart drummed in my chest, as though fatal danger stood right in front of me. I swear, more than it had earlier, when I'd thought I had an intruder.

"I'm afraid so," she said.

"How long has it been now?"

"About a day and a half."

"But they'll find him. Right?" I purposely didn't look at her face as I asked it.

"I certainly hope so."

I squeezed my eyes closed, wishing that pill I'd just swallowed would hurry up and take effect. "Well, anyway," I said, wanting to get back to my anger, which was a less helpless feeling, "it was a flimsy excuse."

"Okay, you want to know the truth? The truth is, I dread coming over here, because you've been so unpleasant to me. Is that honest enough?"

"Then why did you offer to do it? Why not just leave me in the hospital to rack up a bunch of medical bills that might bankrupt me? What do you care?"

I still carefully did not look at her face, so I didn't know if she was angry. I wanted not to care, but I felt defenseless there in bed, and I did care. Whether I wanted to or not.

"Well, the bankruptcy would have been ours," she said. She didn't sound mad. "Paula's already gone to the hospital and signed a paper assuming responsibility for your medical bills."

That just sat in the air for a moment, and I didn't know what to say. I felt some gratitude, and maybe should have said so, but I didn't. I said nothing at all.

"But that's not really why. It's because we feel bad about what happened. Genuinely bad. And we want to do what we can to help."

More silence. I had no idea what to say. Fighting with someone is easy, but this . . . this was beyond me.

"How about that broth?" she asked again, sounding gentle. Which made me enjoy her company even less, if such a thing were possible.

"Maybe later," I said again.

She sighed and left me alone.

It was an enormous relief.

17. Jackie

When I got back into my own dining room, Quinn was sitting at the table drawing with colored marking pens on the heavy tissue paper we'd chosen for our kite. As usual, he was surrounded by all four dogs, who wagged furiously when they saw me.

It seemed almost silly to feel so relieved to be home. That disagreeable old woman probably weighed a hundred pounds and didn't stand five feet tall. And even that's only when she was standing. I asked myself why I let her intimidate me so. If Paula had been there, I know she would have asked.

"Hi, J-Mom. I kept busy while you were gone by decorating the paper. See, I took this frame we made . . ." He nodded toward the stick frame we'd created before I was called away. We'd lashed two thin sticks together in the shape of a *T,* notched all four of their ends, and threaded string through the notches, tying it tightly into a string border for the diamond shape of the kite. Something for us to wrap the paper around. ". . . and I laid it on the paper and I traced around the string. So that way I knew what part of the paper was about to be the kite. So then I knew what part to decorate."

"You continue to amaze me," I said, sitting

beside him and resting one hand on the top of his head.

"Is the lady okay?"

"I think so."

"Did she make you upset? Seems like she made you upset."

"Maybe a little. She always upsets me some."

"Is that why you asked Mando to go? Because we could have worked on the kite later."

"I guess that might have been part of it. Now I feel bad, because I think it wasn't fair to Mando. I didn't think she'd be rude to him. He's just a kid. Did he still seem upset after I left?"

"Sort of. But he knows it's just about her. He knows he didn't do anything wrong. But he didn't like having to go over there. He doesn't like her."

"I don't think anybody does."

"Why'd you say you'd take care of her, then?"

I took my hand back. So I could think better. And because I had to sooner or later. "Because it's our family's fault she's so upset. Well. Star's fault. But Star's part of our family. And because Clementine doesn't have anyone else who'll do it."

"She doesn't have *any* family at *all?*"

"She had a daughter who died a couple of years ago. And her husband moved out . . ."

"She must have friends."

"I've never seen her have friends in as long as we've lived here. And the sheriff's deputies who took her to the hospital . . . they didn't know anybody they could ask to look in on her. I think other people don't like to be around her for the same reasons we don't. I think she just doesn't have anybody."

"Wow." He set down his blue marker for the first time. He'd been coloring blue sky above green fields strewn with semi-sticklike cows in primary colors. "That's sad."

"It is," I said.

"I feel bad for her now."

I made a mental note to try to be more patient. Next time I was forced into her difficult presence.

I found Mando, predictably, in the barn. Sitting on the edge of his bed. Reading. All the furniture from his old room—back when we lived in Napa County and only had the two boys, and they had their own rooms—had been moved out to the barn.

"I owe you an apology," I said.

Then I glanced up to see if the barn owl was watching me. He was. Or she was. I looked away and tried to forget I'd ever seen that stare.

"It's okay. She's not going to be nice to any of us. I can understand why you didn't want to go."

He never looked up from his book. So it was hard to judge his mood.

"I shouldn't have made it your problem, though. Are you still upset?"

"Not about that."

I sat on the edge of his bed with him, and he set the book down.

"Talk to me."

He sighed. "Star always ruins everything."

"I'm not exactly arguing, but what did she ruin this time?"

"I know with all this going on you're not going to take me to that hearing."

"Wrong. A promise is a promise."

"What if they find Star? Right before we're supposed to go? And she's in the hospital, or the police have her, and they set up a court thing for her?"

"If it's on the same day as your mom's hearing, then Paula will have to cancel appointments and deal with it."

"And the lady. Who takes care of her while we're gone all day?"

"We've already arranged for that babysitter to stay with Quinn. She can look in on Mrs. D'Antonio."

We sat in silence for a while as my words sank in. I could feel his mood change. Feel the tense energy drain away. When he sighed deeply, I knew he'd let the last of it go.

"Thanks, ma'am. Jackie."

"A promise is a promise."

"Then I don't mind that you asked me to go to the nasty lady's house. Because you do a lot for me."

I ruffled the top of his hair. Kissed him on the cheek.

"Now if you'll excuse me," I said, "I have to go fly a kite."

We stepped out into the front yard, the seven of us. Quinn, me, all four dogs, and our very impressive kite. The wind was dead flat. Not so much as a whisper of a breeze.

"I could run with it," Quinn said.

The dogs seemed to know the word "run." They started. They tried. They pranced away, then stopped and looked back over their shoulders. Then they massed around Quinn again, disappointed that he did not keep his word.

"When you're flying a kite," I said, "sooner or later you have to stop running. Otherwise, it won't be much fun."

He placed one hand on Jocko's offered head and sighed so theatrically it was all I could do not to laugh.

That was when I looked up and saw John Parno across the road, staring into Comet's empty corral. Just leaning on the top rail and staring, as if conditions might change while he watched.

I set a hand on Quinn's shoulder. "I'm going across the road to talk to our friend John. We'll try the kite later, okay? Make sure all the dogs go in with you."

Then I crossed over to Clementine's side.

John never so much as looked over his shoulder at me. I just walked right up from behind him and leaned on the top rail by his side. Only then did he glance over. Dangling from one of his hands was a plastic bag—filled with water and rubber-banded at the top—containing four gigantic goldfish.

"Now this is a development," he said. "Any idea what's going on?"

"I figured you'd know already. I figured word travels fast in a small town."

"Not that fast, I guess."

"Star ran away. And apparently took Comet with her."

In the pause that followed, I could feel the summer sun baking my scalp uncomfortably at the part of my hair.

"Oh. Oh boy. That *cannot* be a happy Clem. How's she taking it?"

"Hard to tell. The doctor has her sedated."

"Think I'll choose to be somewhere else when it wears off."

"I wish I had that option." I nodded at the bag in his hand. "Why are you walking around with goldfish?"

"Oh." We both stared at the bag for a moment. As if he couldn't understand it any better than I could. "I brought them for Comet's water trough. They eat the algae."

"That's smart."

"Yeah. If there's a horse, it's a good move.

Under these circumstances, I'm not so sure. Think I should drop them in there as a vote of confidence that she'll get him back?"

"I'd appreciate that. I could use a vote of confidence."

He smiled. A little sadly, I thought. Then he unwrapped the rubber band and poured the contents of the bag into the metal trough. The fish disappeared immediately under all that murky green.

"Here's what you gotta do, though," he said. "If there's no horse drinking out of that trough in a week, I need you to come over with a bucket or a pot. Dip some water out of there and pour it on the ground, or in the flower beds. And then it'll fill up with fresh. Otherwise, those fish'll run out of air."

"I can do that."

"And every week after. You know. If . . ."

"Please," I said, one hand raised to stop him.

"Right. Sorry."

We both stood and stared into the tank some more. I have no idea how long. As if the fish were about to put on some kind of show. As if we could even see them.

Then he said, "I keep telling myself if I were a better man I'd go in there and see her."

"She's probably not even conscious."

She might have been. I had no way to know. But he wanted to be let off the hook, and I didn't blame him.

"A better man would go check."

"Run. Save yourself. She never needs to know you were here."

"Think I'll take you up on that." He tipped his battered hat. I thought he was just going to walk away. Instead, he locked his gaze right into my eyes. "Hope this has a happy ending."

"Thanks," I said. "You and me both."

"Don't envy you in the meantime."

"No," I said. "No sane person would."

Clem slept like a corpse all morning. I stuck my head in four times, but she never so much as flickered an eyelid.

By the time I'd fed the kids—and myself—lunch, a good steady wind was up. Just about right for kite flying. And it was past time for Clementine's pill. I left the kids briefly to check on her again. Quinn was busy making a tail for his kite from wide ribbon, at my suggestion, so that bought me a little time.

Clem was still deeply under.

I got into an uncomfortable back-and-forth with myself about whether it was my duty to wake her up to give her the pill. But it just kept going around, with both arguments seemingly of equal weight. I never came to a firm conclusion.

I stepped downstairs—into Clem's straight-out-of-the-1950s kitchen—and called Paula on her cell phone. Not because I'm hopeless at decisions, although I might be borderline hopeless. Because it seemed like a decision a doctor should make.

She picked up on the second ring.

"It's me. Are you in the middle of something?"

"Surprisingly, no," she said. "I'm driving from one place to another."

"Our neighbor has been asleep for hours, and it's past time to give her a pill. So, do I wake her up and give it to her? Or just let her sleep?"

"I'd let her sleep. The idea is to keep her calm, and if she's asleep, she's calm. But I'd stay much closer by until she wakes up. Because she might wake up in a state."

"Right," I said. "Thanks."

I just hung on the line for a moment, wanting to talk more, but not doing it. Because as soon as I hung up the phone I had to stay close to my awful neighbor, who might wake up in a state. Which was pretty much the polar opposite of talking to Paula on the phone, in terms of the feelings they produced in me. But I couldn't get words around any of it.

"You okay?" she asked.

"Yeah. Pretty much. It's just . . ." I guess I was going to say "hard." Or something an online thesaurus would produce if you typed in the word "hard." But I never got a chance to choose.

"Good, because I just drove through the gate for my next appointment."

"No problem," I said. "Bye."

Not exactly a pinnacle of honesty.

"Bye" was true enough.

"Why did we make a tail for it again?" Quinn asked me as he carried the kite across the road, close to my side.

"It keeps it oriented."

"J-Mom . . ."

"Sorry. It keeps the bottom of the kite on the bottom, so the wind doesn't just spin it around in a circle and crash it into the ground."

"Which is exactly what happened to my last kite."

"You didn't have me on your team for the last kite. Now don't go far. And don't go into the road. You'll be tempted to watch the kite once you get it up there, but I'm trusting you to know where your feet are. Stay in the yard and out of the road."

He offered a military-style salute.

"I'll be right inside if you need me."

I opened Clem's door and made my way through the house and upstairs to her bedroom. Her house always felt claustrophobic to me, which wasn't really the right word, because it wasn't small. But it felt dank and closed in. It felt like stepping into a black-and-white movie, because even though there were colors, they seemed faded and drab. It made it hard for me to breathe.

She was still under. Asleep or unconscious. Or

drugged. Or maybe it was impossible to know the difference and it didn't even matter.

I sighed, walked back downstairs. Got a straight-backed chair from the kitchen. Hauled it up to her bedroom.

Just as I was resigning myself to sitting there and staring at her for an extended period, I heard Quinn call to me from outside.

"J-Mom! You gotta come see this! It's flying!"

I was hoping the noise would wake Clem. It didn't.

I walked downstairs again and opened the front door. Leaned out.

Quinn had the kite up so high I couldn't even make out the designs he'd drawn on it. The sun shone through it and made it look luminous, shining, like a white jewel.

I wished I'd brought my camera so Paula could see this when she got home from work.

"Good job," I called.

I watched him for a little longer, wishing—with that childlike belief that wishing should be enough if you do it right—that I never had to go back inside. But I wasn't a child. And it wasn't enough.

"I'd better go sit with her again," I said, and he waved without looking away from his kite.

About ten minutes later I heard Quinn come through the door downstairs. Well, I assumed it was

Quinn. Hoped it was. When I heard the shuffling, light footsteps on the stairs, I was sure.

He had the kite in one hand, the string all properly wrapped around the reel again. His face was red, and beaded with sweat from the sun.

"She's still asleep," he said, his voice a suitable whisper.

"Yeah. I have to stay."

"I think now *I* should stay and watch her sleep and *you* should fly the kite."

"Won't that be awfully boring for you?"

"Doesn't matter. It's boring for you, too."

"What'll you do if she wakes up, though?"

"Run get you."

"I guess if you're sure, but . . . why do you want to do that, honey?"

"Because she's lonely. I don't want her to be lonely. And besides, you should get to fly the kite."

I pulled him close, so we could talk even more quietly.

"But maybe she's lonely because she's not very nice."

"But maybe she's not very nice because she's lonely. Maybe if she wasn't lonely, she'd be nicer."

"Well," I said, "that's actually a plausible theory."

"J-Mom . . ."

"Sorry. It means you just might be right."

I stood, and took the kite he handed me, and he

settled into the straight-backed chair, a fine layer of dust on his bare shins, below his baggy khaki shorts. I kissed him on the top of the head before leaving him alone with Clementine.

"Just yell if you need me."

It would have been easy to go back home instead. Lie down. It was tempting. But a deal is a deal.

So I flew the kite.

18. Clementine

When I woke again, my head was much clearer. But there was something uncomfortable in my midsection—an unpleasant scratchiness, like I'd been sandpapered inside. So I had to assume I was less sedated. I tried to decide if the feelings were better or worse on balance, but that only confused me, so I didn't try for long.

"Don't get scared," a little voice said. "It's only me. Quinn."

I turned my head, with some effort. He was sitting in one of my kitchen chairs, now dragged upstairs, his dusty bare legs not even reaching the floor. It felt charming in a way I wasn't nearly prepared to absorb.

"Yes," I said. "I remember you."

"Okay, good. I thought you might not. Because you didn't remember Mando."

"That's different. I've actually spoken to you. Besides, I was on more medication then."

"Oh! Right! You need your pill. You're late, because you were asleep. I'll go get J-Mom."

"No!" I said, surprised at my own vehemence. The little boy jumped. "No, please. Don't bring her. I'm much happier just sitting here with you."

"But you need your pill. And I don't know where they are or how many you take. I'm eight. I can't do grown-up stuff like that. Besides, I promised J-Mom I'd go get *her* if you needed anything."

"The pill can wait. Right now I'm enjoying being able to think. Just sit here and talk to me for a while."

"Okay. What do you want to talk about?"

"Anything. It doesn't really matter. I just like it when you're here, because you're a polite boy."

"Thanks. Tell my moms that, okay?"

"They don't think you're polite?"

"No, they do. But it's always nice to get a good report from somebody who's not even in the family."

I smiled and closed my eyes, and said nothing for a time. I was almost drifting half-asleep when I heard myself say, "In fact, I wish I'd had a nice little boy like you."

"You had a *girl,*" he said.

That set up a sour feeling like indigestion in my stomach. But it couldn't have been that, because I hadn't eaten anything in a long time.

176

"Yes."

"Do you wish she'd been a boy?"

"No. I had no preference, boy or girl. I just wish I'd had more children."

"Why didn't you, then?"

"We couldn't have kids. Except for that one time."

"But you could've adopted all the kids you wanted."

"We wanted our own."

"They would have been your own. I'm J-Mom's and P-Mom's own. And they didn't even meet me till I was five."

I sighed. Part of me wanted to explain it to him, so he'd see it the way an adult would. Another part of me thought I was the one who wasn't understanding properly, and maybe he should explain it to me.

"Lots of people said that at the time, but I wouldn't listen. Now maybe I wish I'd listened."

Then I decided I didn't want to talk anymore, because I had told this little boy too much already. He was still one of *them*. One of that troublesome brood from across the way. I never talked to anyone about things like that, and I was not at all comfortable with starting now.

Maybe those pills were still hampering me, and that's why I wasn't acting like myself. Then again, maybe not.

"Know what I'd like?" I asked him, hoping to change the mood. "A cup of tea."

"I better get J-Mom, then."

"No. Please don't. Just help me down the stairs and into the kitchen. I'll be careful and hold the handrail. And then I'll sit at the kitchen table, and it will feel good, because I've been in bed too long. And then I can show you exactly what to do to make tea."

I stepped into my own kitchen, shielding my eyes from the light. The little boy waited with me until I was ready to walk over to the table.

In time I took two steps in the right direction. That brought me level with the kitchen window. I looked out and saw Comet's corral empty, with the gate hanging half-open, and the boards Vern had used to secure it still scattered in the dirt.

Something collapsed inside me. Literally collapsed. Or it felt literal, anyway. I just don't know a better way to explain it than that.

I pitched forward and reached for one of the remaining chairs, and steadied myself against it. Then I sank into it, as though I'd just barely saved myself. And then—much to my complete humiliation—I sobbed. It just happened. No warning, nothing I could do to stop it. I was in the process of sobbing before I even realized it was coming. I could hear myself wailing, a keening sound. The sound I used to hear my older relatives make at funerals when I was a child. I felt the little boy's hand on my back.

"Mrs. D'Antonio? Are you okay?"

But I couldn't speak through all the sobbing.

"I better go get J-Mom."

"No," I shouted, forcing myself to deal with the moment. Forcing my verbal ability to return. "No, do *not* bring her here now. I never cry in front of anybody."

"You're crying in front of me."

"Yes, and that's as far as I go. Just give me a minute, and I'll pull myself together."

So he waited.

I put my head down on the table, and the tears kept coming. I couldn't have stopped them if I'd tried. But the audible sobs seemed to have worn themselves down. Either that or I'd thrown up a roadblock so I could speak through them, and they couldn't get around it again.

The polite little boy held my hand while I cried, and it was such a thoughtful and caring gesture that it made the tears come with just that much more force.

When the whole episode had calmed down some, he brought me a box of tissues from the downstairs bathroom, and put on a kettle of water for that cup of tea.

"I'm hungry," I said.

I was thinking I wanted that pill now.

I wanted the relief from that sandpapered feeling. It was worse now than when I'd first wakened up, because I'd allowed myself to cry. Well, I'd had no choice in the matter, really. But I'd cried, and that had only made things worse. My eyes felt grainy and sore, and my sinuses ached. The inside of my gut felt like it had been not only sandpapered but then scraped clean of any leftover . . . anything.

"I can get J-Mom to make you something to eat," he said.

"Soon. Not now. Let me just drink my tea for now."

I raised the cup to my face, and the warm steam greeted me, and I felt as though it was the only comfort I had in my life, maybe the only comfort I'd ever had. I took a sip, and the hot liquid felt soothing running down into my scraped and sandpapered stomach.

I knew my eyes were red and swollen, and no matter how much I wanted food and my pill, I wasn't willing to let that woman see me in this condition.

"You should come to dinner," he said. "At our house."

"Well, I don't know about that."

"Why not? You're hungry. And you're all alone here."

I'm embarrassed to say I had to clamp down on the tears again to prevent them from coming out. See, this is why I never cry. Give the tears a little power and they take over, and then there's just no stopping them.

"You don't know that your mom . . . I mean, your moms would want you to be inviting me."

"I'll go ask J-Mom."

He ran out of the house before I could even stop him. I raised some kind of muddy objection, more a sound than a word, but by then he was too far away to hear it.

I got up and made my way carefully into the downstairs bathroom to get my face together before she came over, on the off chance that she did anytime soon. I leaned on the sink and looked at myself in the mirror. What I saw was really quite shocking.

My hair was more than just messy. It was actually matted. I'd been lying on it without brushing it for so long that I had the beginning of mats, the kind I was bound to lose hair while brushing out. Some were closer to the sides of my head, but most were in the back, where I could only feel them with my hands.

I was wearing the same makeup I'd put on while waiting for the sheriff's deputies to arrive the previous morning, but of course it was a ridiculous mess. Almost all my eye makeup was now puddled under my eyes, black half-circles that made me look like a raccoon.

And my eyes themselves, as I'd suspected, were red and swollen from crying.

I splashed my face with cold water for a long time, trying to bring the swelling down. Then I began attempting to remove the ruined makeup, but I had no cold cream in the downstairs bathroom. I used hand lotion from the bottle beside the sink.

I followed with a soap-and-water wash and looked at myself again.

Now I was completely makeup free, my hair was still a mess, and I still looked like I'd been crying. It wasn't one bit better, and might even have been worse, but there was nothing I could do to fix it in time.

I used the toilet, to avoid the indignity of having to accept help in using it later. Before I could even finish, I heard my front door open again.

"She says it's okay," the little boy called to me.

"I'll be right out," I called back.

"Where are you?"

"I'm in the bathroom. I'll be right out."

I flushed, and washed my hands quickly, then opened the door.

He was standing in the middle of my living room, looking up and all around, his hands jammed into the pockets of his big shorts.

"We're having homemade macaroni and cheese. And salad. J-Mom makes the best macaroni and cheese. But you have to eat your salad first, otherwise she says you just fill up on macaroni and never get any vegetables. Well, she didn't say that just now about you. But that's the rule in our house. And I told her you didn't want her coming over here—you just wanted me. So she told me where the pills are, and she gave me permission to hand you the bottle. And you just take one. She said you should drink a whole glass of water, and then if you need to go to the bathroom, I should go get her."

"I just did."

"Which?"

"Go to the bathroom."

"Oh. Good. Then we don't need her at all. I'll go get your pill."

While he did, I walked to the kitchen, sat down in front of my tea again, and felt vaguely insulted. Yes, I preferred the little boy, but she was clearly ducking out of caring for me as promised. Again. I sat there stewing, reflecting on the reasons she'd rudely given me in our last conversation, and getting angry.

Then the little boy was back with my pill, and pouring a glass of water at the sink, and the combination of his presence and the fact that the pill was about to fix everything put me at ease again. It was a sudden and surprising relief.

I swallowed the pill and then drank the whole glass of water, because I knew it would please him.

"I enjoy your company," I said. Then, before he could even reply, I shouted, "That's it!" He jumped a little.

"That's what?"

"Something I like! I need to tell Vern about this. I need to call Vern."

"Want me to bring you the phone?"

But my heart sank, and I shook my head, because I remembered Vern calling to give me a number, but only for genuine emergencies. This was not a genuine emergency. He'd also said he'd found something—some kind of relief—since leaving, and he wasn't willing to give it up again.

No. His question about my likes and dislikes had come with a time limit. I had finally found something I liked, but now it was too late.

"Do you love the horse?" the little boy asked.

It felt like a thing out of place, and I just blinked for a long time, instead of trying to answer.

"Do you love the horse, and that's why you cried when you saw he wasn't there?"

"Of course not. I don't love a horse. He's not a person. He's only an animal."

"Why did you cry?"

"I don't know. I think the pills were making me emotional."

"But they were wearing off by then."

"And maybe that was just the problem."

"That doesn't make any sense." He wrinkled his freckled nose. "The pills either make it worse or they make it better."

I sighed, and decided I'd liked his company better when he wasn't asking so many questions.

"He was my daughter's horse. I loved my

daughter. And she loved the horse. I guess I feel like he's the only thing I have left of her. And maybe even like he was the only family I had left. But that's silly, because he's just a horse. A horse can't be your family."

"The dogs and cats are *our* family."

"Well, I don't look at it that way. I think it's pathetic to think of a horse as a member of your family."

Then I realized the only thing more pathetic was not having the horse at all, regardless of what you thought he was. He was still the only other heartbeat on the property. No matter what you call that, it's still going from two down to one.

19. Jackie

"J-Mom," Quinn shouted, before he even had the front door closed behind him. "Can Mrs. D'Antonio come to dinner?"

He found me in the dining room, where I'd been stealing an opportunity to work on some of my hand-painted note cards.

"Oh . . ." I said. "Really? Dinner? Here?"

"Is it okay?"

"Well . . . honey . . . I'm not so sure about having her here."

"I know you don't like her. But I like her."

"You do?"

"Yeah. I like her *enough*. And she's all alone over there. And we have an extra place at the table where Star usually sits."

I hid my wince as best I could. "True. But . . . maybe we could just make up a plate of macaroni and cheese and salad and take it over there."

"But I already asked her if she could come."

My heart fell right back into that place it had lived for a couple of days now. Just for a few moments I'd been focusing on something else, and I'd blissfully forgotten to be heavyhearted. But when I heard that he'd already invited her, it all came crashing home.

"Oh. You already asked her."

"Is that bad?"

"Well . . ." I pushed the paints to the middle of the table and pulled him around and sat him on my lap. Because he seemed sad now. Now that I'd let on that he'd disappointed me in some small way. I wrapped my arms around him and set my chin down on the top of his head. Lightly. So I could still talk. "I won't say 'bad,' no. But in the future, it's always best to ask me first. Because if you say, 'I'm going to go ask my mom if you can come,' then if I said no, she'd know I said no. So I can't really say no. I mean, without offending her. Which isn't hard to do. So I guess this time the answer has to be yes."

"Sorry, J-Mom. Next time I'll ask you first."

"I know you will, honey."

"I'll go tell her yes."

He straightened up and slid off my lap, and the dogs ran behind him to the door. I had to call after him with the instructions for her pill and just hope he heard me.

Then the dogs came massing back, and wouldn't stop milling around and staring at me, so I got up and fed them their wet food in the kitchen. A bit of a production, as they each eat in a different corner of the room and they have to be made to wait their turn as the other dogs' dishes are set down.

I picked up the phone and called Paula on her cell.

"Hey," she said when she picked up. "I'm on my way home."

"Oh, good." I felt genuinely better to hear it. "I just wanted to give you advance warning on something."

"Oh, jeez. Now what?"

"No, it's not . . . It's just . . . Quinn took it upon himself to invite our horrible neighbor to dinner."

"Is that all? You really scared me for a minute there."

"Sorry. I just thought you'd want advance notice."

"No, that's you. *You* need to know about things like that before they happen. I'm fine with it."

"Seriously? Fine?"

"Yeah, I think it's great. The more we get to know her, the better. Who's more likely to file a civil suit against us, our friend or our enemy? I'm not saying that's the only reason. I'm not trying to be callous about this. But don't you think this situation could only improve if we had a more cordial relationship?"

"You're suggesting a friendship with Clementine."

"Let's start with cordial and see how far we get. Look, I'm almost home. Five minutes. I'll go across the road and help her over as soon as I get there."

I didn't say a word to either boy about eating their salad first, because we had company. But they both did. Without being asked. Which made me surprisingly happy.

At first we were relieved of the burden of conversation, because the dogs were misbehaving.

The dogs are always supposed to stay outside the dining room while we're eating, but one of the four tends to get carried away and break the rule. Not always the same one. Occasionally, Wendy, but most often Peppy. Then they all do it, because no way are the other three going to be good if they're not all being good. That breaks a code of basic dog fairness.

Wendy came charging in and skidded to a stop between Quinn and Mando. The others followed, milling around the table. Except Peppy. He had better things to do than mill.

Wayne, the huge orange tabby, was sitting in the

dining room with us, on the windowsill, thinking it was a safe spot during dinner. Peppy made a beeline for him and jumped up and down, not quite able to reach him but snapping in the air near his paws. Of course, by that time Wayne was on his feet, back arched, hissing dramatically.

Just as Paula got up to put the dogs back out, Wayne reached down and wacked Peppy on the nose, hard, with claws out. Peppy shrieked and slunk out of the room. Paula followed after him to make sure he was okay.

"My," Clementine said. "So much commotion."

"You don't have pets, do you?" Quinn asked.

"No. Not really. I just have—" But she stopped herself.

Paula came back in and sat down.

"Is he okay?" I asked her.

"I think so. His nose is bleeding. He's licking it, so he'll lick off anything I try to put on it. It's not bad enough to need stitches or anything. I'll check on him again after dinner. He'll be okay. The question is whether he'll ever learn."

Quinn was still focused on our guest.

"Did you *ever* have pets?" he asked her.

"When I was growing up, we had ranch dogs and barn cats. But they didn't come in the house."

"That's weird," Quinn said. "I never had pets before I lived with my moms, but I like them, and I like that they come in."

"It was just different where I grew up," she said.

"It was a different kind of household. There was plastic on the furniture, so it stayed clean, and no kids allowed in the living room, except we called it the parlor. Well, no *me* allowed. I was an only child so no kids meant no me." My head came up at that, and I focused in on her words. "That was back when children were seen and not heard. I was expected to use an inside voice if I spoke inside at all. There was no commotion in my house. It was very quiet. My parents didn't talk much."

I felt Paula look over at me. I could see it in my peripheral vision, but I didn't look back.

"Sounds like *my* house when I was growing up," I said. "Except there was no plastic on the furniture. But it was always so silent. My parents didn't like each other very much by the time I came along, but they didn't fight. They just didn't talk. And they didn't talk to me much. And I guess I was afraid to talk."

"Then why do you have all this commotion now? If we were raised in the same sorts of families, why is my house quiet now and yours chaotic?"

"Seems to work one of two ways," I said. "We either do what our parents did, whether we mean to or not, or we make up our minds to do exactly the opposite."

I expected some kind of reply. I got nothing.

We fell into silence again. As if we'd never broken the ice in the first place.

Just as I could feel Paula gearing up to kick-start some kind of conversation, Clementine spoke. She set down her fork, turned her head, and looked straight into Mando's face. He looked up from his plate, obviously alarmed.

"I'm sorry for our misunderstanding earlier," she said.

I watched Mando's jaw. I won't say it dropped, exactly. But it definitely sagged. "Oh," he said. "I mean, you are?"

"Well, yes. I wouldn't like to be called a thief if I was only trying to help. Those pills make it hard to think straight."

Mando retrieved his jaw and pulled it back into place. "Yeah. I guess it would scare a person to wake up and see somebody in their house. I figured you'd recognize me, but I forgot you were on those drugs the doctor gave you. I said your name when I first came in the door. And before I looked into your room. I was trying not to surprise you too much."

"Oh. Did you? I guess it wasn't enough to wake me. Anyway, so long as you accept my apology."

Mando shot me a desperate glance, as if he didn't know what to make of this sudden development. I glanced over at Paula, but she just looked pleased. Like everything was working out fine after all. She didn't seem concerned by the fact that this was all bizarrely out of character.

"Yeah," Mando said. "Sure. No problem."

Then we all ate in silence for a few minutes, and I saw Clementine's head begin to droop. In between bites, her chin would drift down toward her plate. Then, when it was time to take another bite, she seemed to startle herself awake.

The boys ate with their heads down, but Paula and I watched our neighbor to see if she was going to be all right. I was thinking, *Okay. That explains the out-of-character stuff. She's stoned out of her mind.* Legally, but the effect was the same.

Her head drifted down again until it almost touched her plate, and I saw Paula rise up out of her chair.

"Mrs. D'Antonio," I said. "Are you okay?"

Her head snapped up straight again. "This is very good macaroni and cheese."

Paula said, "Maybe we should wrap that up to go. You look like it might be time to get you back to bed again."

Just at that exact moment somebody rapped on the door.

Of course it landed in my gut to a total panic response, because I wasn't expecting anyone, and didn't seem able to anticipate anything but more trouble. I try not to think that way, but it's more a feeling than a thought, and besides, it's an involuntary response.

"I'll get it," Paula said.

I stared at the open dining room doorway, and so did our neighbor. She seemed wide-awake now.

From the look on her face, I had to think she was expecting only more trouble, too.

A moment later Paula came back into the dining room with Dennis Portman, who was in uniform.

"Can I be excused?" Mando asked, already on his feet.

I looked up, about to tell him he needed to finish his food. But I said nothing, because his face was so tight. He was clearly uncomfortable. Mando is not a big fan of law enforcement. Based on his family history, I can't say I blame him. Besides, his plate was clean. While we'd been watching the neighbor nod off, he'd scarfed down every bite of his food.

"Um," I said. "Yes."

He made himself scarce.

Normally I would have told him to sit with the family while we finished dinner. Well. Normally I wouldn't have needed to. But I was anxious and scared about what the deputy had come to say, and I couldn't handle distractions.

I looked up at Dennis, and he looked back at me and smiled just a little. I could tell he didn't have earth-shattering news in either direction. Nothing disastrous or joyful.

"How about the short version first?" I asked him. "Then I'll invite you to sit down and maybe even have something to eat."

"Short version. We had a sighting. But it did *not* result in our actually catching up with them."

I sighed out some of the tension. "But that's still good. Right?"

"Could be worse."

I looked over at Clem, but she was just staring into space. As though she couldn't make out any significance in our words.

I gestured to Mando's chair, and Dennis sat.

"Eat," he said. "Don't let me stop you."

"How about some macaroni and cheese?" I asked him. "I make it myself. From scratch. It's the kind you bake in a casserole with buttered bread crumbs on top."

"It's really good," Quinn said.

"It is," Clementine added.

We all just stared at her for a moment. As if she'd spoken Latvian or Urdu. Even Dennis.

"That's kind of hard to say no to." Dennis seemed to shake himself back into the moment. "Any chance you could make me a plate small enough that I could still go home and eat the dinner my wife will've made?"

"I'll get him some," Paula said, and she disappeared into the kitchen.

"Scared me to see you come in," I told Dennis.

"Then we're even. Scared me to go over to Clem's and find nobody home. I was knocking on *your* door to tell you we had another disappearance on our hands. I was *not* expecting to find her over here as your dinner guest."

"Right," I said. "It was an unexpected development. Apparently, Quinn had a nice day over there today, and he invited her."

"Next time I'm supposed to ask one of my moms first," Quinn added.

My gut tightened, but Clementine didn't seem to be paying attention.

I wanted to hear more about the Star sighting, but I felt I should wait until Paula was back before asking. And probably Dennis felt he should wait for the same thing before offering.

An awkward lag. Then Paula came out and set a dessert-size plate of macaroni and cheese in front of Dennis, and sat back down at her place at the table, and put her napkin on her lap again.

Dennis took one bite. Closed his eyes. "Now that is comfort food at its pure best." He opened his eyes again and saw that both Paula and I were staring at him. Waiting. "Right. So, this morning we get a call from an old man who lives in the middle of exactly nowhere, at the very northern edge of Franklin County. Says he looked out his kitchen window and there was a big gray horse standing not twenty feet from his house. No saddle, but he said it had a halter, and the halter rope was looped back behind his neck, like reins, and tied on the other side. So he could tell it was somebody's horse. You know. That somebody'd been riding him, not just a horse that got through or over a fence and out of somebody's field. So, he's so busy staring at this horse that it took him a minute to realize there's a girl going through his trash. He'd heard the reports, so he went straight for the front door, but by the time he got out there, they were both gone. He couldn't even see which way.

"So Bobby and I drive all the way up there, thinking we can still track them down. We even called for a search dog. Only, here's what he forgot to tell us. This guy lives twenty miles from the nearest town and he has no phone. Not even a cell phone, not that he'd get reception out there anyway. So he waited until he was going into town anyway, later that morning, to pick up his mail. He gets it general delivery from the post office in Beaufort. Little town you probably never heard of. Anyway, when he called it in, he forgot to mention the sighting was more than three hours old. So it's something, but it's not much."

He stopped. Looked at me, then Paula, then back at me. As if waiting to see what we had to say. His fork hand was still poised, waiting. I noticed he was left-handed, though I didn't know why it should matter.

When we didn't add anything, he took another huge bite.

"How far away is that, where she was seen?"

Paula asked that. I was more or less stunned into silence.

"More than forty miles."

That knocked me out of my statue state. "How

196

did they get more than forty miles from here in only . . ." But then I ran out of steam. Because I was tired, and these last couple of days felt weeks long, and I really couldn't get a bead on how long it had been. At least, not quickly.

"At the time he saw them, it had been about twenty-eight hours," he said, and then shoveled in another bite.

"Doesn't that seem like a lot of mileage in a short period of time?"

"On foot it would be a lot," he said, his mouth still full. "Not if you've got a good horse."

I looked over at Clem, to see how she was taking all this. She was leaning her chin on her hand, as if she literally couldn't hold it up with her neck anymore. I assumed she wasn't hearing a word.

"She's so far from home," I said. "I had no idea she was so dead serious about this. I guess I thought of her as lying beside a stream a couple miles from here with the horse grazing nearby. I wasn't picturing her making tracks. So . . . does this help us at all, that someone saw her?"

Dennis sighed and set down his fork. "It tells us three things. One, they went north. Granted, after that sighting they could have made any number of turns. But of all the directions we've been searching, which is all of them, this eliminates some. Two, they were both still alive as of this morning. Three, they're still together. Not sure if that's a good thing or not, though. We're more likely to apprehend both if they don't have the benefit of each other. The thing that bothers me most is that if they haven't made any sharp turns, they're headed for the mountains. That's not the place I want them. There aren't many roads, so it's a much harder search environment. Plus, it gets cold up there. Snows."

"But it's summer," I said. Pleadingly. As though I could bargain with the weather.

"Still gets cold at night. And it won't be summer forever. Anyway, to get stuck up there they'd have to get another hundred miles or more without getting caught. Let's stay optimistic."

Nobody responded to that for quite a long time. Longer than it took for Dennis to finish his macaroni and cheese. I think we needed the time to work on our optimism.

"Coffee?" I asked him when he was clearly done.

"No, thanks. Best be getting home to the family."

"So, how long ago was that now? When they were seen?"

"Oh. Let's see." He glanced at his watch. " 'Bout twelve hours ago."

"So if they're going in a straight line, and at about the same speed, they're more than sixty miles from here by now."

Dennis opened his mouth to answer. But before any sound could come out, Clementine spoke up suddenly. Said something strange.

"That's so nice for him." Wistfully. And with a voice that sounded . . . younger.

"Who?" Dennis asked.

"Comet."

Paula and Dennis and I looked at each other, and then at Clem.

She had a bite of salad on her fork, and it was partway from her plate to her mouth but stalled. As if it had gotten too heavy to lift. Several beats went by before she looked up and noticed we were all staring at her.

"What?" she asked, defensive now. Much more herself again. "Why is everybody giving me those strange looks? I still want him back, you know."

"Yeah," Dennis said. "We figured that much, Clem. I think it might be time to get you home. I think those pills are going to your head. Maybe one of your nice hosts'll wrap the rest of your dinner up to go."

"Oh," Clem said, sounding disappointed. "Do I have to go back there? It's so . . ."

But she never finished her thought.

"I'll go sit with you," Quinn said. "Till you go to sleep. Can I, Moms? I'm done with my dinner."

So Paula wrapped Clem's uneaten food, and Dennis and Quinn walked her back across the road to her own house. Which left just me and Paula.

"That was weird," I said.

"The drugs make things unpredictable."

"But she was so . . . unlike herself."

199

"Or just the opposite."

"Not following. The drugs made her more *like* herself?"

"Maybe. Think of heavy sedation as something like a truth serum."

"Hmm," I said. I was skating dangerously close to seeing Clementine as only too human.

20. Clementine

I'm embarrassed to admit it, but I don't know if this next part was two days or three days later. My days and nights had gotten muddled by the fact that I slept most of the time.

I woke up because I smelled food. Bacon. That's the smell I could definitely identify. I opened my eyes, expecting to see the little boy standing over my bed. He'd been bringing me meals.

It wasn't him at all. It was Clara Bowe.

"Clementine." She sounded not altogether friendly.

I guess she wasn't my biggest fan.

Then, for some strange reason, I tried to remember who around here was. Chalk it up to the drug, I guess, because who wants to think about a thing like that? Besides, the answer was obvious. Nobody. There were those that put up with me and those that didn't. Just for a second, I tried to remember if it had been any different before the big heartache with Tina, but that was not a place I wanted to go, so I snapped myself back again.

Clara set a tray on my lap, with a plate of scrambled eggs and bacon, and a glass of orange juice. No coffee. Nobody ever brought me coffee, and I would have liked some. It made me feel vaguely insulted, because I took it to mean they didn't want me awake.

"What are you doing here?" I asked her.

She clearly heard it as an affront.

"Trying to help, for what that's worth. But I guess it must seem strange. I'm babysitting for the little boy across the road. The two ladies asked me to look in on you and make sure you took your pills and had something to eat."

"Where are they today?"

"Well, the one of them—the veterinarian—is off doing her appointments, and the other lady and the older boy had to go away. Back to Napa County, where they're from. Just for the day."

"To do what?"

"I'm sure I wouldn't know," she said, with more than a hint of judgment. As if she didn't wonder and neither should I.

She left my room without further comment.

I propped up more, as best I could, and took a bite of bacon. It was crispy and dark, the way I'd always made it for Vernon, which sent a pang of discomfort through my gut when I thought of it.

Clara reappeared in the doorway.

"I forgot your pill," she said.

"I can take it myself. They're right here by the bed." I gestured toward the nightstand with a flip of my head.

"Well, at least let me refill that water glass." But before she took the glass, she opened the bottle of pills and peered inside. "Well, this doesn't seem right. You're to take these every four hours, for a week. You should have enough left for a couple of days still. You only have six. That's only a twenty-four-hour supply."

The news set off a panic in me. I felt it inside my head, like my whole brain was reacting, and in my midsection, which felt cold, and buzzed.

"That can't be right."

"I know how to count. This is only six. You'll be out by this time tomorrow. Maybe they shouldn't have been left here by the bed. You must have taken too many."

I felt a rising sense of resentment, because I didn't much like Clara. I'd never invited her into my home. I'd been given no notice that I might wake up and find a whole new person standing over my bed, judging and counting.

"Well, the doctor will just have to give me more," I said. "Call him, will you?" And then, because I had to rely on her to do so, I added, "Please?"

She put on her reading glasses, which were dangling on a chain around her neck, and peered and squinted at the label. "I wouldn't know how to reach this doctor. I've never even heard of him."

"He's at the emergency room at Tri Counties Hospital."

Clara sighed. "Don't know if this is within my scope of duties. But I guess it can't hurt to make the call."

She shuffled out again, and I picked at my breakfast, though I'd suddenly lost my appetite.

The little boy came in a few minutes later, and sat in the chair by my bed, and said good morning, which I found cheering.

"Good morning," I said. "Did you have your breakfast?"

His hair had been freshly combed, probably by the babysitter, and looked even puffier and bigger than usual, with each curly strand recently separated.

"I just finished. You should finish yours."

"I'm trying, but I'm just not all that hungry. Where's your mom today?"

"Which one?"

"The one who's not the vet." I swear I couldn't remember her name.

"She took Mando back to Napa for a hearing."

"What kind of hearing?"

"I forget the word she used. But it's the kind of hearing where they decide if somebody can come out of jail early."

I opened my mouth to ask more questions, to try to make sense of that, but before I could speak, Clara was in the doorway again, leaning into my bedroom.

"The doctor says absolutely not," she said.

"How can he say that?" I was alarmed, a feeling that appeared immediately and then seemed to expand and multiply with each passing second. I tried to keep it out of my voice. I doubt I succeeded. "How can he just say no if I need them?"

"Well, he didn't use those exact words. But he said no. And he was quite firm about it. He said he's just an ER doctor. He gives people only what they need for that moment, for the emergency. If they need ongoing care, they're to see their own physician. He also said it's a very powerful sedative, and carefully controlled by the federal government, because it has a lot of potential for abuse. He didn't say you were trying to abuse it. Just that it can be quite addictive. And I think he was concerned that you took more than you were supposed to. I could call your doctor if you insist. But I'm thinking he'll say similar things. Except the part about only treating emergencies, I mean. But if they're that tightly controlled and that addictive, and if you took too many, he might say no, too. But if you really insist, I'll call and ask."

I held still a minute, feeling the panic. It was continuing to expand, feeding on itself and growing. I had no idea when it would stop getting bigger, which only alarmed me more. Maybe it never would.

"No," I said. "Thank you. Just go now. I mean . . . I'm sorry, I didn't mean that quite as rudely as it came out. I just want to sit here with my little friend."

She shook her head and ducked out. I felt some slight relief hearing her footsteps fade away down the stairs.

I had no doctor. I'd never been sick a day in my life, so I didn't go to them. Oh, I'd had an ob-gyn for pregnancy issues, and for prenatal exams when I had Tina. And he'd delivered her, of course. But that was well over twenty years ago, that I'd seen him last, and he was long since retired. Or maybe I'd even heard that he passed away. I couldn't remember. And this type of prescription would not have been his department anyway.

For a few years after Tina was born, I had a general practitioner who I'd go to for Pap smears, and to be referred to the hospital clinic for mammograms. But then he'd gotten on me about losing weight, which was humiliating, and really none of his business. Finally, I went in for a checkup and refused to get on the scale, and he refused to treat me, and that was that. I hadn't been to a doctor since, and I was pretty sure that doctor had retired as well.

And if you're going to start over with someone

new, it's probably best not to start by asking for a highly controlled and addictive drug that people abuse, and which you need more of because you used up your first batch too fast.

No, I was just sunk. I had maybe a day to partially enjoy this respite from my current reality.

I focused back on the little boy as a way of trying to think about happier things. He smiled at me curiously, as if he saw on my face that all was not well, and wanted me to know I was quite wrong to believe so. In his world, everything was fine.

It made part of me want to be a kid again. But another part of me knew that even then I hadn't lived in a world like his, where everything was okay. That was a luxury I had never been granted. And this was a boy who'd been in the foster care system, and had been adopted at a fairly advanced age. Were things really so happy for him across the road? That seemed hard to imagine.

I said, "That didn't really make sense, what you told me before."

"What did I tell you?"

"It sounded like you were saying they went to a parole hearing."

"Oh! Yeah! That's the word I forgot."

"But your . . . brother . . . or foster brother, or whatever he is to you . . . he's not in jail."

"No, it's not him. It's his mom."

"Oh. His mother is in jail. That makes more sense. That's why he needs a foster home."

"Right. You should eat your breakfast. The scrambled eggs aren't good after they get cold."

"What's she in jail for?"

"Nothing."

"Can't be nothing."

"No, it is. Really. Nothing. She didn't do anything."

"They don't put people in jail for doing nothing."

"Sometimes they do. Sometimes they think you did something, but you didn't. And you tell them you didn't, but they don't believe you."

"Well, everybody *says* they didn't do a thing wrong, but most of them are lying because they don't want to go to jail. Everybody wants to break the law, but nobody wants to pay a price for it."

"I don't want to break the law." He began swinging his dangling, sneakered feet back and forth in wide arcs.

"I guess I didn't mean *everybody*."

"Do *you* want to break the law?"

"Well. No. But on the other hand, I suppose if there was no price to pay at all . . ."

"I think I still wouldn't," he said.

It may sound odd, or even mean, but I found myself aware of a nagging sense of discomfort about this boy. I think it had been true as long as I'd known him, but I only just realized it. The feeling wasn't always there, just now and then. Because he seemed almost too good to be true, like those little boys on television in the fifties, on situation comedies about families. Families that are always so much happier than your own.

It was just a little much.

I remember thinking if I didn't see a dark side in him soon, something complicated and unhappy, it would argue with my entire view of life. It was more of a general feeling, though. I don't think I thought it out in exactly those words.

Later, after he left, I took all six of the pills at once.

Looking back, it was an amazingly foolish thing to do.

I guess the idea at the time was to throw everything to the wind and plunge into oblivion. But just as I was finishing the last of the water—which the little boy had brought me before going home for lunch—it dawned on me clearly that it would be an all-too-temporary oblivion. Six of those pills would not be enough to solve anything permanently.

I drifted off to sleep quickly, knowing in the back of my mind that I probably would wake up. When I did, the pills would be gone. And the rest of the things I was so unhappy about would not be.

It was a very brief vacation, at a very high price.

21. Jackie

When I looked down, I realized I was perched—tensely—on the very edge of my hard plastic chair. Just like Mando. I sat back and sighed, hoping to set a good example for him. Even though I doubted he was paying any attention to me at all.

We were seated in an almost oppressively small box of a room, with walls that were painted—I swear—a drab shade of gray. They looked for all the world as though made of concrete instead of the usual drywall. I stared at them for a moment and decided they really were. Concrete.

The windows had a metal mesh, a welded wire, fused right into the glass.

There was a long table, like a desk on steroids, at the front of the room. Behind it sat two women and one man, not one of whom had so much as made eye contact with us.

One of the women was wearing a suit so red it looked like it had been designed for highway safety. The other woman and the man were dressed in colors as drab as the walls. They were all three making notes on some papers scattered on the desk in front of them. As though their job functions, their stations in the world, were so indispensable that they couldn't even stop to take a breath.

Speaking of breathing, I glanced over at Mando again, and I swear he wasn't.

He was sitting on the very edge of his chair, as I think I mentioned, both arms straight down, grasping the chair on either side of his legs. Tightly. As if his chair was perched on the edge of a pit of alligators, and he might be about to tip forward.

There were a dozen chairs packed into the tiny room, but nobody was using any of the others. It was only us.

I wanted to reach out and put a hand on Mando's shoulder, but I couldn't decide if that would make things better or worse. I suppose it would have made more sense just to try it and find out.

But that's not me.

Instead, I wrestled back and forth in my head for what might have been a good two minutes.

The clock on the concrete wall above our heads ticked so loudly that each tick felt shocking. It also reminded me that the proceedings were eleven minutes late in starting.

It hit me that I might be about to explode, and I knew the same and then some must be true for Mando, so I tried putting the aforementioned hand on his shoulder. He jumped a mile. I swear he almost fell off his chair. It wasn't my imagination, and I know I'm not exaggerating, because the woman in red briefly looked up. She still didn't meet our eyes.

I leaned in close to Mando's ear. "Breathe," I said.

He laughed, but not the way people do when they're actually amused. And quietly. "I must be breathing. I'm not dead."

"Breathe more. Deeper."

He seemed to concentrate on that for a moment. To draw his energies in to try. I could hear air going into him, which made my breathing loosen up, too. He started to sit back more in his chair. But he never finished. Because Gabriela was led into the room by a uniformed guard, her wrists shackled together.

Mando jumped to his feet, and I had to grab his arm to keep him from going to her, which I instinctively felt must be against the rules.

She looked at him, then looked away in shame. Then she looked at me. At my face. And smiled. Just a little bit.

She appreciated me. And Paula. She'd said so, the only other time I met her.

Paula and I had visited her once in prison. To see if we could talk her into letting Mando come see her. But she was adamant. Prison was a humiliation, and she wanted no witnesses, *especially* Mando. She didn't want her son to see her that way, in that place.

She never relented. We all agreed to weekly phone calls only, which is as many phone calls as she was allowed to make. No seeing her incarcerated. Trapped in that miserably sub-servient position.

And now he was seeing it. I instinctively looked at his face to watch his reaction, but nothing showed. His face might as well have been made of the same gray concrete as the walls.

She turned her back to us and sat in a chair facing the long desk.

I tugged gently at Mando's sleeve. Three times. The third time he reluctantly sat.

The people at the desk kept writing. Kept looking down. As if their only really important work was on paper in front of them. Their physical attitudes had quickly gone from puzzling to infuriating. I could feel stress rolling off Mando, and I hoped things would get under way before he lost his ability to contain it.

Gabriela looked over her shoulder and blew him a kiss, which seemed to relax him slightly. Then she offered me another little smile, so sad it broke my heart. Or bent it, anyway. I could feel the damage in my chest.

She looked away again.

She was a pretty woman with fine bones. Petite. Which had always seemed odd to me. Mando's father must have been a giant. Her hours of labor must not have been any fun at all. Her black hair had been cut short. Boy-short. I wondered if that had been her decision, or if she had no more say in how her hair was cut.

Just for a split second I understood her policy on visits much better.

There was some legal stuff I can't recount exactly. I sat there and listened to every word, but it didn't really add up to something coherent to me. Maybe my brain was too busy, or maybe you have to know the legal system, or both.

Then the woman in drab went on for several minutes about the various factors in their eventual decision, such as prison behavioral violations, or lack of same, character witnesses, petitions of support from the community, or testimony from victims or family members of victims.

I thought, *What victims?* Drugs being something of a victimless crime.

Of course, if it had been a simple drug charge, she wouldn't have been serving fifteen to life.

I remembered the account we'd read of the trial. One of the arresting officers had sworn that Gabriela's late brother, Luis—Mando's uncle—took a shot at him. Which seemed like a perfectly ridiculous claim in light of the fact that no weapon was ever found in the home. Gabriela claimed it was nothing but a sheet pan knocked off the top of the stove during all the panic of the arrest.

I wondered why that policeman hadn't bothered to come to the hearing if he honestly felt he'd been shot at.

I wanted to ask out loud why the arresting

officers hadn't bothered to attend, but I figured I wasn't supposed to say anything. And I worried that breaking the rules might only hurt our case.

While I was trying to take all this in, my brain going miles a minute, Mando's mother began to speak. I'd missed the question she was answering. But, in context, it seemed they'd asked her if she was either remorseful or rehabilitated. Or both.

"I don't know what you want me to say," she said in her heavily accented English. Armando had no accent, but he'd been attending school in the US since he was seven. "Everybody wants me to say I'm sorry for what I did, but I didn't do anything. I lost my job. In the slow season. The restaurant where I worked just laid people off when the tourists went away. You never knew who or when. I couldn't find another job, and I couldn't pay rent, so that's why we moved in with Luis."

Now all three of these people, who hadn't bothered to look up from their paperwork earlier, were staring right into her face. I could tell it unnerved her, even though I was only seeing her from behind.

The bright-red woman said, "You moved your ten-year-old son into a house where methamphetamine was being made. You don't think that's doing anything wrong?"

"Not made," the man said. "Sold. It wasn't a meth lab."

"Fine. Whatever. Sold. You didn't think that was endangering your son?"

"But I didn't know. Luis was not a drug dealer. He was a mechanic. He was my little brother. I loved him. He lost his mechanic job a year before I lost mine. I guess that's when maybe he started selling drugs, but he never told me. He knew I'd be ashamed of him if he told me that, so maybe he didn't say."

"And you didn't see it being smoked?" Red Lady asked. She seemed to be the mean dog at the open gate. She had taken it upon herself to menace poor Gabriela.

"No. It wasn't. Nobody smoked nothing in that apartment. I would've known."

"And you didn't think an awful lot of people were coming and going?"

"No. Never. Nobody ever came over. Luis just went out a lot at night."

"And you never asked him where he was going?"

"It was none of my business where he was going."

"Or where he was getting his money?"

"He said he was getting some bodywork jobs on the side."

"At night?"

"Where I come from, people work during the day."

Red Lady sat back in her chair with a whump sound, looking unconvinced.

"I'm telling you the truth," Gabriela said.

The man took over. He asked, "Did you know there was a gun in the house when you brought your son there to live?"

"There wasn't. There never was. If Luis had a gun, how come they never found it? Where was it supposed to go? They shot him dead because some loud noise scared them. Something got knocked down in the struggle. A pan. I was in the kitchen by then. I watched them shoot my little brother. He had nothing in his hands. Nothing. Of course they're gonna say he shot first, but where did the gun go? It just disappeared, like magic?"

Red Lady said, "I would think the disappearance of the weapon is the reason you were charged as accessory to the attempted murder of a police officer."

"But they were right there in the kitchen with me. Where could I make a gun go where they couldn't see me do it? They were right there. I'm telling you, there was no gun. I did nothing except watch my little brother die. If they hadn't found drugs, I would've sworn he wasn't selling any. But maybe he was. I don't know. People get desperate and do desperate stuff. Maybe he made a bad choice. But all I did was bring my son and me there to stay because we had to have some place to stay. Where were we gonna stay if I couldn't find a job?"

Red Lady said, "There are shelters."

"Where around here is there a shelter?"

"Off the top of my head, I can't say, but the fact that I don't know doesn't mean it wasn't your responsibility to find out. And we're not here to retry this case. We're not here to determine your guilt or innocence. You were convicted, so those are the facts we go on. It says here your brother shot at one of the officers. We can't disprove that in this hearing."

And she said something else, but I missed it. Because my head was filling up with a sudden thought.

Next thing I knew, I was on my feet, and I hadn't even felt myself get up.

"Why doesn't she have an attorney present?" I blurted out.

Absolute silence. Everybody stared at me. Even Mando and his mom. Even the guard with his back to the door.

Red Lady slid off her wire-rimmed eyeglasses. "Who are you?"

"I'm the foster parent who's been taking care of her son. And we were given a pamphlet telling us what to expect at this hearing. It said she'd be provided with an attorney today."

Red Lady just stared at me a moment longer. "I don't even think you have standing to speak." She turned to the man in drab. "Does a foster parent have standing to speak?"

"I'm not sure," he said. "But so long as the

question's been raised, why doesn't she have an attorney present?"

I breathed properly for the first time in a long time, and sat again.

Instead of asking the shackled woman right in front of them, they all three referred back to their paperwork.

"Says here she declined an attorney," the man said.

"No," Gabriela said. "I asked for one. A public defender. And they said they'd send one. But then they came and got me out of my cell, and he still wasn't here. And I asked where he was, and they said something went wrong, like he made two appointments at once or something, and he wasn't coming. But I asked for one."

All three continued to stare at the desk. A couple of papers were flipped over or moved aside.

"It says here you declined an attorney," Red Lady said. And that was it. The proceedings simply moved on. "Does the son have anything he wants to say?"

I looked over at Mando. He brushed his hair back, as if suddenly concerned about how he looked. I could see his hand shaking.

He stood. I watched his jaw work back and forth under the skin.

"If you knew my mom," he said, his voice shaking as well, "you'd know she'd never do anything wrong. I didn't know Tio Luis was selling drugs, either. We didn't know about any of this. She tried and tried to tell the police none of this had anything to do with us. They wouldn't listen. It was just bad luck she happened to be in the house. She—"

Red Lady cut him off. "Were you home when the arrest took place?"

"No, ma'am. I was at school."

"Then you really don't know what happened."

"I know my mom."

"But you don't really know what she did and didn't know. You don't know for a fact that she didn't know your uncle was slinging meth. Maybe she didn't do anything because she needed a roof over your heads."

"She told me she didn't know."

"With all due respect, son, most of the people who come through here tell us they've done nothing wrong."

I watched Mando's face get red. Disturbingly red. I waited to see if he'd say more. But he seemed stuck. Frozen.

Before he could unstick himself, the man said, "We're going to deliberate now. If everybody would please step out into the hall."

Then I got stuck, too. Because I felt like I should say something. Do something. Because she should have had an attorney, and she'd very clearly said she'd asked for one. Because there was no gun ever found, no evidence to suggest that she'd been involved in either the drugs or the alleged assault on the cop. But they'd already said they weren't here to question the details of the conviction. Somehow they'd gotten a jury to find her guilty, which I guess isn't hard. I felt the tug of all of us being railroaded for the sake of time and convenience, but I wasn't a party to the crime, and should never even have spoken.

Next thing I knew, the guard was towing Mando out of the room by his arm, and Mando grabbed my arm to make sure I came along. Then we were out in the hall, between claustrophobic gray concrete walls, sitting on a hard wooden bench.

It was all over.

That was it. The big chance. You wait three years for it, and it's gone just like that.

Mando's mom sat on the bench across the hall from us, because the guard indicated that she must. She tried to sit with us, but that guard straightened her out immediately.

She looked almost bruised, a battered internal condition that figuratively showed on the out-side. Like someone had beaten her within an inch of her life in some ingenious way that left no marks.

"It's good to see you," she said to her son, clearly working hard not to cry.

"You, too," he said.

"You okay?"

"No. I'd be okay if you got out." He glanced over at me, then back to his mom. "Don't get me wrong. It's good where I am. They're nice. But I'm not okay till you get out. Are *you* okay?"

She shrugged, a tight look on her face. And then the door opened, and they called us back in. Yes, seriously. No, I'm not making a mistake and compressing time in my perception. We were in that hall for maybe thirty seconds. If that.

Some deliberation, I thought.

We walked back in and sat down. Mando was crying, but trying to pretend otherwise.

The man made the announcement that surprised no one.

"Due to the serious nature of the crime, and the fact that a police officer could have been killed, and due to the fact that the welfare of a minor child was at stake, and as the inmate shows no remorse whatsoever for the crime—"

"I can't be sorry for what I didn't do," she interjected.

"—our decision is to deny parole at this time. The inmate will come before this board again in two years."

I think he said a couple more things, but I missed them. I was busy thinking that they undoubtedly expected the inmate to somehow grow and mature in the intervening two years. But it was the board that needed to change. It was the process that needed to change. It was the fact that they were all white and she was Latina that needed to change, or at least change into an irrelevant factor.

And the chances of that were not looking good.

About ten steps down the long gray hallway, Mando stopped, turned to face the concrete wall, and punched it with all his strength.

I wasn't really all that surprised. Well, I guess I was surprised in the moment, but only because it happened fast. Something had to give way in him. I was just about ready to punch a wall myself, and she wasn't even my mother.

I heard a thin, whimpery sound come out of him, and he sank to his knees. I crouched over him and took hold of his wrist. I wanted to look at the hand, to see how badly he'd injured it, but he was shielding it loosely with his other hand. Not so much to keep me from seeing, I think, but more as a reaction to the pain.

I looked up to see the guard about ten steps down the hall, watching. He didn't seem concerned. In fact, he had a slight smirk on his face.

"Good thing for him that wall is harder than his fist," the guard said. "Or he'd be responsible for the damage."

Fortunately, I knew the area well. I knew exactly where to find the nearest emergency room. And they weren't the least bit busy.

They x-rayed the hand, and discovered a boxer's fracture on the outside bone, above the joint of his wrist. Amazingly, his knuckles were not broken, but they did require three stitches to stop the bleeding.

While I stood at the cashier's window and dug out my credit card, Mando leaned back against the wall and flexed his hand slightly against the plastic brace, as if to see how much he could move it. He winced silently.

"I'm sorry," he said.

"Don't be sorry to me. You're the one who's paying the price."

He nodded in the direction of my Visa card.

"It's covered," I said. "You're covered."

"All of it?"

"I don't know. But it doesn't matter. It's just what needs to be done."

"It was stupid," he said.

"It wasn't your best decision. But I can understand your frustration. That hearing was bullshit."

I never swore in front of the kids, so I watched his face to see how he would take it. I was surprised when he lit up with something almost like happiness. Almost like relief.

"It *was* bullshit! I'm sorry. I shouldn't say that word."

"Well. Neither should I. But it was."

"It so was," he said.

• • •

"Should we stop and get that prescription filled?" I asked as we drove out of the hospital parking lot.

"What is it?"

"Just Tylenol with a few milligrams of something stronger. I forget if it's codeine or Vicodin."

"Nah. I don't care. I just want to go home."

"I've got some ibuprofen in my purse."

"I'd take a couple of those."

I handed him my purse from the backseat and let him rummage through it himself, left-handed.

"There should be a bottle of water in the glove box."

I pulled out onto the highway toward home as he slowly made his way through the simple task. But it didn't feel like I was headed for home. It felt like this was home. And it hurt to leave it again.

I think we were both feeling emotional.

"I feel like I should have done more," I said.

"Like what?"

"I don't know. Something."

"What could you do, though? They weren't even going to let you talk."

"I just felt so . . ." But I was never able to finish the thought.

After a moment of silence he said, "Me, too."

So I guess I didn't need to.

A mile or two later he said, "You believe me. Right?"

"About what?"

"That she didn't do anything."

"Yes. I believe that."

"Because nobody else does. You heard that lady. Everybody who gets arrested says they didn't do it. And everybody figures they're lying and they really did."

"Look. Mando. I'm not pretending for a minute that I can get inside your experience here. Or that I know what you're going through. But I'm not so stupid that I can't see that a Latina woman with a heavy accent, no money, and a public defender who doesn't bother to show up isn't getting the same break as I would. If that had been me, maybe they would have believed me. Plus, we could scrape up enough money, or at least enough credit, to get a good lawyer. I have eyes. I can see how the system is different for minorities."

Silence for a time. I was wondering if what I'd said had come out right, or like just more bullshit. I wondered if a white person could ever comment on the minority experience and get it right. Or if there was something mildly, accidentally racist in even trying.

"You're sort of a minority," he said after a time.

"Kind of different."

"Different how?"

"Well. Maybe because they'd look at me and not *know* I was in a minority. In some situations I can just hide it. I'm not sure if that's good or bad, though. I mean, there's you, and everybody sees exactly who you are the minute they meet you. Then there's me. If I think I'm down behind enemy lines, I can hide it. So on the one hand, I'm lucky, because I can lie and fake my way out of trouble. On the other hand, I think that's not a good thing. It takes a toll, you know? When you hide. But, seriously, I worry sometimes talking about things like this, because I feel like I don't really know what it means to be you, and maybe I'm saying exactly the wrong thing without meaning to."

"No," he said. "You're not. I'm glad we talked about it. I think I know what you mean. I got no choice that I'm Guatemalan, and I can't make people think I'm not. But if somebody gives me a hard time, I know they're wrong. I know I'm okay and they're just a bigot, like that lady with the horse. But it's like if they can get you to hide it, it's almost like you're ashamed of it."

"Exactly. You get it exactly. It's a choice between getting the crap beaten out of you for being exactly what you are, or avoiding the beating by selling out and pretending you're not, which is like pretending there's something wrong with what you are. I'm not sure which is worse. I don't think it pays to try to figure it out. I think we should agree they both suck and leave it at that."

We rode in silence for a mile or two more, Mando flexing his hand slightly against the brace. Wiggling his fingers, but just at the tips. Not enough to pull on his stitched and bandaged knuckles.

"So, why do you believe me?" he asked suddenly, startling me.

"Oh. Well. I've met your mother. And she just doesn't seem like the type. She doesn't seem like someone who would even drive too fast."

"She doesn't!" he said, suddenly enthusiastic. As if everything were suddenly okay again. "She drives me crazy with that. I say, 'Mom. You're going so slow.' She says, 'I'm going just what the sign says I should go.' She says, 'Why risk getting a ticket?' I say, 'To get there on time.' She says, 'So leave the house five minutes sooner!'" He wound down, a wistful smile on his face. Happy to remember, I guess. Then his smile faded. "But I don't know why I'm talking about it like it's going on right now. Like she said it to me just today. Like she's right here."

A brief pause, an emptiness.

Then he broke down and cried like a baby.

I know he'd rather have cried alone, without me there to see. But we were in a moving car together, so it was one of those things. He just couldn't have it the way he would have liked it.

I pulled off the highway and held him and handed him tissues until he was done.

22. Clementine

Next thing I remember it was light, and I was on my knees on my bedroom floor, throwing up into a wastepaper bin. The veterinarian lady was in my upstairs bathroom, just a few steps away, cleaning up from the last time I didn't make it to the toilet.

She's the one who had handed me the bin. I suppose she was tired of cleaning up after me. I don't guess I blame her.

It's not all that easy for me to report this part of things, because it's a very undignified position for one to be in. It's a disgusting process, emptying our stomachs. There's not always an option to avoid it, but at least one can be afforded the privacy to be disgusting alone.

Not to mention which, my hair must have been a disaster, and my makeup was either ruined or I wasn't wearing any at all. It was definitely not the moment to be seen.

Just as I was having that thought, I looked up to see Denny Portman standing in the bedroom doorway. I was about to comment about more witnesses being somewhat less than welcome, but a wave of nausea struck me again, and I had no choice but to heave dryly in the direction of the bin.

"Oh dear," he said. "I heard you weren't feeling your best."

"May I please be miserable in less of a crowd?" I asked between heaves.

He tipped his uniform cap and walked into my bathroom to have a conversation with the vet.

"Maybe she should go to the hospital," I heard him tell her.

She said, "If you want to take that precaution, I'm not going to tell you not to. But I'm monitoring her vitals pretty carefully. Frankly, if this was going to turn into a crisis, it would have. Twelve hours ago, at least."

I could hear them perfectly well, and I wondered if they knew. I felt vexed because they were talking about me as though I couldn't hear. Also because it reminded me I was being attended by a veterinarian, and not a regular human doctor.

Just as I had that thought, I heard her say, "I realize I'm not quite the doctor the situation calls for, but I did go to medical school and all."

Dennis laughed, which was also vexing. Exactly what part of my misery was so funny to everyone?

"Oh, I don't doubt your ability to treat the mule in question."

"Hey," I shouted, straightening up as best I could. "I'm not deaf, you know."

"Oops," Denny said, sticking his head into my bedroom. "So sorry. I'm going across the street to talk to Jackie, and then I'll come back and check on you again. See if you're feeling any better."

"Do you have any news about—"

"Not a thing, Clem. Not a thing. It's like they beamed themselves out of here. But don't you worry. Everybody has to be somewhere. You just worry about getting yourself back on track and leave the detective work to us."

And with that, he walked out.

I hovered there for a minute or two, trying to decide if it was safe to go back to bed. The floorboards were hurting the bones in my knees. Then suddenly I smelled food, and it made me gag. It was all I could do not to dry heave again.

I looked up to see the little boy standing in my bedroom doorway, holding a paper plate with what my nose told me was a turkey sandwich.

"This is like Grand Central Station," I said.

"I don't know what that is," he said in reply.

"It's a train station. In New York."

"How is this like a train station in New York?"

"They're both crowded."

"Oh."

He looked around for a moment, as though trying hard to see the thing my way. He couldn't see his mom—one of his moms—in my bathroom, but he could hear her rinsing out the towels she had used to clean up the floor after me.

It seemed as though he planned to argue about my assessment of a crowd. I thought he opened his mouth to, anyway.

But all he said was, "I thought you might be hungry."

"Not at all," I said.

"Honey," the vet called in from the bathroom. "Mrs. D'Antonio is sick to her stomach. She probably doesn't even want to smell food."

He looked at the bathroom doorway as she spoke, then back to me. "Do you?"

"Not even a little bit."

"Okay. I'll take this home and ask J-Mom to wrap it up for later."

I knew I was about to vomit again, and I was trying as hard as I could to wait until he was gone, which I very much wanted him to hurry up and be. But then I had to do what I had to do, and there was no holding back, so I was just careful not to look and see if anybody was watching me.

The vet came back out into the bedroom just in time to see that these new heaves were not entirely dry. Where in God's name my stomach found anything more to expel, I will never know.

She was holding the damp towels, which she must have wrung out carefully, because I watched them—as best I could under the circumstances—expecting them to drip onto the hardwood floor. And I was fully prepared to be quite huffy when they did. But they never did.

"I'm going to go put these in the laundry. Where's the laundry?"

I wavered a second to be sure I was done, and could answer. "Garage."

"Let me get you a tissue before I go," she said.

"To wipe your mouth. And a glass of water to rinse."

She disappeared into the bathroom again, still holding the towels. I was vaguely thankful that she thought to prewash them instead of running them through the laundry in that raw postcleanup condition, but I didn't say so, and couldn't even find it in myself to try.

Before she got back, before life even offered me the dignity of wiping my mouth, I saw a movement in the bedroom doorway and looked up.

Vernon was standing there, looking down on me.

Well, I thought, *that's just too much.*

It was a breaking point. It was the straw that broke this old camel's back. I thought, *That's it. I'm officially broken.*

But what good does it do to say that to yourself? Next thing you know, it's a moment later, and you're still there. And you still have to cope with the moment, same as you would if you hadn't broken. Life after the breaking point was depressingly similar to what life had been all along. There just seemed to be no opting out.

"You okay?" he asked. When I didn't answer he said, "Sorry you're not feeling well. I just came by to get the rest of my things."

"Fine. Get them."

"I have some cardboard cartons in the truck. I'll go bring them in."

And he went.

The vet came back and wiped my face with a damp washcloth. It was warm, which almost made me want to cry, but I'd had enough indignity for one day. Hell, for one lifetime. She held the water glass for me to sip and then held the bin for me to spit.

Then she helped me back to bed.

By the time Vern got back upstairs, I was tucked under the covers and at least decently arranged. But it didn't matter. As always seemed to be the case, I had narrowly missed my timing.

At the very bottom of my life, he had been there to witness my shame.

I sat up in bed and watched him pull shirts out of the closet and fold them carefully—even more carefully than *I* folded the laundry—when, of course, he never had before.

Then he fitted them into an open cardboard box on the end of the bed. His side of the bed. Not that there was really a "his side of the bed" anymore, but there had always used to be, and somehow those boundaries had not broken down.

He asked if I had the flu, and I said I thought I probably did. It was a bald lie, but what was I to say?

"Shame about Comet," he said.

There was nothing much to add to that. So instead, I just said, "Did you know? Before you came here today?"

233

"I heard."

Then we fell into an excruciating silence. I felt there must be something worth saying to him, maybe even something that would help my case, but I reached and thrashed in my mind, and couldn't get to it. If indeed it existed at all.

He was the one to crack the silence.

"I know it's heartbreaking. His having been . . . well . . . things being what they were. Are. But . . . well, I don't know, Clem. Maybe I shouldn't even say this. But it seemed like every panicky problem you had last time we talked had to do with Comet. Taking care of him, feeling guilty about him, being afraid of him. Maybe once you get more used to it, you might feel like this was all for the best."

I felt an odd, tingly sensation building up around my ears, and I wondered if they were turning red.

"You're right," I said.

He looked up, quite surprised. "Really?"

"Yes. You're right. You shouldn't even have said that."

He shook his head and returned to his work in silence, moving on to a different box for boots and shoes. The lesser-worn pairs that he hadn't taken with him to begin with. I thought that would be that for our conversation, but a few minutes later he gave it one more game try.

"Seems like you're forced to have a lot to do with those new neighbors. How do you feel about that?"

"I like the little boy," I said, sensing my opening.

Yes! That was what I'd been trying to think of before! That important development I'd intended to tell Vern if I ever got the chance.

He was surprised enough to look up at me. Right into my face. I worried again for my hair and makeup.

"Really?"

"Very much. I really enjoy his company."

Then I waited in the silence, to see if it made any difference to him.

But all he said was, "That's good, Clem. I'm glad you found somebody you like."

Then I started to get mad. Not at Vernon exactly, but not unrelated to Vernon, either. At everything. A creeping sensation came up from the back of my spine, and I understood better what bothered me about the little boy. Why his being so good irked me at times. I still couldn't quite put it into words, though. It was just a feeling that kept getting more and more defined.

"It just doesn't seem right," I said, to vent a bit of the anger.

"What, the two ladies? What difference does it make how it seems to you? It's just how it is."

"Not that, though. Well, not *just* that. I mean . . ." But then I stalled, and wondered if I even knew what I meant. "It's just . . ." I began, without even being sure I knew what it just was. "We did exactly what we were supposed to do."

235

"Us?" he asked.

"Yes. Us. We did exactly what our parents taught us. We got married in the church, and we tried to have a bunch of kids. We lived the life everybody told us was right. And now look at us. Tina is gone. We're apart. Why did we do just what we were supposed to do if it wasn't even going to make us happy? And then those people across the street. They're happy. Well, maybe not now, since that new girl ran off, but in general. They have each other and their family and they're happy. Their kids are happy. Well, that big boy not so much, but I bet that dark cloud over his head was there when they took him in. Do you see what I'm trying to say, Vernon?" I was hoping he did, because I wasn't sure I did.

"I do," he said. "You're jealous of those people."

"I am no such thing," I shouted, drawing myself straight up in bed, covering myself with that outrage as though it were an extra blanket.

"Right. Sorry. My mistake. Of course you're not." But he sounded as though he still thought I was, which was infuriating. "Then what *are* you trying to say?"

I breathed for a moment and tried to get it to come together in my exhausted brain. "I guess I'm saying nothing makes any sense anymore. Everything we learned adds up to nothing."

"Not everybody who marries in the church and has a family the old-fashioned way is unhappy."

"No, but some are. And even if it's just hit-and-miss . . . even if anybody can fall through the cracks, it's still not what I thought I was buying into at all. It still all feels like it makes no sense."

Vernon sighed, and picked up a carton heavy with coats and shoes. "Sorry to say I didn't come back here to help the whole world make sense. Just to pick up some belongings. I'm going to go box up some tools from the garage. I'll see you."

And with that, he walked out.

I listened to his heavy footsteps clomping down the stairs, and realized it was the second time he had ended a conversation that way. By saying he would see me. When what he meant was exactly the other way around. When he was quite purposely arranging his life so he would *not* see me.

I wondered if we had always talked exactly backward, and maybe I just hadn't noticed until that moment.

23. *Jackie*

Dennis Portman showed up right after lunch. Seeing his face at the door made my heart jump up into my throat and fall down into my shoes at exactly the same time. Right, right, I know. That's impossible. But that's the best I can say about how it felt.

"Not a trace of them," he said, purposely pushing it in fast, before I could get my hopes up. Or my fears up.

Of course, he was already too late.

"What brings you by, then?"

"I actually came around to look in on Clem, because I heard about that bonehead play she pulled. But while I was here, I thought I'd check in and let you know everything we're doing. Sometimes when the family doesn't hear from us, they think nothing's going on. Because they don't see it."

"Well, come in. I'll make a pot of coffee."

Before I could even close the door behind him, Quinn showed up on the welcome mat, the sandwich I'd given him still untouched on its paper plate.

"She wasn't hungry. She's *sick*." He said it with a bizarre emphasis on the word "sick." As though he couldn't imagine how anybody could be such a thing. As if nothing like that had ever happened before in his life.

"Yeah, I heard. Do me a favor and cover that sandwich with plastic wrap and put it in the fridge while I talk to the deputy."

"Sure," he said, and made his way into the kitchen, balancing the plate too dramatically, as if it were a raw egg on a spoon.

I looked up at Dennis. Way up. I think I mentioned he was very tall.

"Nice little guy," he said.

"He just amazes me. He's like a dream you'd have about a kid, but you wouldn't expect it to turn out that way in real life."

He smiled crookedly, but didn't comment. Maybe he was thinking of his own kids. Maybe they were more real.

"No coffee for me," he said. "I'm going to get going in just a minute here." I motioned to the couch, but he didn't sit. "How much do you want to know about the search effort?"

"Oh. I don't know. I totally believe you're doing everything you say you are."

"Well, that's good. I could tell you all about how we put out bulletins, and how we coordinate with other law enforcement agencies in other areas. I could tell you what Bobby's back in the office doing right now for this case. But if you're comfortable knowing we've got it covered . . ." He moved to the window. Pulled the curtain aside and peered out. Frowned. "Hmm. I promised I'd go back and look in on her again. Last time she was in the process of being sick into a trash can and didn't much want to chat. But now doesn't look like the time. Vern's there."

"Vern's there?" I asked. As though he hadn't just told me Vern was.

I crossed over to the window and stood shoulder to shoulder with him—except my shoulder was a lot lower—and looked for myself. Which I guess was weird, because I had just told him that whatever he said was happening, I believed. All I saw was an old but well-tended pickup truck parked in the dirt near Comet's empty corral.

"Think he's coming back to her?" It wasn't any of my business, but I was suddenly fascinated. Besides, I hoped so. I wanted Clementine to go back to having all the help she needed, right in her own drab little headquarters.

"Oh, hell, I don't know. If *you* left Clem, would *you* come back?"

I snorted laughter. I opened my mouth to answer, but he got there first.

"Scratch that," he said. "Pretend I never said that. I shouldn't talk like that. It's not neighborly at all. But that woman. Look at me. I'm six foot four. I weigh over two hundred pounds. I used to play football. I work out every morning. And she intimidates the hell out of me."

"Really?" I was enchanted to hear it, and praying he was not exaggerating.

"I think she has that effect on everybody."

"Not Paula. Paula doesn't seem the least bit fazed by her."

"The doc's a different breed. And I hope you know I don't mean that in a bad way at all. She's just a steady sort."

I looked over and up at him, probably drawn by a kind portrayal of the woman I love. I thought, *Kick a dog—or even forget to feed one—and you'll*

240

see a whole different side of her. Of course, it didn't require saying. But that train of thought was how I missed the next development.

"Oops," Dennis said. "He's not coming back to her."

I looked out the window again to see a big, balding, stocky older man with a face frozen into a frown. I realized I'd never so much as glimpsed him out the window before. He was pulling packing cartons out of the back of the pickup.

"Oh, poor Clem," I said, before I even realized I was thinking it.

"This might not be a good moment over there," Dennis said. "I think I'll take you up on that coffee after all."

I sat across from him at the dining room table, running my thumb over the handle of my coffee cup.

"This morning I went and opened the door and looked into Star's room," I said. "I don't quite know how to explain it. It's like I had this image of what the moment would be. Like you look into a child's room, and they're so alive in what they've left behind. Not to talk about her as if she's dead, which she may not be. I mean, probably isn't. Possibly isn't. Hell, I don't know. I don't know what her chances are out there. I just thought it would bring her back clearly in my mind. But the room is so unfamiliar to me.

241

We've only lived here a few weeks. And Star came to us with so little. There's not much left. But it's not so much that *the room* is new. It's that *Star* was new. We had her for a matter of weeks. We barely knew her. And yet when you take on a child, you bond with them. Right away. Even if it's not a cuddly two-way bond. They just become yours. So on the one hand, I feel like we lost our child. And then another part of me feels like she's just a stranger. It's kind of a hard thing to admit. In fact, I don't even know why I'm telling you all this."

"Why not?"

I took a long sip from my mug. The coffee was still too hot, and it burned going down. "It's not that I can't talk to Paula about this stuff. I can. And I do. But she knows already. Whatever's true for me is true for her. So you don't really sit around telling somebody all these things you both know that you both know."

I waited, but he just nodded. I knew I was being too talky. I could hear it. I felt around for the off switch but never found it. Not that I think *he* cared. I was being too talky for *me*.

"If I'm really going to be honest, though, the truth is I *can* talk to her about anything, but sometimes I don't. Because she handles everything so well. So sometimes I think I'm shy to tell her when I'm not handling something, because I think I should be doing better with it. It's my own fault.

I do it to myself. I can feel myself do it. I'm just not sure how to stop. Speaking of not knowing how to stop, I'm going to stuff a napkin in my mouth in a minute to shut myself up."

He laughed a little. "No worries on my account."

Just then Quinn bounced into the dining room, surrounded by dogs.

"I'm going to go back over and keep Mrs. D'Antonio company."

"Well, son," the deputy said. "This might not be the best timing." He got up and walked to the dining room window. "Whoa. That was one quick trip for Vern. Not that I blame him."

"He's gone?"

"Oh yeah."

"So I can go over there?" Quinn asked.

"Tell you what," Dennis said. "We'll go together."

He reached out one big hand and held it out until Quinn caught up to him with his own tiny hand. Then, hand in hand, they headed out of the dining room together.

I got up and followed them to the front door.

"I don't mean to leave without much comment on what we were discussing," he said. "I was listening. I guess all I have to say is you need to get your family back together. And you got a right not to be doing so good until then. I can't promise you it's possible. But if it's possible, we'll do it."

Then he walked across the road to Clem's house, still holding Quinn's hand.

● ● ●

Paula came back in time for dinner.

"How is she?" I asked.

"Mean as a hornet. But you probably meant physically."

"Yeah. I meant physically. But it's nice to hear you admit she's a pill."

"I never said she wasn't. I just have a different approach to that. She'll be fine. She really didn't take enough of those pills to put her in any real danger. She didn't have enough to take. Anyway, she's definitely out of the woods, even if the woods were never very dark and deep. And she's not drugged now, so I see no reason why she can't be on her own."

"Thank God."

Paula sighed deeply, and I could tell it had been a trying day. "I have to reschedule all of today's appointments. But not now. After dinner. I'm starving. I'm going to take a really quick shower."

She kissed me before disappearing down the hall.

"I'll round up the boys for dinner," I called after her.

I found Mando hunkered over his old laptop computer in the barn. Sitting cross-legged on the bed. Typing awkwardly with his left hand.

I dug into my pocket and pulled out something I'd printed off the web for him an hour or two earlier. Unfolded it.

He looked up.

"I thought you might be interested in this," I said.

Then I remembered the barn owl, and looked quickly to see if he was there. And to assure myself he wasn't coming any closer. He stared back at me from the high corner. He blinked, and it looked lazy. Like his film was showing in slow motion.

"What is it?" Mando asked. He was staring at the papers I was holding out. But not taking them. Not even touching them. As if they might sting.

"I printed something off the web about this project that helps people who are wrongly convicted. When you first read this, you're going to see a lot of stuff about DNA. Using DNA to exonerate pre-DNA convictions. Which doesn't help us much. But when you get in deeper, you'll see they help with a lot of different things. Bad lawyering. Shaky witness IDs. I have no idea if they can help, and I hesitated about whether to give you this, because I don't want to get your hopes up if nothing will come of it."

I paused, not sure whether I should go on.

"You did this for me?" he asked. Quieter than usual. A note of awe in his voice. He took the papers carefully in the free fingers of his splinted right hand.

"Of course I did. I'd do more than that for you if I could, Mando. I just don't know if anything will come of it."

A tiny smile broke onto his face. One side only. He turned the computer around and angled it up so I could see the screen. He was on a website for a similar project.

"I've been dealing with these people ever since I got with you and Paula. Ever since you gave me a computer."

"What happened?"

"Nothing came of it."

"Oh. I'm sorry. I guess you know more about this than I do, and I should have just stayed out of it."

"No, it's okay. Really. It's good. I was going to try them again, but I'll try this one you found, too. Can't hurt."

I sank down onto the edge of his bed beside him and promptly ran out of things to say.

"I appreciate it," he said, when the silence got too awkward for him.

"Bad timing, I know, but it's time to set the table for dinner."

I would easily have let him off the hook due to his one-handedness, but he had already refused that offer the previous day. He'd said it was his job, and resolutely performed the task with his left hand and the inside of his splinted right wrist.

"It's okay. I can take a break. Besides. I'm hungry."

"Do me another favor and go get Quinn home from the neighbor's, okay?"

246

"Sure."

He stood and stretched. Then he leaned down and surprised me with a kiss on the cheek. He hurried out of the barn, as if he'd be too humiliated to stay and witness my reaction.

I touched the spot on my cheek, and held my hand there for a moment.

Then I looked around at the owl. He blinked back at me in slow motion.

"You probably know I'm not your biggest fan," I said. Out loud. "But if you're any comfort or support for him, then I appreciate it."

"He wasn't over there," Mando said, sticking his head into the kitchen. "He was in his room."

"Really? I had no idea. I wonder why he came back."

"I don't know, but he seemed a little weirded out."

I headed down the hall to Quinn's room, but he wasn't in it. Feeling my own frown lines in my forehead, I looked around and found him dishing up dinner, the way he does every night, scooping squares of casserole onto plates.

"You okay, Quinn?"

"Sure," he said.

I thought it sounded a little different, but with only that one word it was hard to tell.

Just then Paula showed up in the dining room, dressed in fresh jeans and still toweling her hair, wanting to know where all her clean socks were hiding. And then Peppy came tearing through the room chasing Priscilla, the tortoiseshell kitten.

Whatever problem Quinn might have had got lost in the shuffle.

"All right," Paula said during dinner. "I admit it. I'm exhausted. That is one difficult woman, our neighbor. I keep telling myself it's because she's withdrawing from that sedative. But then another part of me thinks you tried to tell me and I wasn't being a very good listener."

I had to finish chewing before I could answer. Because I've told the kids to do that dozens of times.

"It might be me," I said. "I might be too sensitive to her. On the other hand, Dennis the hulking sheriff's deputy finds her intimidating. But Quinn likes her."

I looked at Quinn as I said it. His head was down, staring at the table. He was stabbing his fork into his square of eggplant parmesan. It wasn't his favorite. But then, you can't always give the kids their favorites.

"Oh no I do not!" he said without ever looking up.

Everybody stared at him. Even Mando.

"You told me you liked her."

"I changed my mind. She's scary and mean."

"What did she do to you?" I asked, the pitch of

my voice rising. Along with the rest of me. I lifted up out of my chair as I asked it, bumping my thighs under the edge of the table in a way that made everybody jump. "I swear, I'll go over there and—"

Paula's hand on my arm stopped me. She gently tugged on the arm until I took the hint and returned to a sit.

"Let's hear what Quinn has to say before we commit any violence."

"She didn't do anything to *me,*" Quinn said. "But she yelled. A lot."

"Who did she yell at, Quinn?" Paula asked.

"The policeman. I mean, the sheriff."

"You mean the deputy sheriff," I said.

"Right. The deputy. She really gave it to him. She said he wasn't doing anything. That Comet was gone and he didn't care and he wasn't doing a thing to get him back, and that all he did was get her all doped up so she couldn't yell at anybody, but now she could. And she did. And I'm never going over there again. Never."

Silence around the table. Except I could hear the clink of Mando's fork against his plate. It was awkward for him to eat with his left hand. And he hadn't paused his eating. Not only was none of this affecting his appetite, but he didn't seem to find it very surprising.

"Well, you don't have to, honey," I said.

"No, you don't," Paula said. "I think we're done

with that. We said we'd look in on her while she was on the medication. But now she's not. So as far as I'm concerned, she's back to being on her own. We can stay on our side of the road, and she can stay on her side, and we don't have to be thrown together anymore."

I would soon wish she had been right about that.

24. Clementine

No one came to see me the following day. Not one single soul. Not even the little boy.

I guess I wasn't surprised that Denny didn't look in on me, because I'd certainly spoken my mind about the "investigation." Which I guess meant "If Comet happens to come trotting into the sheriff's office, we'll give you a call."

But I resented how nobody from across the street came to check.

I guess the only reason they ever bothered was because they felt guilty. Or maybe not even that. Maybe they didn't even care enough to feel guilty. Maybe they just wanted to save on hospital bills.

But the little boy. I'd thought he actually liked me—that he spent time around me on purpose.

My own foolishness, I suppose.

The following morning I took a shower for the first time in a long time. Longer than I cared to figure out, and longer than I would likely admit even if I knew. I got myself properly dressed, got my hair right, and put on makeup.

Like a civilized woman.

Then I walked outside and looked across the street.

The little boy was outside, kicking a ball around. I was delighted, because I did not particularly care to talk to either of his mothers before talking to him.

Silly though it may sound, I used one hand like a shield, like a horse's blinder, so I wasn't looking at the empty corral as I walked by it. Then I hurried across the road. But by the time I got there, he was gone.

For one awful moment I entertained the idea that he'd seen me and run inside, but it couldn't have been as bad as all that. Maybe he'd been called in.

I steeled myself and knocked on the door.

That unruly herd of dogs set up barking. The most awful din, like a ragged wall of sound. I heard the woman yell at them to stop, and they did.

Then she swung the door open. Her face darkened to see me. It was impossible to miss that.

"Oh, you're back," she said, sounding surprised. As if I had been on vacation or some such thing.

"Where had I gone?"

"I didn't mean that. I just meant . . . you look just like you used to."

It was a perfectly ridiculous thread of conversation, and I almost said so, but then I decided if I wanted the boy to come over, I had best tread thoughtfully.

"The little boy hasn't been around," I said. "I was just wondering about that."

"He has a name."

"Quinn," I said, trying not to sound resentful at having to dance to her tune. Though I was. A bit. "I was hoping for a visit with Quinn."

"Not looking good," she said.

Her face was set hard, like it was a wall she knew could keep me out. I felt something rise up in my gut. It felt indignant.

"Did you tell him he may not come over?"

"I didn't tell him anything. He told me. He doesn't want to be around you anymore. You scared the hell out of him, shrieking at poor Dennis, like he's your servant and you caught him being lazy. Dennis was over here day before yesterday, by the way, offering to explain all the different things they're doing to try to solve this case. Did you ask? Did you even give him a chance to tell you, or did you just light into him?"

"I did not 'light into him.' " I could hear each of my words coming out sounding crisp and distinct, separate, the way they do when the walls are up. "I did not 'shriek.' I told him a thing or two that dissatisfied me. I might have raised my voice a bit, but it was hardly shrieking. As if it's any of your concern."

"Well, whatever you did, you scared Quinn, and he doesn't want to see you anymore."

Then she closed the door.

I stood for a moment, just staring at the door, feeling the sinking in my midsection. Part of me wondered why I hadn't felt this openly hurt when my husband moved out in the middle of the night. It was a sick sense of dread that I couldn't seem to shake. Of course, it had only been seconds. But I so wanted it gone.

I walked back to my own house. The sick dread came with me.

A couple of hours later I looked out the kitchen window and was rather startled to see the woman on my property. She had a bucket dangling from one hand, a dark-blue plastic bucket, and she was walking into the empty horse corral.

I hurried through the house so quickly I tripped on the edge of the living room rug and almost went flying. I pitched forward, but then managed to right myself in time.

I swung the door open to see her dipping the bucket into the watering trough.

"What on earth are you doing?" I called.

She looked up but didn't answer. I stamped through the dirt and the heat to the edge of the corral. But I didn't go in. Isn't that funny? The gate was hanging wide open, and there was no horse, but I still couldn't bring myself to go in.

"Well?" I asked.

"I promised John Parno that if the horse wasn't back in a week, I'd bail out some of this water and let it fill up with fresh. So the goldfish won't die." Her voice didn't sound hard-edged, or resentful. Right at that moment she didn't speak to me as though we were enemies. If anything, I'd say she sounded sad.

"Has it really been a week?"

"Give or take a day. Yeah."

I walked around the outside of the corral to the trough. We stood, the two of us, in the hot afternoon sun, the rail fence and the watering trough between us, looking down into the murky water.

"I didn't know he'd brought the goldfish."

"It was that first day, I think. And you were pretty much down for the count."

We looked in silence for a couple of moments more.

"I don't see them. But, come to think, Johnnie said they dive down and hide when a shadow comes over the tank."

"And I started bailing in there, so that probably scared them but good."

"Where did you put the water?"

"It's still here in my bucket." She tipped the bucket so I could see.

The water was just as green with algae as it had been before. I tried to decide if it was any less so. Not from what I could see. It must take them longer to get the tank clean. Well, it would have to, when you think about it. If they could eat all that algae in a week, then what would they eat after that?

"I was going to pour it on something in your flower beds." She pointed to the sad garden that Vern no longer tended. "But then you started yelling at me." A pause. When I didn't fill it, she said, "Anything special you'd like to see watered?"

"Oh, I don't know," I said, frowning at the garden. "Whatever looks saddest, I suppose. But this isn't a very hard job. Why aren't I doing it myself?"

"Oh. Well, you can if you want. I wasn't sure how you were feeling. And I was the one who promised John. But here. You can use my bucket."

"I own a bucket," I said, not meaning it to come out quite as sharply as it did.

She shook her head and plodded the few short steps to the gate.

"Wait," I said. "I don't. Well, I do. But it's in the barn."

She looked into my eyes for a split second, but I broke her gaze as fast as I could. In that very brief window, I thought she looked as though she felt sorry for me, which certainly was unwelcome.

I touched the rail to steady myself in the hot sun.

She walked to one of the flower beds, and poured the greenish water into the dirt. Then she dropped the bucket and headed in the direction of the barn.

"Anything else you need while I'm in there?" she called over her shoulder.

"Maybe that long-handled rake."

Which, I realized a second later, I no longer needed. No horse, no manure.

She came back out a minute later with the rake and Vernon's old tin bucket and set them in the dirt by the corral gate.

"I guess I don't really need the rake right now," I said. "But in case I get him back. I'm still hoping I get him back."

"Me, too."

Then she picked up her bucket and walked off and left me on my own again.

About an hour after dinner I crossed the road again. I worried briefly that I might disturb *their* dinner, but the vet's van wasn't parked out front, and I couldn't imagine they'd eat without her. Besides, I'm not so completely unworldly that I don't know that most people eat dinner later than five.

When she opened the door, she looked at me wide-eyed, like the sight of me was dizzying. Granted, we had bumped into each other quite a bit that day, but it was no reason to stare at me like I was some kind of eight-armed green space alien.

"I would like to speak to Quinn," I said. "I owe

him an apology. If he doesn't accept it, I under-stand. You can't force these things. But I will at least feel better to have delivered it."

She just hung there at the edge of the open door for a moment, as if it were the only thing holding her up.

Then she disappeared. Without inviting me in.

I stood there for a good two minutes in the open doorway, shifting from foot to foot and feeling awkward, before I saw the flash of his red hair.

His mother was actually pushing him. She had one hand behind each of his shoulders and was pushing him toward the door. Not roughly, like forcing him. More like he needed the extra locomotion and would stall without it.

It made me feel about three inches tall, but I buried the feeling again, because I had come to do something important, and it required all my attention.

He stood before me, leaning back on his mom, not looking up into my face at all.

"Quinn," I said, "it was very thoughtless of me to raise my voice with you in the house. It never occurred to me that it would frighten you, because I thought you knew me well enough not to be frightened by me. But I *should* have known. I should have thought of it. I feel very bad, because I was just coming to enjoy your friendship, and if I ruined that, I'll be very unhappy indeed. So I've come to apologize to you, and I hope you'll accept my apology. If you do, and if you ever come to my house again, I make you a solemn promise: I will not raise my voice in your presence. Ever."

Then I stopped, but nobody else started. A silence fell with a thud that wasn't real and couldn't be heard, but which I felt in my gut all the same.

He glanced up at my face once, then quickly looked away.

"Do you think you can forgive me, Quinn?"

He nodded, but shyly. And silently. His mom let go of his shoulders and he retreated to the middle of the living room, where he looked into my eyes for the first time.

I felt like a monster. I know that sounds overly dramatic, but it's the most honest way to say a thing. I felt as though he was the little prince in a fairy story and I was the beast.

The woman mouthed something at me, and I had to read her lips.

What she said was, "Give him time."

I nodded, realizing my mouth was painfully dry.

It struck me that she was almost siding with me by saying those three words. Almost encouraging me. But I had no idea what to do with the sentiment of that, so I just pretended it wasn't there.

"Well," I said, "I'll go on my way now. But I'll lay out some playing cards, and the Chinese checkers set, in case I get a visit from a young friend."

Something dangerously close to tears tickled the backs of my eyes toward the end of that sentence.

Nobody argued with the idea of my leaving. So that's what I did.

I laid out the games as promised. But four more days went by, and nobody knocked at my door.

On the fifth morning I was just rising when I heard someone rapping on *their* door across the road. It was early for visitors. Barely six. My window was wide open to keep the bedroom cool, and it was a hard knocking, so I guess that's why I heard.

I swung on my housecoat and walked to the window to see.

It was Bobby Talbot.

That made my heart jump, and my head swim, because I knew he must know something. Bobby wouldn't come bang on somebody's door at six o'clock in the morning unless he knew something.

I found myself resentful of the fact that he chose to tell them the news first.

I hurried downstairs and started a pot of coffee and waited. But before the coffee had even finished dripping, I heard his patrol car start up. I ran to the window—as best I run these days—and watched him drive away down the road, a cloud of dirt following his car.

Not knowing what else there was for me to do, I sat and drank three cups of coffee, wondering what he could possibly have told them that didn't concern me just as much.

25. *Jackie*

The knock blasted me out of sleep, and I just knew. I knew the coin had flipped and we were about to find out.

Paula was already up and getting ready for work. I didn't see her anywhere, so I grabbed a bath-robe, my heart pounding, and ran downstairs.

She had already answered the door. On our stoop was a deputy sheriff in uniform, but it wasn't Dennis. Maybe it was his partner, or maybe there were other deputies in Easley. Frankly, I'd never thought to ask.

I heard Paula say, "How can you not know if it's good news or bad news?"

"Well," he said, "it's mixed."

I hurried to Paula's side. I already knew it was mixed in a way we wouldn't be happy about. I could tell from his approach.

He tipped his billed cap at me. "Bobby Talbot. Dennis Portman's partner."

I wanted to scream, because he was waiting too long to say it.

"Please just tell us," I said.

"We found the horse."

"But not the girl."

"No," he said. "Not the girl."

I woke Mando, which was never easy. He slept like the dead.

"What?" he said, finally. On the seventh or eighth shake.

"I'm sorry, but you have to get up."

"Why?"

"We have to go somewhere. We have to drive to this little town in the foothills of the Sierras, where the horse turned up. Because law enforcement is searching the area for Star, but there's a community search, too. And I have to be there. I mean, they didn't say I have to be there. But I have to do it for me. And I have no idea how long we'll be gone, so you kids have to come."

He swung his legs off the bed and sat up, his surprisingly graceful bare feet on the cool concrete barn floor. I made a mental note to get him an area rug, a note I didn't figure would stick in all the panic and confusion.

"Is Paula going?"

"She can't. She has an appointment she can't cancel. She has to do an ultrasound on a horse. And if his belly is full of cancer like she thinks it is, she'll have to put him down today. She can't back out of that. He's like a member of these people's family. She'll drive up later tonight."

"Is the horse really in that much pain?"

"I think so, honey. But also the family is on pins and needles to hear whether it's fixable. She just didn't feel she could make them wait. She wouldn't decide that lightly. You know that."

He scratched his head for a weird length of time, the scratches slowing as they went along. I thought he might be falling back asleep sitting up.

"Okay," he said. "I'll get dressed."

I ran back into the house to wake Quinn.

"I don't want to go," Quinn said. "Please don't make me go. *Please?*"

"Why don't you want to go?"

"I just don't."

He had a death grip on the top edge of his Bob the Builder fleece blanket, and he was pulling it up to his collarbone.

"What is it, honey?"

"I don't want to go look for Star."

"Why not?"

"Because we might find her."

"But that would be good if we found her."

"If she's okay. But what if we find her and she's not okay?"

I sat down on his bed with a whump. The springs creaked. Of course, I was terrified of that exact same outcome. But he hit it head-on. I'd been hurrying around, swallowing my heart back down, and pretending the fear had never existed.

"I'm not sure how to leave you here safely. It's too early to even call Clara. And I'd like to get on the road just as soon as we can."

"Please think of something," he said. "Because this is really . . ."

He didn't need to finish the sentence. I could tell what it was doing to him.

"There's the neighbor. But you said you never wanted to see her again. Is it enough that she apologized?"

Quinn sat up in bed. Rubbed his eyes the way sleepy kids do on TV commercials, or in animated fairy tales. "Hmm," he said. I think he picked that up from me. "Maybe if you could get her to promise one more time no yelling. You know. Just in case she forgot. When are you coming back?"

"I don't know. I really have no idea."

"Well. I don't really like her. But I guess I like her better than looking for somebody who might not be okay. So let's go see if she'll promise again."

I expected her to come stumbling to the door with her hair in shambles. It didn't happen that way at all. She was completely put together. Dressed, and made up, her hair in place. As if it were a quarter after noon, not a quarter after six in the morning.

"What on earth is going on?" she asked.

I had no frame of reference for the question, and no idea how she meant it. So I guess I just stood there with a befuddled look on my face. I might have said "Uh . . ." But not much more.

She said, "I saw Bobby come by your house this morning, so I'll ask again. What's going on?"

"He didn't call you?"

"If he had called me, I wouldn't be asking you what's going on. I wouldn't have to."

"He said he was going to go back to the office and call you."

"Why would he call me when he was right here? He didn't call *you*. He knocked on your door."

"He was worried about waking you."

I watched that settle for a moment behind her eyes. "He was worried about *me* if he woke me? Or he was worried about *himself* if he woke me?"

"I have no idea," I said, ignoring the subtext as best I could.

"I'm still waiting to know what's going on."

"They found Comet."

"Where?"

"Quite a ways north and east of here. Not far from Yosemite as the crow flies, but it's not on any major highway that leads into the park."

"How do I get him back?"

"We're working on that. You don't have to do anything. We'll get him back here."

Then we fell silent. I waited for her to ask about Star's welfare, but she never did. I wondered why I was even surprised.

Quinn was holding my right hand, but he kept creeping backward as the tension crackled, so by then my right hand was a foot or more behind the rest of me.

"I came to ask you a favor." I paused, in case she wanted to comment. She didn't. "Quinn doesn't want to go up there with us. I was wondering if he could stay here with you while we're gone."

In the brief silence that followed, I watched her face change. It was something I'd never anticipated. The degree of change was astonishing. Everything softened. Her eyes lost that dead look. I'd always thought of her as a fairly unattractive woman, but suddenly she looked younger. And not at all ugly. Now that I thought about it, it had never been an external ugliness.

"I would be very pleased to spend the day with him," she said.

"It might be more than a day. I have no idea. But if it really drags on, I'll get hold of Clara on my cell phone while we're traveling, and one way or another I'll make a better arrangement for him."

"He may stay as long as he'd like."

"He'll want to be in his own room, though."

"I could watch him at your house."

"I need someone to take care of all those pets, though, too."

"Oh," she said.

And I could see her back down. Part of me was relieved. She was almost too happy to get her hands on Quinn. I wondered if this was how she felt when Star bonded with her horse.

"We may be back tonight," I said.

"Call me when you know. My number is listed. And I promise you again, Quinn, no raising my voice. No anger of any sort while you're here with me."

For the first time since I'd knocked on her door, I felt slack on my right arm.

Mando and I drove the first few miles in silence. I think part of his brain was still asleep.

"Thank you for coming up here with me," I said.

I'd given him an option to stay home once I knew Quinn was settled. Even though I wanted his company. But he'd offered to come along all the same.

"Sure," he said.

"I just think it's nice of you. Because"—I briefly weighed the gravity of saying it out loud—"I know you don't like Star."

"But I don't want her to be lying somewhere hurt or anything."

"I know."

"I don't hate her."

"No. I know you don't."

"I just feel like . . ."

I figured he was doing the same kind of weighing and measuring.

"You can say whatever you're thinking."

"I just feel like we were so much happier before you took her."

"We were."

"Why did you take her, then?"

"You never know what your experience is going to be with a new foster kid. You have to try it and find out. But I do see, looking back, that it really wasn't fair to you and Quinn. But how could we have known going in?"

"But you knew she was a tough case. You knew the last three homes gave her back."

"Yeah. We did."

We drove in silence for a mile or two longer. The scenery was beginning to change. The land outside my car windows no longer looked brown, or flat, or dusty, like Easley. It was a relief. It's not that I was avoiding answering the question. More that I wasn't sure I remembered. Wasn't even positive I had ever clearly known.

"I think it's that our last three placements went so well," I said after a time.

He only nodded.

The third had been a girl named Katie, who overlapped briefly with Quinn. And who was now back with her parents. And who I thought about every day. Wondered if she was okay. Getting what she needed to grow, inside and out. It was a crapshoot. It was never a guarantee.

"It's possible we may have gotten over-confident," I said. Silence. "Too truthful?" I asked him, glancing at the side of his face.

"No such thing as too truthful," he said.

And I smiled.

In my peripheral vision, I saw him turn his face toward mine. "What if you had it to do over?"

"That's a hard question. And it's so theoretical."

"Theoretical means not real?"

"Pretty much."

"But it's not. It's not theoretical. You do have it to do over again. I mean, if we find her, are you going to automatically take her back?"

I felt it like a little punch to my gut.

"We never even questioned that," I said.

"I know. I can tell."

But maybe we should have questioned it. In fact, it occurred to me that maybe I should call Paula as the day wore on. See if she had ever considered it. And if it was something we should consider. But it was a horrifying consideration. Throwing a kid back for a fourth time. My God. You might just as well push her into her grave and throw the first clod of dirt on her.

"Look," I said. "We don't know that we'll ever see her again. I hate to have to say that, but we all know it's true. We might never find her. Or she might . . ." I decided I had trailed off—out loud or in my head—too many times on that sentence, or ones quite like it. I decided it needed to be said out loud. "It's possible that she didn't survive this. So let's cross that bridge when we come to it."

"I'm not saying you shouldn't take her back. I just wondered."

"I understand."

"I think maybe I never should have said that."

"No such thing as too truthful," I said.

26. Clementine

We were playing a game of Chinese checkers when the little boy looked up and me and asked, "Are you happy now?"

It wasn't one of those sarcastic versions of the question. He really wanted to know. Was I happy? I couldn't get the question in context, though. I couldn't imagine why he had brought it up.

Then it hit me that he must be referring to Comet.

"You mean am I happy because Comet is coming home?"

"Yes," he said. "That."

I had no idea what to say. I certainly didn't feel happy, either over this new development, or in general, but that's not the sort of thing you say to someone who's eight.

"I'm certainly glad to be getting him back."

Which was true, but it didn't feel anything like being happy.

In fact, the more I thought about it—well, I didn't think about it, I felt it. You can think about happiness all you want, but it won't get you far. It's not a thinking sort of proposition.

The more I felt it, the more of a mixed feeling it became.

On the one hand was the dread I felt when I looked out the window and he was not there. On the other hand was the dread I had felt—and would likely feel again—when I looked out the window and he *was* there. Pawing the ground, fixing me with that stare, that dark, moist eye, asking without words, *Why are you keeping me here? When do I get out?*

It almost brought a wave of nausea thinking about being back in that bind again. How was I any more prepared to care for him alone than I had been all along?

I didn't realize my brow was knitted into a frown until the boy spoke again.

"You sure don't *look* very happy. You know it's still your move, right?"

Just then the phone rang.

"If it's J-Mom, I want to talk to her," he said.

I got to the phone on the third ring. It wasn't either of his moms. It was Bobby.

"Well, well," I said. "It's about time."

"I take it you heard the news."

"Quite some time ago. Why did you leave here without telling me as well?"

"It was early."

"It was early for them, too."

"She's their daughter."

"He's my horse."

A silence on the line. I wondered if he was on a cell phone, maybe going in and out of range, or maybe he was still talking but cutting out so I couldn't hear. Or maybe he just plain wasn't talking.

"Okay," he said. "You want me to say it? I'll say it. Everybody's been cutting you an extra-wide berth since you tore Dennis a new one."

"I'm not familiar with that expression," I said, "but don't tell me more about it. I don't think I'll like it."

"I knew I had to notify you, and I'm doing that now. But I was not going to drag you out of bed, because even the nicest people don't always wake up friendly."

It wasn't hard to hear between the lines. Even the nicest people. And I, of course, was the meanest.

I opened my mouth to address it. Before I could, I saw the boy staring at me from the dining room, looking a little spooked, so I decided to let it drop.

"How do I get Comet back? I asked my neighbor, but she said I was not to think about it. But how can I not think about it? When is he coming home?"

271

"Dr. Archer-Cummings is going to trailer him home for you."

"She drives a van. How can she tow a horse trailer with that thing?"

"She has a truck at the clinic, with a trailer. You know. For her work. It's the old doc's truck. Vet has to be able to take a horse or a cow into the clinic."

I thought, *It's true. He's really coming home. Today or tomorrow, maybe.*

And I was going to be right back where I started from, too paralyzed to give him most of his care. The only thing I knew how to give him was hay, and that wasn't even the larger half of what he needed.

Bobby said, "You know their girl is still missing, right?"

"Oh," I said, freshly knocked out of my thoughts. "No. I didn't know. I didn't think to ask."

Another one of those silences that might or might not have been purposeful.

Then he said, "It doesn't bother you knowing that little girl is out there all by herself."

I couldn't tell if it was a question or not. Probably not.

"She's hardly a little girl."

"She's fifteen. That's young. How would you have felt if Tina had been lost in the mountains alone at fifteen?"

"Don't you dare bring—" Before I could even

say her name, I looked through the open doorway into the dining room and saw the little boy's eyes go wide. "Don't be scared," I said to him. "I'm fine. I'm keeping my promise. I'm not going to yell."

He settled a little in the chair, but his eyes still looked wide. He looked like a wild rabbit on the trail, waiting to see if your dog is going to take another step in his direction or not.

Meanwhile, I couldn't believe Bobby would compare my beautiful Tina with that difficult girl who had only lived with the neighbors for a few weeks before running off. But I couldn't say so.

"Who are you talking to?" Bobby asked, as though it was impossible that I could have company. As if I must have an imaginary friend, in which case it was probably time to tranquilize me again.

"The little Archer-Cummings boy is here for the day."

"Oh," he said. Sounding insultingly surprised. "That's very nice of you."

I had to bite my tongue again. Such a condescending tone. And I couldn't say so.

"If you'll excuse me," I said, "I have an important game of Chinese checkers to get back to."

27. Jackie

We were driving through the foothills of the Western Sierra Nevada range. The air through my half-open window felt clean and cool. The scenery had changed to those massive light-gray boulders surrounded by evergreen trees.

I thought, *Why couldn't we live in a place like this instead of Easley?*

There was something inspiring about the place. And I'd been without inspiration too long.

I looked over at Mando, who was staring out the window in silence. I wondered what he was thinking. I wanted to connect with him again. But I didn't want to invade his privacy. So I decided to share what *I* was thinking. Even though I knew it was a perfectly crazy thought.

"This is going to sound stupid," I said. He jumped. We hadn't talked for a while, and I'd startled him. "But I'm mad at the horse."

"Why? What did he do?"

"I just feel like . . . I'm not even sure how to say it. Star was so devoted to that horse. She never would have left him on his own. Or at least I can't imagine it. But then they found the horse wandering all by himself without her."

"You think he should have stayed with her."

"I guess that's what I think. Well. What I feel, anyway."

"Do horses even do that?"

"I'm not sure. Some do, I think. Paula would know."

For the fiftieth time that morning, at least, I wished she could have come with us. That I didn't have to plunge into this challenge without her.

"But we don't even know . . . anything," he said. "We don't know she didn't hitch a ride somewhere. Or something. You know. Where he couldn't stay with her. Or if she . . . I hate to say it. But you said it. If she . . . didn't survive. I mean, how long would he stay with her? What good would it do?"

"You're totally right," I said. "I know it's stupid. It's just a feeling. That he let her down somehow. And I have no idea if it's true. I guess I just really wanted her to have someone she could count on out here."

We fell silent again for maybe a mile. I was beginning to think my turnoff, a forest road with a number instead of a name, should be coming up soon.

"It's pretty up here," he said.

"I was just thinking that," I said.

I stood outside the car for a moment, leaning on the roof and just breathing. Not really thinking about Mando or wondering where he was.

We were parked on something like an open, unfenced front yard of several houses. They sat clustered on the side of a hill, tall flights of stairs reaching up to their front doors, partially obscured by evergreen trees.

The air was crisp and cool for midmorning, and the sky was that amazing color of blue. That deep royal blue at the edges, contrasting with the green of the trees and the gray of the huge boulders where sky touched mountains. There was not so much as a wisp of cloud anywhere in that sky. It made me feel free.

I'd been looking up at it for a long time. I think I was avoiding what I would feel when I looked down. In fact, I know it.

I forced my head to adjust. Literally and otherwise.

Dennis's patrol car was parked in the dirt, its light bar flashing silently. But Dennis was nowhere around. There was a state highway patrol vehicle parked closer to the paved road, but it wasn't exactly a car. More like an SUV. And there was one other black-and-white I couldn't identify. It had a star on its door, like a sheriff's car, but I was too far away to read it, so sheriff of what I didn't know. A uniformed man stood inside its open driver's-side door, talking on a handheld radio.

Otherwise, the scene was disturbingly free of people.

I looked around again and saw Mando. He was

leaning on a board fence that sectioned off the side yard of one of the houses. On the other side of the fence was Comet. I hadn't seen the horse when we'd first pulled up, when I'd first tried to find somebody—anybody—who could tell me where to go or how to help or how to keep occupied before I exploded. The horse must have purposely come to the fence to allow Mando to stroke his long face.

I walked to them, too aware of my own movements. As if I were no longer quite real. I expected the horse to toss his head or take a few steps back as I approached. He didn't.

I stepped right up beside Mando, not a foot from Comet's face. All the horse did was move his head an inch or two in my direction and make a rumbly noise. It sounded almost contented. Which, right in that moment, struck me as the most foreign mood imaginable.

"He's such a pretty horse," Mando said.

"He is." I reached over and stroked his neck, to no reaction. "He seems different."

"He's calm. That's not too surprising. He's probably tired from all the traveling."

"He even looks different, though."

"Different how?"

Then I had to figure out what I'd meant by that. He seemed more muscular to me, though it's entirely possible that was my imagination. Can a horse visibly build up his muscle tone in less than ten days? I had no idea. His coat looked shiny and smooth, as though he'd been brushed every day. I wanted to say he looked the way I always thought he'd been meant to look, but I worried it would sound strange.

"I guess I'm just not used to seeing him so calm," I said.

I was still stroking his neck. In time, Mando stopped stroking Comet's face and just watched me.

"Thought you were mad at him," he said after a time.

"Oh. That. Well, that was pretty stupid, wasn't it? He's just a horse."

"Still. If you feel it, then you just do. Stupid or not."

"I suppose you're right," I said. "But I don't feel it anymore."

When I finally saw Dennis, I felt saved. In fact, until I did, I was completely out of touch with how lost, scared, and out of place I'd felt just the moment before.

"You're here," he said.

"You didn't know we were coming?"

"I didn't. Actually. But that's fine."

"Your partner, Bobby, said there were some members of the local public searching. So we thought we should join in."

"Oh." He sounded almost disappointed. "There

were. But the search dog is going to be here in less than ten minutes. So we called that off. That's really looking for a needle in a few hundred haystacks compared to what the search dog can do."

"Right," I said, suddenly feeling helpless and sad. Like I was there for nothing. Like the whole trip had been for nothing. Like my whole life didn't add up to much of anything. I just felt as though all was suddenly lost.

I think he heard that in my voice, or saw it on my face. Or both.

"No law says you can't look around while we're waiting, though. Let me tell you the one direction we hadn't gotten to yet." He pointed across the road to a very steep, very rocky incline. "Nobody scrambled up the side of that thing. Not because it's so impossible to get up there, but because we figured it might be close to impossible for *her,* if she was hungry and sick. So it seemed like a less-than-likely bet. But if you want to look around up there, at least it'll give you something to do. But don't get lost. We don't want to have to send out a search party for you, too."

"I won't let us get lost," Mando said from just behind my left shoulder.

It startled me. Because I hadn't known he was back there. And because it was such a dependable Mando response to make himself scarce when there were uniforms around. I guess I'd figured it was a safe bet he was nowhere near.

"I used to hike all the time around Napa," he said. "I never got lost. I always looked at rocks and trees and memorized them. And I turned around to see how they looked from the other side. So I'd know them again when I headed home."

I hadn't known any of that about Mando. I wondered whether he meant before he came to live with us. He must have.

Just for a minute, it reminded me that Mando was not our kid. He'd had a whole life before we met him. It made me sad to have missed all that. But that's what we'd signed on for. That was the kind of parenthood we'd chosen.

By the time I'd managed to scramble to the top of the rise, I could barely breathe. Mando was standing at the top, waiting. The slope was so steep and rocky that I had to use my hands as well as my feet. I had to find handholds on the rough granite boulders and use them to pull myself up. So I wasn't looking up much, and when I finally saw I was on the same level as Mando, I was surprised.

I stood for a moment, nearly doubled over, my hands on my thighs, trying to get my breath back. Then I gave up and sank onto a smooth rock, and Mando came and sat with me.

I noticed he'd gotten a lot of dirt on the ACE bandage that held his hand brace in place. Not that it really mattered.

We looked down over the area in silence.

A new red SUV was parked by the patrol vehicles, and I wondered if it belonged to the search dog's handler. But there was nobody around. Not a human being as far as the eye could see. Over the board fence, I could see Comet grazing in the flower beds in the side yard of that house. I wondered if the owners of the house had found the horse. Or if somebody else had offered to confine him. And if they would be mad when they saw all he had helped himself to eating.

"You ready?" Mando said.

I was not. I was quite definitely not. I couldn't remember when I'd felt a stronger resistance to moving on to the next segment of my life.

"Does it feel like she's here somewhere?" I asked him.

He paused a moment. Like it was worth trying to feel that.

"I'm not sure I know what you mean."

"I'm not sure I do, either. But . . . I mean, does it seem to you like she's right around here somewhere?"

I watched his forehead furrow. I think he knew what I was asking. That I was talking about some kind of sixth sense knowing. Which made my question nearly impossible to answer. I think the only reason I asked was because I didn't want to get up and search.

"I'm no good at things like that," he said.

"No," I said. "Me neither."

We looked over the scene in silence for a few minutes more.

Then he asked it again. "Ready?"

I pulled to my feet, then sank into a sit again. Dropped my head into my hands.

"You okay?" He moved in to put a hand on my shoulder.

"I can't do this."

"Can't do what?"

While I was gathering myself to answer, I thought about Quinn, lying in bed, clutching the blanket to his throat, nearly in tears. Or maybe it wasn't right to say I thought about him. Somehow I just made the connection. I knew in that moment that my resistance was exactly the same as his.

"I can't walk along this ridge looking behind every boulder, knowing at any moment I might find her body."

He didn't respond at first, except to sit next to me again.

"I could go look," he said after a time.

"If you want. Or . . . you remember what Dennis said. It'll probably be the search dog that finds her."

"It can't hurt," he said. "You wait here."

I'm guessing about thirty minutes passed before I saw Dennis scrambling up the slope. It surprised me. There'd been no action near the parked cars, and I hadn't seen him approach the bottom of the hill. I guess I'd been a million miles away.

He stopped, cupped his hands, and called out my name.

I stood and waved frantically until he saw me.

Then I scrambled down the hill as fast as I could, sliding on small pebbles and loose dirt, because I thought that would be faster than just waiting. Before I could reach him, I slipped, twisted my ankle, and went down hard, bruising my hip on a stone. I felt around on the ankle as best I could until he caught up to me and helped me to my feet.

"Can you put weight on that?"

I tried. It hurt, but it held. "Pretty much."

"Good. Because we only have one ambulance coming."

"You found her?" I had a lump in my throat so huge and tight that I was surprised I could force the words around it.

"The search dog did."

"Alive?"

"Yes. Alive."

"Oh, thank God." I sank onto the ground again. And just breathed. "What did she say?"

"Say?"

"I mean, was she happy to be found, or did she fight you?"

He didn't answer for a second, so I looked into his face. And that lump came back to choke me.

"I didn't mean to give you the wrong impression, Jackie. She's alive. But not much more. Not by a comfortable margin."

Just then we heard the siren. We looked to see the ambulance tearing down the road in our direction.

"You have to go," he said. "See if you can get down there in time to get into the ambulance and go to the hospital with her. If you miss your timing, jump in the car and drive there. See if you can follow them. If not, you're going to have to get on your cell phone and try to find out where she's gone."

I got up and took one limping step downhill. "I can't," I said.

"You can't walk on that ankle? Let me help you."

"No. It's not that. I'll manage with that. I can't leave Mando. He's out there searching. I can't just abandon him."

"Just go. I'll see to Mando. I'll find him, or I'll wait for him to get back, and I'll bring him to the hospital."

It seemed like a long pause before I spoke again, but I'm sure it wasn't. It might have been a fraction of a second. But in that fraction, a lot ran through me at once. I wanted to say, *No. I can't do that to him. Leave him in the hands of law enforcement? He'll die. It isn't fair.*

Well, maybe it wasn't fair. But it was going to be that way. Because Mando wouldn't actually die.

Star might.

284

28. Clementine

The little boy was napping on the couch when Bobby Talbot came back. I had been sitting in my old easy chair, half thinking I should have Vern's recliner carted to the dump, half watching the child's sweetly sleeping face.

I jumped up and ran to the window, wondering whose tires were crunching on my gravel driveway. I pulled the curtain aside. When I saw Bobby's car—not the patrol car, but his regular off-duty station wagon—I tried to swallow but couldn't.

What else could he possibly have to tell me? They'd found Comet. What more did I need to know? Was he here to tell me they'd lost him again?

I watched him step out into the wavy heat. He was wearing his uniform, and it seemed odd that he should be dressed as though on duty while driving an off-duty car. Maybe Denny had the patrol car. Yes, he must. He must have gone to that place where Comet was found.

Bobby didn't know I was watching him out the window. I could tell.

I watched him stop halfway across the yard to my door. Watched him . . . I'm not sure of the word for this. Steel himself? Something like that. I

285

watched him pull himself up a little straighter. Fill his chest with extra breath.

I watched him prepare to do an abhorrent thing.

I know it sounds like I couldn't have seen all that, but I did. I just can't quite explain it. But I saw it with my own eyes, and it was very plain.

I got that feeling again, the one I'd had when the little boy backed all the way up into the middle of his living room before daring to look into the face of the monster.

I thought, *I'm abhorrent.*

I thought, *I didn't used to be. At least, not so far as I know.* I thought, *I guess I used to be difficult, but it was nothing like this.* I wondered when it had snuck up on me, and where my attention had been at the time, so that I hadn't noticed.

I dropped the curtain, and a moment later he knocked on the door.

I looked quickly at the little boy, but it didn't seem to have wakened him.

I opened the door, purposely not looking at Bobby's face so I wouldn't have to see a reflection of what he saw when he looked at me.

He tipped his uniform cap, a little too formally.

I held a finger to my lips, and then opened the door wider so he could see that the boy was taking a nap.

I stepped outside into the searing afternoon heat and closed the door gently, and not completely. Not enough to latch it. So I wouldn't lock myself out.

"Don't tell me you lost him again," I said.

He frowned.

I swear I'd meant it more as a joke. But I guess I could see how it was just the kind of comment that made people steel themselves before knocking on my door. I felt deeply chastened.

"We have the girl," he said.

I blinked a few times and wondered why he was telling me this. She wasn't my girl. Then I caught myself again. I could see exactly why I was so dreaded and unpopular, but I couldn't seem to stop myself.

He waited for a moment, then said, "Well, you don't seem very interested in her condition, but I'll tell you anyway. We found her just in time. Few more hours and we'd likely have found her dead. She's severely dehydrated—"

"It's not hard to get water from a creek," I said, doing it again.

"Seems that's exactly what she did. Drank from the creek until she got so sick with giardia that she probably couldn't even hold down water. And then she got so dehydrated and so malnourished that her body couldn't fight the infection. She's in bad shape."

"Is she going to be okay?"

His eyes came up to mine for the first time in a long time. "Glad to hear you've got some questions about her welfare. We don't know. Hopefully. I mean, now that she's in the hospital they can pump her full of fluids and antibiotics and monitor her situation. But if we hadn't found her when we did . . . well . . . she was pretty close to the line."

I waited. I didn't dare say a word. I wanted to know what this had to do with me, but I knew I couldn't ask. That would be one of those things, those typical Clementine things. The ones that make people step back. Roll their eyes. But this time I saw it before it was too late. It seemed like a breakthrough, some wonderful shift in my control, but I didn't have time to congratulate myself on it in that moment.

"So . . ." he said. As if I should know what came next.

I didn't.

"So?"

"We need to know what you plan to do."

"About what?"

"Charges, Clem. We need to know if you're going to press charges."

"Oh."

My brain ran in several directions at once. I wondered why I hadn't thought of that before, in all this time while they were gone. I wondered what would happen if I made this hard decision and the girl didn't even live. I wondered if nearly dying should be all the punishment she needed. Or even deserved.

"Do you really need to know that right now?"

"Well. Yes. We do. We need to know if she's in custody. If she should be handcuffed to the rail of her bed in case she comes to, and gets itchy to take off again. So . . . yes. We need you to decide. Let's be optimistic and say she'll pull through. Will you be pressing charges?"

"She shouldn't just get off scot-free. Actions should have consequences." Then I wished he could have heard the other, gentler thoughts I'd had on the matter. But he couldn't, of course.

"So that's a yes."

"I'm not sure." I leaned on the pillar of my little porch awning, because the heat was making me swoony. "Couldn't we do something in between?"

"In between what?"

"Like community service."

"I can't sentence her to community service, Clem, and neither can you. You either press charges or you don't. If you do, the judge decides what price she'll pay. You can urge leniency, as the victim, but the judge will still basically do what he—or she—wants. We can't control sentencing."

I leaned a moment longer. Pressed my eyes closed.

I thought, *Comet is really the victim, but he can't very well address a judge.* Then I thought maybe that wasn't true at all. The part about his being a victim, that is. Maybe Comet was having the time of his life. Maybe the worst thing that could have happened to him was being caught and trailered home.

I thought about the time the girl snuck over in the middle of the night and brushed the burrs out of his coat and the tangles out of his mane and tail. And the time I saw her in his corral in the dark, dabbing thrush medicine into his hooves. I wondered if she'd brought the thrush medicine and the curry comb with her when they ran away. If his thrush was all cleared up by now.

"I need to see the condition he's in before I decide."

"Dennis told me he never looked better."

"Couldn't she just work off the debt over here at my place? There's a lot of stuff to do here now that . . ." I stopped, wondering if he knew Vern had left me. Of course he did. The whole town undoubtedly knew by then. But I still couldn't bring myself to say it. "There's a lot to do on this big place. It seems fairer than putting her in juvenile detention. Especially if she took as good care of him as you say."

Bobby lifted his cap and scratched at the hairline of his forehead with the same hand, all in one motion. "If your answer is no, you don't want to press charges, you can put any kind of condition on it you want, but the law can't enforce it for you. It's not a legal arrangement. You can make some deal with her foster parents, but it's got nothing to do with us. And you can't change your mind and press charges if something goes wrong. Understand?"

"I really can't decide until I see his condition."

"I told you. Dennis says he never looked better."

"Did he look in his hooves, though? I'll bet he didn't. He had thrush when he was stolen. And the girl knew right where the thrush medicine was. It was right in the dirt by the corral gate. And I haven't seen it since. So maybe you took it as evidence, or maybe she took it along and has been treating his hooves every day. And maybe the thrush is all cleared up by now. In which case I'll just talk to her parents about some labor when she's recovered, so she isn't getting off with nothing. But if she didn't have the medication, and his thrush has gotten bad, then I'd be inclined to press charges. I know you say you need to know right now, but I need to find these things out first. When will Comet be back?"

"The vet said she'd wrap up work between four and five and then drive up there. More than two hours each way. And I'm sure she'll want to stop and see the girl in the hospital. But tonight, anyway. It should be tonight. I guess we can wait that long to know, since the girl is still unconscious."

"I'll call Denny when I decide."

"No," he said. Firmly. Actually, harshly. "You call *me*."

"I'm not even to speak to Denny?"

"Oh, you spoke to him plenty enough for one lifetime, Clem."

"I don't see why everybody's making such a big deal over that. I might have said some difficult truths—"

Bobby's temper flared. I could feel it even before he spoke. It made me want to take a step back, but I forced myself to stand my ground. Well. Lean my ground.

"Truths, Clem? Truths? You said all we were doing was sitting on our lazy derrieres eating doughnuts when we should have been looking for your stolen horse."

"I never said anything about derrieres or doughnuts."

"You might just as well have. You said we weren't doing squat. You had no idea what all we were doing. You didn't ask, and you didn't give him a chance to tell you, which is what he'd come to do. And now you stand here and you've got the nerve to say all that was true. If it was true, how do you figure your horse is arriving back here tonight? You think that happens by luck?"

I was stunned to be spoken to that way. But then it hit me that I spoke to others that way often. I remembered once, when I was a little girl, my mother saying I could dish it out but I couldn't take it. It made me feel unsalvageable, as though I had been born unlikable and had no hope for being any other way now.

"I . . ." I said. Then had no idea how to finish. I

had to stop and regroup. "I guess I was wrong in what I said. I'm sorry."

I expected it to make some kind of a difference. It didn't.

He just shook his head, turned away, and walked toward his car. "Call *me*," he shot over his shoulder. "Not Dennis. Me."

He got in, fired up his noisy engine. He drove away without looking back.

I turned to go back inside, and saw the little boy standing, frozen, one hand on the partly open front door. He had obviously heard a piece of that conversation, but I had no idea how much. I felt deeply ashamed, and my cheeks burned. I looked at his face, then quickly looked away.

"Why are you like this?" he asked.

In that moment I would have done anything to get away from him. If we had been anywhere but my house, I would have run. If his parents had been home, I would have dropped him back to them in a heartbeat. But I had agreed to watch him for an indeterminate length of time. I was well and surely trapped.

I ushered him back into the air-conditioned living room.

"That's a very foolish question," I said.

"Why?"

"Because I don't even know what you're asking. Why am I like what?"

But I knew.

"Mean," he said.

I kept ushering, moving him into the kitchen. I thought I'd sit him down at the table and make us a snack. I thought if I just kept moving I could keep all this away. Keep ahead of it somehow.

"I'm not mean," I said.

"Yes, you are."

"Well, I'm not trying to be."

"But you really are."

I sank down into a kitchen chair and let my head fall into the cradle of my arms. It was dark in there, and a little bit closer to safe. I stayed there for what seemed like the longest time. How long, I can't even say.

I wondered if the boy knew his foster sister had been found. If he'd heard that part. If I should tell him.

But there was an even more important matter at hand. I was a mean old woman. I'd never meant to be, but it was unquestionable that I was. Up until that moment, I'd half known, but I hadn't cared what other people thought of me. I guess I cared what Vern thought, but somehow I'd considered him grandfathered in. I guess I'd thought he had to put up with me regardless.

I cared what Denny and Bobby thought of me, because they're responsible young men. But they're paid to serve the community, so I guess I thought I was something like their employer, and their respect was guaranteed.

Beyond that, I just hadn't cared. Hadn't cared much, ever. Hadn't cared at all of late.

But I cared what this little boy thought. And he thought the very worst about me. And, worse yet, what he thought was true.

I wondered if there was a way to change anything at this late date.

I felt his small hand touch my back.

"I'm sorry if I hurt your feelings," he said. "I thought you knew."

Less than an hour later, his veterinarian mom came to pick him up. To take him with her on the drive. I hadn't known she was going to do that. I'd thought he would be with me much longer. Probably overnight.

It hurt more than I can put into words.

He didn't say much as he was leaving, and he didn't look at me. The vet told him to say thank you to me for looking after him. And, when instructed to, he did. But not with much feeling.

I had thought I would have more time to redeem myself in his eyes.

Seems I had thought all kinds of things.

Seems like everything I had ever thought was plain wrong.

29. Jackie

I held myself together pretty well until Mando came into the hospital room.

I just sat there, in a slant of sun shining through the window, and watched Star's face. It didn't do anything. But still I watched it.

Her skin looked gray and papery, and she'd lost more weight than she could afford to lose. Her hair was hopelessly greasy, and so tangled I thought we might have to cut it all off and start over. *If.* If starting over on any aspect of her life was an option we were lucky enough to be given.

That's what she looked like. Here's what she didn't look like: A brat. A rebel. A troublemaker. An emotionally disturbed teen.

Lying in that hospital bed, somewhere between unresponsive and comatose, she didn't have a smart mouth or a bad attitude. She didn't roll her eyes or talk back. She was just a helpless kid.

Which meant she was just a helpless kid. It didn't really matter what she pasted on. It was what she pasted it on to that told the real story.

And yet my mind kept going back to the inevitable. Or at least what I hoped was inevitable. Bringing her home. It terrified me to think of taking her back into our family. How long could we keep living under this kind of stress? And the question was one thing for Paula and me, because we were running the show. It was something else altogether for the boys, who had no say in the matter.

For one silly moment I toyed with the idea that Star's social worker would take her back. Find her a new placement. Because we'd carelessly misplaced her. But it was a ridiculous thought. Star had run away from every placement. We were hardly unique. And no one else was waiting to take her, especially not now. No. We were Star's last stop in the foster care system, and everybody knew it.

Then there was the other option. The one where she didn't survive to be brought home. I think that was even more terrifying, but by then it was hard to know for sure.

I'm ashamed to report it, but when it dawned on me that she might be on her way to a juvenile detention facility, I was undeniably relieved. Hurt and relieved, all at the same time. It always made my chest ache to feel two things at once, each so strongly.

Just at that moment, Mando walked in, his face open and calm.

I burst into tears.

I'm not sure I'd ever burst into tears before. At least, not in my adult life. I'd cried some tears, let some leak out, held back more than a few. Probably more than it was healthy to stifle. But I don't think I'd burst into any. Until that moment.

Mando raced to my side. "What? What is it? Are you okay?"

But I was crying too hard to answer.

He pulled a plastic chair right up to mine, until it bumped hard, and sat with me. And held my hand, and patted it.

"Did she die?"

I shook my head.

"Oh, thank God. Why are you crying?"

I took a moment, and gathered myself up as best I could. It wasn't enough to stop crying, but at least it was enough to start forming words.

"I think I didn't realize until just now how scared I've been," I said. "I don't think I could let myself know that until it was over."

He didn't say anything in reply, but I think he knew what I meant. I got the feeling he did.

He brought me a box of tissues from the bedside table near the empty bed on the unoccupied side of the room. I cleaned up my eyes and nose as best I could.

"I'm so sorry I had to leave you alone with that deputy."

"It's okay," he said.

"No, I mean it. I know that was very uncomfortable for you."

"Not really," he said. "He's a pretty nice guy."

I have no idea how much time elapsed before I looked up to the door and saw Paula standing there. A couple of hours, I'd guess, but the divisions of time had gone on vacation, leaving just a crush of constant moments.

And she had Quinn with her. Wonderful Quinn.

I flew to her, and held her, and she held me in return. After a minute I felt Quinn squeeze in between us and hug me around my waist. I looked over my shoulder at Mando, but he didn't take the hint. He just sat slumped in his chair, like we were all one thing and he was something else entirely. So I held out an arm to him, and motioned. After a few frozen moments he hesitantly joined us in the embrace.

"Has the doctor been around?" Paula asked me, feeling Star's bony wrist for her pulse. I heard her mutter something under her breath, something shocked, sympathetic, affected. The only actual word I made out was "poor."

"Yeah, he was here."

"What's the diagnosis?"

"Severe dehydration, mild hypothermia, malnutrition. A very bad case of waterborne illness that her body just wasn't strong enough to fight."

"Did he give you a prognosis?"

"He's not making any guarantees, but he's optimistic. He feels that Star's in a controlled environment now, and things can be handled. You know. Things that would have killed her if they hadn't found her when they did."

"Her pulse is fairly strong," she said. "I wish I could stay, but I have to go give Comet an exam and then trailer him home."

"You're leaving?" I tried to say it like a mature grown-up. I failed miserably. "You just got here!"

"Star's got doctors," Paula said, gently pushing limp strands of that ruined hair off Star's closed eyes. "She's in good hands. I'm the only doctor the horse has."

"Dennis said he never looked better."

"Yeah, he told me that, too. I ran into him in the lobby. But there's another reason I want to get over and see to the horse." She looked at the boys. First one, then the other. They looked back, their faces open and a little scared. "Guys, could you give us a minute?"

They looked at each other, then shuffled out into the hall.

"What?" I said, feeling like one more piece of bad news would kill me. I'd just turn into a little cloud of dust and blow away. Poof.

"He told me his partner went over and talked to Clem. About whether she's going to press charges."

My stomach went icy cold. "And . . . ?"

"It hinges on whether the horse's thrush has cleared up."

My brain swam wildly for a moment, and I looked at Paula as though she were crazy. Though really I knew it was Clem. Paula was just repeating craziness from Clem.

"That makes absolutely no sense."

"It makes a degree of sense," she said. "If Star took good care of the horse, she's less inclined to press charges. If she took the thrush medicine with her and looked after his hooves, and his thrush is all cleared up, that's one situation. If she stole him knowing he had a potentially serious hoof condition and just let it get worse and worse, that's another thing altogether. That's what she's basing her decision on. Whether Star took good care of the horse."

I sat back in my chair. It squeaked.

I looked at Star, as though she could tell me. End the suspense. Again, she just looked so perfectly innocent. Whether she technically was or not.

"I hate to say this," I said, "but that makes total sense. Which, coming from Clem, makes no sense at all. It's almost . . ."

But then I couldn't find the word for what it almost was.

"Fair?" she offered.

"Something like fair."

We sat and stared at Star for a few moments more.

"I can't stand that you have to go." I hate to be a complainer. Always have. But it needed to be said. "It was so hard to do all this without you."

"Come with me," she said, pulling to her feet.

"How can I? I have to stay with her."

"She doesn't know you're here, Jackie."

"What if she wakes up?"

"You were going to go home later tonight anyway. Right?"

"Was I? No, I don't think I was. How can I go home?"

"It's two hours, Jackie. A two-hour drive. Come home. Eat a late dinner. Get a good night's sleep. You can drive back in the morning."

She reached her hand out to me. But I didn't take it. It was welcoming and familiar. But it was also wanting to tow me out the door.

At that exact moment—I swear—a male nurse or orderly stuck his head into the room. "Visiting hours are over," he said, punctuated with a little knock on the doorframe.

So I took Paula's hand. On our way through the hall, I grabbed at Mando's hand. Mando grabbed Quinn's hand. And we all allowed ourselves to be towed.

"Will you call Janet?" I asked. "Tell her the news?" I still hated to talk to the social workers.

"Sure," she said.

"And I'll call Marcie and Fran."

"Marcie and Fran?"

"Well . . . yeah. They were in on the beginning of this mess. I think they'll want to know."

"Right," she said. "I hadn't thought of that."

302

Which surprised me. Because normally I'm the one who hadn't thought of that. Whatever "that" happened to be.

The sun was on a long slant when Paula led Comet through the gate in the board fence and up to the trailer.

"Now is this a perfect gentleman or what?" she asked me.

"He seems like an entirely different horse."

"You heard what John Parno said. He just needed to let off some steam. Here, take his lead rope. I want you to walk him toward me, and then away from me. So I can be sure he doesn't have any kind of lameness or injury."

I craned my neck to see that the boys were okay where we'd left them. Mando was sitting in the passenger seat of our car, his shoulder belt on, as if the car might be about to drive away on its own. Staring off into space. Quinn was fast asleep in the backseat, his head half dropped back and half leaned in to the window, his mouth wide open. I knew he was snoring, not because I could hear him, but because I know Quinn.

I took Comet's lead rope. Which I would have been afraid to do at one point. But I was not afraid.

Paula nodded as I walked him back and forth. It was obvious he was walking fine. Even to me.

I brought him back to her, and she took his lead

back, tied it to the outside of the trailer, and lifted one of Comet's front hooves.

"Do horses feel loyalty to people?" I asked her. It was a stupid question. Well. It was a stupid time to ask the question. The real question should have been, *Did Star take care of the horse's hooves?* But that's not what I asked.

"Hard to say what an animal feels."

"Do they *display* loyalty?"

"In what way?"

"I guess I mean the way a dog would. You know how a dog will stay with his owner? Even if the owner dies?"

"Not quite like that, they don't. Or usually don't. I don't know. It's a hard question. I know a lot of horses who seem to have genuine affection for their owners." She set down the hoof, moved along his side, and ran her hand down the hock of his rear leg. He lifted that hoof for her, politely. "But as far as staying with them . . . some will and some won't. Then again, a lot of people train their horse to stay where they leave him, even if he's not tied up. So it's hard to know what's loyalty and what's training. Why? Why are you asking this?"

She set down the rear hoof and moved around to the other side. Between Comet and the trailer. She pushed gently but firmly on his flank, and he moved over, so Paula could occupy that space without being dangerously trapped.

"I guess I'm trying to understand why he left Star."

Her head popped up, and she looked at me over his broad gray back. "He didn't."

"He didn't?"

"No. She turned up not fifty feet from where the horse had been found grazing."

"Then why did Bobby Talbot come to our house and say they found the horse but not the girl? They must have searched the immediate area before saying that."

"They did. Twice. But then the search dog found her where nobody else could. Apparently, she'd crawled into a culvert pipe and covered herself with leaves. Everybody missed her but the dog."

I thought, *That's weird. Why would someone who was that close to death crawl into a culvert pipe and camouflage herself?* Surely she was ready to give up and be found by then. Unless she didn't know what bad shape she was in. Or didn't care. Or didn't want to be found even with death as the only alternative.

I didn't say any of that out loud. All I said was, "How do you know all this? I've been here all day, and I didn't know that."

I couldn't see most of Paula. Just her jeans and boots. But I heard her voice. "I asked Dennis, and that's what he told me. I have the hoof verdict. Want to hear it?"

No, I thought. *Of course I don't. Why would I be babbling like a fool if I wanted to hear the verdict? Can't you tell?*

"Sure," I said.

"It's good news. His thrush has cleared up beautifully. She definitely continued to brush that medication in. I can see the reddish color of it around the frogs of his hooves. I doubt it's more than a day old."

"Good news," I repeated.

But in my gut, where I just can't lie to myself, I wasn't sure that felt like good news at all.

I followed the trailer on the road back to Easley. It was almost dark. Quinn was snoring like a miniature buzz saw in the backseat. Mando was staring through the windshield, and occasionally tapping at the hard plastic of his brace.

Just when I least expected it, he said, "Know what I was thinking just now?"

It startled me, but I kept that to myself. I'm not sure why.

"Not a clue," I said.

"I was thinking about that deputy."

"Dennis."

"Yeah."

"What about him?"

"He's a nice guy."

I knew there was more to his thinking than just that flat, obvious statement. But I chose to give him time. I needed time, often, before I could wrap words around what I was thinking. Maybe everyone else did as well.

"I like him, too," was all I said.

After half a mile of silence, he said, "I used to get so mad at people, because they would look at my mom and me like they knew just exactly what we were. But they didn't know anything. They just figured, we're brown. She's a waitress. We don't have much money. They just figured we were the same as everybody else like us. Like she was every Latina waitress they ever met. Me, I don't care so much what they think about me. But I got real mad when they judged *her*."

"I don't blame you," I said.

"But I did it, too."

Again, I waited.

"I hated that deputy so much. I was so mad that he kept coming over. Even when he didn't need to. I thought he was trying to make trouble for us. But he's a nice guy. He's not like the other cops. What does it mean, that I thought that? That I hated him so much?"

"That you're human?"

"Isn't that really bad, though? I mean, what does that say about me?"

I sighed. "Considering you just saw yourself doing it . . . made that observation all on your own, at age thirteen . . . I'd say that puts you quite a bit ahead of most of the adults I know."

• • •

My headlights lit up the back of trailer, and I could see the long hairs of Comet's tail. They were half inside the trailer, half hooked over the back gate and blowing. I could see down one side of him as well, and now and then I saw him reach over and pull hay from a feeder. Paula must have loaded that feeder with a flake of hay before she drove up to get him.

Paula thinks of everything.

I thought Mando was looking out the window, but when I glanced over I saw he was fast asleep. I picked up my cell phone and called her.

"Hello back there," she said. She sounded a bit too jovial. As if all the bad stuff were over.

"I'm going to say something," I said. Maybe more gravely than necessary. Maybe just gravely enough. "And it's going to sound like a really unthinkable thing to say."

I waited in silence. Looked up at the side mirror of the truck, as if I could see her reactions somehow. But I couldn't see Paula in the side mirror.

"Okay," she said, sounding unrattled, and I realized she'd just been waiting for me to go on.

"We're treating it like a given that Star will come back and live with us. And I'm not sure we should."

Again, in the silence, I watched the back of the truck for some reaction. Which was ridiculous. All I could see was the horse's butt, and he looked

308

relaxed enough. Then again, what did he have to lose?

Just for a split second, I wished I was a horse.

"That's some pretty radical thinking," she said.

"I know."

"We're probably her last chance. Especially after this."

"I know."

"But you still think maybe we should be the fourth family in a row to throw her back?"

"Maybe. I don't know. It's kind of unimaginable to me, too. I actually didn't think of it on my own. Mando brought it up. How we weren't even questioning the decision. And ever since then I've been thinking about it. And wondering if it's fair to the boys. We were such a happy family before we took Star. And we're so miserable now. And I just worry about them. It's not really fair to Star to throw her back, but it's not really fair to the boys to keep her. And they didn't do anything wrong. They didn't create this trouble. She did."

A brief silence. Then she said, "You're serious about this."

"At least about considering it. Yes. I don't think we should thoughtlessly, automatically take her back. I think we should weigh the decision."

"How do you make a decision that hard?"

"Oh, crap, Paula, I have no idea."

"Let's let the boys decide," she said.

"Is that a joke?"

"Well. Not decide. That's the wrong way to say it. Let's give them a chance to weigh in honestly about how much this is hurting them, and we'll decide based on that. We have to know if it's fair to them, and how do we know that? We have to ask. We can't just guess at what they're thinking. Ask them."

"Now?"

"Why not now?"

"They're both fast asleep. Besides, I don't want to do that alone. That's something I'd want us to do together."

"Okay. In the morning, if they're up. Or after my appointments tomorrow. We'll talk to them together."

I wanted to stay on the line with her, just to keep her close. I really wanted us to be riding in the same vehicle together, but this was the best I could do. But roaming cost money on our cell phone plans, and besides, it was illegal to talk on a handheld cell while driving. And it still didn't put us in the same vehicle together.

So I let her go.

I kept running it around and around in my brain. All the rest of the way home. Letting the boys break this tie of indecision. It seemed like a strange plan. At best. But I didn't have a better one.

30. Clementine

That night I had a vivid dream. It seemed odd that I would, because it was fairly rare for me to dream, vividly or otherwise. Although I remember Tina telling me she'd learned in school that we all dream all night, but maybe we don't remember what we dream, or even that we do.

Anyway, I surely remembered this.

In the dream I heard a gentle clopping of hooves outside my bedroom window, and I knew it was Tina and Comet home from a ride. I heard the hoofbeats stop in the front yard, and I heard her voice call up to me.

She called, "Mom! Hey up there! I'm home!"

I ran to the window to greet her, because I knew, even dreaming, that it was a remarkable thing that she was home, that she hadn't been for a long time, and that I had accepted that she never would be again.

Then I woke up, and I was standing at the window, holding back the curtain. So I guessed the part about hurrying to the window wasn't part of the dream.

Comet was standing in the middle of his corral. I craned my neck to see more of the front yard and saw those two women, my neighbors, walking back across the road to their own house. So apparently the part about hearing hoofbeats wasn't a dream, either.

I stood there, blinking at the dark scene below me, and letting the miserable truth sink in: the only part of the dream I cared anything about was the part that hadn't happened in real life at all.

I stepped out into the dark night. I didn't even bother to put on the porch light, because sometimes that just makes it harder for my eyes to adjust. I walked across the dirt in my bedroom slippers, which don't come up very high around my feet. So I had to scuff along carefully to keep from getting that dusty brown dirt inside them.

I stopped by Comet's fence and placed my hands on the top rail. For some unexplainable reason, I expected him to walk over to greet me, which is a very strange thing to expect, since he never had before.

"Well, at least *you're* home," I said to him.

His ears flicked forward and out to the sides again at the sound of my voice. Nothing else moved.

I looked over at the gate, suddenly wondering what was keeping him in. I knew it would have wakened me if they had nailed that gate shut again, and the latch had never been any too strong. Vern had promised a dozen times to put on a better one, a horseproof one, but he never had. What difference did it make? Proper latch or two-by-fours nailed into place—it doesn't matter if you never plan to open the gate. There was always something more compelling for Vern to do, even if that was only drinking coffee and reading the paper.

The ladies from across the road had secured the gate with two cable locks, like the ones people use to lock their bike to a tree.

I breathed a sigh of relief and looked back at the horse, thinking I should be thrilled to have him back, but feeling only unsettled.

That's when I noticed he had deposited two loads of manure—not one, but two—right in the very center of the corral.

Now, first of all, he couldn't have been back for more than twenty minutes, so where a horse finds that much to eliminate in so short a time I couldn't imagine. Second, there are only about four square feet of that corral that can't be reached by leaning through the fence with that long-handled rake, and he had hit that tiny target. Twice.

"You did that on purpose!" My voice was full of outrage and resentment. I knew it wasn't my imagination, because he backed up two steps.

Then it hit me, the lunacy of what I was saying.

How on earth is a horse supposed to know where the rake does and doesn't reach? It's absurd. He couldn't possibly have done that on purpose. If I'd honestly thought so, I should be locked up.

So I didn't really believe it, but I had hurled the

accusation at him all the same. Everyone who came into contact with me, whatever they did, I thought the worst and took it as a personal affront.

But doing so with a horse was simply carrying a thing too far.

"I take that back," I said, in more like a whisper. Not that I thought anyone could hear, but I wasn't taking any chances. "I shouldn't have said that. I'm going to try to be a nicer person. I mean, I *am* trying. I just haven't made very much progress with it so far."

I stood at the rail another minute, still somehow thinking he would come to me. That my earnest admission would cause him to trust me more.

He stood his ground.

I sighed, realizing that things don't turn around in an instant. Everybody says they're going to change, but the people around you have heard that so many times before. They're smart enough to hang back and wait to see if you really do.

I couldn't even put that one over on a dumb animal.

Two cups of coffee into my morning, I heard some noises out in the yard. I was afraid it was Comet getting restless and banging around. It froze me through and through, and I realized I'd been on pins and needles waiting to see how he'd react to being penned up again.

I'll never understand that. How can I be on pins

and needles and not even know it? It sounds like a thing that shouldn't exist in the world at all, but there it is. It's discouraging to be in the middle of a life that's impossible to explain.

When I got to the window, I saw that the vet was in the corral with him, giving him some kind of checkup. It must have been her making the noises, because Comet was just standing there like a horse statue. She had her big leather bag in the dirt near his front hooves, and she was listening with a stethoscope, but not to his heart. More like under his barrel, in a number of different places, like she wanted to hear if his intestines were rumbling. And he was letting her. She didn't even have a halter on him. They were just standing side by side.

I left my coffee on the table and rushed to the door.

Then I had a thought that stopped me: nice, neighborly people bring the vet a cup of coffee when she's looking after their horse early in the morning. I didn't know what she would take in her coffee, though, so I opened the door to find out.

She looked up immediately.

"Coffee?" I called, trying to make my voice sound bright.

"Thanks, but I've had mine," she called back.

I walked to the rail to join them.

"I would have knocked," she said, "but it's early. I didn't want to wake you."

"I was already up, but that's fine." That sounded good. Like what any nice person would say.

"I hope we didn't wake you when we brought him in last night. We parked the trailer at our own house and walked him across the road to be quieter."

I didn't feel like addressing that, because I didn't want to think about the dream again. It hurt to think about that. I just said, "I would have thought the exam would have been the very first thing. Before you even brought him home." But cheerfully, so as to sound less like a complainer.

She straightened up and took the stethoscope out of her ears. Let it hang around her neck. "I gave him a pretty good going over before I trailered him up. Mostly made sure he wasn't lame and didn't have any injuries. But I was losing light by then, and I wanted to get him home. I did make sure he was well first thing. But I think the sheriff will want a pretty extensive accounting of his condition. So I wanted to do more of a full exam in the light of day."

"How are his hooves?"

"All cleared up. And it's kind of remarkable, too, because when they found Star and took her to the hospital she was practically comatose. But the thrush medicine . . . I could still see it, dried into the grooves around his frogs. It was fresh. Less than a day old, I'd guess. Which means she kept applying it even when she was in pretty bad shape."

316

"I'm not going to press charges," I said. I almost went on to say something more, something like *You can stop campaigning now,* but I caught myself in time.

"Well, that's good of you. Thank you."

"I'm trying to be a nicer person."

She looked at me briefly from the corner of her eye, but nothing more. I stood and waited, but nothing happened. It reminded me of the previous night, with Comet. You try and you try, and the best you can get is the other party reserving judgment.

"May I ask you a favor?" I needed to say something, to fill the uncomfortable void in which nothing encouraging was being returned to me. "So long as you're in there, if I bring you the rake, will you at least move those piles more toward the rail, where I can get at them?"

"Sure," she said, and then went back to listening to the inside of the horse.

"Thank you. There's one other thing."

She seemed to be able to tell it was a big thing. Anyone would have known, I think. She straightened up again and freed her ears for what would follow.

"Yes?"

"I'd like the girl to do some work over here, as a fair way to pay me back for what she did."

She looked at me strangely. There was a little bit of a breeze, which was unusual for so early, and it blew her hair around her long, narrow face, because her hair was wispy—blond and baby-fine. I wondered if my life would have turned out all differently if my hair had been blond and baby-fine. If I'd been naturally pretty and tall like the ladies across the road.

"Star can't even get up out of bed."

"Not now, I didn't mean. When she's able. She'll come back to health, won't she?"

"We certainly hope so." She reached out, almost unconsciously from the look of it, and put a hand on Comet's withers, and he allowed it.

"I'm sorry. I didn't know she was so bad off."

"What kind of work did you want her to do?"

A voice in my head said I should have prepared an answer for that. But my gut said I already knew. That I had known all along.

"She's good with the horse. And you know I don't do well with him. So I thought she should come over and do all the work of his upkeep. Groom him, keep his corral clean. Keep him exercised . . ."

It made my throat close up with fear to think about letting him walk through that open gate every day. But I calmed the fear until it lay back down again. He'd been out for days, and he was as docile as a puppy, and would continue to be if someone kept him tired out.

While I was thinking and feeling all that, the vet's mouth twisted into a rather strange grin, but on one side only. It looked a bit wry. I couldn't read what it meant.

"What?" I asked.

"Nothing." But we both knew it wasn't nothing. "It's just . . . isn't that more of a reward than a punishment?" Before I could even open my mouth to answer, she said, "No, never mind. I'm looking a gift horse in the mouth. No pun intended. When she's back on her feet, we'll have her over here tending the horse every day. Except . . . Unless . . ."

I watched her as she trailed off, and I thought I could see her deflating, fast, like a tire with a steak knife plunged into it instead of just the usual small road hazard like a nail or a screw.

"Unless what?"

"Assuming she's still living here with us."

"Why wouldn't she be?"

I couldn't help noticing that she avoided my eyes. Also that she began plowing through her veterinarian's bag but couldn't seem to find what she was looking for. It reminded me of that moment when you open the fridge but you've already forgotten what you wanted.

"Why wouldn't she be?" I asked again. It was too important a question to let drop. I had to have help with Comet. The thought of going back to being on my own with him again was nearly unbearable.

"Star committed a crime," she said. "She may have to go back. We're waiting to see."

"Well, that's awfully harsh. Rip a girl out of her foster home? That's pretty extreme. Isn't it only a crime if I press charges?"

I could feel her discomfort growing. I could see it in her body language. She wasn't good at masking things. Probably one of those people who usually didn't try.

"I don't know," she said, still rummaging around in the bag. "We're waiting to see, like I said. But if she doesn't live here, and you can't get any work out of her . . . then what?"

"Well, I suppose if she gets yanked out of her new home and has to go back to living in some kind of . . . orphanage or something . . . I guess I would figure that's punishment enough."

She looked up, right into my face, still from that crouched position in the dirt. At least she had given up pretending there was something she needed in the bag.

"That's a very understanding attitude," she said. It sounded sincere.

"I told you. I'm trying to be a nicer person."

She smiled a little, pulled to her feet, closed up the bag, and slung it over her shoulder. She ducked out through the rails of the pen.

She walked right up to me, close, and I felt alarmed. Nobody ever walked right up to me.

"So far, so good," she said, and put a hand down on my shoulder, and smiled again, albeit a little sadly. She gave my shoulder a pat.

Then she walked back across the road. She must have forgotten she was going to move that manure for me.

I didn't bring it up.

I wanted to, but it was a nice moment, and I hadn't had many nice moments of late. I didn't want to ruin it.

31. Jackie

Paula came back across the road around seven thirty, just as I was about to serve breakfast. I could tell something was off with her. It was just there in her energy. When you've been with someone for years, you know.

"What? Don't tell me the horse is sick."

"No. He's not. He's fine."

"Thank God. Explain that to me, though. Seriously. Star is on death's door, and the horse has never been in better health."

"Star can't graze for her food. And her system isn't set up for unfiltered water. Look, I need—"

"I'll call the boys for breakfast."

I hadn't meant to cut her off. I'd thought she was done before she started to say she needed something. We just ended up both talking at the same time.

"Not yet," she said. "We need to talk. The two of us."

"Okay." I felt mostly hollow where I should have felt scared. "But hurry up and talk, because you know how I hate the waiting."

"She's not pressing charges. She just wants Star to work it off in horse care."

"Oh my God. Star will love that. So what's the bad news?"

"I just did something I never do. I lied."

"About what?" I didn't have to ask to whom. That much was obvious.

"About the fact that we might be sending Star back. I couldn't bring myself to say the truth of it. The neighbor was going on about how harsh and horrible it would be for her to have to lose her new home. I couldn't bring myself to say it's our decision. I just left her thinking they might take her away over this. Through no fault of our own."

I poured milk into my coffee and plunked myself down on a stool by the kitchen counter. "Oh, hell, what difference does it make, Paula? You don't have to tell her personal things. You don't have to tell her anything you don't want to. I know you're the honest type, but I don't get why this is a big deal."

"Because now I'm feeling like if you can't bring yourself to say you would do a thing, because it would just sound too awful, then maybe you shouldn't do it."

That sat between us for a moment or two,

heavy and awkward. Needing to be sorted out somehow. I sipped my coffee and stalled for an answer.

"Or maybe," I said in time, "the reason it would sound awful is because no one who hasn't been in our position could possibly understand."

"Maybe. How do you tell the difference?"

"Damned if I know. Ask *you,* usually. I thought the plan was to let the boys have a vote."

"Yeah. That was the plan."

"Is it still?"

"I guess so," she said. "I just feel . . . *bad* about all this."

"That's because there's no way to feel good about it," I said. "There's nothing good in there. There's bad and badder. Take your pick."

We waited until after breakfast to have our family meeting. The timing was something that required no discussion. We never held meetings on difficult family topics and ate at the same time. As a person whose appetite and digestion are easily swayed by my emotions, I'd drawn the line on that policy years ago.

Quinn was on his feet and picking up his breakfast dishes when I said it.

"Family meeting in the living room."

He froze in midclearing. I looked at his face, then at Mando's. And wished I never had to say anything that struck fear into the heart of anyone I loved. But parenthood isn't like that. Hell, life isn't like that.

"Is this about Star?" Mando asked, sounding more apprehensive than I would have thought possible.

"Yes," Paula said.

"That figures."

I looked again at Quinn, who looked like he was about to cry. He sank back into his chair, despite my having said we were moving to the living room.

"Did Star die?" he asked, his voice shaking on the last word.

"No," Paula and I said at almost exactly the same time.

"No, it's nothing that bad, Quinn," I said.

"You sure she didn't die? What if she died in the night but nobody from the hospital called yet?"

"I called the hospital first thing this morning," Paula said, "to check on her. She's more stable than she was yesterday."

I heard a batch of air leave poor Quinn's little lungs, as if for the first time in a long time. He still looked like he was just about to cry, but this time more from relief than that sickening crush of tension.

"So maybe we have our meeting right here," I said, because I felt for them. I know how much *I* hate those moments between knowing there's something bad afoot and hearing it spelled out.

Then I couldn't bring myself to go on.

"I'll start," Paula said, rescuing me. "It hasn't escaped our notice that things have been hard for you guys since we brought Star into the family. We're beginning to worry now that having such a . . . difficult foster kid isn't fair to you boys."

"But she's ours," Quinn said. "Nothing we can do now."

"That's not necessarily true," Paula said. A bit too solemnly, I thought.

Mando pulled his napkin off his lap and whipped it down onto his empty plate. But it was a light paper napkin, so the move fell short of drama. "This is about what I said, isn't it? I wasn't trying to get her thrown out of here. I don't want to be the one who gets her thrown out of here."

"Star's getting thrown out of here?" Quinn's voice had taken on that frightened whine.

"Order in the court," Paula said firmly, and the room fell silent. "We're trying to be good parents to you boys by making sure we don't totally destroy your happiness with the decisions we make. So we want to know if it's fair to you to keep bringing all this turmoil and heartache into the family."

"So *we* have to decide?" Mando asked. "That's too much responsibility."

"I'll say," Quinn added, looking a little green.

"Maybe this was a mistake," I said, looking over at Paula.

"Maybe. But maybe *not* doing it would have been a mistake. I have to fall on the side of asking everyone to weigh in. I'd rather make *that* mistake. We just want you guys to weigh in."

"On whether she gets to live here," Mando said.

"On how much it's hurt you to have her here," Paula said, "and how much you think it would hurt you to have her back."

"Maybe she learned her lesson," Quinn said, sounding weak, like a cornered baby mouse.

"Maybe," I said, trying to bring some softness back into the meeting, for his sake. Well, for all our sakes. "We'll certainly take into account whether this trouble has changed how she behaves. But sometimes it takes a lot to change a person, especially when they've had a really bad time, like Star has."

"If she had such a bad time, we should help her," Quinn said. And his tears started flowing.

I pulled him onto my lap and wrapped him up in my arms.

"We don't want you to answer off the top of your head," Paula said. "We want you to take your time and think it through. And if the answer is that it really has hurt you a lot, we don't want you to feel guilty for what we decide."

"But we will," Mando said, and got up and walked away from the table.

I looked at Paula and she looked at me. We

silently compared notes on whether we should let him walk away.

We let him walk away.

"Is the meeting over?" a sniffly Quinn said from my arms.

"I think so."

"Good," he said.

Paula went off to her appointments, and the boys and I drove the two hours to the hospital. In absolute silence.

Star's eyes were open when we stepped into her room.

There was still nobody in the other bed, so the boys pulled chairs over from that side of the small double room, and we sat around her bedside, not knowing what to say. Well. I didn't know what to say. And they didn't say anything.

She looked cleaner, like someone had washed her face and neck and hands. Or maybe all of her, but I couldn't see all of her. But her hair was still a matted disaster. Probably none of the hospital staff wanted to take responsibility for cutting it all off. It sure as hell wasn't going to comb out.

It struck me sad that she'd brought along a curry comb and kept the horse perfectly groomed while her own grooming fell apart. It made me love her more. That selfless devotion. But it also made me mad, because I thought Star deserved care, too.

From me, if available. From herself, in a pinch.

I think it made her uncomfortable that I was looking at her. I wondered if she could see I was viewing her with empathy. Then it struck me that she might consider that worse. She squeezed her eyes closed.

Out of the corner of my eye, I saw Mando tug at Quinn's sleeve. "Come on, Quinn. Let's go outside and have our meeting."

For a split second I wondered why they hadn't held the meeting on the long, tedious drive. But the answer was obvious. It was a two-person, no-parent event.

"We won't go far," Mando said to me.

I watched the two walk out of the room together. Watched how comfortable they seemed with each other. How much Quinn trusted Mando. It showed in the closeness, the ease with which they walked together.

Like brothers.

"I feel disgusting," Star said. I could tell how weak she was by the way she said it. Nothing moved but her lips, and barely even them. She didn't manage to produce much volume.

"I'm not surprised."

"When do I get out of here?"

"We don't really know yet. You're still a very sick girl."

"Yeah, that's what everybody always says about me."

"Not funny, Star."

A long silence.

"Am I under arrest?" she asked weakly.

"Apparently not. It seems the lady isn't pressing charges. She just wants some work from you when you're on your feet again."

"What kind of work?"

"Taking care of the horse."

A noise came out of her, a burst of breath. I couldn't quite interpret it. "Only if they find him," she said, sounding a bit stronger. "And I hope they never do."

"He's home. He's back in his corral right now."

No verbal response. At first. Her mouth dropped open. Then she squeezed her eyes shut again. Finally, she said, "Are. You. F-ing. Kidding. Me." Each word its own individual sentence. None of them a question.

I found it mildly commendable that she obeyed the no-cursing rule even at a moment like that.

"What did you think, Star? Did you think you were just going to quietly die in that culvert pipe, and the horse would live free? Did you really believe that?"

"Free is good."

"Oh my God, Star. You are so naive. Do you really not see how naive you are?"

I stopped, a bit stunned at my own vehemence. I hadn't realized an attack on this poor sick girl was about to burst out of me.

I had a sudden rush of memory: The first spanking I ever got from my mother. For bolting out into the street. Her fear of being unable to protect me had morphed into rage in an instant. Of course, I hadn't understood that at the time. Star probably wouldn't, either.

"Let me start over," I said. "More calmly. You thought you could survive out there alone, and look what happened. You nearly died. And you thought you could turn a tame horse loose and he'd become a wild horse."

"There's such a thing as wild horses."

"Yes. But they're born that way. Wild horses travel in herds to keep themselves safe—well, saf*er*—from predators. And they don't all survive, even so. And that's in a herd. Where did you think Comet was supposed to find a herd of wild horses to join in Central California? He was born in captivity. He never had to fend for himself a day in his life. His idea of knowing how to survive is walking over to the feeder when a flake of hay is dropped in."

I paused for a breath. Star said nothing in her own defense. She lay perfectly still, eyes squeezed shut. Before I could open my mouth to continue, I saw the first of her tears leak out. I couldn't let them break my heart. But they were trying.

"I'm not meaning to be cruel, Star. I'm sorry. But I'm trying to make you see that you don't know as much as you think you know. That's why you were put in a foster home, instead of being set free. I'm sure free sounds nicer to you. But the truth is, we know things you don't. We know the horse across the road can't live wild. We know it gets too cold in the mountains for you to live outdoors. And that you can't drink unfiltered water from these creeks without getting sick, no matter how clear it looks. You were sent to live with us because you need help. You're a kid. You need taking care of. Just like the horse. You're not wild. You need parents. You need care."

I braved another look at her. She was crying freely now, tears streaming down her cheeks. The tears got into my heart, no matter how much I tried to protect it. They made some cracks in there. I thought, *She's a helpless kid. What if the boys say it's not fair to take her back? How will I live with that? She needs a family.*

"Okay, I get it," she said. "I'm stupid and worthless. Are you happy now?"

"You're not stupid and worthless, Star. You're a kid. It's not that you can't learn, it's that nobody's born knowing everything. You're fifteen. You've got a lot to learn, that's all."

Her nose needed wiping. I tried. I pulled a tissue from the box by her bed, but she pulled her face away. Even though she was weak, and the face didn't go far.

"Don't," she said. "Leave me alone."

331

"We just got here, Star. We drove two hours to see you."

"I didn't tell you to come. Please. Go away. I'm begging you. Go away and leave me alone."

I froze there by her bed for a time. The better part of a minute, I'd say. I was wondering if that was really what she wanted. If that was what I was really going to do. If she would regret it the minute I walked out the door.

I walked out the door.

It hurt me to do it. Every damn step. But I figured Star needed to know that when you tell people to go away, they do.

I met up with the boys coming down the hospital hallway. Coming back.

"Done with your meeting?" I asked.

They both nodded.

"We're going home."

"We just got here," Quinn said.

"Star wants to be alone. She insisted."

I thought I saw a slight eye roll on Mando's part, but they turned around and walked out with me. Out into the bright sunshine on the traffic circle in front of the hospital lobby. We all squinted into the light.

I said, "I guess you want to wait until we're all together before you tell us what you decided."

"No," Mando said. "We'd rather tell you now. We can tell . . . Paula when she gets home." It was still hard for him to call us by our first names. He still had to catch the "ma'ams" before they could slip out.

We began walking to our car together. Quinn slipped his hand into mine as we stepped off the curb. Neither boy said anything. I remember desperately hoping they never would. I felt raw, and unable to hear whatever they had to say.

We arrived at the car, still in silence, and I unlocked the doors. We piled in. Silence. The boys put on their seat belts. Silence.

When the pain of not hearing got bigger than the pain of hearing, I said, "Go ahead and tell me." Then I fired up the engine and shifted into reverse.

"We think Star should come home," Mando said.

"You do?"

"Yeah," Quinn added from the backseat.

I shifted back into park and looked over at Mando. He looked away.

"Are you sure?"

Mando said nothing.

Quinn said, "We're positive."

"Why? I mean, if it's okay for me to ask why. I mean, however much you want to tell me about your meeting."

"Because she needs us," Mando said. "Even if she doesn't think she does."

"Truer words were never spoken," I said quietly. I'd meant that to be only a thought in my head, but it came out of my mouth instead. It sounded corny, but I'm not sure why that mattered.

"And because living in this family should be a no-matter-what kind of thing," Mando added.

I mulled that over for a moment. I could understand how Star's security in the family might reflect on their own. I'd considered it before.

"Nothing is really no matter what, though," I said.

I glanced at Quinn's face in the mirror. Watched it fall.

"It should be," he said.

"Think about this. What if Paula and I brought home a foster kid who actually tried to hurt one of you? I mean, seriously injure someone? You know we couldn't put up with violence in the house."

"Okay," Quinn said. "It should be no matter what so long as nobody gets hurt."

I thought, *There are more ways than one for a family to get hurt. It's not always physical.* But I was so touched by their decision that I decided not to go there. Besides, they knew. The original premise had always been to judge if the hurt was too much or not. And they'd made their decision.

I pulled in a long, deep breath.

"You boys are amazingly good people. Do you know that?" I looked at Quinn in the rearview mirror, and he beamed back at me. I looked over at Mando, but he turned his face away. I took hold of his chin and turned it back. "No ducking this, Mando. You're a good person."

He squirmed, but didn't try to take his chin back. "Please. You're embarrassing me."

"So what? So freaking what, Mando? So be embarrassed. You won't die."

"I might."

"You're a good person. Whether you like it or not."

His face reddened, but he squirmed a little less. A moment later I thought I saw the beginnings of a faint smile.

I let him go and shifted into reverse again. And we began the long drive home.

We drove the two hours in silence. Again. But it was a far different, far more comfortable silence.

32. Clementine

And, just that suddenly, everyone and everything was gone.

The little boy stayed on his own side of the street. Comet was back, and my hospital bills were paid, so the ladies owed me nothing. The girl came home two or three days later, but was still too weak and sick to work. Or so I assumed—nobody came by to tell me what to expect and when.

Vernon didn't call, or think of anything else in the house he needed.

For eight days or so, it was just empty and silent. It was just me.

It was quite a challenge, filling all that time.

I played a lot of solitaire and watched a lot of TV. I cleaned things, including things I'd cleaned the day before and likely hadn't dirtied in the meantime. I went to the window every couple of hours, sometimes more, to check on Comet—including in the night—though I had no idea what I thought might happen if I didn't. I fed him and stared over the fence at him by day, watching him grow more restless by the moment.

Once I even embarrassed myself by driving into town for groceries and lingering too long over the scanner in the checkout line, asking the checker, Geraldine Franklin, about her roses, her husband, and her cats. The embarrassing part is that she finally had to indicate with a flip of her head that there were people waiting in line behind me. I left quite ashamed, yet feeling it was something I might be compelled to try again. It was an uncomfortable combination to say the least.

I learned two things that I don't see myself forgetting anytime soon. The first is that watching TV and playing solitaire is not a proper life. It's not living. It's killing time, and that's hardly the same. You start asking yourself too many questions when your day is reduced to these rote activities that accomplish nothing. You start to wonder at the purpose of it all. Why be given hours and days if all you want to do is make them go away again?

I found myself wondering what I'd always done to fill up a life before.

Well, I'd raised a daughter. But that wasn't the real answer.

Here's the answer, and it's the second thing I learned: my life had been full, all right. It had been full of people I didn't get along with. It had been full of resentments, harsh words, misunderstandings, arguments, complaints. These things had filled my days and had seemed to give my life a sense of purpose.

Without them, my house was a very quiet place indeed.

Turns out the dreaded neighbors across the street were more my type than I'd realized. They were just that right amount of irritant to keep things from getting too unavoidably real.

It might have been the eighth day, or it might have been the ninth, when I looked out my window and saw the little boy playing in his side yard with one of the dogs—that hyperactive dog who looks something like a beagle, but really not enough like one to be purebred.

The boy had one of those long-handled plastic devices that help you throw the ball extra-far for your dog to fetch. It gives you much more leverage. He was standing on the driveway side of his house, sailing that ball all the way back into the ribbon of trees that lined both sides of the creek where it ran through. The dog was finding it and bringing it back every time.

I watched them for a while. Three or four throws and fetches. I wanted to go talk to him, but I wasn't sure if I dared. I wasn't sure if it would hurt. And I think I had accepted the fact that none of those people across the road had any responsibility to entertain me, or to fill the giant hole that was my life these days. Either in a positive or a negative way. It just wasn't their job.

But in time I walked over to talk to him all the same. It seemed inevitable, as though I could stop myself for a time, but not forever.

They had some outdoor furniture placed in a grouping in the dirt, some webbed chairs and two chaise lounges. I sat on the edge of one of the chairs and waited for him to notice me. In time I began to realize that he had noticed me all along. It just hadn't stopped him from what he was doing.

"I've missed your company," I said, which was a very bad place to start. It sounded like I was trying to make him feel guilty. Or beholden. And though I hadn't meant it that way consciously, even I had to admit that those were the words I had chosen.

"My moms say you're all better now and you have your horse back."

"You can still come over and play Chinese checkers."

"I guess," he said, flinging the ball as he said it. The wild motion of his arm changed the tenor of the word "guess," and made it sound wheezy and strange.

"You still think I'm mean, don't you? Even when I don't yell."

"Yeah. Kind of." His arm and the long ball-thrower sagged to his side. He never looked at me, not once. He just kept watching for the dog to come back. I had the feeling it was taking too long this time. "I mean, I don't mean it in a bad way. Well. I guess you can't really mean that in a good way. What I mean is, I know you can't help it."

It was hard to know how to gather a response for that, especially without crying.

Before I could even try, he said, "Oh! Oh! You know who should be visiting you if you're lonely? Star!" He seemed quite proud and excited to have thought of it.

"Why Star?"

"Star's kind of mean. And she yells. And she doesn't like much of anybody, either. Maybe you two would be just right for each other." A brief silence. Then he said, "Shoot. Peppy's not coming back. He might have seen a squirrel. I gotta go check."

He ran toward the creek and disappeared down the slope and into the trees.

And that was that. A tiny punctuation in the endless blank pages of my days. Already over.

That night I woke in the dark and walked to the window to check on Comet, the way I'd been doing at intervals throughout the night. But this time what I saw was different. This time what I saw broke my heart. And you know, when you think about it, it's amazing there was any of my heart left intact to be broken. I certainly wouldn't have believed it a moment before it was proven.

Comet was sleeping standing up, as horses do. Draped along his back was the girl, fast asleep. She was lying on her stomach, her thin arms trailing down, as if to hug the base of his neck, but of course they would never reach around. Her legs dangled well beyond the hems of her pajama pants, her bare feet brushing the sides of his barrel. Her face was pressed against his neck on one side, just forward of his withers. Part of his mane trailed over her face.

I watched for a moment or two, trying gamely not to feel my heart ripping. But there's really not much you can tell your own heart. It tells you, not the other way around.

You see, we'd brought Comet home the night before Tina's twenty-first birthday, and surprised her with him in the morning. She rode him almost all day, and when she wasn't riding, she groomed him, and fed him apples and sugar. When the sun went down, I insisted she leave him and go to bed. But I woke up before dawn, and she wasn't in her room, so I put on my robe and slippers and went down to the barn. That was back in the day when Comet used to stay in a stall in the barn, because he got lots of exercise by day. I thought maybe she'd gotten up early and gone to see him. But she was fast asleep on his back, much the way the girl from across the road was now, only in warmer pajamas. And she'd clearly been that way for quite some time.

Now, back in the present moment, standing there in the window, I thought, *Star loves him the way Tina loved him. Which might explain why he loves her back.*

I didn't say anything, or go downstairs. I didn't disturb the scene. I made no plans to let on that I even knew. I just went back to bed.

I didn't get up to check on him again, because he had someone nearby who would know if there was anything he needed. Someone who could give him far more than I ever had.

Fairly early the following morning I heard a faint knocking on my door.

I opened it, and the girl was standing on my welcome mat.

Her hair had been cut off short—very short— which I hadn't noticed from upstairs and in the dark. But it was clean. She was wearing jeans and

341

an untucked bright-red shirt, and black lace-up boots. She looked pale and thin, and really not well at all. If I'd seen her on the street in town, I might have said, "Oh dear. Are you all right? You look like you need to go lie down."

"I'm here to work," she said. She seemed subdued. If she still had that same defiant attitude, she'd left it across the road. Or maybe she was just too tired and sick to trot it out.

"You don't look like you're ready to. You look like you're still just about to fall over."

"I'll have to take it easy the first few days. But the mom-types cleared me to come over. I'm not really sure why."

"Have you had your breakfast?"

"Right," she said. "Like they'd let me get out of there without breakfast."

Then she grimaced slightly, and bent forward, as though it were no longer possible to stand up properly straight.

"Are you all right?"

"I still get these . . . they're like cramps. Like the cramps you get once a month, only higher. And . . . not that. But I still get these pains in my gut."

"Maybe you should come back when you're feeling better."

"Look, I'm here. I finished the antibiotics and I'm here, and I'm going to ride him. I rode him feeling much worse than this, and he's been locked up in that little pen for days now, and I don't want him to think he's back to just how it was before. I may not do a full groom today, but I'll get the tangles out of his mane and tail and pick his hooves and then take him out and let him run. He'll feel better and so will I."

"All right. If you're sure." Of course, I was much relieved. I swear every pang of impatience Comet had ever experienced I'd felt in my own gut, like we were joined at our most impatient parts. "His saddle is in the barn," I added, hoping to make it clear that I was not going to go fetch it myself.

"I don't need the saddle."

"It's safer with the saddle."

"He wouldn't throw me. We ride like we're all one thing."

And with that, she turned away and walked to his corral. I wondered how she planned to get through those locks, so I waited at the door and watched, but they were combination locks and she seemed to know the combinations.

I heard Comet talking to her as she unwound the cables, that earthy horse talk from deep in his chest. It made me jealous, quite frankly. Anytime I saw somebody loving something or someone and being loved in return, I felt that way. I just hadn't admitted it before.

I went back inside and poured another cup of coffee. Then I watched out the living room window near the front door as she combed his mane and tail, and picked his hooves, which he lifted politely for her.

The halter and lead rope were hanging on one of the posts of the rail fence, and she took them down. I watched him hold his head still for her to slip it on, and then she tied the rope to the other side of the halter and brought it back over his neck like reins. She led him over to the fence to make it easier to get up on his back.

I set down my coffee and stepped outside again. I was afraid for that moment when they both burst free. It made me want to hover and worry.

She looked up at me as she swung a leg over his back. "I used to be able to jump up. I was good at it. But I think I need to be feeling better before I try that again. Open the gate for us, okay?"

I jogged through the dirt to the corral gate and undid the rickety latch.

She squeezed his sides with her jeaned legs, and they trotted out of there, trotted right by me, her hands entwined in his mane.

They broke into a gallop when they hit the road.

I stood and watched them—watched the figure of them get smaller and smaller, and watched Comet's lovely galloping gait, especially that split second between steps when all four hooves left the ground at once.

Then they rounded a bend in the road, and that was that.

I turned back to the corral. I thought it would

bother me to see it empty again, its gate hanging open. I was wrong.

Turns out there's empty, and then there's empty. There's "I'm going away forever," and then there's "I'm going to be out for a while." One had been tearing me limb from limb for what seemed like ages. The other was quite a bit more comfortable than I might have imagined.

33. *Jackie*

I woke in the middle of the night because Paula wasn't in bed with me. Sometimes my sleeping self seems to know if she's there or not. I sat up and rubbed my eyes and looked to the bathroom, but the door was open and the light off.

"You should come see this," she said. She was standing by the window wearing a strappy sleeveless tee and pajama bottoms. Holding back the curtain.

I got out of bed and joined her at the window.

Across the street, I saw our foster daughter, Star, sleeping on the back of the horse, her skinny bare arms and lower legs exposed to the night.

"She looks cold," I said.

"It's like sixty degrees out there."

"Oh. Why did you even wake up?"

"I have no idea."

She put her arm around my shoulders, and I

moved closer, until our hips bumped comfortably. I wrapped an arm around her waist and set my head down on her shoulder. Then all was right with the world, even if Star was across the street and we hadn't even known she was gone.

Paula said, "I can't decide if that's the saddest or the most beautiful thing I've ever seen."

I mulled that over for a moment. "You sure the two are mutually exclusive?"

"Please. I just woke up. Don't overtax my brain." We watched in silence for a moment longer. "There has to be hope for her," she said, "if she loves something that much. If she's capable of that kind of devotion. Even if it's not to us. Even if it's not to anyone human. If a person is incapable of loving anything, themselves included, then I wouldn't be so sure. But that doesn't seem to be our situation."

"I hope you're right," I said, and sighed. "Think we should go get her back?"

"I don't see why. It's not like in the old days when our neighbor didn't want her on the property. She's been waiting for Star to get over there and start taking care of the horse. I say we let it slide."

"Fair enough," I said.

But we didn't go back to bed at first. We watched. Even though it was a little like watching grass grow. Not exactly an action-packed scene. But worth seeing, all the same.

Eventually, we went back to bed.

Star showed up for breakfast like nothing had ever happened. I had no idea when she'd wakened up and snuck home.

Paula was already sitting at the table having her coffee. "Maybe today you should go over and take the horse out," she said to Star.

Star stared at her as she sat down at her place at the table. "Mean it?"

"When did I ever say something I didn't mean?"

"You said I was still too sick."

"I think maybe it's time to get your hand in over there. You should take it pretty easy at first. But I expect you could take him out for a ride. Right?"

"Yeah! Definitely! He's the one doing all the work. All I have to do is hold on."

I sat down with my own coffee. The boys hadn't quite made it to the table yet, probably still stuck in the ritual of dressing while half-asleep. It was just the three of us girls.

"Are you still having stomach cramps, though?" I asked Star. "You sure you want to ride with cramps?"

"Wouldn't be the first time," she said.

"I think it feels right," Paula told me quietly.

And, after all, she was the doctor. Not me.

"Thank God," Star said, "because I am so incredibly bored with sitting on the couch watching TV all day."

"I can imagine," I said.

I watched Star pour milk and shovel fresh berries onto her cereal and then scarf it all down at the most astonishing rate. Mando came in and sat down, looking barely half-awake. He said good morning, but without the aid of context I'm not sure I could have identified the words. He looked up at Star. Watched her for a moment.

"That's the fastest I've ever seen anybody eat," he mumbled.

Star didn't take time to respond.

"She's in a hurry because she gets to take the horse out for a ride," Paula told him. "So he gets some exercise."

Not three seconds after the last word in that sentence, Star was on her feet and out of the dining room, still chewing.

In between the time we all finished eating breakfast and the time Paula was out the door for work, someone knocked on the door.

Paula kissed me good-bye as if we hadn't just heard that.

"I have to go," she said. "I'll be opening the door on my way out anyway."

I walked her to the door all the same, because I was curious.

Standing on our welcome mat was Dennis Portman, in street clothes. Jeans and boots.

"Now you are the last person I expected to see," I said.

"I hope you won't take this personally," he said. "I'm not here to see *you*. I'm here to see Armando."

"Oh," I said. Of course I wanted to know. But it seemed better to let the thing play itself out first, whatever it was. "Mando," I called. "You have company."

His face appeared in the dining room doorway, and lit up like the streetlights suddenly switching on at dusk. "Oh, you're here! That's great! Come in the barn with me. That's my room. I got all my stuff in the barn. And my computer."

Then they were both gone.

I looked to Paula, who hadn't quite left yet. She was on the outside of the door at least. But curiosity has its glue-like qualities.

"Should I even ask?" I said.

"I wouldn't interrupt them to ask. I'm sure Mando will tell you later. If you ask him."

She kissed me again and headed for the van.

I looked across the road, and it made my heart miss a beat to see that corral empty. Not that it shouldn't have been empty. Not that I hadn't expected it to be. It brought back bad memories, though.

But this time Star would definitely come back. That was the difference. She would definitely be back. Definitely.

When I caught myself saying definitely one time too many, I forced myself to go back inside and think about happier things.

• • •

I didn't hear Dennis leave. He didn't come through the house again on his way out. But half an hour or so later Mando turned up in the kitchen in search of something cold to drink.

"Is the deputy gone?"

"Yeah. He had to go. He had to go on duty."

"Mind if I ask what that was all about?"

"We're trying to get an investigation opened for my mom's case. Like, to see if the conviction was done right or not. Which we pretty much know it wasn't."

I felt my eyes go wide. Then I realized it was me who didn't want to get my hopes up if nothing was going to come of it. "Can he help with that?"

"Yes and no. I mean, maybe. He can't make another county do something. But he knows people, and he knows about the law. He thinks the whole part about the gun—I mean, the *no* gun— might be prosecutor bad conduct. I think he said it some fancier way. See, I'd never even heard of that thing, but he's teaching me. And he's made a couple calls already. He's a smart guy. He knows how to handle things. Like he knows who's going to defend the sentencing that's already happened and who's going to question it. Just by their job. You know, like their title. And by the first few things they say. I don't know if it'll work, but it's awful nice of him."

"It really is. It's nice to have a friend in law enforcement."

"Yeah," he said, with a crooked smile. "Who'd have thought it, huh?"

Star was gone for close to three hours. It was beginning to worry me.

Then I heard the most delightful sound. The clopping of that horse's hooves. I looked out the window and watched them ride up from quite a way down the road. And I breathed for what felt like the first time in a long time.

I realized that until Star was either sent to another placement or aged out of the foster care system, I would never completely relax. Never fully let my guard down.

But at least I could enjoy that moment, watching her ride home.

She was riding bareback, looking like she'd been born up there. One hand was woven into Comet's mane, down by his withers, almost more an absentminded gesture than an attempt to hold on tightly. Her black boots swung slightly, easily, along the horse's side.

Quinn, who I was pretty sure had been out flying his kite, stuck his head in the front door and yelled out, "Star's home!" Then he disappeared again.

I thought it was telling, and interesting, and just like Quinn. I hadn't said I would be nervous until she got home. I guess I hadn't needed to.

• • •

When she stuck her head in the door, she looked sweaty and exhausted, but she stared right into my eyes, and something in her face seemed to shine. It reminded me of someone, but at first I couldn't place the memory.

Then I did.

A year or so before, Paula and I had gone to the hospital to see a friend of ours who'd just had a baby. And I do mean *just*. She was barely two hours out of labor, and holding the baby in her hospital bed. Her husband was standing beside the bed, holding her free hand. When she looked up and saw we were there, she had the most astonishing look on her face. I remember thinking I'd never seen anyone look so tired, so sick, so wounded, so drained . . . and so purely happy.

Star looked at me curiously, as if trying to gauge what I was thinking. Then she stepped inside and swung the door closed behind her.

"Good ride?" I asked.

"No such thing as a bad one."

Then she came in my direction. Very fast. I had no idea why, and I confess it alarmed me. She threw her arms around me and hugged me tightly. I was so completely taken aback I couldn't even raise my arms to hug her in return. She was slight and fairly small, so her head only came up to about my shoulder. I realized I'd had no idea how it felt to hold her, because I never had. I'd never dared.

352

In time the shock wore off enough that I could wrap my arms around her shoulders.

"I'm really sorry I did so many stupid things," she said.

I opened my mouth to say something. But I have no idea what it would have been. And it didn't matter, because I never got that far.

She let go, and she was gone. I heard the door to her room slam, almost like the old days. Almost as though that odd miracle had never happened.

34. Clementine

It was three or four days later, and I was watching her work. I was outside, in the shade of the porch awning, sitting on the swing chair and drinking a glass of iced tea. Star had Comet haltered and out of his corral, his lead rope tied to the top rail of the fence, and she was raking out the manure and small stones with amazing care, so that no square inch of dirt was left ungroomed.

She had just led him out and tied him to the rail. She made it look so easy. Was it really so easy?

Every time she had been here working, I'd stayed close and watched her. I think she might have assumed I didn't dare leave her alone, but if that had been the case I would never have allowed the two to gallop away each day.

Truth is, I wasn't fully sure why. I hadn't really

thought it out, other than the obvious truth that I was in no position to waste human companionship.

"You're always staring at me," she said suddenly.

"I didn't think I was staring."

"Well, you're always looking at me when you think I'm not looking. It makes me nervous."

"Sometimes I think you remind me of someone."

She stopped and leaned on the rake. She was using a normal rake, with a normal handle, not that ridiculous thing Vern had fashioned for rakers who are terrified of horses. She looked right into my face, albeit from a good distance off. "Who?"

I looked away immediately. And in that split second, I knew. "I don't know," I said.

She shook her head and went back to raking.

"Well, *maybe* I know," I said. "Maybe I just figured it out. Sometimes you remind me a little bit of Tina, my daughter. But that's an odd thing to say, because in most ways you're almost her polar opposite. She was very quiet and shy. She never broke the rules or raised her voice to anyone. She would have been afraid to. But there's some little aspect of you that reminds me of her, and I can't even put my finger on what it is."

"Aspect? What's an *aspect* of a person?"

"It's probably not the right word, but I don't know what would be."

Then it was time for her to stop raking and go haul the wheelbarrow over and load it up with manure, for its eventual use in the flower beds. I watched her and thought, *"Energy" is the word I mean.* There was something familiar in her energy. And yet I didn't want to use that word, because it sounded too flaky and new-agey, and I didn't even know if I believed that people had an energy. But there's something in a person you can feel, so that you know a little bit about him before he even opens his mouth. I just wasn't sure what to call it.

I wondered for a while what could be so similar between this wildcat lawbreaker and a bashful little mouse like my Tina. But, oddly, I didn't wonder for long. It was right there, like a thing that was sitting on the table in front of you while you were focusing your eyes on everything else but.

Disturbance.

They were both disturbed. Not in the same way, but it felt the same. Tina's disturbance seemed to have been inborn, and had been inside her from the start. This girl in front of me, as best I could figure, had been born average and then abused or neglected. But somehow they both exuded the same need.

Need. That was another important word, I decided. Suddenly I understood perfectly why the girl and the horse had clicked together right from the start. Because Star approached him the same way Tina did, with that depth of need, as though he were the only thing in the world that could save her. It was something he recognized. Maybe even something he had missed.

I looked up to see her walking by the porch, hauling the wheelbarrow behind her rather than steering it in front, and staring into my slightly downturned face. She pulled up short, the wheelbarrow banging into the backs of her knees.

"Why do you have that weird look on your face?" she asked me.

"I don't know what look you mean."

"You look like you're trying to do the world's hardest math problem in your head. Were you thinking about your daughter?"

"Yes."

"I'm sorry about that. Your daughter, I mean. That's really sad."

"Thank you."

"So what about me reminds you of her?"

"I honestly couldn't say."

And that *was* honest. After all, I didn't pretend I didn't know. I only said I couldn't say.

After she came back from her ride, I asked her in for a glass of iced tea and some cookies. She looked at me suspiciously. Maybe I was the wicked witch. Maybe I had poisoned the cookies.

"Why?" She stood there with Comet at her side, one hand lightly on the rope rein. Again, making it look so easy, so unfrightening. So not a thing you need worry yourself to death about.

"Well, that's a strange question. Why not? It's hot in the sun, and you've been out for a long ride, and you worked hard today, and you looked sweaty and tired, and it seemed like a neighborly thing to do."

That was partly true. But also I had come to look forward to the company, and to dread the moment when she finished up for the day and left me to my enormous silences.

She just kept giving me that look, as though she were reading a newspaper located at the very back of my brain, through my face.

"What kind of cookies?" she asked at last.

"They're store-bought, I'm afraid."

"Aren't all cookies store-bought?"

I laughed, and she didn't seem to know why. "They're the kind that are lemon-flavored, but with that rich layer of chocolate in between the halves."

"Ooh. Yes, please."

She put Comet away in his corral and unhaltered him, and locked the gate with the cables. Then she joined me inside. She followed me through the living room—a bit hesitantly, I thought.

"You seem so comfortable around horses," I said, indicating a kitchen chair and wordlessly suggesting she sit. "Have you had experience with them before?"

She eased herself down slowly into the chair, as if I might have wired it with explosives. "Tons," she said. Just as I thought she never planned to elaborate, she did. "My cousin Jimmy had horses. Lived on a ranch in Northern California. Thoroughbreds. My uncle raised them and trained them for racing. They weren't very good. I mean, they were good horses, but they didn't go out and win the Kentucky Derby or anything. A few of them had some seasons on the track. Thoroughbreds are kind of high-strung. So that's why when you said Comet was high-strung and I'd get hurt, I knew I wouldn't. I'm totally used to that. You just have to be someone calming for them."

"Sounds like you spent quite a bit of time with them," I said. I was taking out my little footstool, to retrieve the cookies off a high shelf. I purposely kept them up higher than I could reach so I wouldn't eat so many. I was hoping she would offer to help, but she didn't seem to notice. She was staring at Comet out the window, and I might as well not have existed.

"Yeah. I never liked Jimmy. Or his parents. So I pretty much spent the whole summers with the horses. Slept inside, but that was about it. My mom used to send me there every summer, because she couldn't stand it when I was home. She said me being there in her space from the time school let out to the time I went to bed was trouble enough. She used to put me to bed right after dinner. At, like, seven. Because she couldn't stand to have me in her space."

"That's terrible," I said, wrapping my hand around the cookie package. "That's an awful way to be forced to grow up."

I set the bag down on the counter and watched her bristle. Watched it and felt it. It crackled in the air, and I thought, *If that's not energy, what is it?*

"It's just the way she was. She couldn't help it. People always judge like that when someone is mentally ill."

"Not me," I said.

She laughed, and it came out rudely. A snort, really, like the kind a pig might make. "Is that a joke? You judge everybody."

I didn't answer at first. I got down a plate, which was easier to reach, and fanned out some cookies in a nice pattern. I set them in front of her, but then I noticed her hands were filthy from grooming and riding Comet.

"You should wash your hands in the sink."

She did, without comment.

I poured her a glass of iced tea.

Then she sat down, and we sipped and ate in silence for what might have been a minute, or even two.

"My daughter was mentally ill," I said. "So I know. It's an illness, just like it says in the phrase. It's not a moral failing. It's funny how people have empathy for a physical illness. They see it as bad luck, and they never question whether you can help it. But mental illness we still treat with shame."

"I know, huh?" she said, sounding enthusiastic.

Then we fell silent again, and I wondered if I had been wrong to share that. But her mother was mentally ill, so I couldn't imagine her using the information against me.

"These cookies are good," she said.

"I'm glad you like them."

Then more silence.

"Why are you doing this?" she asked suddenly.

"Why am I doing what?"

"You know very well this is not a punishment to me. Coming over here and taking care of him and riding him. You know it's the thing I wanted most."

"Then it's a win for both of us, because I desperately need it done."

She stared at me in that uncomfortable way again, as if the truth were there in me to read if she could only focus.

"You're acting like a nicer person than you used to," she said.

I slapped a hand down on the table, and it seemed to startle her. "Yes!" I fairly shouted. "You're the first one to notice. I've been trying and trying to be nicer, and not one person has said a thing, except one of your moms, but only when

I pointed it out. Of course, there's never much of anybody around to notice, and those who are . . . I think people are slow to believe in any kind of change."

"That's 'cause nobody ever changes," she said.

"Do you really believe that? Not ever?"

"Well. Hardly ever. I guess you could be the exception to the rule."

She still sounded as though she planned to wait and see, but it was marvelous progress all the same. It made my whole day.

"So if you understand so much about mental illness," she said, breaking my congratulatory train of thought, "why did you say that was an awful way for me to have to grow up?"

"Because it was. Whether she could help it or not."

Just before she left for the day, just as I was walking her to the door, she said something rather surprising.

She said, "I'm really sorry I stole your horse."

I was too surprised to answer.

"I know that sounds stupid," she added.

"It doesn't sound stupid. Remorse for a bad act is admirable."

"But it was such a huge thing. And here I say, 'Sorry,' like I accidentally stepped on your foot or something. But I just want you to know that I only did it because I really thought it was the best thing for him. No matter what happened to me. But one of the mom-types pointed out that it wasn't very good thinking, because he didn't know how to live out there. Which is why I'm sorry. The last thing I wanted was to do anything that would be bad for Comet."

"I know," I said. "I can tell by the way you are with him."

Then we ran out of things that weren't too uncomfortable to say, having said everything that was right on that line, and a few things slightly over it.

I opened the door, and she stepped out onto my porch, then paused there on the mat as though there was something else she wanted to say. But if so, she never did.

"If you ever want to come over and play a game of cards or something . . ." But I never finished.

I was positive she never would want that, and I didn't even blame her.

35. Jackie

Right around the time dinner was over, but before anybody had gotten up from the table, Star broke a fairly comfortable silence among the five of us.

"I'm going over to the neighbor's," she said.

I wrinkled my forehead. Then I looked at Paula, whose forehead looked exactly like mine felt.

"It's late for riding," Paula said. "Dusk is a hard time for drivers to see you on the road."

"I'm not going riding," Star said. She held her gaze down, as if fascinated by an empty plate.

"Is she asking you to work inside the house now?" I asked.

On the one hand, I would have found it aggravating if Clem's demands had grown beyond the original deal. On the other hand, the original deal was pretty sweet. And how much was too much for Star to owe her? We certainly hadn't hit that line yet. So I was torn.

"It's got nothing to do with work," she said, still avoiding all eyes. "I'm just going to go over there to play cards."

Silence.

I guess there were a lot of things I could have said. I told myself there were. But I didn't know what they might have been, or where they were hiding.

"Is that so strange?" she asked.

"Oh, yes," I said.

"It's kind of strange," Paula said.

"Weirdest thing *I* ever heard," Mando added.

"Yes!" Quinn said, pumping one small fist. "I was right! Score!"

I didn't know what he meant, but as is so often the case in the setting of a good-size family, I had no time to follow up and learn.

I said, "I understand you must have some guilt—"

"It's not guilt!" she shouted. "It's not weird! It's just cards. Why am I getting the third degree? God! I knew you guys wouldn't understand."

"Help us understand, then, honey," Paula said. "Why are you feeling inclined to spend time around Clementine voluntarily?"

Star was half on her feet by now. She hadn't even stepped away from the table, but I could almost hear the door to her room slam in my head—a weird combination of memory and anticipation.

"Why not? Why shouldn't I? You act like she's horrible."

Silence.

Someone had to say it, so I volunteered. "She's *kind of* horrible, honey. Everybody thinks so."

"Well, *I* don't think so. She's trying to be nicer, and you never even noticed. She just gets frustrated and yells, like my mom. That's not a death-penalty crime or anything, you know. So we're going to play cards. So what? I'm bored. I need something to do."

"We would play cards with you if you're bored," I said.

"But that's not good enough!" She slammed the table hard, and Quinn jumped the proverbial mile. "It's different with you. You're so . . . normal!"

Then she stomped out of the dining room. We heard the front door slam.

Both the boys looked to Paula and me, as if for help in what to think. How to react.

"I think that's the first time I ever lost points for being normal," I said.

I got up and walked into the living room. Over to the front windows. I watched Star stomp across the road. I thought maybe she'd look back, but she never did.

Paula joined me a moment later.

"Is that the weirdest damn thing ever?" I asked her quietly.

"I don't know. I'm not sure I think it's as weird as you think it is. They both feel completely alone."

"But Star's *not* alone. She has us."

"But we're too normal."

We both laughed. We couldn't help it.

"But Clem is so unpleasant and disagreeable," I said. Or whined, to be more honest.

"Unlike Star?"

"Oh. I guess that's a point. But she hated Star more than she hated any of us."

"They definitely got off to an explosive start. Probably a nicely familiar feeling for both of them. Besides. Star misses her mother. The fact that life was hard with her mother doesn't mean she doesn't miss her."

"She has two mothers on this side of the road, though."

"But we're nothing like the mother she grew up with."

"And Clem is?"

"She just said so. She just said, 'She gets frustrated and yells like my mom.' The devil you know being a safer bet than the devil you don't know. Or however that old saying goes."

"I completely missed that. Why do you catch these things and they go right over my head?"

"Just two different kinds of focus," she said.

She took my hand, and we walked back into the dining room.

Both of the boys had made themselves scarce.

I found Quinn lying on his bed playing a handheld video game. Surrounded by dogs. How four dogs and Quinn fit on that tiny single bed I could never quite fathom. But they always found a way to utilize the space.

"You okay?" I asked. I didn't sit down because there was no room.

"Sure. Fine. Why wouldn't I be? She can be over there as much as she wants. Makes it nicer over here. See? I was right about them."

"Yeah. What did you mean by that, honey?"

"I told that neighbor lady if she was lonely it should be Star visiting her. Not me. Because Star is mean, too. And she yells. And she doesn't like anybody, either. That's why they get along."

I suppose it should have made a degree of sense to me. But, based on where we'd all started off with each other, any friendship between them still seemed unimaginably weird.

• • •

When I got out to the barn, Dennis was there, sitting cross-legged on the concrete floor with Mando, head to head over a carefully arranged group of papers.

"Sorry," he said. "You must think I've just about moved in. I drove around the side and didn't knock because I thought you must be sick of the sight of my face."

"We're not," I said. "And it's nothing to apologize for."

"He got the trial transcript," Mando practically shouted.

"Yeah," Dennis said. Like it was no big deal. "I pulled some strings."

"So . . ." I moved closer. Peered at the papers as though they might tell me something. Either that or jump up and say "Boo!" to startle me. "Do you think there was prosecutorial misconduct?"

"Right now I can't tell. I can't make heads or tails of this just yet. All I know so far is that the presence or absence of a gun never came up during the trial. Which is a pretty glaring omission. I take it to mean something went very wrong. But whatever happened, it didn't happen during the trial. Probably beforehand. If the DA buried that information, it's prosecutorial misconduct. If not, it was the public defender's job to bring it out. In which case you have an incompetent defense. Both would yield the same result. It's some type of misconduct either way."

"What result? You said it would be the same result. What would that be?"

"First it has to be proven. It goes before a judge to decide. Then the judge decides on the remedy. He could overturn the conviction, or bump it down to lesser charge. Or he could just reduce the sentence. Which is good for us, because it's pretty likely he'd reduce it to time served. Three years is a lot for first-offense drugs, especially when the drugs appear to be somebody else's."

I realized I was squatting to get closer to the papers, which had been placed in neat stacks, some purposely crisscrossing each other. But I swear I didn't remember getting down there.

"How do you prove a thing like that?"

"Bad news is, I'm not sure. It's really not my field of expertise. I've never done it before, and this happened outside my jurisdiction. Good news is, I don't exactly have to prove it. I mean, not personally. I have to convince somebody in Napa County to open an investigation into the prosecution of the case. I think I've made some good allies, but you never really know until the chips are down."

I looked up into Mando's beautiful face. He looked back as though he might burst before our gazes unlocked again. I couldn't decide if he looked more happy and hopeful, or more afraid to let himself be. Probably it was a tie.

It's ignoble, what I felt, but probably ultimately human. I thought, *We're going to lose him.* And it made me terribly sad. Well, happy and sad at the same time. Probably it was another tie.

I thought of the day Star was found. That moment when Dennis came up the steep slope, and I came down it. And a minute later I agreed to abandon Mando into the care of a man in uniform. I thought it was the worst thing I'd ever done to him. Turns out it might have been the best.

That is, if this worked. If this wasn't another heartbreaking dead end.

"What do you think, Jackie?" Mando asked. It was one of the few times he'd used my name, and maybe the only time he'd used it with no hemming and hawing, and no visible discomfort.

I crossed my fingers on both hands. Under the circumstances, it was all I could bring myself to say about it.

"So what did you need?" he asked.

"Need?"

"You came out here for something."

"Oh. That. I was just making sure you were okay after that little dinner squabble. And I guess I wanted to hear what you thought about this Star and Clementine thing."

"Fine in my book." He punctuated that with a shrug. "She can go over there all she wants. Better her than me."

I noticed Dennis staring. "Star and Clementine?"

he asked. Then, quickly, "No. Never mind. None of my business."

"It's okay. It's fine. We're talking right in front of you. She's over there now. Playing cards."

"Because . . ."

"I have no idea. She just said she wanted to go."

He shook his head. Then sat still for a split second. Then shook his head again. Then laughed one short burst. "The meanest lady in the whole county is across the road playing cards with the girl who stole her horse."

"I know. That's pretty much what I thought."

"People never cease to entertain me," he said. "Just when I think I've heard everything."

36. Clementine

"Here's what I'm wondering," I said to the girl. "I know you'll say it's none of my business, but I might just go out on a limb and ask anyway."

She was staring intently at her cards. Frowning at them. I didn't know if she had a very bad poker face—except we weren't playing poker, we were playing gin—or just wanted me to think so.

I expected her to look up in response to what I said, but I was wrong.

She kept me waiting a long time for an answer.

Finally, she said, "If you're going to ask, why don't you, then?"

"I know you weren't taken away from your mother because she put you to bed too early and sent you away summers."

"That's not a question." She picked up another card and fanned her hand out on the table, cards face up. "Gin."

I frowned and marked it off on the sheet of yellow lined paper I was using to keep score. She was much harder to beat than Vern, which was mildly irritating.

"Your deal," I said.

I watched her shuffle the cards and knew she'd had prior experience with this, too. She knew all kinds of things for one so young.

"So what you're asking," she said, dealing cards onto the table with a crisp snap on each one, "is why my mom got locked up, and what she did to me that was so terrible that I got thrown into foster care and turned into somebody who would steal a horse."

"You certainly know how to make a question sound worse than what was intended."

"No matter how you say it, it's a pretty personal question." She fanned her cards in her hands, rearranged them, then discarded one and drew from the pile.

"Yes, I suppose it is. If I was wrong to ask, I'm sorry. I don't much like it when people ask *me* personal questions, either."

We played our hands in silence for a few

minutes. Might have been three, might have been five.

Then she spoke, startling me. "Make you a deal. I'll tell you what happened with my mother if you'll tell me what happened with your daughter."

I didn't answer.

I had no intention of accepting that deal. And yet, puzzling though it may seem, I was sorely tempted to. I couldn't tell whether it was because I wanted to hear her story or tell my own. Whichever, I had no intention of doing what the feeling told me to do. I hadn't survived this long by listening to the whims of every random feeling.

"Okay," she said. "I'll go first, and then you'll *have* to go. You'll have no choice. Every now and then . . . well, pretty often actually, she'd get into these really psychotic moods. And then she thought I was a demon. Well, not that I *was* one, exactly. More that I *had* one. That a demon was coming to catch her, but it was getting to her through me. So she'd lock me out of the house for a few days at a time. Or she'd light something on fire and use it to chase me off. Twice she took a shot at me."

"With a *gun?*"

"Well, of course with a gun. What does anybody shoot at somebody with? A bow and arrow? A slingshot?"

"Did she hit you?"

"Nah. I was pretty fast."

"I'm surprised the neighbors didn't notice and do something about it."

"Well, obviously they did, didn't they? Eventually. Or I wouldn't be *here*."

I shook my head, as if to sift my worldview back into order. I had a sudden appreciation for my own mother. She hadn't done nearly all I thought she should have for me, but at least she hadn't done anything overtly against me.

"Too bad she didn't want to protect you both from the demon, instead of just protecting herself from you."

"Yeah. I thought that a couple of times. Well. More than a couple. But you're stalling, you know. It's your turn to tell."

"I never agreed to that deal," I said, feeling my insides turn cool.

"Oh, cheat!" She slapped her cards onto the table face down. "Are you really that much of a cheat? You should have stopped me if it was no deal!"

"I really don't know why things turned out the way they did with Tina."

"That's a major cheat. That totally sucks."

"I'm sorry, but it's true. I've never understood why anybody wants to take her own life," I said, carefully ignoring my little incident with the sedatives. "I doubt I ever will. What about you? Can you help me understand it? When you crawled into that culvert pipe and covered yourself over, what were you thinking? You must have known if you'd stayed near the road instead you would have been saved."

I looked up from my cards gingerly. She was staring me down.

"Who told you that?"

"Doesn't matter. It's a small town."

Bobby had told me. Probably hoping it would inspire me to go easy on her.

"I don't know what I was thinking. If I even was. Haven't you ever felt like it's not worth it? Like there's nothing here for you in the world?"

"Often," I said. "But I keeping slogging along."

"Maybe you're braver than me."

"Or just the opposite. Maybe I feel like it's not worth it to stay but I don't have the guts to do anything about it. I've only felt that way in the last couple of years, though. I didn't feel that way before Tina died."

I was relieved when she didn't respond. She seemed to have backed off on pressuring me to speak, to tell. I breathed a huge sigh, but quietly. We played our gin hands for a few moments in silence.

"I blame myself," I said. I swear I hadn't known I was about to say that. But I'd known it was true all along.

"For what? Oh. Your daughter. But you said she was mentally ill. So maybe it wasn't your fault."

"There was so much I could have done better."

"What would you do different, then? You know. If you had it to do over."

"I *don't* have it to do over, and I never will, so what difference does it make?"

"If you did, though."

"I wouldn't extend the silence."

"I have no idea what that means."

"When I was over having dinner with your family . . . your foster mom—the one with a J—said she was raised in a silent house, and I said I was, too. She said sometimes we turn out like our parents without meaning to, and other times we do just the opposite. She grew up and broke the silence. I didn't."

"When were you ever at my house for dinner?"

I looked at her as though she were being foolish, but it was me. I was the foolish one. "Oh. That's right. That was while you were gone."

Minutes dragged by, and I thought the conversation was over, and I was quite glad for that.

Then she said, "You could have it to do over. Not with the same girl, but still."

I snorted laughter. "I'm over sixty years old. Don't you think it's a bit late for more children?"

She flipped her head in the direction of home. "They can have all they want."

"Oh, you mean I could foster or adopt. Everybody told me to adopt at the time, but I wouldn't listen."

"Yeah. No offense, but you don't strike me as the world's best listener."

"Well, isn't that just the pot calling the kettle black?"

"Right," she said. "I guess that's true."

It seemed like a perfectly ridiculous idea. Open my door to a troubled stranger? Why would anyone do that? Then I looked across the table and realized I was doing that already, quite voluntarily, in hopes that it was better than being alone in the huge silence.

And it was.

It was late, and dark, and clear she had to go home. I walked her to my door. When I opened it, I saw Denny Portman parked across the street, which made me feel peevish. I had lived in this town since before he was born, and suddenly *they* were his friends?

He was standing by his car—his off-duty car—dressed in street clothes, and talking to both of the ladies.

"I'll walk you over," I said to the girl.

"I'm not five."

"I didn't think you were. I need to talk to the deputy."

Unfortunately, the deputy saw me coming and made a break for it. He jumped into his car and fired up the engine and backed up in a wide arc into the road.

"Dennis Randall Portman," I shouted. "You know very well I want to talk to you, young man! You just stop right there! I'm still your elder!"

He slammed on the brakes, half into the road, because . . . well, what difference did it make? We didn't have much of what you might call traffic.

I hurried across, slightly amused that I could talk to a big, hulking man in that tone, as if I were his mother or schoolteacher, and receive submission in return.

Over the roof of his car I saw the girl go into her house with the foster moms.

Dennis had powered his window down, and was looking pouty behind the wheel, his huge arm dangling out along the side of the door. "You owe me an apology, Clem."

"Well, of course I owe you an apology. Why else would I be shouting at you not to move?"

"Oh," he said, seeming shyer now. "I didn't know you knew."

"Of course I know. Hush up and let me get through this. It was unfair of me to suggest you weren't really looking for Comet, especially since you found him. I was in a terrible mood, and I never should have taken it out on you. I'm sorry."

He sat still for a moment, then shifted the car out of gear.

"I'm not sure I've ever heard you say anything like that before, Clem."

"I'm trying to learn to be a nicer person."

"Commendable," he said. "Now what's with you and the horse thief?"

"She's not a horse thief."

"Beg to differ. All you have to do to earn the honor of being called a horse thief is steal a horse."

"You still shouldn't call her that."

"Well, I wouldn't to her face. Or to her moms. But I'm trying to make a point."

"I'm sure I don't know what the point might be."

"Why aren't you furious, Clem? That's my point. Answer me that. It's not really my business, but I'm asking all the same, and we've established that you owe me a little something after that recent outburst. So tell me. Everything makes you furious. Everything always has. You were furious with me because you thought I wasn't trying hard enough to get your damn horse back, but you're playing cards with the girl who stole him. It just doesn't make any sense in my head. So help me out here."

I sighed. It was dark, at least outside the beam of his headlights. So I couldn't see his face well, nor could he see mine. I was grateful for that.

"She loves him," I said. "She loves him the way Tina loved him. That's no small thing."

"No," he said. "I suppose it's not."

Then he shifted into gear and drove away, leaving me standing in the middle of the road, once again alone.

37. Jackie

I can't say exactly how much later my feelings about the Clem/Star situation broke wide open. At least two weeks. Maybe almost three, but I'm thinking not quite.

Star had been spending nearly every waking moment across the road, grudgingly appearing for family meals only because I insisted. And I'd said nothing. But I'd taken to grinding my molars silently, and I wasn't even sure why.

Then came the evening when she found me in Paula's and my bedroom and announced that she might just as well spend the night over there.

"She has a guest room," she said. "It's just easier."

"Easier how?" I wasn't even trying to hide my irritation. "How much trouble is that saving you? You stay at someone's house to save yourself the long commute home. How many steps is it from there to here? How many seconds does it take you to walk back to your own room for the night?"

"You're always doing this. You never understand. I should have asked Paula."

"And you should know that Paula and I don't make decisions without talking to each other."

I watched her hands turned into balled-up fists at her sides. Her hair had reached an awkward length

379

where it wanted to lie down in some places but not in others. Her face was reddening, and I remembered thinking she was something of an unappealing package at the moment. Well, at most moments. It only underscored how strange it felt that I was trying to keep her closer to home.

Still, we'd signed up to care for her. It was a legal arrangement, and it came with responsibilities. We couldn't just sublet her to someone else.

"Why are you being like this?" she shrieked, and I heard Paula run up the stairs immediately.

"You live here, Star," I said, remaining calm. Well, that's a lie. Keeping my *voice* calm. Well. Pretend calm. "You live here with us. Not there with her."

"I can't be myself here!"

"Why can't you?"

"I told you already. You guys are too normal. All of you. I hate it! It makes me feel terrible! I don't belong here, and you know it! Everybody knows it!"

Paula walked in about halfway through those shouted sentences, and stopped near Star. She knew better than to cross to my side of the room, to physically align with me in that moment. That might only make Star feel even more like the odd person out.

"I'm getting a little tired of that line," I said. "I

have no idea what you mean by 'too normal.' You need to use better words."

"I don't know any other way to say it," she whined.

"Take a big, deep breath, Star," Paula said, "and tell us why you feel like you don't fit in here."

"It's so obvious."

"Not to us," I said.

To Star's credit, she actually seemed to try the big-deep-breath thing. Her fists loosened slightly. "You're all one thing and I'm different. And I hate it. And I don't feel that way when I'm over there. I feel like I can be myself with her."

"What are we that you're not?" Paula asked.

I found myself growing impatient with Paula for being so unflappable. I would have felt so much better if she'd gotten mad right along with me. Raised her voice. No one can be reasonable all the time.

"Normal," Star said.

"That word's not working. Try a new one."

A long silence. Paula moved closer to my side of the room, which made me feel better. Big, grown-up parents need support, too.

"Happy," Star said. "There. Now do you get it? You're all happy. Even Mando is happy, now that there's that investigation thing going on with his mom. Or about to go on. Or whatever. And I hate it, because I'm not, and it makes me feel terrible, and I'm going over there now, and I'm spending the night in her guest room, and if you want me back you're going to have to come over and drag me back, and don't think I won't fight you."

She stomped out of the room and down the stairs.

I started after her, but Paula reached one hand out, touching my arm.

"Let her go," she said.

"But she's *ours*."

"Is that what you're so angry about? Ownership? We don't own her."

"I'm not angry!"

"She said angrily." The comment was a rare flash of sarcasm for Paula.

I paced a couple of laps in the small room. "Okay, I'm angry. I feel like I want to break something." I actually stopped and looked around for something, but everything I saw seemed either useful, precious, or irritatingly unbreakable.

"Please don't. I think we need to figure out why this triggers you."

"Damn you, Paula," I shouted. "Would you please stop being so damn calm and reasonable for once? Can't you back me up on this? Can't you show some emotion for a change?"

Quinn stuck his head into our room, eyes wide. "Where's Star?"

"Across the street," Paula said.

We still hadn't looked into each other's eyes since my outburst.

"Then why are you yelling? You never yell unless Star's here."

"We're just working something out," I said.

"Go back to your room, honey," Paula said. "I promise we'll be there in a minute."

He slipped away without argument. But he was clearly spooked. Which took most of the fight out of me. If not all of it.

Paula sat down hard on the end of the bed. "Really? You're seriously going to blame this on me?" She sounded tight and scratchy, maybe even hurt, which was something like the emotion I wanted from her. I needed to hear that. It helped me.

I sighed and flopped down next to her. "No. Of course not. I'm sorry. I just get frustrated at being the only one who gets frustrated."

"Listen. Jackie. Remember why we had that big family issue over whether to take Star back? Because it was so hard to have her here. Because she was tearing the peace in this house apart. And she still is. Except when she isn't here. Which is mostly. So I'm wondering why you're not happy she has somewhere else to go and the house is quiet and calm again."

"Wasn't very quiet and calm just now."

"Because you tried to stop her. Why did you try to stop her?"

"She said she's *staying* there tonight. It's like she doesn't even live here anymore."

"I'm still waiting for the bad news," she said.

We both laughed.

I leaned forward and put my elbows on my knees and my face in my hands, still laughing. "Oh, crap, Paula. I don't know."

"Tell the truth now. Why so mad?"

"Because we did so much for her and we went through so much with her, and she doesn't even appreciate it. She doesn't even like us or want us."

"In case you hadn't noticed, dealing with messed-up kids isn't always big on immediate gratification. Maybe years from now we'll find out she really did care. Or not. I don't know. I'm not sure she'd have any idea how to show that even if she felt it. Meanwhile, she's found something that works for her. She wants to go be unhappy with the neighbor. Let's let her."

"What about her social worker? What if Janet finds out she barely even qualifies as living here anymore? Clem's not in the foster care program. It's not an official arrangement."

"Want me to call Janet on Monday morning and get her thoughts?"

"That would be good, yeah. Thanks. I'm sorry I—"

"I'm sorry I—" she began at the exact same time.

Then we laughed again. What choice did we have?

"I'm sorry I can't get mad when you do," she

said. "I know it's frustrating for you sometimes. That I can't be more . . ."

"No, it's me. I'm the one who should be sorry. You don't need to be more anything. I was wrong to say that."

We sat a minute, sighed deeply. Well, I sighed deeply. She sighed, but it was more restrained.

Then we stood up, sighed again, and walked into Quinn's room to assure him that nobody was shouting at anybody now.

38. Clementine

It was dark by the time I heard her coming back, so I thought we might abandon our plan, or maybe postpone it until the next day. I couldn't decide if it would be better or worse in the dark. Frankly, though, I think I was just looking for a way out, and thrilled to have perhaps found one.

But when she got back inside she said, "Okay. Let's go."

"We'll need a flashlight." I thought my voice would shake, but it sounded steady to me. I sounded steadier than I felt.

"You don't have lights in there?"

"We did. But they haven't been on in so long I don't know if the bulbs are still good. Plus, you have to see to walk out there. You have to see the switch."

"Do you have one?"

"A flashlight?"

"Yes, a flashlight. What else are we talking about besides a flashlight?"

"I think I have one in that kitchen drawer where I keep all the nonsense I can never figure out where to keep."

"I'll go see," she said.

I sank onto the edge of Vernon's chair, which I still had not had carted off to the dump. I was thinking I'd just tell her never mind, that it was too late at night to try this. I'd say it casually, like there was nothing very wrong.

But then I thought maybe this was the best night to do it, because she'd be staying. I hoped she'd stay again, of course, but I didn't know for a fact that she would, and it seemed frightening to do such a thing and then be left alone with my dreams all night. I couldn't imagine it. Or at least I didn't want to.

"Okay," she called in from the kitchen. "I found it."

She took me along on her way to the door by grabbing one of my elbows and pulling. Maybe she knew I needed a good pull. I was so frozen that I didn't resist. I guess that sounds like a contradiction in terms, because frozen usually means you can't move, but in this case it meant I couldn't mount any kind of decent defense.

We stepped out into the only barely cool night. It

wasn't fully dark yet, but too dark to be walking around without a handheld light. It was August by then, no longer the shortest nights of the year. I remember thinking she'd have to go back to school in a handful of weeks. Would she still come over for more than just the horse? And, if not, what would I do?

We walked carefully through the dark yard together, as if anticipating land mines. She held the flashlight with one hand. With her other hand she held my elbow. As if I didn't walk ably. As if she were escorting a feeble elderly woman across the street. None of that seemed to fit my case, but it felt like some kind of support, so I said nothing and let her.

When I saw the open barn doors, I stopped dead, while she walked on another step or two. Then she bounced back when her grip on my stationary elbow stopped her. There was a blackness on the other side of that doorway. It was inky in there. It felt like the kind of dark that could swallow a person alive.

Well, it had. It had taken one of us already.

"Don't stop," she said. "If you let yourself stop, you might never start again."

Then she pulled me hard. At first I didn't move my feet at all. In fact, I tried to plant them. But she pulled my upper body forward. I never really took any intentional steps. I just moved my feet out of necessity, to keep from falling.

She shone the light inside, and I saw Comet standing patiently in his stall. She'd been keeping him in since he got ridden every day. She thought he'd be happier there, and that it would remind him of better days.

He rumbled a greeting to us from deep in his chest. Well, to her, probably. But it helped all the same.

She switched on the overhead light, and I winced and squinted. Then she towed me a few more steps into the center of the barn. I had no idea why. Maybe to give her more chance to catch me if I tried to take off like a scared rabbit.

I blinked until my eyes adjusted to the light. Then I looked around. Well, not around, really. That's not quite accurate. I looked *there*. I expected her to ask where it happened, but she didn't need to. All she had to do was look where I was looking.

There was nothing there. Just a dusty wooden beam over the empty middle stall. What had I expected? Of course there wouldn't be anything there.

My insides felt buzzy and shocked, as if a mild electrical current ran through the middle of me, but we stood in silence, and in time it subsided. Still she was holding me by one elbow.

"Talk to me," she said.

"I hate it," I said. "I think I hate it as much as I thought I would, except it turns out I only hate it a little bit more than I hate everything else. Because I still remember, even when I'm not here. I still wake up every morning with that image in my head, and this is only just a little bit worse, so even though it's bad, it seems strange to have avoided it for so long."

"It's like I told you. Don't put too much stock in where things happened. *Where* isn't really the problem. The *where* isn't to blame for the *what*."

I looked down at Comet again, all freshly groomed and calm, his jaw working a mouthful of hay. He was certainly unconcerned by the place. It seemed pitiful to just be learning something your horse had known all along.

"So you're not sorry we did this?" she asked, sounding a bit timid.

"No. There are some things it doesn't feel good to do, but there shouldn't be things you can't do. It gives the world too much power over you."

"Want to go back now?"

"In a minute."

I closed my eyes and explored the most frightening thought of all. That some aspect of Tina might still hover—"aspect" not being quite the right word this time either—and that, if so, she might hold some of my flaws against me. But I felt nothing malignant in the air around me. Nothing at all.

Then I realized it was silly to think Tina would harbor ill will toward me, because she'd loved me.

She'd loved me as best she could and I'd loved her as best I could, and the fact that our bests weren't nearly good enough was no cause for resentment, what with us being in that same boat together.

I heard myself let out a deep breath.

"I hate those moments we can't ever undo," I said.

"Who doesn't?"

"How many times have I gone back to that moment and just beat myself bloody against the fact that nothing in the past can be undone?"

"Everybody does that," she said.

"Really?"

"Yeah. Of course. Didn't you know that?"

"No. I thought it was only me."

And that, I realized, is the worst price we pay for living in a dearth of true communication. We go through our whole lives thinking it's only us. And that has to be the deepest, most bone-chilling definition of the word "alone." You can have a crowd around you, a circus, but they can't spare you from that brand of loneliness.

I made up the guest room for her, because Tina's room was untouched, and would remain so.

Maybe that was our next big project, our next excursion with a flashlight and a tightly held elbow. But enough for one night was enough.

She stood with her shoulder leaned in the doorway, watching me put fresh sheets on the bed, a job much better suited for two. When I became resentful that she wasn't offering to help, I glanced over my shoulder at her. I didn't mean it to be a glare, but it might have come out that way.

She raced over and grabbed the other end of the top sheet, and we shook it out together. Then I wondered if half the time when I thought people were being rude by not helping they were actually unsure about me, and afraid to approach.

"You must have had a place like that some-time in your life," I said. "Your own barn." I knew because we don't learn in our heads, or by imagination. We learn when life forms a brick wall in our path and we smack it hard enough to bleed.

"I used to," she said. "But I got over it."

"How did you get over it?"

"I didn't have any choice. It was in the kitchen. If I hadn't gotten over it I would've starved."

"Didn't your mother go in the kitchen and make meals and bring them out?"

She looked at me as if I'd just suggested we fly to Africa without the aid of a plane. "Um. *No*. I was lucky if she put stuff in the fridge for me to go get."

I signaled for her to bring me the pillows from where I'd set them. She did, and we each took a pillow and put a pillow slip on it.

"What was it about the spot?" I said. "If you don't mind my asking."

"One time she set some newspaper on fire, and she burned the linoleum. She would roll up newspaper and use it like a flaming torch to keep me away. You haven't lived until you've been chased out of your own kitchen like some kind of Frankenstein's monster. A big piece of burning paper fell on the floor, and it left this black mark on the linoleum. For years I wouldn't step on that thing. I'd jump over it, or walk way around it. But then I got older and figured out it was the mom that was the problem. Not the floor."

"Then you were years ahead of me," I said.

I thought I would never get to sleep, but I fell quickly, and slept soundly, probably because I wasn't alone in the house. I knew if I had a horrible dream, and screamed out, she would come running.

I had no dreams at all. At least, none that I could remember.

In the morning she had to go home for breakfast. There were deals in place, unspoken deals, and it seemed best that we keep them.

I watched out the window as she scuffed through the dirt of my front yard, her boxy, unfeminine boots kicking up dust clouds. I was thinking how strange it felt that she didn't feel strange to me. I tried to remember how long it had been since the first day she came over here to work, but it just felt like something that had always been. I knew in my head it was a matter of weeks, but my gut had accepted it utterly.

She stopped at the mailbox and opened its little front door, and it jarred me out of my acceptance of her, suddenly thinking she was invading my privacy or going through my things. Or even stealing from me! Maybe she was after my monthly check.

She pulled out an enormous stack of catalogues, envelopes, and junk mail and carried them back to my door unexamined. Then I felt quite ashamed indeed.

I opened the door to greet her.

"You didn't bring your mail in," she said. "Looks like you haven't brought it in for days. You could see stuff sticking out of the box."

She dumped the stack into my waiting arms.

"All I get is bills, and I can't pay them until my check comes. If anyone wants to steal my bills, they're more than welcome. They can pay them while they're at it." I dropped the stack on the table and began to sort through it. She stood in the doorway and watched me. I'm not sure why. "I get all these catalogues because I made the mistake of buying two dresses and a pair of shoes from one. It seemed to make more sense than driving into one of the cities that have clothing stores. Now they act like I have enough money to buy new things every couple of—"

A big manila envelope caught my eye. I never got anything in big manila envelopes. I pulled it out. It bore no return address. I ripped it open too hastily, my heart hammering in my chest.

In it were some legal papers, with a yellow sticky note in familiar handwriting that said, simply, "Clementine, please sign and return. Thank you. Vernon."

I sat down hard in the nearest chair, which was his.

"What is that?" she asked.

I don't think she was snooping or prying, frankly. I think she saw my panic and stayed out of some kind of concern. Or maybe I'm putting the best possible face on the situation.

"My husband has begun divorce proceedings."

"I didn't even know you still had a husband."

"It would appear that I don't."

She hung in the door in silence for a moment, just watching me. Then she said, "Is that, like, the worst thing ever?"

"No. It isn't. The only good part of what happened with my daughter is that I can safely say I've already lived through the worst thing ever. This feels bad, though. But not for the reasons I thought it would." I expected her to ask about that. When she didn't, I volunteered. "I haven't missed him as much as I expected to. I've definitely missed having another living soul nearby, but when I think of him, I mostly think of all the things that irritated us about each other, and then I wonder why we lived that way so long, like it was the most normal thing in the world. So I don't exactly feel like I lost the great love of my life, but it feels bad because it doesn't feel that way, and because it now seems he wasn't. If that makes sense."

"It might," she said. "I'm not sure."

I slid the papers back into their envelope to be dealt with at another time. A more civilized time, when I'd at least had coffee and breakfast.

"It just seems like all those decades of marriage should add up to more of a loss. I'm not sure what we've lost. Something, yes, but not all a marriage should be. It doesn't feel right that all those years could turn to dust in your hands, like it was never what you thought it was. Do you know what I mean?"

"Yes," she said, and seemed to mean it. "Did you think he would be back? Or did you *expect* to get those papers?"

"Neither one. I knew he wouldn't be back, and yet I never really thought about this next development. I should have. Sometimes it seems I keep myself in a place that's different from where all this real-world activity is happening. Does that make sense?"

"Oh, yes," she said.

"You don't have to stay. Really. Go have breakfast. I'll be all right."

She took me at my word and left for home. And it was okay, because it was only for breakfast. If it hadn't been only for breakfast it would not have been even remotely okay.

39. Jackie

Paula was on the phone with Janet, Star's social worker. Quinn was sitting at the breakfast table swinging his feet in such a way that the heels of his sneakers hit the chair legs with an irritating clunk on every swing. Wendy, the poodle mix, was begging for Quinn's toast, which was strictly against the rules. But I didn't want to leave the fried eggs in the pan long enough to fix that, because I knew if I did, I'd miss my over-easy moment.

In other words, it was a typical morning.

"Quinn," I shouted. "Don't let her do that!"

Paula pressed the heel of one hand over her free ear.

Star stepped into the kitchen at the exact moment Quinn set down his toast and escorted Wendy out of the kitchen by her collar. Also the same moment Paula took her phone call into a quieter room.

"Who's she talking about me to?" Star asked.

"Janet."

"Why?"

"Don't panic. We're just reporting the fact that you're spending most of your time somewhere else."

"So she can stop me?" she asked, her voice rising to a near shriek.

"Star. I said don't panic. Janet can't stop you from spending time with a neighbor, and she isn't going to try."

"Then why are you even telling her?"

"Because we have a legal arrangement to take care of you, and now we're sort of . . . not."

"I don't like this at all," she said, and flopped down unnecessarily hard on her kitchen chair.

I was fiercely tempted to ask her what she did like, since I hadn't heard many entries from that list. I kept the thought to myself.

Paula reappeared, off the phone now. She set the receiver back on its base and sat down for breakfast.

"What did she say?" Star asked immediately.

"She's not too worried about it. She likes it when kids bond with someone. She pretty much gave us two choices. Just make sure of your welfare every day, or see if you and Clem want to enter into an official foster arrangement."

"Yes," Star shouted. "We do!"

"Have you talked this over with the neighbor, Star?" I asked, serving the first of the eggs to Quinn and Paula.

"I want scrambled, not fried," Star said.

"I realize that," I said. "I've met you."

Mando wandered into the kitchen, silent, and still mostly asleep. As usual.

"I haven't asked her, but I know she'd say yes. I mean . . . I think she'd say yes."

"We should be the ones to talk to her," Paula said.

"What did I miss?" Mando mumbled.

I said, "Star's social worker thinks we should talk to the neighbor about whether she wants to legally foster Star. Since they're practically living together as it is. How do you want your eggs, honey?"

"However you're making them is fine," he said, and sank into his chair.

I walked over and kissed him on the temple.

"What was that for?" he asked.

"Never mind. It was just on general principles."

"Why would you want to live there instead of here?" Mando asked Star.

She never looked up from the table. "Bad enough I had to explain it to *them,*" she said, running her thumbnail along a natural flaw in the wood.

Mando looked to me instead.

"She thinks we're too happy," I said.

I realized it sounded critical, but I hadn't done it on purpose. I was just repeating what she'd told us. I didn't add ridiculousness to the statement. It was built in.

"If you're looking for unhappy," Mando said,

vaguely in Star's direction, "you hit the jackpot over there."

"Shut up, Mando," she barked. "Everybody stop picking on me."

"We aren't meaning to pick on you," I said.

"I just can't be as good as you guys. When I'm over there, at least I feel like I'm good *enough*."

A shot to my chest. That most vulnerable of real estate. I knew plenty about how it felt to think you're not good enough. I had never imagined myself on the other side of the equation. Worse yet, I had no idea how to fix it for her.

"Maybe we could talk about something different," Paula said.

"Wait," Star shouted. "I'm not done talking about this. So if you're the ones supposed to talk to her, when are you going to?"

"It'll have to be after my appointments," Paula said. "Six thirty or later."

She grumbled, but said nothing audible.

I got to work scrambling four eggs.

Shortly after Paula left for work, Star pulled me aside into the hall to ask something privately.

"So . . ." she said, and paused. She definitely seemed more humble than the usual Star. Or maybe "scared" would be a better word than "humble." "I'm going back over there now."

"And . . . ?"

"Am I supposed to not talk to her about it at all?"

"We didn't say that. Just that we have to hear her thoughts on the matter. Not only you. We have to hear it with our own ears."

"That just makes me more confused. Do I tell her, or don't I?"

Yes. "Scared" was the word. Star was scared. I'd never seen Star scared. I'm sure she had been. In fact, I suspected she always was. But I hadn't seen it. I wanted to reach out to her, maybe even hold her, but I was sure she would vehemently reject the gesture. So I didn't. And then I felt guilty. Because I should have done it anyway.

"We can't control what you talk about over there, and we're not trying. I think you need to decide that for yourself."

She hung there in the hallway, as if wishing I would say more. But I didn't, because I had no idea what to say. So she let herself out.

I walked to the window and watched her cross. She stopped right in the middle of Clem's front yard. She looked at the front door of Clem's house, then in the direction of the barn. Then back at the door. She took two steps toward the house, then pivoted on one boot sole and trudged off to the barn.

Not a minute later she came riding out on Comet's bare back, and they galloped away.

"I was so hoping we'd never cross this road to her house again," I said as Paula and I crossed the road to her house. "Why did I let myself believe that? Wait. Here's a better question. Why are we so tied in with this woman, and how do we untie?"

"I guess in time we'll move on to a new practice in a new town."

"I'm glad to hear you say that. Can we hurry?" I glanced over at her face. She didn't look seriously miffed, or hurt, but I said it anyway. "Sorry."

Paula knocked on the door, and Star answered, which seemed mildly surprising.

"Thank God you're here," she said. "Finally."

"We're an hour earlier than what I told you this morning," Paula said.

"Oh. Didn't seem like it."

"Who is that?" Clementine called in from the kitchen.

"It's the mom-types," Star called back. "They want to talk to you."

Clem hurried out of the kitchen drying her hands on a dish towel, her brow furrowed into worried lines. "What about?"

"About this arrangement," I said. "About Star and where she's going to be."

The brow furrows deepened, which I wouldn't have thought possible. "Star, take Comet out for another ride," she said.

"But—"

"Do as I say, please."

Star dropped her head and shuffled to the door. She wore her discontent clearly, and exuded it for all of our benefits, but she didn't argue. Which is more than *we* ever got from her.

She slammed the door behind her. At least that much was painfully familiar.

"Sit down," Clem said.

We did.

Before we could even gear up to speak, Clementine said, "I know what this is about. I know exactly how you feel, but I'll thank you to think carefully before acting on those feelings. I felt the same way when she started coming over here to spend time with the horse. Before I even knew her. Before I even knew any of you. I felt like something was clearly mine and someone was treating it like it wasn't. But Star is not an it or a thing. She's a girl. I'll tell you something, and it's candid, and I haven't always spoken candidly to you in the past. But I'm about to. Ever since you moved here, I've been quite miffed, and I would never admit it was jealousy, but it was. I didn't understand how you were such a happy family with happy children. It's not as common as I used to think, and it's not as easy as the Christmas specials make it look. But now I have one consolation: that not every parent is best for every child. I wouldn't say such a thing to you if she were your child, either by birth or adoption. But she belongs to the state, or the county, or whatever, and she's happier here, and I want you to think about that before you do something to pull that apart."

402

I looked at Paula and she looked at me. Neither one of us found the answer we were looking for.

"I thought you knew what this was about," I said.

She didn't answer. Just sat and blinked too rapidly.

"Star didn't tell you?" Paula asked.

"No. She didn't say a thing."

For some reason I was the one to launch in. "Paula had a talk with Star's social worker this morning. We wanted her to know that Star is here more than she's home, because we signed on to look after her. She needs to hear about changes like that. She asked if you were open to the idea of an official arrangement as Star's guardian, but we didn't know what to say. That's what we came to talk about."

"Yes!" she said. "But I'd have to be part of that program, right? What if they don't accept me?"

"That doesn't seem too likely," Paula said, "but it's not crucial either way, because her social worker is also open to the idea of Star spending time here less officially, provided we're over-seeing her welfare."

Clementine looked first relieved, then suspicious. "Why are you doing this?"

I shrugged, and looked at Paula.

"We don't understand the question," Paula said.

"Didn't it make you mad that I just sort of . . . took over with her?"

"It made *her* mad," Paula said, pointing sideways at me.

"Not enough to do the wrong thing for her," I said.

Clementine frowned slightly, and it was hard to know what to make of that. I thought, *I wonder if I just made her feel not good enough?*

"What do I have to do to make this happen?" she asked.

"Tons of stuff," Paula said. "Get ready to be deluged. And asked a lot of questions. There'll be home visits and interviews, and probably some background checking. You'd best be serious about this, because it's not a simple process."

"What kind of things will they ask?"

Paula looked over at me. "What did they ask us? It's been so long now."

"The thing I remember best is that they ask a lot about why you're making the decision to foster. What you think you have to give to a kid, and what you expect to get out of the experience. That kind of thing."

She began winding her hands around each other in her lap. Then she dropped her head and began looking where she was winding.

"Do you have thoughts on that?" Paula asked. "You don't have to say, but you can run something by us if you want."

She looked up immediately. Right into Paula's face. Then right into mine.

"I want another chance. I know you can't have anything to do over, but you can try again with someone else and do better than you did before. And I know what I want to do differently this time. Well, everything, really. But I don't know if that's the sort of thing the social worker wants to hear."

"I think she wants to hear whatever's true," Paula said. "So I'd go with your gut on that."

When we got home, Quinn informed us that we'd missed a telephone call.

"I didn't pick it up. I tried to call Mando, but he didn't get in from the barn in time."

Then he padded back to his room, leading a small sea of dogs.

Paula called our voice mail.

"The prison," she said, her ear still pressed to the phone.

I looked at my watch. It was after six. "Collect?"

"Yes. Collect. So we only got the recording that an inmate was calling, and asking if we'd accept the charges, but nothing else."

"Weird time of day for her to be calling."

"I know. I thought that, too."

"I thought she wasn't allowed to call after five."

"Which makes me wonder about extenuating circumstances."

We blinked at each other for a moment.

"Mando!" we both bellowed at exactly the same time.

Quinn and Mando skidded into the kitchen simultaneously, from opposite directions, both looking quite shaken.

"What? What happened?"

"That was your mom trying to call," Paula said.

"That call you missed while we were gone," I added.

"No. Couldn't be. It was almost six."

"I know," I said. "But that's who it was."

"Did she leave a message?"

"You know she can't leave a message. Unless we accept the charges. You're not thinking straight. I don't blame you," I added so as not to seem critical. Poor guy. How *could* he think straight? "We're not, either."

He stood, wobbly but still, for a couple of beats. He looked as if he'd just stepped out onto a tightrope. Accidentally. "What does this mean?"

"We don't know," Paula said.

"How do I find out? I have to know. I have to know now. I can't wait till morning. I'll die. I'll explode and die."

"Maybe Dennis knows something," I said.

"Dennis! Of course!" He grabbed up the phone. Punched numbers by heart. I didn't know if they'd been talking a great deal, or if Mando had made a special effort to memorize the number.

Paula hooked one hand around my elbow. "Let's give him a little breathing room."

I hooked Quinn's elbow, and we moved off into

the dining room, where we could listen without hovering.

"What *could* it mean?" Quinn asked, looking a little seasick.

"It could mean she heard something about the investigation," Paula said.

"A good something?"

"We don't know."

"Is Mando going home now?"

"We don't know, honey," I said.

"Dennis," we heard him say. "Do you know anything?" Brief pause. "My mom called, and it was late. She never calls that late. I thought she actually couldn't." Silence. "Okay. I'll be here." He clicked the phone off and stared at it. Then he looked into the dining room at us. "He doesn't know." He sounded like some hybrid of tremulous and deflated. He walked in and sat down at the table. "He's going to make some calls and try to find out. How can he not know?"

Paula said, "Just because he asked someone to open an investigation doesn't mean they'll necessarily tell him the results first thing."

"But *she* would have known," he said, tilting toward deflated. "If it was going to a judge, she would've known that before it happened."

"Not necessarily," I said. "Somebody could have opened an investigation, seen something they didn't like, sent papers to a judge for some kind of determination. I'm no legal expert, but . . ."

"Or maybe she knew," Paula said, "but she didn't want to get your hopes up until she was sure."

The phone rang, and Mando jumped. Literally, I swear. He was sitting and then he was standing, with nothing in between. He levitated. He grabbed up the phone before the second ring.

"Dennis?"

Silence.

Mando sank to his knees. His legs just melted right out from under him. Then he started to cry. But the tears were anything but sad tears. He fell apart into relief. "Oh my God. When?" While he was waiting for an answer, he wiped his eyes with one sleeve. "Oh my God. Dennis. I can't believe you did it. How many days, do you know?"

I looked at Paula, then at Quinn.

"Mando's going home," I said.

"I'm going for a run," Mando announced.

"Now?" Paula asked. "It's almost dark."

"I can't help it. I can't hold still. I have to do something."

"Wear something white. Or bring a flashlight. Or both."

I put one arm around Quinn's shoulder and ushered him into the bathroom for his nightly tub. I started the water running, took down a washcloth and towel, then let myself out. He wasn't a toddler.

Before I could close the door, he said, "I'm gonna miss Mando."

"Oh, honey. You and me both."

I joined Paula on the couch. Flopped down hard. She slung an arm over my shoulder.

"I have empty-nest syndrome," I said.

"We still have Quinn."

"I have semi-empty-nest syndrome."

"The goal was always to give them back."

"True. Also unhelpful."

Mando stuck his head into the room. He was wearing a white T-shirt. "I want you to make me a promise. I want you to promise after I'm gone you'll take another kid."

"Uh," I said. Not exactly an articulate response. "Paula and I might have to discuss that."

"No," he said. It was the firmest and most definite "no" he'd ever said in our presence. "You have to promise."

I looked at Paula and she looked at me. Without a sound, I passed it off to her. I was tired, and more than overwhelmed.

"Why is it so important to you that we take another kid?"

"You have that extra room. Star's room. But that's not really why. It's because, just think if you'd decided not to take any more after Katie. I never would have met you, and you never would have met me."

Paula and I exchanged glances again.

"He makes a good point," I said.

We both nodded at him.

"Okay," Paula said. "We promise."

A lopsided grin took over most of his face. "I knew you would." Then he left for his run.

I breathed deeply, followed by a huge sigh. "Is it possible that we just went from three kids down to Quinn in the space of about an hour?"

"Don't worry. We're about to have a new one. We promised."

"Maybe someone less challenging than Star this time. Actually, strike the 'maybe.'"

"Amen to that," she said.

40. Clementine

It was almost dark when she came back from that second ride, and I was waiting, and watching. I stepped out onto the porch just as she swung her leg across Comet's rump and slid to the ground.

"Why didn't you tell me what they wanted to talk to me about?"

"I don't know," she said, leading Comet up to the porch. "I guess I figured *they'd* tell you."

"That doesn't sound like a very honest answer. I thought they had come to accuse me of stealing you. I read them the riot act, I'm afraid, and it was very embarrassing. Well, not the riot act by my old standards. But it was still embarrassing. Why didn't you tell me?"

I tried to read her face in the dim, but I couldn't

see it well. But her energy—and yes, "energy" was the right word—was tight and defensive.

"I was scared, okay? Happy now?"

"Of what?"

"Oh, come on. Of what? I'm supposed to just come over here and say, 'Oh, by the way, do you want me?' What if you said no? It's one thing to have me over here to take care of Comet and even to play cards or talk. Or stay the night because we were going to do something that's scary to you. But asking if you wanted to be my foster person is kind of taking things to a whole new level, don't you think?"

"You must have known I've come to rely on your company."

"I wasn't sure *enough,*" she said. "I mean, I was. Until it came time to ask you. Then I wasn't."

"Well, you should have been."

"Come down here," she said.

"Why?"

"Trust me. You're about to take another big step."

"What kind of step?"

"You call that trusting me?"

I wavered a moment, then stepped off the porch. She untied the rope from one side of Comet's halter, turning it from reins back into a lead. She reached the end of it out to me. "Time to stop being so afraid of him."

I stared at the rope for several seconds in silence.

"He's not going to do anything," she said. "What do you think he's going to do?"

I took the rope in my hands.

"Lead him around."

"I don't know—"

"It's not brain surgery. You walk. He follows."

I took a few steps, and he ambled along behind me, his hooves making that clopping sound I'd grown to like. I glanced at him over my shoulder in the gathering dark. Then we circled around and came back to where she stood.

"See how easy?"

"It wasn't so much that I was afraid of him," I said. "I'm not saying I wasn't, but that wasn't the biggest problem between us. I was angry with him."

"For what?"

I cleared my throat. I'm not sure why. "I think I felt that he was supposed to be enough."

"Enough?"

"For Tina."

"Oh. He's just a horse, you know. How can you be mad at a horse? All he can be is exactly what he is."

"I didn't say it was logical. I didn't say I was proud of it. Just that it was."

"Past tense?"

I looked back at him again, and he returned my gaze steadily. And of course he was only a horse. "Yes. Past tense."

41. Jackie, Three Months On

Paula is the natural cook in our family. I know it doesn't seem that way, because she works so much and the job falls to me. But she's the expert. So on that Thanksgiving, as with any major holiday when she doesn't work, she handled all the food.

I didn't just sit around smelling the turkey roasting. I drove more than twenty miles to the nearest train station to pick up Mando and his mom.

Their train was a few minutes early, so they were standing on the platform when I drove up. I stopped the car along a curb that was clearly marked to discourage such behavior, and jumped out. He hugged me, and laughed. Yes, laughed. Somehow it was a moment that ran to merriment.

"I swear you got bigger," I said. "Is that possible?"

"J-Mom. It's only been three months."

I held him at arm's length by the shoulders. "What did you just call me?"

"J-Mom?" He asked it timidly. As though he might be wrong, and hadn't called me that at all. "After I left I decided I should totally have called you guys J-Mom and P-Mom. Because it's not the same as just plain mom. It's perfect. Sorry I didn't see that at the time."

"We're ignoring your just plain mom," I said.

Gabriela and I gave each other a more brief and reserved hug. Then we piled into the car, Mando swinging an overnight bag into the backseat. He grabbed the shotgun seat and left his mother to sit in the back.

I shifted into gear and pulled away toward home.

"You realize you just silently called shotgun on your own mother," I said.

His mouth twisted. "Oops. Sorry, Mom. I was used to grabbing this seat from the other kids. Guess I got carried away."

"I'll remember on the way back," she said. "I'll have to stand up for myself."

Mando turned to face me again. "I can't wait to meet Rose."

"She's dying to meet you. Seriously. You're like a household legend. We're always 'Mando this' and 'Mando that.' She probably sees you as some kind of mythical figure."

"Uh-oh. She's in for a letdown. Are Star and the lady coming for dinner?"

I rolled my eyes. I shouldn't have, but I did. "Unfortunately, yes. Mando, you don't tell a soul I said that."

He held up his right hand like a juror swearing in.

I met Gabriela's eyes in the rearview mirror. "Please?"

She made a lip-zipping motion.

"So they haven't changed," Mando said. It wasn't really a question.

"Well. They have and they haven't. I honestly think Clem is better about not being downright nasty. But she's still not exactly my favorite person to have around. And they fuss at each other constantly. They're like an old married couple. They speak to each other with such disrespect sometimes. But I guess at least it's good that they speak to each other."

"But are they happy?"

"Now that's a damned good question. I'd say they're happy for *them*. They seem to have found some strange version of happy that they can make work. Which I think is nice. But don't be too surprised if it doesn't seem like any kind of happy you'd choose for yourself."

When we first came into the house, Rose ran and hid. The dogs wagged furiously at Mando, and jumped up, which they're not supposed to do. Owing to the circumstances, I didn't correct them.

Quinn played host and brought them drinks. Soda for Mando and wine for his mom, which I poured. I began to set the table, watching Rose creep back down the hall and peek out at the company.

I said, "It's Mando, Rose. You've been wanting to meet him."

She wandered into the living room, not in the

world's straightest line. Stopped in front of the two guests on the couch, leaving a few feet of safe space.

"I know you," she said to Mando.

"Well, we haven't met each other exactly."

"But you're Mando. Everybody talks about Mando."

"Well, that's good, I guess. I mean, I hope. How old are you?"

He knew. But everybody always likes to get kids to say.

She looked down at her right hand, tucked in the thumb, and held up the remaining four fingers.

"Good age," he said. "You're the only member of the family I haven't hugged hello." He held his arms wide.

I winced, bracing for it.

Rose let out her signature ear-piercing shriek, ran into the dining room, and hid behind my legs, leaving several inches of space so we didn't accidentally touch.

"Totally my fault, Mando. I meant to warn you on the drive, and I was so happy to see you I forgot. Rose doesn't like to be touched." I twisted around and looked down into her huge brown eyes. "Mando didn't know."

Paula leaned out of the kitchen wearing both long oven mitts. "Everything okay out here?"

"My fault," I said. "I forgot to warn him about Rose's . . . issues."

She nodded and disappeared again. Not three seconds later, I heard the knock on the door that could only be Star and Clementine.

"I'll get that," Mando said.

I tried to pretend the house didn't jump ten lines on the stress-o-meter when they walked in. Mando held his arms out to his former foster sister, but she just rolled her eyes and sidestepped him.

I sighed from the dining room.

Mando came in and found me. "I totally blew it with Rose," he said.

He looked around for her, but she'd run off to be in the kitchen with Paula.

"It was my fault. But it'll be fine, really. People make mistakes with her all the time. She gets over it. Once she sees you're staying away, she'll give you another chance."

"Do I even want to ask about the touching thing?"

"No. You don't. It'll spoil your whole holiday. Did you ever get through to Dennis?"

"I did. He said I should come by his house after dinner. I was hoping you or P-Mom could drive me."

I felt my face twist into a smile. "Go in the kitchen and tell her that. Right now. Tell her, 'I was hoping you or J-Mom would drive me.'"

Just as he disappeared through the kitchen doorway, Clem and Star began fussing at each other.

Clem said, "It's very rude when you know people and I don't, but you don't introduce me."

"You know Mando!" she said, already raising her voice.

Clem indicated Gabriela with a flip of her head. "I don't know *her*."

"I don't know her, either," Star shrieked. "Jeez. Make everything my problem, why don't you?"

I hurried out to the living room to make introductions.

"Star, Clementine, this is Armando's mother, Gabriela."

"Happy to meet you," Gabriela said.

She held her hand out to shake. With either of them. Neither one took it for an uncomfortable space of time. Then Clem reached her hand out to shake just as Gabriela gave up and turned away, and I felt a pang of hurt for both of them.

Mando came back to join us.

"Excuse me," I said.

I found Paula in the kitchen. She took one look at me, set down the big spoon she was holding, and offered me a hug. I gratefully accepted. I let out a few previously unexhaled breaths.

"You seem positively frazzled," she said. "And the day's barely started."

"Thanks so much for reminding me."

"Star and Clem?"

"Who else?"

"They're exactly who they are, Jackie."

418

"I still like it when they're exactly who they are at *their* house." I pulled out of her arms and looked around. "Where's Rose?"

"Quinn took her and the dogs out to play so I could have a moment's peace."

"I should do the same. Give you a moment's peace, that is. I just wanted to ask you a question. You know how I always said I wanted the big bustling house full of family? All that lovely chaos? Can I take that back now?"

She let out a snorting laugh. "You can wave a magic wand and see if we all disappear," she said. "But frankly, I think you're stuck with us."

"I'd better get back out there and referee."

"Hey. Before you go. You won't believe what Mando just called me."

"Actually," I said, "I have a pretty good idea."

It was quite a bit after dinner, right around the time I was hoping the crowd would thin, when I noticed Star was missing.

Rose was giving Mando a tentative second chance, after his promise to remain on a no-hug basis. Clementine was watching the child's timid approach, and continually making unwelcome comments, mostly along the lines of, "My, but she's a jumpy little thing." Despite my having caught her eye and silently shaken my head to discourage it.

I thought Star might be in the bathroom, so I waited.

When she didn't come back, I asked no one in particular, "Where's Star?"

"Oh, who ever knows?" Clem said. "She's such a slippery devil. Every time I look around she's gone off someplace without saying. Usually I look in the barn first, and that gets it. She loves to go off and be with Comet."

"Excuse me," I said.

I let myself out into the nippy dark. I stood and breathed a moment, watched my clouds of steamy breath, and looked at the many bright stars, happy to have all that chatter out of my ears. Even though I liked or even loved most of the chatterers. It was nice to enjoy a rare moment of peace.

The light was on in the barn across the road, so I walked over.

Not surprisingly, Star was in the stall with the horse, leaning on his shoulder and feeding him carrots with their green tops still on.

She heard me, and looked up. "Don't tell me, let me guess. You're mad because I left."

"Not really. I just wondered if you were okay."

"Why wouldn't I be okay?"

"Just that you and Clementine had that little fight . . ."

"What fight?" When I didn't answer she said, "We didn't have a fight. That's just how we are. I just wanted to come over here and be with the person I have the most thanks for. Well, okay, I know you'll say he's not a person."

"I didn't say a word. I'll leave you alone with your horse."

"J-Mom," she said before I slipped through the open barn doorway.

I laughed out loud.

"What's funny?"

"Nothing," I said. "What?"

"Don't think I didn't notice you and Paula did a lot for me, too. Put up with a lot of crap. You know. You know I knew that, right?"

"I think I knew. But thanks."

"It's just hard to . . ."

"I know," I said. "I get it."

I walked out into the cold again. "Cold" really said it better than "nippy." I was thinking, *Why are all the places that are ghastly hot in summer also ghastly cold in winter?*

I hovered for a moment under the stars, savoring that rare solitude.

Then I walked back into all that noisy chaos. And I really wasn't sorry.

About the Author

Catherine Ryan Hyde is the bestselling author of twenty-four novels, including the 1999 smash hit *Pay It Forward*, which has been translated into more than two dozen languages, and was made into a major motion picture starring Kevin Spacey, Helen Hunt, and Haley Joel Osment. In addition to her novels, Hyde is the author of more than fifty short stories and is founder and former president (2000–2009) of the Pay It Forward Foundation. During her years as a professional public speaker, she addressed the National Conference on Education, met with AmeriCorps members at the White House, and shared a dais with President Bill Clinton.

Center Point Large Print
600 Brooks Road / PO Box 1
Thorndike, ME 04986-0001 USA

(207) 568-3717

US & Canada:
1 800 929-9108
www.centerpointlargeprint.com